A Way Of Life, Disrupted

Bert Scorgie

authorHOUSE®

AuthorHouse™ UK Ltd.
500 Avebury Boulevard
Central Milton Keynes, MK9 2BE
www.authorhouse.co.uk
Phone: 08001974150

First published by AuthorHouse   8/17/2010

ISBN: 978-1-4490-9272-6 (sc)
ISBN: 978-1-4490-9273-3 (hc)

This book is printed on acid-free paper.

Contents

Chapter One

S ANDY COULD FEEL A COLD SHIVER run down his spine as he swung his legs over the side of the bed, he was preparing to spend another hard day fighting the elements. As he looked at the window after lighting the hurricane lamp which supplied the light and heat in his sparse room, little had changed over the last fifteen years; he could just make out the frosty flowers that nature had patterned overnight on the window. He had to wriggle his legs into his ex-bobbies breeks, it was a bit of a struggle over the top of his thick winter long john drawers. He could hear his sister Meg raking the cinders from the firebox of the black range fireplace in the kitchen as she prepared to get heat to boil the kettle for a quick cup of tea before they faced the cold frosty early morning.

It all began for Sandy and Meg when their father was awarded the tenancy of a seventy two acre croft Hillside, or Hillies as it was locally known, it was well named as the only good crop it produced every year from its sloping fields were stones they seemed to appear from nowhere. The Second World War was over things were getting back to normal, except for the battle of trying to keep up with rising prices and inflation, money was very scarce. To go back to the start, Sandy was eleven when his father excitedly announced that his offer to take over the tenancy of Hillside had been accepted by the Laird, they would be moving on the 28th of May the following year. There was great excitement at the prospect of the Duncan family becoming part of the farming elite, one of fifteen families who crofted in the Glen. If only they knew what lay ahead they might not have been so enthusiastic. Alexander Hugh Duncan to give him his full title was born some twenty five years ago to Peg and Sandy Duncan the eldest of their seven children, alas there are only two of them left to carry on the struggle for survival at Hillies, Sandy and his sister Meg the rest have long flown the nest and were scattered around the world, mainly due to the war and their quest for better paid employment, it is not unusual; to find Scots in every corner of the globe migrant workers seems to be the name given to them. Sandy was not a happy man only nine of the original crofters still scratched a living out of the hostile landscape they lived on, rumour had it that others were on the verge of throwing in the towel as rising prices was causing strangulation, for all their hard work the rewards were pretty poor. What with the price of animal feed, rent increases and soon they were to get mains electricity and bathrooms fitted, Sandy was at the end of his tether fair worried how to make ends meet. It looked as though extinction for the crofter was just round the corner, what then?. The only skill he had was being a farmhand, so his scope for employment was very limited, but it's only five-o-clock in the morning too early to worry about things that have still to take place. Meg and Sandy had a special routine in the morning that being that they never spoke to each other for at least an hour as she could be a right girny bitch at times, she soon came round after a good blaw of frosty air as she crossed the yard on the way to the byre to milk the coo, Sandy was usually on his way back to the house when they met and exchange pleasantries their first of the day. He was ready for his bowl of brose his daily breakfast, six spoons of oatmeal salt pepper, and a knob of butter topped off with the thickest cream he could lay his hands on (good healthy eating). As he sat alone at the table that morning his mind was in turmoil as he tried to figure out the outcome. He tried various formulas but there didn't seem to be an acceptable answer.

Meg would soon be back from the byre so he put his thoughts to one side no need to have her worried as well as himself. Going back to the day they moved to Hillies Sandy could clearly remember the excitement as they loaded their belongings on a flat cart in preparation for the three mile journey; it needed two carts to transport their possessions and the family. It was the start of a great new adventure for the Duncan family especially the children, Sandy was allowed to ride his bike alongside the carts as they made their way to Hillies, ringing in his ears was the warning from his father,"Nae bloody nonsense remember you are on the main road". It was a slow journey and took two hours to complete but soon their new abode was in sight, Mrs Duncan had kept the young ones amused with songs and poems, but that was forgotten as they eagerly waited for the grand entrance to the Hillside farmyard. The excitement was at fever pitch as the family dismounted from the cart the young ones anxious to explore their new surroundings, one of the main attractions was the toilet it straddled a small burn which made it slightly more hygienic than a bucket, that is if the burn was in spate. Mrs Duncan was soon in command delegating jobs to the kids it was a race against time to have the house habitable before bedtime; she herself also had the added task of milking the cow.

It was close to midnight by the time everything was in place the two extra bedrooms made a world of difference. To-morrow would be the start of a long hard battle with the unfriendly terrain of Hillside, or the more appropriate name Hillies. Before we go any further this would be the right time to introduce the Duncan family, the head Honcho is Sandy Duncan (senior) his good wife Peg both in their late thirties, at that time there were seven bairns including two sets of twins they were Sandy eleven, twins Meg and Willie ten, Betty nine, Jim seven, Mary and Peg twins aged two. The fist morning at Hillies was like an Army Command post as Mother Duncan allocated tasks to the youngster's this had to be completed before going to school woe betide any one of them who didn't adhere to the rules by not completing their allotted task.

Everything around Hillies was pretty handy the shop/post office, school, Kirk, Village Hall, and then there were numerous vans selling all the essential needs, at first the vans were mostly horse drawn affairs but they were regular and dependable. So the move to Hillies had a lot of plus points. They managed to survive the first weekend and on Monday morning the youngsters were ready to face their first day at the New School, young Sandy had done a bit of exploring over the weekend and discovered that they were only twenty minutes from the small fishing village of Covie. This would open up a whole new world for Sandy as he had a fascination for the sea, many hours of his life would be spent in that lovely little village, he soon became well know to the villagers, Sandy Hillies was a well loved visitor. He was less than two years away from leaving school, his father was about to start him on a learning curve of how a farm was run, training that would stand him in good stead when his time came to leave school . The Blacksmiths shop was the main hub of activity in the village the Smiddy as it was called, every plot and prank was hatched in the smiddy that included scandal and gossip it all stemmed from the on goings round the Anvil.

The Blacksmith William J. Watson big Will to his many friends was a huge jovial man mountain full of devilment but the back bone of the community if a thing was broke Will would fix it, he was a few years older than Sandy but through their love of music they became firm friends, a friendship that lasted until old age and finally death parted them. Sandy didn't have a lot of free time as his father was a hard taskmaster also a bit of a perfectionist who aimed to give his sons a thorough education in the finer arts of farming. They moved into the croft at the busy time of year the crops required a bit of attention as they needed the highest yield possible so that they were practically self sufficient both for the animals and themselves right through the winter months. Willie was a year younger than Sandy, they were complete opposites in nature he tended to be rather strong headed, when Willie made up his mind nobody could change it he was a very determined young man, this often caused friction between the two brothers. Willie had no interest in the croft or farming and was sure he was destined for greater things thus he spent much of his time helping Will Watson in the smiddy, before his fourteenth birthday he could shoe a horse as good as any grown man, any work about the croft was carried out grudgingly but his father was the boss and Willie had to toe the line along with the rest.

Bye the time their first winter arrived everything was under control there had been an exceptionally good harvest and the summer weather had been excellent the only thing that was lacking about Hillies was money but it was a common ailment in the glen it was pretty much a hand to mouth existence but they were all in the same boat. It was a fairly frugal way of life, their food was basic using as much of what they produced on the croft as possible to keep the cost at a minimum when there were shortages it was not unusual to live solely on dishes made from oatmeal starting off with Brose, Lunch would be Skirley and mashed Tatties supper would possibly be porridge made with milk and instead of bread they would eat oatcakes. Meg being the oldest daughter was also being groomed to help her mother and of course prepare her for life after she left school; she already helped look after the younger family members and was well educated in the skills needed to run a home such as baking a very important skill in the early part of the century. Everybody had to muck in and help, as there were no fancy appliances available every chore had to be done manually and very hard work it was, whether it was in the house or on the croft there was a lot of blood sweat and sometimes tears required to survive. In the house everyday was earmarked to carry out a specific chore, Monday was usually wash day, Tuesday would be spent ironing, Wednesday would be making butter and cheese, Thursday was spent cleaning and packing eggs ready for the grading station anything up to twenty dozen, Friday was the most important and possibly the heaviest day of the week that was baking day everything had to be mixed by hand oatcakes, various kind of scones, pancakes and there were always some fancy cakes, the women had also to fit in seeing to the family cooking meals mending clothes and possibly knitting socks and a very important chore milking the cow twice daily, great supplies of elbow grease were required.

Sandy Duncan senior had a terrible up bringing he was boarded out, an orphan, born in Glasgow his parents died when he was just a toddler his early life was very vague as there was no information available, he met Peg Morrison when he was twenty two, she was the first person in his life who showed him any affection, the people who had raised him and there were a few as he had been shunted from pillar to post used him as cheap labour, he was one of hundreds of these bairns, they were treated little better than the animals raised along side them on the farms and crofts all over the North Of Scotland. In a lot of instances they were treated dreadfully bearing in mind the traumatic start they had in life, a life often blighted by drunken parents, on the farms they were probably better fed but they were shown absolutely no affection. some of them were complete families, if they were all placed together it helped but lots of them were loners probably thrust into parts of the country where they couldn't even understand the local dialect, completely different from what they were used to in the likes of Glasgow where the majority started life. Sandy doted on his family and tried to give them as correct an up bringing as was humanly possible, polite, mannerly and helpful, they attended church every Sunday so that they had a good Christian knowledge of life. When they moved to Hillies there was seven of a family, Peg hoped that was the family complete as she was having niggly little health problems, but it was not to be and she found herself pregnant once again, it happened so easy, there was no Wireless or Telly you had to find something to pass the time it was also a great cure for insomnia. One story that was often told was of another crofting family the Fraser's, Bunty the mother was proud of her seven sons and her goal in life was to complete the family with a girl. One day the Vet called to look at one of the animals, it was at dinnertime so he was promptly invited to join the family and have dinner, which was the norm. He was the guest of honour so the drill was that he and Auld Davie would be seated first Bunty then called the boys to enter the dining room as each took his place at the table she announced his name when the last was seated the Vet said, " By gosh Mrs Fraser that's seven strapping lads you have, was it a loon every time". Bunty replied "Na Na there wiz lots of times that nothing happened" I presume that was not what the Vet had in mind. Every family in the glen had at least six youngsters the highest number was a family of fifteen so they were never lonely always plenty company, everyone was equal as far as wealth went, maybe I should have said poverty, one thing that was plentiful was kindness and what ever one family had in abundance they would share it with the rest, the workload was shared although there was some friction at times as is common in most communities. Everything was going hunky dory until a madman by the name of Adolph Hitler caused mayhem and changed the way of life forever, all the able bodied men were called up and many never returned for various reasons, getting killed, getting married, and different reasons for settling down around the world. Many of the young men who survived the war had learned new skills that were never to be of benefit if they returned to the Glen so they settled down where they could find work appertaining to their new found skills. Families were decimated and the way of life pre war was gone for ever, for better or worse only the individual can answer that.

Hillside was situated about a mile from the turnpike as the locals called the main road, it was a B class road which continued past Hillies for a further four miles where it ended at the gates of the Mansion House, the lairds residence he owned the Glen also a huge expanse of arable land known as the Home Farm, they had an enormous walled garden which in later years was to become a market garden, the whole estate amounted to three thousand acres the five main farms with the best land covered about two hundred and fifty acres each, then the tiddlers, fifteen crofts about eighty acres each with ground that was inferior to their larger cousins, the crofts required a lot of hard work to get them to produce.

The laird was steeped in Military traditions being ex army, the Rt Hon Spencer Tracy MM was a stickler for getting things correct so everything was done with Military precision, if not the Major would be on your top, but apart from that he was a very amiable sort of guy who was kind and approachable, his passion was running around with the local Territorial Army, he was always on the look out for new recruits, and was in his element up to his arse in mud shouting encouragement to his troops to get stuck in.

Sandy's mother was six months pregnant when she started to feel very unwell, she suffered from severe high blood pressure, and was confined to bed a lot, this meant that young Meg had to carry the burden of seeing to the family she had just turned twelve so it was a big responsibility for one so young but she was more than capable. Her schooling had to suffer but most of the girls in the glen went on to work in service where education was not a big factor very few of them became academics so what they learned at home was adequate to see them through life, this was the start of a catalogue of difficulties to plague the Duncan family over the next few years. Every family in the glen attended the local Kirk on Sunday morning it was the main source of keeping abreast with World Affairs, the minister usually had a ten-minute slot where he discussed important matters especially complicated items that could probably affect their lives, it also saved them trying to understand the complexities of what was happening around them. The Rev Jim Kerr was one of the main stays of the community always ready to lend a helping hand when needed carrying out duties far beyond what was expected of him, he turned out to be a true friend to the Duncan's in their times of need. Then there was Bill Findlay the local doctor another pillar of strength in the community, in those far off times the doctor had to be paid for his services by his patients this was often a struggle due to lack of hard cash so in many instances he would receive –part payment and some produce to cover his fees, if he had owned some land he would have had the biggest gathering of livestock in the Glen as he was often offered a sheep or maybe a pig as part payment. Another one of the community stalwarts was Bob Paterson the headmaster he was a formidable character who put the fear of death into his wayward pupils, he ruled with an iron fist, he was also a justice of the peace so it was his duty to maintain law and order. Last but not least was Dod Simpson the local bobby he was getting on in years so all he looked for was a quiet ending to his long police career, his usual threat to any young person who tried it on was that he would sink his foot up his arse until the third lace hole had disappeared, this threat was never used but it was always on the mind of any would be offender.

Chapter Two

LIFE ON THE FARM/CROFT WAS A very repetitive lifestyle and followed the four seasons of the year starting off after the New Year as soon as the weather was favourable and the frost and snow had cleared they would start carting dung to the fields in preparation for the ploughing to begin, it had already been started late autumn so it just required to be finished off, every chore had to be carried out using brute force and ignorance no fancy labour saving tools, it was back breaking work, as well as moving dung there was still plenty livestock to be looked after cattle, sheep, pigs and of course there were hens and fire wood to keep the home fires burning, their only source of warmth so there were never idle hands. As soon as the ground was suitable the ploughs would be in action a lot of palaver went into the art of ploughing it was the only function on the farm where the final article would be on show until it was flattened out by the harrows. The idea was to get the first drill or the feerin as it was called dead straight that was the lead to leaving a work of art. There was a lot of leg pulling and general banter about who was the best ploughman, Auld Jockie Grant was the butt of many jokes as his feerin was likened to a dog pissin in the snow but poor Jockie had very bad eyesight so he had an excuse anyhow his would look the same as the rest in a few days time when flattened but it was a source of hilarity as long as it lasted. One of the highlights of the crofting calendar was the twice-yearly visit of the steam driven threshing mill, late on a Sunday afternoon the beginning of March and November she would suddenly appear on the horizon hissing steam and belching smoke as she laboured to pull her load over the brow of the hill towing the Mill and the attendants accommodation and of course a tender full of coal, the usual plan was that the two men would get their meals on whichever farm they were working on so all they needed was a place to sleep. The glen folks looked forward to this fortnight as they would catch up with the gossip the two men had collected in their previous places of employment so long evenings were envisaged when the Mull

Boys were around telling tales into the early hours of the morning. Frankie Smith had the first croft off the main road so this was the first port of call for the men to set up the mill ready for off first thing Monday morning. The Glen folks got a rude awakening with a blast from the steam whistle letting people know they were ready for action. It would take two weeks to complete the task then it would be all over for another six months the excitement over it was back to the mundane tasks about the farm on the one man crofts it could be a lonely life. Sandy helped his father as much as he could but he still had a few more months in school and had to attend for the amount of time specified by the authorities, Meg had to get an exemption so that she could help her mother so from thirteen years of age she never attended school her mother was due to give birth soon. Willie was still being his usual pain in the arse, disagreeable and awkward, continually at loggerheads with Sandy and his father he just hated having to work on the croft but would spend hours on end at the smiddy helping Will Watson. Sandy tried to get over to him that he would be leaving school soon, he would need to get paid employment as the croft could not sustain two of them drawing wages, Willie would just have to knuckle down and become his fathers helper.

Willie narked back at Sandy he would only be here for a year because as soon as he could leave school he was going to train to be a blacksmith it was a daily argument, the niggling raged back and forth very near coming to blows at times Willie was thrawn and stubborn nothing would change his mind. The community struggled on trying to make ends meet as they braved the elements their fate lay in what the weather threw at them some years they would have magnificent crops with ears of corn in abundance, wheat and barley hanging heavy, then they would have a deluge of rain that would flatten every crop for miles around, this would cause a lot of additional work as the flattened areas would have to be cut with a scythe, if it was really bad the bottom layers would be lost due to them rotting it was a vicious circle, but even with the drawbacks they were happy people and enjoyed a laugh and any devilment that would lift the spirits. The early summer was fairly easy going as they waited for the crops to ripen there was still plenty work to be done, and the long summer evenings were a bonus, Sandy made the best of this and spent any spare time in the village of Covie where he could fish off the rocks not that this was really essential as the small fishing cobbles always had an abundance of freshly caught fish he often supplied half the Glen , in return the fisher folks would get eggs milk and butter.Soon the hay would be ready to harvest all this work was carried out using horse drawn implements and of course brute force courtesy of the humans. The turnips had been hoed and the potatoes were beginning to show above ground it was a real merry-go-round. In between times fences were repaired wood work to be treated with creosote and the next set of implements checked and greased ready to go to work.Mrs Duncan was rushed into hospital and gave birth to another boy, the baby was fine but she was in very poor health, the doctors were worried that she might not pull through, her husband was sent for and it took forty eight worrying hours for her to respond to treatment, Mrs Duncan was never to enjoy full health again, her young daughters had to carry the burden. Sandy and his father decided the crops were ready to start harvesting the next Monday morning weather permitting, on the Sunday morning before Church they spent a couple of hours cleaning and polishing the horses harness as the next six weeks would be hectic as they gathered the harvest before the bad weather set in, then it would be time for another visit from the threshing mill to stock up for winter. They were heading fast to-wards the winter the dark nights would soon be upon them the only crop left to harvest was the potatoes, this usually lasted about six weeks, it was a combined effort with all the kids over twelve exempt from school for a couple of weeks over and above their Tattie holidays. As soon as the ground was clear the crofters would start preparing again for next spring it was vicious circle. Sandy decided to have a heart to heart talk with his father regarding his future it was getting close to his fourteenth birthday, he was well aware the croft could not carry two men drawing wages, even though he would only be entitled to about two pounds a month it was just out of the question, it was decided that Sandy should start looking for a fee (job) in preparation for the next May term. Willie and Jim would have to take over the task of helping their father run the croft, as usual Willie showed disapproval but was left in no doubts that what had been agreed was how things would happen.

Mrs Duncan was not a well person and was having to take to her bed more and more leaving the burden of running the house to her daughters especially the oldest Meg, life was not easy for the lassies as they struggled to cope but other options were non existent so they just had to get on with life.

Christmas Day passed without a lot of fuss, in this part of the world

Auld Years Night and New Years Day were the important days in their calendar, Hogmanay night was the night Santa delivered the presents so New Year's morning was always a bit of a stramash as they emptied their stockings and unwrapped their meagre presents many items were handmade, knitted or sown but it was the thought that counted. The house was decorated, again lots of the streamers and things were made in the school classroom; their father had killed a goose for the dinner. Will Watson arrived in the afternoon, he had his trusty fiddle with him, Sandy Sen got out the Button Key accordion and they soon had a bit of a concert going, one or two drams were taken and a good time was had by all.

The month of January was never very fruitful in the N.E. of Scotland where they are prone to heavy snow falls so nineteen thirty eight was normal, a couple of feet of snow chaos on the roads as they were blocked, but the locals were used to such conditions they had plenty food for the house and the animals so it was a case of batten down the hatches and ride the storm out, the male members of the Duncan family passed their day carrying out maintenance where ever it was possible there were always bits and pieces that needed repairing. The horses were getting well rested although whenever possible they were taken out and exercised to avoid them stiffening up. At the Kirk on Sunday Jim Kerr had a very special message to his congregation telling them that there was signs of unrest in Europe reminding them that it was only twenty years since the last conflict with the Germans but he was praying it would be resolved round the conference table this time. They were told as they left the church at the end of the service to stop at the War memorial and look at the names and ages of the young men of the Glen who unselfishly gave their lives the last time, this must not be allowed to happen again. Old Spencer made sure he was first at the memorial; he was at his dramatic best as he recounted the horrors of his wartime experiences to anybody who was prepared to listen to him. As the Duncan's waded through the snow Sandy turned to his father and said "You would think Auld Spencer was the only bugger who had any input to the last war they way he goes on". "Aye replied his father the chances are that the Auld bugger was in charge of the Canteen or some thing like that but according to him twa or three men and him leading won the bloody war. Every Sunday before dinner Sandy and a couple of the younger ones would walk the perimeter fence of the croft to make sure all the fencing was still intact, he also had a few snares set, sometimes his walk would be quite fruitful with a few rabbits and occasionally a hare this would add a treat to the dinner table, they would occasionally be allowed to take the gun and would down a few pigeons but father wasn't too keen to allow them the gun incase of accidents. Bye the middle of February the ground was clear enough to get the plough going again the dung had been carted when the frost was hard, the days were still pretty short but it allowed them to progress slowly.

Sandy's father arrived home from the mart one day and he rather excitedly told his son that he had more or less fixed him up with a job, Dod Wilson the farmer at Burnside one of the larger two hundred and fifty acre farms needed a loon (junior worker) to start at the May term and if he went along and spoke to Lang Dod as he was affectionately known because of his six foot six frame the job was his. The very next Saturday afternoon Sandy borrowed his father's bike and headed for Burnies that was all of six miles away, his heart was thumping as he knocked at the door about a minute passed before the door was abruptly opened by a haughty looking woman aged about forty, she demanded to know what he wanted, Sandy was a bit taken back by her hostile attitude and stammered out that he was here to speak with Mr Wilson, she again asked abruptly if he was expected and what nature his business was, Sandy thought what a bitch but explained why he was there. As she closed the door she said she would see if Mr Wilson was ready to see him. Two minutes later she was back told him to follow her and make sure his boot's were clean before he walked on the linoleum in the boss's best room, Sandy felt really uncomfortable with the attitude of this stuck up bitch she had him on edge even before he came face to face with Lang Dod. He tapped on the door rather timidly and near jumped out of his skin when this rather gruff voice told him to enter. As Sandy entered the room he became aware why people called the man Lang Dod he was standing up behind his desk all six feet six inches of him he held out his hand for Sandy to shake, told him to sit down and make himself at home. Sandy was still trying to come to terms with his surroundings when Dod Wilson started to speak outlining the duties that would be expected of him if he wanted to come and work at Burnside. "I used to always go for an older man to do the job I'm offering you but I have kent yer father for many years so I ken your pedigree". Sandy would be reporting directly to the farm foreman Jake Thompson, his wages were to be twelve pounds every six months and he was expected to keep toon (cover the week-end cattle feeding etc) every second weekend at no extra remuneration he would have to share the Bothy with Eck Davidson the cattleman. After Dod was sure Sandy fully understood his commitments he stood up and shook his hand saying he would look forward to his starting work at the term. He was on top of the world as he cycled home whistling at the top of his voice it was not easy to land a job like the one at Burnies so he had reason to be happy with himself.

As soon as he reached home he excitedly told his father he had been successful and proceeded to relay the story of his interview and he was due to start work on the twenty ninth of May, which was six week away. They discussed all the gear he would require clothes etc , firstly new tackity boots a pair of moleskin trousers and a decent working jacket, his father was talking and at the same time heading for the shed beside the house, he opened the door and inside stood a nearly new bike Sandy's reward for all the hard work and help he had given his father, Willie arrived to have a look and congratulated his brother on landing his first job he also reminded him that in eleven months he would be following him away from Hillies to start his apprenticeship with the Blacksmith. Father let Willies remarks pass without comment young Jim was coming along nicely he was interested in the croft so a readymade replacement would be in place over the next year.

Sandy kept his nose to the grind stone over the next six weeks as he tried to get his father as far ahead as possible, he had been given a young calf to rear a year ago it was now ready to be sold the money would be real handy and help finance his new working gear what was left over would be the start of a bank account.

Mrs Duncan was very unwell and was totally unable to be of help to her young daughters the doctor had recommended as much rest as possible to try and build up her strength so she was constantly in bed only able to advise when the lassies needed advice, it was decided to employ a local woman a few hours weekly to help Meg with the heavy work, Sandy often milked the cow to try and make life easier for his young sister.

His final day at school arrived he was over the moon, but he still had a month to go before he started work, but as usual there was plenty to do at home as they were approaching the busy period again. The month soon passed and before he knew where he was he was days away from leaving his father, on the Saturday he borrowed the horse and cart to ship his Kist over to Burnside, being Saturday afternoon his big pal

Will Watson gave him a hand and to keep him company. He arrived at Burnies and knocked on the kitchen door, the door was answered by the same obnoxious female he had spoken to at his interview she was about to flaunt her authority again when Big Will butted in, "Aye Aye Lizzie Smith that's an awful way to welcome a young man to his first job it would be more helpful if you just showed him where the Bothy is". She squinted up at the figure on the cart as her eyes focused on the huge figure she began, "Oh! It's you Will Watson; it's awhile since I have seen you around how are you?" She then winked at Will and whispered you have to start on a right footing if they are scared of you they get every thing richt. Lizzie grabbed the halter and led the horse to the chaumer door, she opened the door and pointed to the bed on the left, that's yours, she told Sandy, the ither een belangs to Eck Davidson the cattleman, her parting words were keep the place clean and tidy as you no longer have yir mither rinnin efter yir erse. As Sandy and Will headed for home Sandy passed a remark, " That Lizzie seems a richt vicious bitch", "Aye Will replied that's what yea call a chip on the shoulder to put you in the picture, Lang Dod never married, his mother kept the place going until she died two years ago, Lizzie has been hoose keeper for over twenty years she has a son aged over twenty he is teacher doon in England somewhere, the story goes that the Lang fellow is his father, Lizzie thought she would get married after the loon was born, but the old mother thought Lizzie being a skivvie wasn't good enough for her Dod, but it was ok to have his evil way with her, it looks like Lizzie is still trying to get the big man to the alter. She more or less runs the place she is ok yea'll just have to try and get in her good books when you start work.

Will then burst into song and serenaded Sandy all the way home, he sang about every cornkister that was ever recorded Sandy was familiar with a lot of the words and joined in where he could, the journey soon passed and they were home in no time at all. Next morning Sandy was up at the crack of dawn he had a few things to get sorted out before it was time for the Kirk he was unsure when he would get the chance to attend from now on until his work pattern was established.

Late afternoon with all his meagre possession in his haversack he was ready to mount his bike and head for Burnside his new abode, all the family were waiting to wave him goodbye and wish him luck in his new venture, his mother even managed to drag herself to the door so that she could give her personal hug, it was very emotional as he felt the hot tears running down his mothers cheek he was swallowing hard as he tried to maintain his composure. As he swung his leg over the crossbar his father walked over and told him to close his eyes and hold out his hand, he then placed a silver watch in his eldest sons hand. "That ma loon is yir grandfathers watch it is very old so make sure you look after it." To the ringing of the cheers of his family Sandy mounted the bike and set off he had a huge lump in his throat as he waved goodbye, his pent up emotions got the better of him and he felt a couple of tears run down his cheek, he wiped them away as he was afraid he may just meet Will Watson or one of his old school pals who would make sure he was dogged about his tears. An hour later he was entering the farmyard at Burnside he went straight to the Bothy door, he knocked then tried the handle it opened and there perched on the end of the bed was his new roommate Eck Davidson, he introduced himself to Sandy and let him know he had worked at Burnies for fifteen years there are four of us and everyone has over ten years service so you can understand Mr Wilson is a good man to work for so if you are willing and show interest you'll have a job for life.

He started to unpack his few possessions and stack them on the shelf above the bed, Eck watched his every move with interest, as Sandy removed an old Button Keyed accordion his new mate enquired if he could play Sandy nodded shyly yes but quickly added that he was still learning being taught by his father, Eck was delighted and told Sandy he better get practicing, " Once a fortnight the lads from the fairms round aboot gather here and we have a Bothies nicht, we have feats oh strength like pullin the swingletree, games of cards then end the nicht we an oor or so oh cornkisters so your services will be in big demand." At eight-o-clock Eck announced that it was time to head for the kitchen for a cup of tea before bedtime, this was a nightly occurrence if you felt like it, on entering the kitchen Sandy was shown where to get the oatmeal for his brose in the morning, Eck pulled the cover off the table and Sandy could hardly believe the spread of food laid out for them, all they had to do was boil the kettle and mask the tea. As they sat at the table Eck turned to Sandy and said " I'll give you a bit of advice, what ever yea dea before yea leave the kitchen mak sure it is the way yea found it if not yea will feel the sharp end of Lizzie's tongue, she is a rough diamond and would soon kick you up the erse if you get on her wrong side." With that in mind Sandy used to grab the dishtowel and did the dishes as soon as he finished his meal this seemed to keep him in her good books as she never said a cross word to Sandy, he soon got to realise that her bark was worse than her bite, she turned out to be a good friend and on numerous occasions he asked Lizzie for advice. Back in the chaumer Sandy started to get ready for bed about to wind up his alarm clock he was informed by Eck there was no need for an alarm as he had never needed one and had never been late for his work ever, Sandy was taking no chances and went ahead and set his clock. He had a very restless night, new bed, new job his mind was in turmoil most of the night. He must have fallen into a deep sleep as he leapt out of bed the minute the alarm burst into life his heart was near jumping from his chest with the fright he got.

Chapter Three

HE WAS GETTING DRESSED WHEN ECK arrived in the door with a grubby looking towel slung over his shoulder, he pointed Sandy in the direction of the horse trough where he could have a swill before heading for the stable. He hurried across the yard his stomach churning with nerves, it was the first time he had had to face such an ordeal, the top half of the stable door was open he could hear voices so he tapped on the door, a head appeared round the side of a big brown Clydesdale horse and asked what the hell he was chappin at the door for, "Jist come awa in and mak yirsel at hame nae need to be shy aboot here". Sandy was pleased to see it was a kent face this put him at ease right away it was Jake the foreman, he was already dishing out oats so Sandy grabbed some loose hay and started to dish it round the stalls there were seven horses in the stable, two more men appeared, Jake introduced Sandy to brothers Bill and Tam Scott they both nodded in acknowledgement, Bill asked Sandy if he was sure he shouldn't still be in school as he was pretty small alongside the huge Clydesdales he was about five feet four, after the horses were seen to the men made their way back to their homes to have their breakfast which would be brose, Eck was already at the table, he advised Sandy to have a bloody good feed as it was a long time till they ate again. With a satisfied stomach and a cup of hot tea Sandy was ready to face what ever the foreman could throw at him, there was a wee stagger in his step as he walked to-wards the stable. The foremen was already harnessing up his pair when Sandy got back, he told Sandy he would be assisting the others for a few weeks till he got into the way they did things at Burnies. This morning he was to assist Eck tend the cattle, then spend the day with him repairing fences, it was also pointed out that he was responsible for Robbie the spare horse making sure he was fed, groomed and exercised if he wasn't working a lot. Eck was still mucking out the cattle when Sandy got to the byre so he grabbed a fork and got stuck in. The work in the byre complete Sandy went to the stable to get Robbie harnessed up ready to cart the fencing material up the hill to where they were going to work. He was glad the stable was empty as he needed an old fish box to stand on to reach Robbie's head he was huge, as they passed the kitchen door there was a tray with a teapot and some home baked scones, Eck made a beeline for the tray motioning Sandy to follow it was the half yolkin, "we better have it before we hit the hill" said Eck. As they wound their way up the hill Eck pointed out all the boundary fences on the Burnside farm, they stretched for some considerable distance some of the ground was suitable for grazing only, the arable land was fenced off in huge fields, there was absolutely no comparison with the croft at Hillies. The twosome worked away fencing until near dinner time Sandy had to make sure Robbie was fed and watered ready for the afternoon stint. Sandy had his first real encounter with Lizzie as she ladled out a huge plate of Tattie soup; "Weel ma loon fu did yir first half day turn oot"? She asked. " Oh it wis aw richt" Sandy replied. Much to Sandy's embarrassment she turned to Eck and asked how he had performed. "Weel he kens aw aboot fencing he kens fu tae work so there's nae muckle wrang wie him as far as I can mak oot." Eck replied, just at that moment Lang Dod appeared in the door and before anybody could speak Lizzie butted in, Eck says the loon is dean affa weel Mr Wilson and kens fit he's dein" Dod was put in an awkward position but he had an instant answer.

"Weel I'm pleased aboot that but I never expected anything else because his father is a first class teacher." Even though Sandy was thoroughly embarrassed he was almost certain he had passed the first test of acceptance at Burnside. At one-o-clock they were heading back up the hill to carry on the fencing until it was time to feed the cattle for the night , Eck passed comment on that nosey auld bitch Lizzie for butting in when the boss was present and her telling Lang Dod about Sandy's first morning at work, he explained that that was her way and one of her bad points, on the other hand he was quick to point out her better side for example, "You'll never gang hungry as lang as Lizzie is doing the cookin". Sandy was back in the stable and had it all tidied up before the other three horsemen returned, as the foreman entered he exclaimed, "By gosh Sandy lad you've been busy! I hope yea hivna been hiding in here all day". He was famed for his little sarcastic remarks, Sandy had been warned by Eck who told him the Foreman was an ignorant sort of bugger at times so his remark was like water off a ducks back, but he did let him know they had repaired a good length of fence in between times. The foreman's closing remarks were that he had done a grand job and doubted if he had ever seen the stable so tidy, the Scott brothers nodded in agreement and gave Sandy a pat on the back as he passed them bye. After the horses were fed and watered it was off to the kitchen for their supper, Sandy could hardly move by the time he had finished, a quick wash and he crashed out on his bed, the next thing he was aware of was Eck shaking him as it was time to eat again the last cup of tea before bed time, as they passed the stable door he heard movement in the stable and having a look inside he spotted Jake Thompson having a final look round before heading home to his family in their cosy little cottar house. Sandy called out that he would start feeding in the morning if he was first in the stable, his foreman nodded his approval and muttered that he likes a loon who showed willing. His job at Burnside was pretty mundane as they were in a quiet period waiting for the hay to ripen; the cattle were feeding in the field's full time so a lot of time was being spent on repairs. He was able to go home every fortnight and occasionally weekly

he needed to get his washing done, so the most favourable idea was to get home as often as possible as the crotch and oxter areas of his under clothes could become quite ripe. There were very few men who wore pyjamas in those days so the semmit and drawers were worn twenty four seven, they were in need of a fortnightly turn around worse still most people only possessed two sets one on and one in the wash.

Quite often when Eck and Sandy were at their meal the boss would sit and have blether with them over a cup of tea. Eck maintained he was a very lonely man and needed a bit of company, Sandy asked what Lizzies role was and Eck told him that Lizzie kept him fed and attended to all his other needs he said this with tongue in cheek. Lang Dod was very up-to-date in his thinking he was one of the few farmers who owned a car, he also had a wireless and it was said as soon as there was tractor available that would be his next purchase he had already attended a few demonstrations. He loved to talk about World affairs and relate to what he had listened to on his wireless, as he stirred his tea he announced "Aye the news is nae very good fae Europe ower the last few days".

"Oh! Man fits wrang asked Eck"? " There's a bugger oh a German mannie called Hitler he's causing a lot of grief especially among the Jews he seems to have a spite against them, oor politicians are predicting another war shortly if he disna settle doon and behave himself, but it winna effect the thee of us, Eck and me are ower auld and Sandy is ower young. " He then asked Sandy if he knew Spencer Tracy the Laird, Sandy nodded his head and asked what about him, Dod told them that Auld Spencer had the Territorial Army out every weekend digging trenches and shooting at everything that moves. The feel auld bugger will start a war himself if we dinna watch him.

Sandy finally finished his first two weeks at Burnside and at one-o-clock on the Saturday he tied his laundry on to the carrier of his bike and set off for home, he felt rather excited as he entered the road leading up to Hillies it felt good to look forward to an evening with the family again it would only be for the one night so he intended to make the best of it. He was half way up the hill when he heard his name being called and a squad of youngsters racing down the road to meet him; he dropped the bike and spread out his arms as he caught the youngsters in a bear hug. Willie was the next to meet him "Ah hope yir nae wantin to kiss me" Willie said in his own dour way. Sitting round the kitchen table Sandy was bombarded with questions regarding his new job, his mother although very frail and ill looking managed to get herself dressed so that she could be part of the welcoming committee for her eldest son's home coming. Meg had produced a bit of a spread for her elder brother so there was a bit of a party atmosphere as they sat down to the meal she had specially prepared for Sandy, cooking some of his favourite tit bits. After lunch the young ones wanted to play it was a lovely evening, Willie divided them into two teams and they soon had a game of rounder's in full swing, friends and neighbours started to arrive and before long there were about twenty a side the older folks sat around and watched the youngsters enjoying themselves. As the evening wore on the young ones started to drift off home while some of the parents moved into the house before long there was a bit of a concert in full swing with Sandy Sen and Will Watson supplying the music, Sandy had left his box at Burnies so he had to be content with a stint on his fathers box while he had a dram. By midnight the last of the revellers were heading for home with parting words," I'll see you in the Kirk the morn."

Crack of dawn next morning Sandy made his way to the kitchen he could hear his father coughing as he opened the door he was asked what the hell are yea dein up at this time of day, Sandy's reply was that he didn't see any point in lying in bred missing out on the good weather they were experiencing and if the two of them got stuck into the animals they would be finished all the quicker, they were near ready to head for the byre when Meg appeared looking a bit dishevelled still in her dressing gown. "Why don't you give me the milk pail I'll milk the coo you have a long lie"? Sandy said to his sister, " you look like you could use it". Meg let out a squeal and wrapped her arms round her brother giving him a big kiss on the cheek she said "Sandy Duncan you are a saint". With that she disappeared back through the house to her bedroom shouting that she didn't want disturbed for an hour. As usual the Kirk was full to capacity all the wifies competing to see who had the most ridiculous hat on their heads.

Sandy met a few of his school pals, the pupils from his class were all working, only two had opted for further education big Durno Smith who went on to study Marine Engineering and Isobel Findlay the local doctors daughter she would probably end up studying medicine. He spent about an hour after the service discussing his job and listening to others telling of their experiences and general chitchat. He arrived home as Meg was overseeing the setting out of the dinner table, she had spent a bit of time getting her mother washed and dressed so that she could join them at the table. Father stood up to say grace before they were allowed to eat, he put up with no nonsense even baby Tommy had to toe the line at meal times. After dinner Sandy asked for volunteers to have a stroll down the brae to Covie he was inundated with offers his father even suggested that he would stay home with mother to allow Meg a rare break, her first line of thought was what about the dinner crockery it needs to be washed and tidied away so she was surrounded by helpers as they rushed to get the place tidy before they left for their walk. The return trip to Covie lasted some time with the bairns playing on the beach for a while, Sandy also spent time chatting to the friends he had in the village they were all concerned as to where he had disappeared too he had to explain he was now working and his abode was six miles away, it was well over three hours before they arrived back home. Little Tommy was flat out the sea air must have taken its toll on him as he was sleeping like a log in his pushchair.

It was soon time for Sandy to pack his small case and say his goodbyes as headed off to return to Burnside it was a grand evening so he cycled at his leisure admiring the animals and the crops on either side of the road, he opened the Bothy door and there was Eck indulging in his favourite pastime reading the latest batch of comics his sisters kids kept them for him. He told Sandy he had exchanged his motorbike at the weekend and the new bike had a sidecar attached to it. Burnside was a self contained unit it had its own threshing mill its own bruising machine for processing the oats into animal feed so there were quite a few new skills to be learned, he would never have had the opportunity if he had stayed with his father, everyday he was furthering his knowledge on how farming should be carried out. It had been a fruitful year crop wise even Hillies had excelled in the amount of crops it had produced all the fields were now bare, as everything was stored away for the winter. Lang Dod had decided to allow one of his fields to be used for the annual ploughing match a highlight in the farming calendar it was a great entertaining day so they were all looking forward to its arrival. It was such a popular event that a second field was needed to accommodate all those wanting to compete, and because of Lang Dod's enthusiasm for modern technology he insisted that there would be a section for tractors, it would be interesting to see how many would enter. Match day arrived and the place was like a cattle market there were over thirty pairs of horses and much to Dod's delight three tractors turned up and boy did they attract some attention. The match kicked off at ten-o-clock and had to finish at two this was to allow the judge's time before darkness fell; Sandy's father was a recognised champion ploughman so Sandy acted as his second man making sure that no divit was out of place. One of the bigger hotels from the town had set up a bar in a marquee tent they sold snacks and drinks for the hungry ploughmen.

It was a good autumn day so the ground was dry the competition would be keen, after the initial palaver of getting the first furrow straight and level Sandy had little else to do except keep his father company, the time soon passed and they were ready for the judging to begin that would take place when auld Davie Morrison had finished there is always one who disrupts the plans but as Davie said to the ones who were barracking him, " Somebody has to finish last", there was a lot of hilarity among the spectators of course the drink was taking control some of them had been at the bar for a good couple of hours and when drinks in the wits oot. The judging lasted over an hour finally all the placing was in order, from a rowdy mob to utter silence as the Chairman Rt Hon Spencer Tracy mounted the make shift platform to announce the winners and his wife Lady Tracy would hand out the prizes and certificates. You could hear a pin drop as the tension mounted of course auld Spencer had to give a spiel before getting down to the nitty gritty but this was the style of the man he did get heckled a bit but it was water off a ducks back. At last the business of presenting the prizes got under way, tension was mounting as the name of the Supreme Champion was announced the cheer was deafening as the name of Sandy Duncan Hillside was announced a very popular choice. As soon as he had presented the prizes Spencer managed to squeeze in his favourite subject membership of his beloved Territorial Army he had a new spiel as he outlined the mounting threat from Germany of a Second World War, there was a lot of wisdom in his speech but it didn't save him from severe heckling, but to Auld Spencer it was more water off the old ducks back. After the presentation people began to drift away, one of the tractor owners asked Lang Dod if he could park his machine overnight as it had no lights, Dod was over the moon at this request and on the Sunday morning he was up early and going over the tractor with a fine tooth comb, he even started the engine but didn't attempt to try driving it As Sandy and Eck made their way to the kitchen for breakfast Eck commented that the boss would be like a bairn wie a new toy, he also added that Dod would have had a tractor but his horses were all young and he would be severely out of pocket if he had tried to sell them at the moment, but he was sure that Burnside would mechanise just shortly. He advised Sandy to get interested in the tractor as it was without a doubt the way forward, just look at the time they spent ploughing their stint yesterday and compare that with the horse ploughing, "jist nae comparison." There is only one problem for us the tractor will cost jobs.

Monday morning after the ploughing match the Burnside work force had a lot of tidying up to be carried out, all the loose ends of the field had to be tied in and there were many items left lying about they were kept busy most of the day. The dark evenings were well and truly established and the long winter evening were just round the corner, Eck decided to pay his sister a visit she was married to the local fly man the type that tried to avoid work and lived on his wits he was the official mole catcher, but anything edible was fair game to Jimmy Lindsay he was from a family of travelling people although Jimmy preferred to stay put, Eck said he was too bloody lazy to move about like the rest of his tribe, Eck was the only member of his family who had any contact with his sister the rest of family referred to their brother-in-law as Jimmy –The-Tink and often said the bugger would steal the sugar out of your tea.

Sandy was invited along for the evening he knew of the Lindsay's but had never been to the house, he was also about to experience his first encounter with a sidecar. The Lindsay house or maybe hovel would have suited it better was at the back of beyond a broken down shack of a place in modern times it would be condemned. Sandy was in for the shock of his life as the door opened the stench was overpowering, you could hardly see the rafters for rabbit skins they were hanging everywhere, the room was full of smoke from the fire, there was a menagerie of dogs and children, Jimmy was sitting at one side of the fire a clay pipe in his mouth as he laboriously weaved a willow basket, his wife was breast feeding a tiny baby quite oblivious to the circus taking place around her, Jimmy addressed everybody as Cove a dead give away to his travelling background, they seemed quite contented even though their lifestyle seemed a bit pre historic, Sandy was dreading that he would be offered tea and was quite relieved when Eck decided after half-an-hour it was time to be going, before they left Jimmy tried to sell some of his wares but was unsuccessful.

It was getting close to the November term and all the farm workers had to wait to see if they would be engaged for a further six months or would they be on the look out for another job. About a week before the term Sandy was told by Lizzie that the boss wanted to see him after his tea break, " Mind and remove your beets before yea gang through the hoose", she scolded in her rather brash manner. He knocked on the boss's door and was told to enter, as usual he was a bundle of nerves he couldn't understand why as Dod was one of the easiest people he had ever talked to, he told Sandy to be seated. " Well ma boy how have you enjoyed your first six months at Burnside," Sandy replied that he was fair enjoying himself and found the rest of the staff had been a great help. Dod was delighted with the response he got and asked Sandy if he would consider a further six-month contract, Sandy grabbed it with both hands and he was delighted to hear his wages were to be increased by half-a crown a week (twelve and a half pence), he was told this was his reward for all the effort he had put into his first six months, he was floating on air as he went to join Eck topping and tailing neeps ready for winter storage. Eck was over the moon that his young companion had been kept on, they had formed a wonderful partnership, but then Sandy was a very level headed polite young man it was a pleasure working with him, Sandy could now settle down for the winter knowing that he had six months work ahead of him, work was quite scarce the only place you would get a quick start was the army a lot of young men were forced to join up either that or they were libel to starve there were no government hand outs as we know them to-day. Sandy had to miss Hogmanay that year, as it was his turn to look after the animals. On New Years morning they turned too at six-o-clock as usual there was a good covering of snow and Eck was moaning and groaning he was suffering a hangover from the drams he had had the night before. He was little better than useless and kept repeating never again much to Sandy's amusement as soon as they were finished Eck headed back to his bed unable to face breakfast.

Chapter Four

JANUARY NINETEEN THIRTY-NINE A NORMAL N.E.SCOTLAND winter snaw up to yir oxters cold frosty days everything was at a standstill, the work force at Burnside had to find work indoors it was the one time of the year that they were all working in the same area, making new reins and winding up discarded rope a general overhaul of the out buildings, it was not exciting work but the banter with the older men helped pass the time. Sandy got to know his workmates a bit better the first time since he was engaged to work at Burnies. The boss spent some time with them relaying his fears about the troubled times in Europe as he shook his head he repeated over and over things are not looking good., " Its aboot time somebody put a bullet in this Hitler bugger he seems intent on starting another war our Politicians are back and forth trying to keep the peace, for what its worth but he is keeping the potty boiling." Another worry is that the government are on about every male between the ages of eighteen and thirty nine having to register in case there is quick call up, this is not official yet but it would affect the Scott brothers but Dod assured them that he would do his best to resist any call up.

Sandy finally managed a week-end at home with the bad weather and him having to keep toon over the Hogmanay it was six weeks since his last visit his clothes were beginning to get a bit ripe, he was given the welcome of a long lost explorer, Willie couldn't wait to tell him that he only had eight more weeks schooling then he would start his apprenticeship as a Blacksmith, Megs schooling had finished nearly a year ago so that she could look after her mother and the youngest member of the family baby Tommy, she had more than a full time job with very little reward for her efforts, she was lucky in the fact that her younger sisters were very helpful, Betty shared the burden but she was due to leave school in eight weeks time and the croft could not support any more of them so she would have to get a job. She had set her sights on being a nurse. Jim was quite capable of taking over from Willie as his father's assistant and with him being interested in what crofting was all about he was maybe a better bet than Willie. Back at Burnside with all his clothes newly laundered Sandy was ready to get stuck in again, the weather was improving but after the frost the ground was like a quagmire, so they were restricted in what functions could be carried out, Dod gave a daily bulletin on the latest happenings in Europe it was getting real serious, information was scarce and events had taken place days before they were broadcast. Dod was invited to attend yet another tractor demonstration, at the last minute it was cancelled due to the uncertainty, put on hold was the phrase used to over come the problem. Eck ever witty and sharp passed comment "Nae doubt the boss will blame this Hitler gadgy for cancelling the tractor show". Lang Dod was a shrewd operator and he must have been continually scheming and planning ahead, Sandy was called to his office and told to take a seat the stomach nerves were playing up as he wondered why he was being given this audience with the boss. The reason for this little get-to gither is that I have been thinking in view of the progress you have made since you started with us its time to further your skills so as of Monday I want you to go wie Jake Thomson for a few hours every day and get some ploughing tuition.

When asked how he felt about that plan Sandy said " He was really looking forward to that, he had done a bit with his father, but he was quite small at the time and had problems but he had stretched quite a bit since then and would find it a lot easier now". He was over the moon, what an opportunity, little did he realise that his boss was covering his own erse, he was sure to loose the Scott brothers to the forces, getting replacements would be virtually impossible, there's nae heid like an auld heid.

Between excitements in this part of the world there were often long stretches of boredom, life just ambled along with most folks trying to scratch a living of sorts from the land, suddenly overnight the peace and tranquillity was shattered ? Dod Wilson had a spring in his step as he entered the stable door that morning it was unusual for him to be out and about so early, what could be wrong? " Well lads that's the hostilities started Germany invaded Poland last nicht, oor government have warned tham that if they dinna withdraw we are gan tae tak sides wie the Poles, its hard tae say where all this bloody nonsense will end". " We'll ken better on the midday news our government are gan tae mak an updated announcement". The BBC news at midday had the biggest audience ever recorded especially at Burnside Lang Dods sitting room was packed to capacity as they awaited the latest bullitien, Lizzie was the least worried about the outbreak of war as she fussed about making sure there were nae dirty beets walking on her clean fleer. Suddenly the room went silent as Winston Churchill started to speak letting the nation know that the Germans had ignored the ultimatum given by Britian, this left the British with no option but to throw their weight behind the Poles and drive the Nazi's back to where they belong. "Sadley we British Citizeans are at war once again", a loud gasp reverberated around the room, Lang Dod was the first to speak, "Weel, weel folks there could be a lang hard struggle ahead with difficult times to overcome but I'm sure we'll manage to handle the situation.

Auld Spencer was the first to re-act to the fact that war was imminent, he had done a great job recruiting the young men to join the Territorial Army, a ready trained fighting force therefore the first to be called up. With-in hours of the Prime Ministers speech the terriers were being wired instructions to report to their nearest drill hall. The Glen was devastated at least three quarters of the men were Terriers, before the end of the month most of them were serving Soldiers of the King. Lang Dod had played his cards right when he trained Sandy how to use the plough, because the Scott brothers were called up he was now two experienced ploughmen short. Dod did his best to get his men exempt but according to government legislation there were enough bodies left at Burnside to keep it going they included himself in the headcount. But there was a reprieve for one of the brothers, Tam was deemed unfit due to colour blindness , but brother Bill was not so lucky after sweating it out for over a week he received his instructions advising him to head for Woolmanhill barracks in Aberdeen where he was to join the Gordon Highlanders and become a member of the fifty first Highland Division. For the first time in his life Bill Scott was about to leave his native Glen and head into the unknown, Tam was worried about his younger brother but it was maybe just right as he had a wife and three bairns. Sandy was promoted to third ploughman quite a step up for one so young but he was highly regarded by the Boss and his work colleagues, none of them had any doubts that he couldn't handle the situation, Dod managed to hire a semi retired man to fill Sandy's post.

Everything was in turmoil as the government struggled to gain control a lot of new rules and regulations had to be implemented, there was a lot of movement of troops and one of the most magnificent sights Sandy had ever witnessed was the fleet of ships sailing up the Moray Firth, somebody suggested they were sailing for the deep water anchorage at either Invergordon or Scapa Flow where ever that was, it was certainly a formidable sight.

Sandy was glad he had the next week-end off he would get home and find out who had been called up it was serious the regular army were engaged in a Battle along the Maginot Line in France and were suffering casualties. It was quite a shock when his father rhymed off the names of all the young men of the Glen who were either away or waiting instructions. " Yon auld bugger Spencer has a lot to answer for he pressed all the boys into joining the T.A. and then what happens they are the first to go?" "Of course his own twa loons are both in the forces Adrian is a pilot and Roddy is an army officer". Willie had started work with Will Watson training to be a Blacksmith; Jim was now helping out on the croft everything was running fairly smoothly, Tommy was getting big and into everything now that he could walk. Mother was very poorly and quite a handful as she needed assistance with everything she did, the doctor was back and forth but never gave any idea of what caused the deterioration in their mothers health, his usual remedy was plenty rest and sleep.

News of what was happening in Europe was very sketchy the Minister tried to get the most up-to-date news so that he could tell the congregation the latest bulletin at Kirk on Sunday; he was one of about six people in the district who owned a wireless, they were powered with a wet and dry accumulator, the wet one had to be charged frequently this was done at the Smiddy so if you were to maintain continuity you needed at least two wet accumulators as they needed about thirty six hours on the charger, you can appreciate the hassle owning a humble Wireless caused. The year was wearing on again it would soon be Hogmanay; Sandy was due to be off this year so he was looking forward to having time with his family. The news from Europe was not good and a casualty list was published in the Peoples Journal every Friday, every week it seemed to be getting longer, how long before the first son of the Glen would loose his life, the government were having to implement their latest rules and the first of the rationing would take affect in the New Year the shortages were beginning to bite. The Glen was having its annual fall of snow it was fairly mild causing the minimum of disruption, a few of the boys managed to sneak a couple of days leave, most were clueless as to what their next move would be according to the individual they were living from day to day with very little advance notice of when or where they were going. Hogmanay day arrived and Sandy was allowed to leave early the roads were pretty dodgy which meant he had to walk a lot of the way it was getting dark as he neared the crossroads. Sandy near collapsed when a huge guy in Army uniform jumped out in front of him pointing his rifle very menacingly and ordered him to stop, Sandy didn't hesitate it was his first time looking down the barrel of a gun and he didn't relish the feeling. This roadblock was new to Sandy and he had no idea it was there, he was held up for twenty minutes as he was quizzed about his business asking the most ridiculous questions eventually they were satisfied he was a genuine young man in a hurry to get home.

As soon as he got in the door Sandy related to his father what had happened at the cross roads, his father said they were a bloody nuisance and if you had to pass them a dozen times a day they would stop you, he was sure they just did it to annoy people, on the other hand they were there twelve hours a day so boredom maybe played a big part in it. Meg was busy as she with the help of her sisters prepared the feast for New Years Day; even although things were scarce they had managed to get enough rations to have the usual fare along with a goose. The house would be in turmoil in the morning as the younger ones played with what ever Santa had brought there were only three believers, the twins Mary and Peg along with little Tommy. The New Year and everything was at a standstill for about a month due to heavy snow the roads were impassable so everybody had to sit tight until things improved. Bye the middle of February things were on the move again, suddenly all hell was let loose when the Military took over the moorland behind the Mansion House they had all sorts of machinery and guns, the noise was horrendous and made even worse when the Air Force decided to get involved the animals on the crofts and farms were terrified and were prone to stampeding which didn't do them any good. Auld Spencer was the only happy man in the Glen and he spent hours at his upstairs bedroom windows with his binoculars as he tracked every move the Military made. Rumour was rife in the Glen that there had been quite a few casualties but everything was hushed up in other words top secret, all the approaches were heavily guarded which made it difficult to gain access and if you tried to get in across the fences you were libel to get shot. The Glen folks were just about getting used to the racket, then one morning they awoke to the sound of silence, not a squeak it was near as bad as the noise they had had to put up with, the silence didn't last long and just as dawn began to break the Military burst into life and a huge convoy of vehicles started to trundle down the hill heading for the main road where they went from there was anybody's guess. Will Watson and young Willie Duncan stood in awe as they watched the different lorries, cars, motorbikes, tractors, buses and tanks they must have stretched for a couple of miles and it took about an hour and a quarter for them to pass, quite a few of the residents of the Glen lined the roadside and watched them passing.

Lang Dod looked to be in a bit of a hurry as he crossed the yard head down in his unmistakable gait he arrived at the stable door just as the men were about to leave for their afternoon stint. " Well boys I have jist listened to the midday news and the prime minister mannie Chamberlain has resigned and the ither mannie Churchill has taken over, it is maybe for the best I dinna think Chamberlain had a lot of bite aboot im, bit Churchill is a bit mair determined and hopefully will pit that Hitler bugger in his place. They soon found out where the troops were headed for, as the papers were full of the happenings in the St Valery area of France the Fifty First Highland Division had been slaughtered and there welfare was unknown there were many casualties even though many thousands of men had been rescued from Dunkirk just hours before the demise at St Valery. It seemed the Fifty First had suffered the brunt of it all and was more or less wiped out as a fighting force. The news was very vague but it appeared that many thousand had been taken prisoner when they surrendered. It would be weeks before the exact figures were known but most of the Glen boys were in the 51st so there was an anxious wait to know their fate.

The main topic of conversation that summer was the miracle of Dunkirk even in defeat the heroics carried out were something never to be forgotten every man had a different story to tell some were funny some very sad some just down right lucky. There were at least fifteen local boys involved only five returned of the other ten six were P.O.Ws and the other four were presumed killed in action. The war was beginning to bite and rations started to get scarce, rationing was very prevalent mainly on imported goods sugar was a prime example. But the farming folks didn't have a big problem as they were more or less self sufficient, they were supposed to send all their eggs to a Ministry of food pool for distribution but soon discovered that eggs were a good tool when it came to bartering for rationed goods or even bribery what ever the case may be. When any of the fisher folks would arrive at the croft with a bucket of fresh flounders (they were often still wriggling about) in return they would get eggs, butter and cheese, occasionally an animal would be slaughtered if this was the case it would be shared around, there was never any shortages as far as food was concerned. At the Kirk on Sunday it was announced that a meeting was to be held in the village hall on the following Friday it was strictly a meeting for men but the ladies could come along if they so wished. On the Friday evening the Glen folks began to gather it was surprising the amount of people that turned up considering that a good percentage of the young men were away fighting in various parts of the world. The stage of the hall was lined up with eight chairs, on the walls were draped the Union Jack with a picture of the King on one side and Churchill on the other. The first person to appear on stage was the local headmaster Bob Paterson he started by thanking the outstanding number of people who had taken the time to attend the started to explain the reason for the get-to-gether, "Gentlemen and ladies as you are aware as a country we are at war, a very grave and dangerous war going by the results we achieved at Dunkirk a few weeks ago, the Germans seem to be a very powerful enemy so while our troops are engaged in Foreign lands our country is very vulnerable so the reason for this meeting is to discuss the probability of the formation of a voluntary unit that is to be named the Home Guard , I will now hand you over to the experts." He received a rousing round of applause as he stood back and invited the others to come on stage via the side door. The first to appear (in full uniform) was the commanding officer from the training ground at the Mansion house Cornel Davis from the Welsh Guards he stood to attention in front of the flag and saluted before he was introduced by Bob Paterson, the rest of the seats were filled with the local dignitaries, the doctor, minister, bobby and finally there was one empty seat. Bob Paterson pointed to the door and announced that the final guest was a weel kent face, "Please welcome the Rt Hon Spencer Tracy". He was dressed in full Military uniform complete with a huge sword dangling from his side, he stopped in front of the flag and executed a salute as if it was just out of the text book, he got a standing ovation and was in his element he just loved playing at sojers. Cornel Davis was the first to speak, he explained that the government had to form a home defence force using men who were no longer fit for active service they were called the Home

Guard, its function was to keep an eye on the coast and be prepared to defend their patch if called upon.

"One of the main things to look out for is any strangers going about if you should see anybody that's not local call somebody in authority and they will be investigated there are many spies in our midst, at the moment in this area apart from the training on the moors you would hardly know there was a war going on, but in the south our cities are being raised to the ground as the Germans mount nightly bombing raids thousands of civilians are being killed and maimed. Finally Cornel Davis continued I would like to give you some hard facts as to why we need a defensive unit. The Germans control every country from the Mediterranean to Finland, from Norway to the Scottish coast is about one hour flying time, if the plane was loaded with super fit paratroopers we have very little defence against them at the moment, lets hope Hitler is not thinking along these lines and uses his resources to continue his battle against Russia. This gentlemen is why we need volunteers and as many as we can muster, I thank you all for attending and listening to what I have had to say". He was given a hearty round of applause for his effort. The headmaster proposed a vote of thanks to Cornel Davis for his time and advice, he then handed the floor to Auld Spencer. "Gentlemen I do hope you have all digested Cornel Davis's words and in our quest for recruits we will be inundated with volunteers", a few hands shot up requesting some questions to be answered, Auld Spencer held his hand up and assured them that there would be a time allocated for questions when the briefing was over. He cleared his throat as he prepared to continue, "We would like as many of you as possible to register to-night, and we need to get the unit off the ground as soon as possible so the quicker I get through my speech the better". He rambled on for a further twenty minutes more or less reiterating what had already been said by Col Davis, he finally ran out of steam and thanked everybody for taking the time to attend then handed back to the chairman Bob Paterson he offered the floor to the rest of the panel but they all declined as they felt all the points had already been covered. The meeting was then thrown open to any questions the fist one asked was "Dea we get paid"? It was pointed out that volunteer meant free of charge this brought a ripple of laughter. It was agreed that the first get together would be the following Tuesday evening at seven thirty and again on the Thursday same time they were told to bring any firearms they possessed as there was a shortage of weapons, with that the meeting was closed and everybody in the hall signed up much to the delight of the committee. The following Tuesday evening Auld Spencer was at the Hall bright and early dressed in full uniform waiting for his new recruits to arrive, they began to arrive in dribs and drabs some of them straight from the byre their boots still covered in cows sharn, the array of weapons was something to behold, twelve bore shots guns point two, two rifles air guns and four ten shot guns one old guy even had a huge sword a souvenir of the first world war, but nothing Mien Furher need worry about, if Charlie Chaplin had made an appearance it would have been a real comedy. But as the saying goes you can only pee with the stroop given to you. Auld Spencer would have his hands full trying to knock them into shape. They didn't have long to wait for their first Red Alert it was reported that the Germans had landed spies along the coast at Portgordon, three in total a woman and two men, two were quickly caught but the third managed to get to Edinburgh before capture. Spencer had two or three days of glory before standing his men down.

The rest of the year was pretty uneventful for the home Guard the guys were very enthusiastic at their training Auld Spencer was in his element, as he strove to knock them into shape, he was full of beans and this seemed to rub off on the rest. They had the usual winter fall of snow and before long they were into another year the war was causing a bit of disruption but the glen folks soon adapted and carried on as usual. It was the time of year for the threshing Mill to start its rounds by the time Sandy had his next week-end at home the Mill was half way through its two week stint in the Glen on the Saturday they were threshing the stacks at the Morrison croft they would work through till they finished. Sandy was still a couple of miles away from home when he heard the old Steam Engine and soon he could see the smoke belching from her funnel, he would just call in past Hillies and say hallo to his mother then head on up the road to offer help and to have a banter with the guys. There was only just over half-an-hour and they would be finished for the day so Sandy grabbed a bag of barley and headed for the loft, as soon as the last sheave had gone through the operators would start to strip the mill ready to move and get set up for Monday morning it was a tight schedule. The work now complete the men and boys gathered round and the banter and leg pulling began, "Frankie Smith started on Sandy " Aye Sandy there's a rumour goin roon that Lang Dod's getting a Land Army Quine (girl) fit div yea ken aboot that." Sandy was taken aback and said he hadn't heard a word aboot it, this didn't stop the ragging he got aboot keeping it secret so that he could maybe get off his mark with her, he was left quite embarrassed. They finally broke up and started to drift off home, when Sandy got his father on his own he asked what the story was about the Land Army Quine. His father explained that due to the shortage of men the government had set up a unit of women and they were being slotted in to jobs where agriculture was suffering due to lack of manpower. Sandy burst out laughing causing his father to look in amazement and ask what was funny," Father can yea imagine Lizzie Smith, she runs efter Lang Dod like he was a young boy, the men at Buries maintain she wipes his erse so another possibly younger woman there should cause fireworks, but there may be truth in the rumour you see the old semi retired guy is struggling to keep going and he is always threatening to leave so we'll just wait and see what develops." When he got back to Burnside on the Sunday evening he couldn't wait to tell Eck Davidson his news aboot the Land Girl, he was over the moon about it and was desperate to broach the subject with Lizzie when they were at breakfast in the morning even if its nae true it would wind her up and maybe take the cocky bitch doon a peg or two Eck's words. Sandy made sure that he was in the kitchen at the same time as Eck was that morning this piece of banter would be too good to miss. They were seated at the table as Lizzie entered in her usual early morning grumpy mood, the bouncy Eck was at his best and greeted her with his usual cheerful manner, " Aye Lizzie yea can fair keep a secret", " Whit dea yea mean she snapped"? " Aboot the new Land Girl, Sandy and me were wondering if she would be sleeping in the Bothy between us two." " Eck Davidson fit the hell are yea haverin aboot she scolded, aye have never heard such nonsense coming oot a man your age in my life, it would be over my dead body that the boss would employ a Quine tae dea a mans work she said tossing her head in the air.

Chapter Five

L IZZIE KEPT CLEAR OF THE KITCHEN for a few days so that she would avoid further confrontation with Eck, but over Lizzie's dead body or not a Quine did arrive a few weeks later but that is another story. Back to the present and the early spring was starting to appear, Sandy was doing his least favourite job gathering loose stones from the field farthest away from the farm steading it was a very noisy morning as the RAF flew constantly overhead going about their unknown business, Sandy's head was full of thoughts one was that his father would be at the threshing mill they still had a few days before everybody in the Glen had been seen too. Through boredom he would whistle a tune and it was always his ambition to compose a tune but that was easier said than done, suddenly amid the over head racket he heard a car horn being blown quite continuously he looked to-wards the road and there was the boss's car, horn blasting and the head lights flashing, as soon as he was level to where Sandy was standing he jumped out of the car and started to run across the field, bye the time he reached Sandy he was near to collapse and out of breath having great difficulty trying to speak. Sandy could tell his normally placid boss was distressed what ever could be wrong; Dod was leaning against his young prodigy and finally managed to tell him what the problem was. "Sandy there has been a dreadful accident at the threshing mill your father has been seriously injured, at the moment how seriously I don't know but my instructions were to get you to the hospital as soon as possible", Sandy asked what about the horse, " Never mind the bloody horse just make for the car, on second thoughts we better let the horse loose he'll graze away till we sort things oot. Forty minutes later they were entering the front door of the hospital the smell of disinfectant nearly knocked them over, suddenly Sandy felt a vice like grip take over his stomach he felt like throwing up his mind was in turmoil wondering what was ahead of him. At the end of the corridor was Jim Kerr the local minister he met Sandy and shook his hand telling him his father was still in theatre and had been for over three hours, as they stood in silence they were joined by a man wearing green overalls, Jim Kerr introduced him as Mr Brown the theatre surgeon, he told them to follow him to his office where he asked a secretary to provide some tea. Once they were all seated Mr Brown started to speak, " Sandy your father is badly injured, because he is a big strong man and has managed to survive so far, he is a fighter, we are still working on him and will be for a wee while yet, don't ask me if he will pull through because I could not give you a truthful answer, he has lost a lot of blood and is very weak", Sandy felt like he had been felled with a huge boulder he just couldn't think straight he felt physically sick and asked to be excused while he made his way to the bathroom. When Sandy got back to the office Mr Brown had gone back to the theatre both men in the room asked Sandy how he was and was he managing to cope, Sandy shook his head and assured them he would be fine. Dod Wilson had decided that he would be better at home as his men were short handed so it was decided that Jim Kerr would stay with Sandy until they knew what was happening, his parting words to Sandy were that if he was needed just get on the phone and he would be here as quickly as he could, he put his arms round Sandy's shoulders and gave him a sort of hug but said nothing. Sandy thanked him for his support and kindness he was close to tears his world was suddenly upside down.

What seemed like hours passed and still they were working on Sandy senior, eventually Mr Brown arrived in the waiting room he looked exhausted, "Well Sandy that's as much as we can do at the moment it is the waiting game now the next forty eight hours will be critical. We have had to assist your father with his breathing other than that we have to wait for the healing process to take over he will remain heavily sedated for the foreseeable future." Sandy asked if he could see his father, the surgeon said he could have a brief visit and then he would like Sandy to go home there was nothing he could do here and should there be any developments he would contact Mr Kerr immediately. With that he motioned Sandy to follow him, Sandy was bracing himself for what he was about to witness but it was way beyond his wildest dreams the shock was difficult to handle, about a minute passed before Mr Brown asked them to leave. Sandy Duncan was swathed in bandages from head to toe there was evidence of blood seeping through the heavy layer of gauze Sandy could only shake his head he had never had to face a crisis like it in his life. Jim Kerr put his arm round Sandy's shoulder's as he lead him towards the car, making conversation on the way home was difficult but Jim said he would phone the hospital first thing in the morning and then come up to Hillies and let them know the latest happenings. As they approached Hillies Sandy had a look at his watch he could hardly believe it was past eight-o-clock he had been at the hospital for over ten hours, as soon as the bairns heard the car stop they came flooding out of the house anxious for news of their beloved dad, the minister insisted he accompany them into the house so that he could say hallo to Mrs Duncan and say a prayer wishing Mr Duncan a speedy recovery he also asked for God's assistance in their hour of need, he then left as he had had a very long harrowing day. When the family were finally alone Sandy gathered them round the kitchen table, before he could start to tell them what he knew Meg asked when he had eaten last, Sandy rolled his eyes and said his last proper meal was breakfast. She told him to carry on and she would listen as she prepared some food for him. He then asked Willie if all the chores about the croft had been carried out they assured him everything was up-to-date, Sandy started to tell his siblings that there dad was seriously injured he tried to keep as near the truth as possible without causing the younger ones too much distress. The rest of the evening they had a steady stream of caller's and well-wishers anxious to know the latest bulletin on one of their most popular neighbours, the Morrison's were extremely anxious, as it had happened on their croft. Finally with the clock nearing midnight the older members of the Duncan family sat round the table and tried to make some plans as to where the future would lead them, Meg, Betty, Willie and Sandy were devastated the croft was now like a rudder less ship, Willie was the first to speak he told Sandy not to worry about the croft as Will Watson told him to stay at home until things were sorted out, Betty was due to take up a post in the hospital in Aberdeen shortly but she would cancel it if she were needed, so they were sort of in control. Sandy was sure his father would never work again but at the moment he kept his thoughts to himself. He was about to have a last look at the cattle in the byre when Meg suddenly burst into tears the rest of them rallied round her embracing her thinking that the grief was too much when she exclaimed that she had forgotten to milk the coo so it was roll up the sleeves and get stuck in!!!.

Next morning the family were up at crack of dawn getting stuck into the chores around the croft before it was day light, nine-o-clock sharp and the minister drove into the farm yard he gathered them all in the kitchen and let them know that their dad had survived the night and according to the doctor at the hospital he was holding his own. He told Sandy that the surgeon had asked if he could get to the hospital as soon as possible but he had no idea why such a request had been made. Sandy was ready to go Willie could handle any thing that arose at the croft, as the minister and his young companion drove along the road it was hard to make conversation but Jim Kerr did his best to assure Sandy that the medical people could work wonders and on no account to give up hope. Mr Brown the surgeon was waiting for them as they entered the main door of the hospital he shook hands and than ushered them towards his office got them seated and ordered some tea. " Sandy I will come straight to the point we have had a battle on our hands all night to keep your dad going he is very low and weak it is my duty to inform you that he could slip away at any moment." Sandy felt as though he had been kicked in the stomach, his head was spinning and he was speechless, Mr Brown continued to talk but his words were just a blur and making no sense to the young man seated in front of him, it took Sandy a couple of minutes to gain his composure and continue, he asked if he could see his father, there was not a lot to see because of the bandages and the only sign of life was the sound of his father gently moaning, within a minute he turned on his heel and left the room . He was in for a surprise when he reached Mr Browns office because seated in the corner was Dod Wilson drinking a cup of tea, he stood up and gave Sandy a hug and asked how things were looking to-day Sandy shook his head and his eyes filled with tears, he was unable to speak. Dod asked the minister if he had things to do at home as he Dod had come prepared to stay with Sandy and see he got home, the minister took up the offer as he was behind with his chores what ever they may have been, he assured Sandy he would be in touch later in the day.

Dod decided to get Sandy away from the hospital for a while and suggested they go for a drive along the cliff top road just out of town, he parked the car and got out, "Come on young man lets go for a walk and let the wind blow away the cob webs", as they walked in the strong breeze breathing in the clean salty air Sandy began to feel a bit better. Dod told him he had spoken to the doctor and was well aware the predicament the young man was in. Sandy started to apologise for all the inconvenience the Duncan's were causing and also the fact that he was having to neglect his work, the big fellow rounded on him and in no uncertain terms told him he didn't want to hear any more bloody nonsense like that again, "We are all put on this earth to help each other and don't ever forget that". He was fair taken aback with the severity of the big fellows rebuke so he thought better of continuing along that lines and was quite glad when it was suggested they make tracks back to the hospital. As they entered the main access they were met by Matron she said Mr Brown wanted Sandy immediately and to follow her, he could feel the knot in his stomach tightening as they walk behind this very elegant efficient lady. Mr Brown seemed quite relaxed as usual, he motioned them to be seated, suddenly his mood changed as he put on his hospital face this was part of his job that he detested but it had to be done.

Clearing his throat he began " In the last hour your fathers condition has deteriorated at the moment he is just clinging to life by a thread his strength has been keeping him going but his strength is ebbing away, I thought it would be better to tell you the truth and it may be less of a shock if the inevitable happens the odds Sandy are very poor." Sandy was numb he had been bracing himself for this to happen but now that it was a reality it is difficult to handle, he was fighting back the tears when he felt Lang Dod put his arm around his shoulder to offer some comfort but nothing seems to help in these situations. His young head in turmoil Sandy had no idea what to do next, Dod asked if he would like to be alone for a few minutes as he felt maybe a good greet would clear some of the pent up emotions gripping this young boy, they left Sandy on his own he stood up and gazed out to sea which was flat calm, suddenly he burst into a flood of tears and cried for a good two minutes, it felt like the world had been lifted off his shoulders, he made for the bathroom and washed his face, now he was ready to face the world again. Sandy Duncan senior passed away later that evening his oldest son was by his bedside a boy not yet sixteen, he had never experienced death before but could not believe how calm and subdued he felt as he gazed at the lifeless figure lying at peace on the hospital cot, he was surrounded by medical people and his boss Dod Wilson, but the feeling of loneliness that engulfed him was almost unbearable. The Doctor and his medical team along with Dod Wilson moved out and left Sandy alone as they were sure that is what he wanted, he said a silent prayer touched his father's still warm forehead and left the room. Shortly after that Dod Simpson the bobby and Jim Kerr arrived they both shook Sandy by the hand and expressed how sorry they were at how things had turned out. The minister said he would take care of the funeral arrangements and would talk to Sandy next morning about the service etc. With everything more or less in hand Sandy decided he was better off at home at least he would have a better idea of how the young ones were coping, the three elder men told Sandy not to worry they were there to help whenever he needed them he only had to ask, as he neared home the knot in his stomach was beginning to tighten he felt quite sick, one thing that did brighten his life a bit was the sight of his friend Will Watson he had young Tommy in his arms and if Sandy knew him he would have kept the family amused, Dod Wilson decided to carry on home he didn't fancy Sandy's task of telling his siblings that their dad would not be coming home ever again, he took his leave and promised to call next day.

Sandy inhaled a deep breath as he faced Big Will who put his arms round his shoulder and said he was sorry he then tried to soften the impact for the family by cracking a few cheery jokes but nobody was in the mood for laughter, the youngsters were all red eyed from crying the girls were in a terrible state it was heart breaking, Sandy was soon engulfed with arms and legs as they all tried to get round him at the same time, he tried his best to hold his composure as he tried to explain that their dad would not be coming back home, as he was now in heaven with Jesus, the ice was broken when young Tommy said in his child like voice " Tandy fit will Jesus dea wie him"? It brought a bit of a snigger from the rest a hard question for Sandy but he dealt with the whole situation admirably.

Overnight barely sixteen Sandy Duncan junior became an adult as he grasped the enormity of the task ahead of him, his father had been an orphan with no known relatives, his mother had one brother who was in the forces somewhere around the world so it all rested on Sandy's young shoulders, but with the help of his friends and neighbours he was sure he would cope, at the moment he was washed out as he had had very little sleep since the accident. Mid morning and the minister arrived he told Sandy he had all the arrangements in hand except for any special requests they may wish. They retired to the sitting room where Sandy invited Meg, Willie and their mother to sit in and make sure they all agreed what was going to happen. Jim Kerr ran through the procedure with them, fist thing was that their fathers remains would arrive around five-o-clock that day and they could have him lie in state in the sitting room that was normal practice unfortunately the coffin would have to remain closed due to the injuries their father sustained, then the funeral was arranged for Saturday at one-o-clock, as was the local tradition the funeral service would take place at Hillies with the interment at the Churchyard, Jim Kerr took his leave saying he would return in time for the arrival of the remains. The dreaded hour arrived and the family watched as the hearse turned in at the shop and slowly made its way up the road to Hillies young Tommy had been sent to neighbours to save him the ordeal. Will Watson was they're lending his support he helped Sandy and Willie along with the undertakers to carry the coffin through the house to the sitting room they were amazed how light it felt considering their father was a big hefty man. They had a steady stream of visitors as friends and neighbours came to support the young fatherless family the Duncan's were grateful, as it would have been difficult to manage alone. Dod Wilson arrived and told Sandy all his mates at Burnies had sent their condolences and they would all be attending the funeral on Saturday. Dod called Sandy aside and had a bit of a chat he said they would have to meet early next week and discuss what route Sandy would be taking he apologised for springing this so soon but as far as Dod was concerned it was just one of the major hurdles life threw in front of you and had to be tackled, he assured Sandy that what ever was decided he would give his full backing. A couple of sleepless nights later and it was Saturday morning not a day that the Duncan's were looking forward to but it had to be faced.

One good thing it was a nice autumn day, the mourners started arriving just after twelve thirty, the undertakers set up the coffin at the back door so that people could get pretty close and hear the service. Jim Kerr was there early and said a few comforting words to the family, at two minutes to one he led them to the back door where they stood behind the coffin facing the multitude of mourners who had gathered to pay their final respects to a very popular man who at the age of thirty nine had had his short life taken from him, Jim Kerr did his best not to sound too mournful and kept his service to forty minutes. The coffin was then loaded on to a flat cart and surrounded with loads of flowers Sandy Duncan's favourite animals his beloved pair of Clydesdales were yoked to the cart and they pulled their late master to his final resting place, this was Will Watson's idea it rather brightened up a very sad occasion. As they lowered the coffin into the grave a Squadron of spitfires screamed across the sky a rather fitting tribute to a well loved son of the glen.

Chapter Six

THE PROCEDURE AFTER THE INTERMENT WAS that the mourners lined up and shook the hands of the deceased persons family in this case it was Sandy, Willie and Jim, by the time the last one had shaken their hands they were beginning to have cramp but it was uplifting to see so many well kent faces some of whom they hadn't seen for some time, it took over an hour for the cemetery to return to peace and quiet, as the three brothers headed for home Sandy reminded the others that the house would be packed out the door as the women had stayed behind to make sure any mourner who so wished could have a cup of tea and a bite to eat. Meg was doing a sterling job dispensing cups of tea and she had baked plenty of eats, she had many willing helpers so its was well organised, as people had their tea they then began to drift off home until there were only the Watson's and another couple of neighbours, Sandy asked if any of the family would like to go to the cemetery and look at the grave, the flowers would be nice and fresh, they all wanted to go so it was decided that Mrs Watson would stay with Mrs Duncan while the kids said a final farewell to their beloved dad.

Sandy found out what like it was to be on his own as of the Monday after the funeral it was strange and difficult having to make decisions and not have the backing of his father he had no option but put on a brave face and get stuck in he was lucky in as much as it was heading towards winter and not a lot could be achieved. Sister Betty had flown the nest to take up her job as an auxiliary nurse in Aberdeen; she was the first to leave home, could this be the start of the break up of the family. Dod Wilson arranged a meeting for the Wednesday some sort of plan needed to be thrashed out so that Sandy could get back to a settled way of life it might not be all plain sailing. Sandy cycled to Burnside his meeting was at two pm , Eck was clearing a blocked ditch along the farm road as Sandy approached he got a great welcome from his old pal but he was running very close to the agreed time so he shouted to Eck see you on the way back, the welcome at the kitchen door from Lizzie was a bit more fiery as she reminded him to make sure his boots were removed before he entered the best room. Dod was reclining in his chair and belching smoke from his pipe the aroma of St Bruno reminded Sandy of his father, that was his favourite tobacco. He welcomed Sandy and motioned him to be seated, just as Lizzie was closing the door he called "Could we have a couple of cups of tea Liz please" " Yes Mr Wilson that will be no problem", Seated behind his desk Dod looked the gentleman farmer part, he opened his note pad and wrote Sandy's name and the date, he paused while Lizzie entered and placed the tea tray on the desk " Will that be all Mr Wilson" " Fine thank you Liz just fine", she glowered at Sandy as much as to say this is all your fault you little runt, Sandy just stared her out and gave her a cheeky grin as she closed the door nearly pulling it off its hinges. Right Sandy doon to business lets try and get to-days session over in an hour and a half," "Will you start or will I" Sandy told him to carry on, " Ok we have three options as I see it , one me being a selfish sort of man I could offer you a cottar house and you could carry on working for me. The second option is to ask Spencer Tracy if you can carry on the lease at Hillside."

"I have taken the liberty to have a chat wie Auld Spencer his only concern is your age he thinks your a bit young for such responsibilities, bit I jist pointed oot that in another twa of three months yea'll be auld enough to go and fecht the bloody Germans." "The third option and the one least best suited to you is that you get called up, that's not impossible with your next birthday being your seventeenth. Well dea yea want time to think it over or have you already got an answer." Sandy was a bit taken aback the last option had never entered his head but it was a re-ality especially the way the war was going , he thought he had gone through all the options but this one was a bit of a body blow. He retorted to his usual mannerism scratching just above his left ear. His mind was set on staying put on the croft he didn't fancy the cottar house as they would have less room than the croft house, so he gave Dod Wilson his answer without much thought other than to fight the good fight at Hillside. He thanked Dod for all his help and guidance over the last few difficult days and hoped that his decision would not alter the bond that had grown between them because he opted to work the croft. Dod gave him a long silent look and said I knew what your decision was going to be before we even started this meeting and I am glad that's the decision you made, I like men who want to be independent, now my boy we have a lot of planning to do so that we get you up and running. First we need to speak to Spencer I'll try him on the phone, the phone rang for a couple of minutes, " Is that you Beldie he holds the phone away from his ear, oh! its Mrs Forsyth is it funny it wis always Beldie Smith when we were in the school but maybe you hiv an elevated status in life noo hiv yea he was beaming from ear to ear how he loved taking the rise out of people". "Can a speak tae the mannie"? "do you mean Mr Tracy"? She replied and have you an appointment. "Look nivver mind the appointment bit jist tell him Dod Wilson needs to speak till him urgently" . No doubt Beldie was giving as good as she got and soon came back on the phone to say she was putting him through to her boss. A well-educated voice started to speak "Yes Yes Mr Wilson and what can I do for you to-day." " Aye Spencer I have young Sandy Duncan here we have just gone through the business you and I discussed the other day about Sandy taking over the lease at Hillside". "Yes I have given a lot of thought to the request and as you are well aware of my in put to the welfare of our youth of the Glen I will go along with entrusting the lease to Young Sandy, I have peace of mind in the fact that you will pick up the pieces were things to go wrong, just go ahead and get the solicitors and the Bank to draw up an agreement and we will proceed from there." Dod could just imagine the auld bugger having a good giggle to himself after his dig about picking up the pieces, they always did try and outsmart each other, Sandy had only heard one side of the conversation but by the expression on Lang Dod's face he was sure it was a favourable decision, Dod dropped the receiver back on the rest and looked at Sandy "Weel ma loon apart from the formalities you are now a fairmer, Auld Spencer was nae bother and spoke highly of you and your family so its up to us nae tae let him doon seeing he has been so helpful." "I'll contact the banker Hamish Watt and the solicitors to make appointments and will let you ken what's happening", with that over Sandy thank his now ex boss and took his leave. As he entered the kitchen Lizzie was at the table baking scones she near wrapped herself round Sandy as she started to fish for gossip, Sandy told her nothing, even the offer of tea and a fresh baked scone wouldn't tempt him.

Eck was still working at his ditch so Sandy stopped for a chinwag he told Eck about Lizzie trying to quiz him about what was going on, Eck said he was quite right to tell the auld bitch bugger all as everybody in the Glen would be told. He went on to tell Sandy about the New

Land girl and how Lizzie was spitting fire with jealousy to wind Sandy up he told him he liked working with her better than him, when asked why that was Eck replied "Because she isn't as bloody ugly as you are"? They both had a good laugh before Sandy mounted his bike and headed for home telling Eck to call in at Hillies so that they could have a crack and yea can bring this good-looking quine wie yae.

It was a week since the Duncan family had buried their beloved dad Sandy had never stopped since and felt he didn't have a chance to grieve properly for his father, his sisters and his mother had cried buckets of tears and were now accepting that dad was gone for good. So Sandy called his dogs and set off to the far corner of the croft and behind the dry stane dyke that formed the boundary with the moor he sat down and surveyed all that had happened over the last week or so and then burst into tears he cried his heart out for a good three or four minutes the dogs sensed something was wrong so they snuggled up to Sandy as if trying to offer some comfort, Sandy gave them each a hug before getting to his feet and heading for home but first he had to call in past the cemetery to assure his dad everything would be ok. There was a message for him from Dod Wilson to say they had an appointment at ten-o-clock on Monday morning with the Banker and then at mid-day with the solicitors. He had an uneventful weekend the highlight being a walk on Sunday as far as the village at Covie the bairns just loved it and could spend hours hunting for crabs and minnows among the rocks. Lang Dod was sharp half nine on Monday morning but Sandy was used to his punctuality and was waiting for him and jumped in the car the minute it stopped. After exchanging pleasantries they were on there way as usual Sandy had the heebie jebies worried sick about what lay ahead. This was a first for Sandy he had never been inside a Bank before so he was unsure of what to expect, his mentor Lang Dod just steamed in he seemed to know everybody and everything, he just crashed through the bank door and confronted the rather stern looking female seated at the reception. "Good morning Jeannie fit like the day"? She kind of glowered at him but didn't return his enthusiasm but of course it was Monday morning. She eventually decided he was due a reply and rather sarcastically said, "Oh! Good morning Mr Wilson I will find out if Mr Watt is ready to see you." Up until then she had more or less ignored Sandy but just as he was passing her she leaned over and said in a lowered voice how sorry she was to hear about his fathers accident Sandy could feel his cheeks starting to burn. She held the door open as Dod and Sandy entered the office, seated behind a rather untidy desk sat a rather overweight gentleman in a pin-striped suit. He stood up and offered his hand to Dod Wilson who in turn introduced Sandy to the Banker he expressed his sorrow about loosing Sandy Duncan a very honest and reliable customer and his yearly visits would be greatly missed. Hamish Watt asked if they would like some tea they both nodded he pressed a bell and as if by magic Jeanie appeared with a tray. On his desk was a folder, Sandy could make out his fathers name and the croft name of Hillside in bold capital letters on the front cover, Hamish proceeded to open the first page.

"Well Sandy you have nothing to worry about your father's account is in very good shape, all we need is to go through the formalities of transferring the account over to you, because you are so young we have to implement a couple of clauses, you need to consult us when you need to draw money of course this will only last until we are sure that you have a good grip on how things function", Dod Wilson butted in and said he would be acting as Sandy's advisor until he was up and running so he would be keeping an eye on things. Hamish Watt then asked about the Legal side Dod told him that there next port of call was the solicitor's office. They all stood up and shook hands as he held Sandy's hand he told him he was looking forward to doing business with him. As they passed the reception Dod had another dig at Jeannie Robertson asking if there was any sign of her getting a man as she was getting on a bit noo. At that point Jeannie dropped her mantle and hissed, "Why don't you just bugger off yea Lang streak of misery", with a peal of laughter the big fellow passed through the door pleased that he had hit a raw nerve poor Jeannie, Dod was in his element winding people up especially if it were of the female sex. Bang on time they reached the door to the solicitors office Sandy's stomach nerves were playing up again, as this was his first encounter with anything to do with the law and he really felt out of his depth, but he got a pleasant surprise when he walked in the door the young lady at the reception desk was none other than one of his old class mates from school Shelia Morrison, she had been all through school with Sandy her father Davie Morrison was a couple of crofts along the road from Hillside, she soon put him at ease as she told him all the people in this office were very friendly and helpful. They were ushered along to an inner office and were met by yet another long lost pal of Lang Dod his name was Davie Still, Sandy was introduced and again told how important his fathers custom had been to this company, they then got down to business the necessary paper work was drawn up signed and witnessed as per procedure with-in an hour it was all done and dusted. As they drove home Dod asked Sandy if he was quite satisfied with the proceedings so far Sandy shook his head he was still rather bewildered by it all, Dod said they would meet in a month to see how things were progressing and if he had a need for any advice just come along to Burnside he said he would tell Lizzie that he had top priority if he called, finally he told Sandy not to heed anybody else as they would all be wanting to add their tuppence worth and would only cause confusion, with that advice ringing in his ears Sandy expressed his gratitude and bade the big fellow goodbye.

Sandy was working at a fence at the roadside it was just a couple of weeks before Christmas his father had been dead for just on two months he was thinking about their New Years dinner without father it would be another sad occasion, no matter how he tried to put things to the back of his mind something would crop up and dad would be foremost in his thinking. He heard the sound of an engine and looked round there was the Laird chugging up the road he stopped opposite Sandy and got out, by the time he reached the fence he was peching (panting), "How are you Sandy it's the first chance I have had of speaking to you since your fathers unfortunate accident are you managing to cope with everything". Sandy told him he was ok and once he had mastered the accounts and book keeping he would be fine.

Sandy thanked him for showing his concern and was about to carry on when Auld Spencer started to speak again. "Bye the way lad now that you are at home and settled in can we count on you attending our Home Guard meetings on Tuesday and Thursday evenings, now that you are over sixteen we can certainly use your body", Sandy was in a corner and had to agree, Spencer was a fly old codger. As he started back to his car he brought up the subject of paying the rent for the croft, he explained that it was paid twice a year at the term and it was appreciated if it were in advance instead of arrears, as some people took great delight in doing, he had a bit of a chuckle to himself as he boarded the car. Sandy shook his head and thought the Auld bugger never misses a trick. True to his word Sandy started to attend the Home Guard Parades and was amazed at how enjoyable an evening it turned out to be, the Laird was pretty officious and tried his best to run it along Military lines but with all the young men away in the Regular forces he had to make do with middle aged and elderly men who's co-ordination was long gone, their sense of timing was abysmal causing Auld Spencer a lot of frustration, one or two of them had shotguns but most were armed with wooden replica guns, if we were invaded they would have to wait till the Germans were close enough to be clubbed to death. At every meeting they were reminded of the drill if there happened to be an emergency, the siren mounted on the outside wall of the hall would be activated, as soon as it was heard they had to get there as quickly as possible what ever the time of day or night may be, the men used to have a good laugh at Spencer's expense as they were sure he was just dying for an emergency so the he could set off the siren, as usual they were becoming complacent almost sure an emergency would never happen around here. Everything had settled down the Duncan's badly missed their father but life had to continue, Sandy and Meg had a lot of responsibility looking after the croft and looking after the younger members of the family and of course their mother needed constant attention she seemed to deteriorate daily. Willie had matured quite a bit he enjoyed his job at the Blacksmiths shop but he was a great help to his brother on the croft, but there were black clouds on the horizon for Willie in just fifteen months he would be old enough to be called up his job would not save him so he would just have to wait and see the out come. Betty was enjoying Aberdeen and looking forward to the day she would start training as a nurse. It was amazing how the family were growing up Tommy would soon be starting school he had been badly spoiled by Meg and without their father to show discipline, he could be a bit of a handful at times.

The Glen folks had survived another severe winter and were now well into a new spring crops were growing and the weather was good this allowed the work to progress. Sandy had just finished feeding his animals and was making for the kitchen to have his breakfast, half way across the yard he met Meg she was heading for the byre to milk the cow they exchanged pleasantries and Sandy took stock of what was going on around him the birds were singing and building nests for so early in the morning it was a wonderful feeling, Jim and Willie should be at the table having breakfast before heading for their jobs Willie to the Blacksmiths and Jim to carry out his chores around the croft before he went to school. Sandy had one foot in the back door when all hell was let loose the dogs were going mental it was a real circus. Sandy cocked his head and listened.

49

Chapter Seven

IT SUDDENLY DAWNED ON SANDY THAT the noise was the emergency siren calling them to muster at the village hall as there was some sort of scare, he mounted his bike and with the dogs running ahead he peddled like mad and with-in minutes he was in the parking area at the hall, Sandy looked back up the hill and it was quite comical to see all his neighbours on push bikes streaming down the road. As the breathless crofters arrived one by one each had the same question, "Fit the hells wrang"? Each was given the same answer take a seat in the hall and all will be revealed when the full compliment arrives. Auld Spencer was satisfied that all the men who should be attending were here, he mounted the platform and in his usual flamboyant manner proceeded to tell the assembled company that he believed that Britain was about to be invaded, "Fit maks yea think that" he was asked. Well at around midnight last night a German plane landed in Scotland it was carrying Hitler's Deputy a man by the name of Rudolph Hess it's all very secret at the moment but my way of thinking is that he is only a smoke screen for the main attacking force so we must be prepared, I have decided that we start by digging some defences at the cross roads if they attack by air they would come from the east if by sea it would be more a south easterly direction. If we dig a line of slit trenches along the edge of the field behind the cross roads at least we may be able to contain the enemy until re-enforcements arrive. Somebody in the audience shouted, "That's Frankie Smiths hay field and Frankie is away visiting his sick mother yea jist canna start digging with out asking him." Spencer pulled himself up to his full height and replied "that field is now the property of the M.O.D and we can use it as we see fit". There were rumblings of disapproval among the assembled crowd and the next question was asked by auld Davie Morrison " Fan are we expected to start digging", Again Spencer decided on a show of strength when he told them they would start digging with-in the next ten minutes, Auld Davie a stubborn sort of a man stood up and said, " I for one will nae be diggin in ten minutes I hivna hid my breakfast yet, I have nivver worked on a teem (empty) stomach in my life and I'm nae startin noo" there were rumblings of here, here through out the hall Auld Spencer had just suffered his first defeat and was soundly told that they would start digging at nine-o-clock. Bye the time the crofters returned the area of diggin had been marked out and a big sign erected along the bottom of Frankie's field announcing that the ground belonged to the Ministry Of Defence Keep Out. It was easy digging and with in a couple of hours they were down over three feet about half way, it was a welcome change from the usual routine of the croft and they were having a good bit of banter, some of the female volunteers had made tea and sandwiches so they had a good blether while eating. Some of the diggers had reached the depth of six feet and were leaning on their shovels awaiting the others to finish there was now twelve six foot by eighteen inches by eight feet trenches along the edge of Frankie's field, they had destroyed a ten feet wide area of his next winters hay he should be really chuffed about that. It was envisaged that they would be finished at twelve noon and they would just go home and await further instructions. About quarter to one the sound of a motorbike could be heard somebody said it sounded like Frankie's B.S.A there was a hush as they waited in anticipation.

Frankie's face was a picture to behold as he gazed in amazement at his hay field some of the guys were still tidying up the bottom of the trench and all you could see was shovels full of muck appearing over the top the digger was below ground level, Frankie blew his top he had a bit of temper anyway. He demanded to ken what the hell wis goin on, his good hay absolutely ruined, Spencer asked for calm as he explained to Frankie that the Germans had landed in Scotland and fearful of an attack he had ordered the defence of the glen to be implemented. Frankie let rip again " Div yea ken where the Germans hiv landed and it is one German nae Germans, one man and he landed on Eaglesham Moor just oot side Glesga twa hunner mile away dea yea think that warrants my hay park tae be destroyed". Auld Spencer had been caught out his face was rather crimson as he faced the troops he began to apologise and said he may have jumped the gun but he felt it was a worth while exercise, he near had a riot on his hands as Frankie persisted about the damage to his park, " Yir worthwhile exercise winna feed my cattle in the winter am needin compensated for the loss of at least one haystack. Waving his hands up and down trying to calm the situation Spencer told Frankie that when it was time to harvest the hay to come up to the Home farm and he would replace his loss at his expense, that was enough to satisfy Frankie but there were rumblings from the rest about wasting six hours playing at bloody sojers. To compensate for his rather over enthusiastic blunder Spencer offered his tenants an olive branch in the form of a garden Fete to be held at the Mansion house on a date yet to be decided he called on two or three people to form a committee so that they could set out a programme Will Watson, Bill Paterson and Jim Kerr were elected, Spencer added that he would ask Col Davis if his troops would participate in some sort of challenge match i.e. tug-of-war or something along that lines, with that the crofters dispersed to carry on with tending their crofts, one remark over heard was that they hoped there were no half wits like Auld Spencer in charge of the front line. The rest of that year passed without any major crisis the war was still raging and young men were loosing there lives Bill Scott and Roddy Tracy were prisoners of war they were two of the more fortunate ones. An announcement was made at the Kirk one Sunday where the minister told his congregation that there was a residents meeting to be held it was hoped there would be a good turn out no inclination was given as to why the meeting was called but local wit Will Watson decided that maybe Auld Spencer wanted to dig mair holes this brought a few adverse comments. The meeting was held on a Friday evening and the hall was packed to capacity, Bill Paterson was the man in the chair, he rose and welcomed everybody and also commented on the turnout. Looking at his notes he said he would outline their plan and then ask for the assembled audience for their verdict, " Ladies and gentlemen it is getting near to a New Year due to the ongoing war there is not a lot of cheer and goodwill about so we the local residents committee decided that we should have a concert to try and give ourselves a bit of a boost", hands up all those in favour, nearly every hand in the hall was raised. Bill Paterson carried on and emphasised the fact that they would need performers so if any of the audience had any stage skills to give their names to a committee member so that a programme could be implemented.

Will Watson persuaded Sandy to put his name forward as a musician, it turned out that there were at least six people with musical talents also a couple of singers, ones that could recite poetry so yes they could raise enough people to hold a concert. Lizzie Smart said the W.R.I. would put on a sketch but they may need a couple of men to help out so it was agreed that as soon as a programme was arranged rehearsals could begin at least it was something to pass the long winter evenings. There was a dark cloud on the horizon for the Duncan family the threshing mill was due shortly a reminder of the tragic death of their father it was now a year since it happened, but the threshing mill was a necessity to allow the crofters to have enough feed over the winter for their precious animals. Sandy was finding out he had very little spare time on his hands with two nights of Home Guard duties and two nights getting his musical talents up to scratch his spare time was at a premium, Will and him would get set up in the Blacksmiths shop where it was nice and warm and practice for a couple of hours at least twice weekly, if Willie was there he would give the bellows a pump to keep the furnace glowing so it was happy times. The threshing mill came and went without incident and mid December the snow appeared, before Christmas it was probably over a foot deep it was causing havoc with the little transport available at that time but the crofters were used to this annual snow fall and were well equipped to cope with it.

The night of the concert arrived, in the afternoon the school kids had a party complete with Santa Will Watson. The hall was then cleared and set up for the evening concert followed by a dance but being Saturday evening they would have to be finished by midnight. Sandy and Will were the first act so along with there fellow musicians they were set up ready to play Sandy had a peek out of the slit in the curtain and near collapsed he had never seen a crowd like it, as well as the locals there were three rows of soldiers at the back of the hall, Sandy began to have his usual bout of butterflies. The laird (no show without punch) had to carry out the introductory speech before the concert could start he was quite brief and told the people he had a special surprise but it was a secret until later on in the programme. The curtain rolled back and the musicians started a programme of Jigs and Reels the audience participated and kept time to the music the noise was overwhelming no doubt the evening was something different to the usual run of the mill evenings they were used to. It was getting near to the end of the concert and the stage was cleared the curtain shut, Auld Spencer appeared and announced that the special treat was about to take place, he asked how many have a wireless, if so you may be familiar with the next act if not just sit back and enjoy a session of American Jazz played by a small swing band from the Army Barracks at the Mansion House. Will Watson applauded, he was a jazz fanatic and to hear a real live band was beyond his wildest dreams, the band played for about half an hour Glen Millers In The Mood, American Patrol and many more the audience were reluctant to let them leave the stage so it was promised they would return during the dance and do a stint. The consensus of opinion was that it had been a great night , they still had to contend with struggling through deep snow on the way home but most of them had taken a pair of Wellington boots with them, there is no substitute for experience it was not the first winter that the glen folks had encountered deep snow.

Hogmanay came and went and still it continued to snow and it would be with them for another eight weeks. The only thing of any significance that happened that spring was the opening of a new Observer Hut on top of the hill it had a clear panoramic view of the Moray Firth and with powerful binoculars you could see clearly for about eighty miles of horizon so they could look out for ships and aeroplanes it was to be manned round the clock eight local men had been picked to man it. At last Lang Dod was getting his new tractor so it should be in place for the spring ploughing, Sandy was desperate to see it in action as the elder states men of the glen were sure the tractor would be a Pink Elephant and would never beat the horses especially in the small fields around the crofts, how wrong they were to be proved.

Although the North East of Scotland was not as heavily involved in the war as our counterparts in the East Coast of England we were probably just as close to the enemy, with just over an hours flying time to Norway and possibly Holland but the Germans only paid us an occasional visit although they dropped bombs from Wick right down the East coast the damage was minimal, the boys in the Observer Station could tell by the engine noise when the Luftwaffe came calling. The crofters were busy harvesting the hay on a lovely bright Saturday afternoon Sandy, Willie, Jim and Will Watson were working away in the field at the back of Hillies steading they were having a good spell of weather hence the reason for working on the Saturday afternoon the saying goes make hay while the sun shines. Young Tommy was after getting a telling off from his brothers for jumping on the hay colls and knocking them over he was warned if he did it again his erse would be dirling. Suddenly from nowhere an aeroplane came screaming out of the sky the Duncan's looked at each other as that plane was too close for comfort Will was the first to speak "It'll be that bloody idiot of a boy Adrian Tracey showing off again he will have forgotten the telling off he got the last time he frightened all the animals with his antics. As Will shaded his eyes against the sun he heard the plane begin to dive suddenly an awful thought struck him it could be bloody Jerry and he would be heavily armed, Will started to scream down, down, down, he hit the deck followed by three mesmerised young men and a bairn screaming that they had hurt his arm, how true Will's thoughts were when the plane started to spew out shells meaning to hit the men they eventually began to hit the small hay coll they were lying behind there was about six feet between them and sudden death they could feel the down draught of the plane as it passed over head, Will made sure he got a close look at it and there was no doubts in his mind it was Jerry. Even in the face of the most dire situations there is always a jink of humour, Sandy terrified as he was decided to have a quick peek round the side of the little haystack to see if any of his neighbours were still around he near burst out laughing when all he could see were heads behind the haystacks on every croft his neighbours were also lying flat on the ground they were not taking any chances either, this enemy plane was just about to make another pass over the terrified Duncan boys when suddenly another screaming engine could be heard the cavalry had arrived.

From out of the blue a good old spitfire appeared on the scene and immediately engaged the enemy in deadly combat all the crofters appeared from their hiding places and witnessed and enjoyed a grandstand view of real live dogfight this would probably never happen again, somebody described it as like being in the front row at the pictures. The two planes were locked in a deadly battle there would only be one winner, from the ground it was hard to tell who had the upper hand as they twisted and dived and fired their cannons, they were lost in the rays of the sun the audience were peering from shaded eyes when a cheer went up the tail plane of the German plane had been shot away and he was heading for the ground still a few thousand feet up, a tiny speck was seen to jump clear of the crashing plane seconds later a parachute opened and started to float along in the still air, the spitfire although damaged managed a victory roll as he left for his station, he got a fantastic cheer as he passed over his awe struck audience. The German was able to drift at a good height so he was soon clear of the glen some of the crofters tried to follow but he came down about three miles away an army lorry from the Mansion house had kept pace with him so he was captured immediately his feet hit the deck, he was armed with a revolver which he handed over as soon as he saw he was out numbered, the local people who saw him described him as a young arrogant boy who looked terrified. The Dog Fight above the glen would be talked about for years to come and some of the youngsters who witnessed it would no doubt tell their Grandchildren of what happened that day. After the fuss had died down the Duncan brothers stripped down the hay coll it was about six to eight feet in diameter, it was then they discovered how close they had come to meeting their maker the cannon shells were with-in eighteen inches of where they had been lying it sent a shudder down their spine.

Sandy had passed all the stages that Dod Wilson had asked of him when he took over the croft he had also satisfied the Bank so it was plain sailing he had received his exemption from the Military due to his circumstances, he now had a job with the Timber Control which he had been advised to take as it was included in the list of things that were a great help in the struggle to keep the country going as long as the war raged in Europe. Jim also got a job with the Timber Control when he left school, Willie was just weeks away from being called up. Sandy now needed another helper around the croft Tommy was too young so he was out of the question, Sandy hadn't long to wait his young sister Mary who had no notion to work in the house offered her services she had always been a bit of a Tom Boy, she turned out to be as good as any of them and eventually could possibly have ran the croft single handed. After lunch one Sunday Sandy decided to have a walk around his perimeter fence he had a few snares set and it was always a good idea to keep an eye on the fences and drystane dykes, Tommy wanted to go with him so they set off accompanied by the dogs, at the far end of the croft behind the hill stood a disused Quarry as Sandy approached the rim he could see smoke curling up in the still air he crept forward and was quite taken aback to discover a tinkers encampment with three or four tents the tink's were sitting around the fire and there in there midst sat Jimmy the Tink Eck Davidson's brother-in-law. Sandy was sure they had no right to be there but as long as they didn't bother anybody best leave them alone.

Sandy put his fingers to his lips and told Tommy to keep quiet as they moved away without being spotted; Sandy had noted that all his snares were empty that day he had a good idea why. As the two brothers walked the fence at the road side Sandy heard a motor bike approaching he was sure by the engine sound it was Eck Davidson, he skidded to a halt on the gravel road and asked his friend how he was getting on, with a grin he said he was on his way to meet his kin folk they had a camp in the quarry he told the two Duncan boys to get in the sidecar and he would introduce them Tommy was aboard in a flash so Sandy mounted the pillion curious to find out what lay ahead. When Jimmy Lindsay saw them he greeted them like long lost brothers, he started introducing his cousins, Sandy was amazed as they all had Biblical names like Solomon, Isaac and Joseph but they seemed a jolly bunch there were numerous bairns all looked badly in need of a good wash but they soon had Tommy running around with them, as they played various games. Everyone of the adults were smoking clay pipes the aroma didn't smell like ordinary Tobacco so it was hard to make out what it was but they all seemed to enjoy it, one of the men asked if anybody was interested in a game of pitch and toss a favourite tinker gambling game, the idea was to place a stick in the ground and from about ten yards you pitched pennies after they had all pitched as many as they wanted the one nearest threw the pennies in the air all the ones that landed heads he kept the tails were handed to the next nearest and he followed the same routine until all the pennies were won and they started again, Sandy was sure there was a lot of dishonesty in the game as he never seemed to win and he pulled out when he had lost one and sixpence. As they were leaving to go home some of the male tinkers were trying to sell their wares home made baskets, clothes pegs boot laces etc but Sandy was having none of their wares, Eck dropped them off back at the croft on his way home, the tinkers were moving shortly back to the Perthshire area in time for the Tattie howkin. The war was really beginning to bite with many casualties being reported on a daily basis, young men from the glen and surrounding area who would not be returning when this awful war finished, there was a constant reminder that there was a conflict all be it that it was many miles away, the air traffic was constant as there were at least two airfields with-in ten miles, and just as a real reminder of the horrors of what could happen would land on their door step. Sandy often watched the bombers returning from a night time raid at times he wondered how they managed to stay in the air they were so badly damaged their engines would be very sick it just seemed a miracle they could stay aloft but one morning the miracle failed to materialise and a catastrophe was about to unfold. Sandy had finished his breakfast and was about to head for the stable and get the horses harnessed up ready for work Willie and Jim were on their way to work. They could hear the drone of a squadron of heavy bombers about to pass overhead the brothers halted in their tracks and gazed at the sky shaking their heads in amazement at the damage the planes had sustained in their latest raid but they limped on by probably thinking not far to go now. Willie held up his hand telling his brothers to listen, straining their ears they could just make out the noise of a very sick engine as it spluttered and back fired, suddenly it came into view just missing the top of the farm steading the boys ducked thinking the buildings were about to be flattened but the pilot managed to clear the highest point, Sandy shouted she will never make it over the hill.

Behind Hillies there was a hillock possibly six to eight hundred feet high the Pilot must have been fighting to clear it as the engines began to rev, but they were doomed and hit about twenty feet from the summit, the carnage was heart breaking the plane disintegrated on impact and within seconds was a fire ball setting alight an area of moorland. The Duncan brothers ran towards the wreck hoping they might manage to help save lives but it was an impossible task the heat and exploding shells kept them some distance away, with-in minutes half the men folks in the glen had arrived to see if they could offer any assistance, Dod Simpson the bobby came puffing up the hill but he stood shaking his head his eyes filled with tears, he muttered, "what a bloody awful way to end your life". Next on the scene was Auld Spencer of course he had to throw his jacket in the ring and would have liked to throw his weight about that was until an officer from the Mansion house arrived with a squad of soldiers and told the locals to go home the show was over. Sandy began to realise that the plane had crashed just short of the quarry and wondered if the tink's were still there he managed to evade the troops and worked his way round the edge until he could peer over the rim he near had a heart attack, the tink's were gone but where the camp had been lay a huge wheel complete with tyre and a conglomeration of hydraulic pipes attached to it Sandy's blood ran cold thinking what might have been. The locals began to drift away heading for home they were heart broken for the gallant crew of the aeroplane it turned out to be Canadian and there were at least six of a crew what a start to the day, Will Watson reminded them that what had happened in the glen to-day was happening everyday down south and added "Aye maybe two or three times a day we are very lucky here compared to other places". Jim Kerr had a special service for the crew at the Kirk service on Sunday he also mentioned their grieving relatives somewhere in Canada.

Late that afternoon a RAF jeep arrived with a couple of NCOs on board they had to drive through Sandy's fields to get to the crash site, they stopped at the croft house to clear it with Sandy and to let him know they had a couple of heavy low loaders that may leave fairly deep tracks in the fields they also said they would take about a couple of days to clear the site, they would be erecting a small tented camp and would require fresh water, Sandy asked how many would be in the camp he was told about a dozen, he told them about the quarry as it was nice and sheltered also thinking if it was good enough for the tink's it would be good enough for the RAF, he said they could get fresh water from the croft. Once the two guys had surveyed the site they came back to the croft and were sitting by the gate waiting for their colleagues to arrive, Sandy went over and asked if everything was ok they said it was but until reinforcements got here they would just have to wait, he offered them a cup of tea and was near knocked over in the stampede towards the kitchen door, the weather looked as though it was about to break not really ideal for camping out. The RAF lads sat down and were soon tucking in to home made scones and pancakes, Sandy asked Meg if she had a minute when out of hearing range he asked her what she thought about letting the lads use the sitting room instead of having to sleep in a tent it was quite cold at night, she couldn't see any problem with that, they told their plans to the two boys and showed them the room they said they would keep it in mind if conditions got too rough.

It was late when the convoy of RAF vehicles arrived they headed straight to the crash site their instructions were to get the gear ready so that they could start at first light it would be rather a gruesome task as the burnt remains were still in the plane. The Duncan's were settling down for the evening all doing their different hobbies and tasks to pass the time, suddenly there was a loud knocking on the door, Willie was the first to reach the door standing in the fading light was a huge man sporting a mighty handlebar moustache he had the loudest voice the Duncan's had ever encountered little Tommy was quite scared of him. He introduced himself as Taffy Williams the second in command of the rescue detachment, his senior officer would arrive in the morning, and he had the driver of the water bowser with him and asked where they could fill up. When the task was complete they were on their way, Sandy said to the others he was glad he didn't have that noisy Welshman bawling in his ear all day as it would get a bit aggravating eventually, worse still it was hard to make out what he was saying in his heavy

Welsh accent, mind you they had no problem with his swear words. Meg was the last to go to bed she got her mother settled about midnight she felt very tired it had been a long tiresome day, she felt quite weepy as she thought about the poor Canadian lads killed in that awful crash, as she tossed and turned she could hear the storm brewing and the wind howling round the gable of the house, she wondered about the lads sent to clear up the crash site, what it would be like trying to sleep in a tent finally she drifted off to sleep. Sandy was the first to rise in the morning he crept quietly down stairs trying to be as quiet as possible, he made his way cautiously it was pitch-dark but he made this journey daily so he used to say he could see in the dark and anyhow he was aware of all the obstacles or so he thought. That morning he encountered eight pairs of RAF issue boots of various sizes he tripped and landed his full length in the lobby, the stramash he caused had everybody in the house leaping out of bed to find out what the hell was going on. Sandy was lying on his back moaning about the pain in his hip being hellish, then big Taffy Williams appeared at the sitting room door the noise he made would waken every house in the glen, if he got any louder the residents in the cemetery would be in danger of being wakened. After limping around the kitchen a couple of times Sandy's pain began to ease, he was thankful nothing seemed broken, he was getting plenty advice from the bold Taff as they sat having a cup of tea Taff explained, " Around o- one hundred hours this morning it was howling a gale the tents were starting to blow over, one of my lads said you had offered us a room Boyo it seemed to be the only answer to getting some shuteye, when we got to the house I told my boys to remove their boots trying to be as quiet as possible then this appens you cant bloody well win can you boyo". Sandy left to feed his horses he could hear big Taff shouting at his men it was time get out of bed and go to work. Meg appeared and asked Taff if the lads would like a plate of porridge before they left she said it would be ready in ten minutes, he said they would appreciate that, she filled eight plates and gave them a jug of thick cream she near threw up when she saw them wasting precious sugar on top of her good Scottish porridge. Apart from the ragging Sandy got he was none the worse of his tumble and it was soon forgotten the RAF boys were there for close on a week it was a gut wrenching task.

It turned out that there were only three crewmembers in the plane the other five had managed to bale out; the bodies were recovered from the wreckage. It was confirmed that all three lads were Canadian they had only been flying for a matter of weeks the Glen people were truly saddened by the incident and arranged with Jim Kerr to hold another service this time at the crash site just as a token of gratitude to these brave young lads who unselfishly gave their lives trying to make a better world for the survivors of this awful war , a contingent of the RAF lads who cleaned up the crash site also attended the service. Within weeks all that remained of the crash site was a scorched area of scrubland when the spring would come round there should be a nice green area of new grass a kind of memorial to the gallant crew. Everything had settled down once again and the crofters were plodding on trying to get the last of the crops home safely before winter set in, to break the monotony and liven things up a bit it was decided to hold a ploughing match this year it was now three autumn's past since the last one, the Bremner family offered two of their fields for the event they were one of the rich families who farmed a two hundred and fifty acre farm on prime land their fields were as flat as a billiard table it was great to be rich but their money didn't save their sons two of whom didn't survive the war the oldest son had been exempt to help his father run the farm, a committee was formed and the plans laid out, Lang Dod being a committee member insisted they should have a section for tractors his suggestion was approved, he was able to enter both sections having both a tractor and two pairs of horse. The Saturday of the match soon arrived and they all headed to the Wards as the farm was called there was a huge turnout of competitors ten were tractors and twenty five pairs of horse. Competition was stiff as they competed for a host of prizes the most sought after being the cup for the best overall ploughman. Old Davie Morrison won the cup Sandy managed to come second in the horse section while one of the Bremner lads won the tractor section with Tam Scott coming second Lang Dod was delighted as Tam was quite inexperienced. In the evening they held a dance in the barn, as usual Will and Sandy supplied the music and again they managed to engage a small swing band from the Army base at the Mansion house, the special guest was a piper his stint went down a treat. The Army boys had acquired a bottle of whisky so the musicians managed to get a bit tipsy before the end of he dance, it was the first time Sandy had participated in the demon drink he was rather unsteady on his feet on the way home and spent the rest of the night throwing up. The ploughing match was a good pointer that the end of another year was close at hand; they could expect the weather to break at any time, the winds were getting colder as they swept in off the North Sea. The inhabitants of the crofting communities were normally fit and healthy people very seldom needed the doctor, but with troops arriving from all over the world it was noted that some unfamiliar illness's were starting to affect the local inhabitants there was an out break of scarlet fever and various other unfamiliar ailments. During a routine visit at the school by the district nurse the teachers pointed out that the kids had recently started to scratch their heads and bodies the teachers had checked for lice but didn't find any, the nurse decided to have a look and she was shocked to find that some of them were red raw from scratching she had no problem identifying the cause.

Chapter Eight

THE NURSE HAD COME ACROSS THIS nasty little bug before and soon told the teachers the bairns had contacted scabies it was more than likely the whole school would have them, she decided to call in Dr Findlay for a second opinion. He duly arrived and within seconds had confirmed the nurses findings, the school and every residence in the Glen would need to be fumigated this was done by closing up the doors and windows and feeding blocks of sulphur onto the fire and of course everybody having a complete wash with carbolic soap, it was also found that there was lice in some of the kids hair it looked like the lice epidemic was just taking off, the normal cure for getting rid of lice was to shave the victims head so that there was no hiding place for the nasty little bugs, for the next few weeks the school looked more like a Penitentiary than a school. The source of the outbreak was never discovered but the soldiers at the Mansion house got the blame. The entertainments committee from last years Christmas doo were called to a meeting in the hall and it was proposed that in view of the success of the concert and dance the previous year they should hold another this year, it was pointed out that they were very low in funds, the WRI were asked if they would be interested in holding a sale of work to raise funds. It was promptly pointed out that most of the baking and tablet etc needed lots of sugar which was the scarcest commodity in their lives due to the rationing it is more precious than gold one woman pointed out.

Early in November Willie was hammering away at a white hot piece of metal as he shaped yet another horse shoe, suddenly he was aware of a tap on his shoulder, turning round quickly he was confronted by Jock Mitchell the postie, he was taking great delight in waving a brown envelope, in bold capital letters it stated O.H.M.S., " Aye Willie they've caught up wie yea at last" stated Jock he was hanging about waiting for Willie to open it, he would then gossip about the contents with everybody he met that day, Willie was well aware of

Jocks gossip so he slipped the envelope into his pocket much to the delight of Will Watson who winked at Jock and carried on hammering at his work piece, as soon as Jock cleared the smiddy door Willie ripped open the envelope he was quite up tight about it. He had to report to Woolmanhill Barracks in Aberdeen on the following Monday morning at nine-o-clock, Big Will said that would be no problem he could get the first train and he would be in Aberdeen for eight thirty plenty time to get to the Barracks, Willie had never been further than Banff and had never been on a train in his life already he was starting to panic, Will told him to go home and tell the family. Meg his twin sister was overcome with grief at the thought of her beloved brother having to go away to war and probably never come back, Sandy quietly told her to get a grip as she was upsetting the rest of the family.

The train journey to Aberdeen was quite uneventful as the old steam engine wheezed and coughed with her load of passengers bound for the Granite City, they arrived dead on time, Willie asked a porter how to get to Woolmanhill, he was told just jump on a tram bound for the barracks (Willie scratched his head wondering what the hell a tram was) and within ten minutes you will be there, the sheer size of the city was a bit of a culture shock for Willie. Most of the passengers on the tram were young men and funnily enough they all disembarked at the barracks.

Willie was apprehensive, he entered the Barracks it was teeming with people mostly in Khaki uniforms, he was met at the gate by a guy with two stripes on his arm his regiment was the Scots Guards so it said on his shoulder flashes. He asked their names ticked a piece of paper and ushered them along to a door marked knock and enter, inside on the wall were huge letters A to I, J to R and S to Z, Willie was in the first group they were shown into a room with about a dozen chairs they were told to be seated, suddenly the door burst open and the most loud mouthed ignorant little man entered, right away he started throwing his weight about, Willie was sure the animals at home were not talked to in such an ignorant humiliating manner as this little runt used, he was English and the boys had great difficulty understanding his accent. When he had finished his tantrum and was sure he had convinced his charges that he was a sergeant in his Majesties forces and a person to be looked up to and be respected they were each handed a form to be filled in, again loud mouth tried to humiliate them by asking if they could all read and write, his question was ignored until he demanded each one of them answer individually just to further their humiliation, the form filling complete they were told to move to the door at the far end of the room form a queue and wait further instructions. Ten minutes later the door swung open to reveal a room with ten booths along one wall similar to a phone box, the first ten were told to strip off to the buff and stand outside the booth awaiting their medical examination, Willie had never revealed his naked body to anybody in his life not even his brothers had viewed anything below his waist, he was absolutely horrified and asked the regular on duty if it meant his under pants as well, he got a mouthful of abuse that was unimaginable and was asked if he had difficulty understanding the Kings English, or was he just plain stupid, he was then asked if he was different down below from the rest and didn't want anybody else to see it, Willie felt very embarrassed and humiliated and things got worse, he was first in line to be examined he was told to face the booth and bend over, the doctor then started to poke around his rear end, Willie asked the orderly what was going on the orderly told him the doctor was having a gander at his Dukes, " Fit the hells ma dukes"Willie asked , Duke of Argyles (Piles), Willie said he was wasting his time as he didn't have any, the final humiliation for Willie was when he straightened up, he was told to face the front as he stood up straight the doctors hand shot out and grabbed Willie by the googlies and told him to cough Willie got such a shock he near spewed never mind cough, he was never so glad to be told to get dressed as he was at that moment thankful his ordeal was over. They had been told not put on their shirts or jackets just yet, they were moved to another room it contained a few chairs and a table two guys were seated they looked rather groggy they had just been inoculated and had passed out Willies squad were next but they all survived the ordeal and were told to dress. They were then moved to another small room where yet another guy with a clipboard was ready to tell them their final destination. Willie was the third name to be called he stepped forward and was ushered to a corner where another guy was standing they were soon joined by another two all four had been together since morning, they were given instructions to go along the corridor and enter the fourth door along they were told to report to Sgt Macdonald this they did and were pleasantly surprised to find this N.C.O soft spoken and very mild mannered a change from the first ignorant pig.

Sgt Macdonald shook all four by the hand and welcomed them to His Majesties Armed Forces he said they would soon be sworn in and would be the property of the government. Sgt Macdonald was a Scot who made the lads feel more at ease than their previous encounters with

NCOs, he looked at his notes and asked who William Duncan was Willie raised his hand, well William I see you asked to join the REME or the Royal Engineers, the bad news is you are going to neither, the four of you are being sent to the Royal Military Police. Willie was quite excited about the prospect although he had no ideas what the M.Ps did in the army no doubt he would soon find out. The four guys were then chased off to the canteen so that they could have some lunch they were told to report back in one hour to await further instructions. It had been a day of surprises and humiliation for young Willie Duncan, when he arrived back in Sgt MacDonald's office after lunch he was in for the biggest surprise of the day, the sergeant told them to be seated he then proceeded to tell them their fate, they would be given travel warrants and expenses then catch the train for London at eight-o-clock that evening, they should arrive in London at approximately eight am to-morrow, then make their way to Woolwich Transit Barracks where they will receive their kit and instructions where to go for training. Willie was gob smacked he thought he would be going home to Hillies before being posted. He had made plans to meet his sister Betty at the railway station she was going home for a few days leave from her nursing job they had arranged to travel together on the four thirty train he would need to get to the station before the departure time to let her know what was happening. Just after two thirty they were allowed to leave the barracks with the threat be on the London train to night or else, they headed for the Railway station arriving around three pm, they found seats in the buffet and for the first time that day they managed to do a proper introduction, Willie was first, then Sammy from near Foggieloan he worked for a fencing contractor, Jimmy worked on a farm in the Buchan area and Davie came from Turriff where he was a joiner introductions over they ordered a cup of tea and discussed the future in their role as Military Policemen, Willie let them know he really wanted to carry on his trade as a blacksmith but they had ignored his request to be enlisted in the REME, Willie was keeping an eye on the time as it would soon be time for Betty to catch her train for home. He was getting anxious less than twenty minutes and still no Betty as he scanned the station suddenly he noticed her waving for all she was worth and Betty being the smiler of the Duncan family was beaming from ear to ear she threw herself at her brother giving him a big hug, her joyfulness soon turned to tears when Willie told her he was not coming home, she howled even louder when informed he was bound for London that evening. Willie held her tight and told her not cry and it was good that she would be able to tell the rest of the family when she got home, with that she boarded the train . Betty was still leaning out the carriage window and waving as the train rounded the first curve on leaving the station she would be home before Willie started his journey into the unknown. The three new mates were still in the buffet when Willie got back so he joined them they still had about three hours before they were due to leave but they had been advised to get on the train as early as possible as it would be busy and seats would be at a premium, twenty to seven they headed for their platform.

The lads were quite taken aback by the number of people already on board the train, the majority were in uniform, they did a bit of hunting along the carriages and eventually found four seats together, Willie was fascinated by the different emotions shown by the people on the platform married couples hugging and kissing while their kids tried to get in on the act some laughing some crying then the whistle blew warning everybody they were about to leave, dead on eight-o-clock they started to chug out of the station there were hundreds of people on the platform waving for all they were worth until the last carriage had disappeared from view, one of the guys mentioned it must be relations seeing their fowk awa. The other two seats in the carriage were occupied by a couple of sailors they were going to join a ship in Portsmouth, this had been some day for Willie so many new things had happened to him and he was about to experience another first in as much as he had no bed to go to that night they would have to make the best of the railway carriage, Willie soon fell asleep they had pulled down the blinds and extinguished the lights so falling asleep had been easy. Around one am and the train stopped Willie looked out the carriage window and spotted a sign saying Berwick-on-Tweed he knew from his History and Geography lessons at school they were on the border with England, one of the lads produced a package of food which he shared around the carriage somebody else had a bottle of lemonade so they had a wee picnic as the train pounded its way to London, Willie would have liked to go for a good stretch as he was stiff and cramped but in the confines of the carriage it was not possible, maybe at the next station he would jump out and have a stretch, one of the Navy boys said the next stop was Newcastle where they had a twenty minute stop is anybody fancied a cup of tea they would have plenty time that sounded good, a couple of them armed with enough money for six cups of tea was ready to jump out as soon as they stopped, it was like a rugby scrum trying to get near the little kiosk to get their refreshments. Back on the train and the six young men were soon sound asleep the next time Sandy wakened he felt worse than the first time as well as being stiff and cramped it was quite cold he looked out the carriage window and noticed they were steaming through some sort of town, one of the Navy boys said they were in the outskirts of London, Sandy pointed out they still had an hour before their arrival time, it was pointed out London was a huge place and it took near an hour from the outskirts to the Station, he was taken aback the nearer he got to the city centre, seeing all the devastation that had been caused by the bombing the lads had never envisaged anything quite like it one of them remarked that they didn't know what a war was about back home.

Willie had never seen so many people in the one place as he did in King's X station it looked like millions they were bumped about from pillar to post as people hurried about their business, the lads had now to find a tube station to get to Woolwich again the hundreds of people packing the underground was unimaginable Willie was flabbergasted and terrified he would get lost from the rest, when the Woolwich train arrived the surge of the crowd soon had everybody on board, Willie had grown up over the past twenty four hours he could just picture his brother Sandy ambling his way to a field to begin work totally oblivious to how things happened in London. With-in minutes they were leaving the Underground and heading for the Woolwich Barracks.

Chapter Nine

Woolwich Barracks was another shock to Willies system the sheer size was mind boggling, everybody dressed in Khaki, shouting and bawling orders at each other the din was overpowering. From the reception office the boys were directed to an office where again they had more form filling more or less giving the same info as they had given in Aberdeen they were then taken to the stores where they were given their kit it was just heaved at them if the fit was near enough they kept it. It was getting near lunchtime and the lads had never even been offered breakfast so the pangs of hunger were starting to bite, Jimmy asked a very officious looking Corporal when they could eat. Jimmy was a very quiet polite sort of lad who didn't really deserve the ignorant, obnoxious answer he received, it went along the lines that the NCOs in Woolwich asked the questions and the buckshee privates just did as they were told, Jimmy was quiet but obviously had a bit of a temper he was about to retaliate when the others closed ranks and pulled him away, from between clenched teeth he hissed " When I qualify as a Red Cap I'll come back here and personally crucify that ignorant little bastard" After being kitted out they were shipped to the M.P training depot to begin their basic training.

Back at Hillies they were waiting for Betty and Willie to arrive, Betty was spotted walking up the road the young members started running to meet her shouting "Fars Willie is he nae cumin hame"? Betty just shook her head her eyes again filling with tears, " Na Willies on his wie tae London he is a sojer noo its hard tae say when we will see him again", bye the time she reached the house the whole family were there demanding answers as to how she was alone, she had quite an emotional time explaining that Willie had been sent to London, in fact she added the train will still be in Aiberdeen it disna leave till eight-o-clock, Meg was overcome with grief Willie her twin brother gone and she had never really said goodbye properly, they fully expected to see him home for a few days until it was decided where he would be sent. A couple of weeks later they received a postcard type note with his name and army number telling them he was alive and well but no forwarding address, still it boosted the morale knowing he was ok. Everyone was beginning to feel the pinch none more so than Will Watson the Blacksmith due to the war effort it was impossible to purchase iron, most of his work now was patching things up using scraps of metal found lying around the workshop, he was missing his young apprentice for company but as far as the work went he was quite glad he only had himself to cater for, Sandy and Jim were both employed by the Timber Control, Sandy hated it because he thought dragging timber was hard work on his horses so he worked them day about this allowed them to rest every second day. Mary who was now twelve years old took over the running of the croft when Sandy was working she was as good as any man which was a burden off Sandy's back as the timber was hard work and work he wasn't accustomed to. They had a bumper harvest that year the stockyards were full to bursting, at least this looked like a lucky year for a change but you can only ride your luck for so long. The animals at Hillies had been around for as long as Sandy could remember and one old timer Dolly the cow was beginning to show wear and tear not producing as she used to, a real predicament for Sandy what should he do about it.?

Sandy decided to consult his mentor Lang Dod Wilson for advice, "Sandy the trouble with you crofters is that yea treat the beasts like they were family and yea get ower close to them then, when they hiv to go its heart breakin I ken foo yir feelin aboot Dolly bit yea'll jist hiv tae tak the bull by the horns (pardon the pun) and get rid o the beastie its as simple as that. Sandy could just hear the hullabaloo the rest of the family would kick up when he said he wis getting rid of Auld Dolly a faithful friend for as long as he could remember. The only difference between Dolly and the family was that she slept in the byre and ate hay while the family slept in the hoose and ate cooked food otherwise they were all Duncan's. Sandy had always been quite shrewd when buying and selling his animals until one day a dealer arrived at the croft and Sandy unwittingly mentioned he was on the outlook for a young heifer to replace his old milk coo, within days the dealer was knocking at his door telling him he had a young heifer and if he was interested part of the deal would be he would take the old beast off his hands. Sandy asked for time to think about it and was given the usual spiel about big demand for breeding heifers and if he delayed too long he might lose out.

Sandy had a restless night as he tossed and turned wondering if he should take a chance and buy the dealers cow by the time morning came he was as far from a decision as he had been when he finally fell asleep, one idea he had was to keep Dolly and feed a calf off her if she were short of milk he could always supplement with milk from his new beast, which ever way he went it would put a strain on his bank balance. Jimmy the Swick (cheat) as he was known locally soon made an appearance telling Sandy he had received another offer, this was his last chance he couldn't afford to wait any longer, an old dealer trick but amazing how often it worked as it did now, Sandy told him he would take the young heifer but he was keeping hold of Dolly, he would be expecting to have a few pounds knocked off the price seeing The Swick didn't have to dispose of the old beast, he agreed this was a fair deal, he would return later with the beast, he reminded Sandy how he wanted the cheque made out just incase he forgot. Will Watson looked like a man on a mission as he legged it up the croft road, Sandy started out to meet him but he could see Will was not in his usual jocular mood so he asked, "What the hells bathering yea Will? Yea wid think somebody had stolen yir scone or is it something else batherin yea". Will replied, " Oh aye there's plenty batherin me can yae tell me what the hell that Jimmy the Swick was needin I noticed he has been back and forth all week, dinna tell me yea have been daft enough to have dealings wie that slimy little bugger have yea"? Sandy could feel his blood pressure rising and no doubt his face was beetroot red, he could'nt tell his friend a lie, so he came clean and told the truth, then the guilt set in as he began to wonder if he had blundered, he thought big Will was about to explode when he said he had bought a beast off him. Will tried to calm down he felt there was no point getting at his young mate he shook his head and looked Sandy straight in the eye. " Sandy I hope this works out ok for yea, but I thought you would have more sense than deal with that low life he would swindle his mother if there was few bob to be made off her".

Will then asked a few questions about the animal, Sandy told him the price he had paid, Will thought it was reasonable if the beast was healthy and had a good yield of milk. Sandy was starting to get a bit apprehensive the day was wearing on and it would soon be dark. no sign of the Swick maybe he had changed his mind, this wouldn't matter to Sandy as he had now learned a lesson not to deal with shady dealers in future, suddenly out of the darkness he could hear the sound of footsteps and the unmistakable sound of hooves on the hard road, peering into the darkness he could just make out the shape of Jimmy The Swick and walking behind him an animal on a halter, as he closed in on Sandy he said " That took a lot longer than I thought it would it's a fair walk fae the ither side of Burnside". Sandy was anxious to get a close look at the beast so that he could confirm if he had been conned or not. When he finally set eyes on her he near fainted she was just a bag of bones looked as though she hadn't been fed for months, Jimmy started to explain she belonged to an auld wifie who was unable to look after her animals properly the cruelty people had closed her down so I offered to find good homes for them, a week of good feeding and she'll be right as rain, Sandy had his doubts and let Jimmy know he was not amused, but all he was interested in was getting his cheque, Sandy being an honest human being dwelt on the fact that he had made a deal which they shook hands on and he felt it his duty to honour the deal. Jimmy grabbed the cheque and as he was about to leave he again offered to take old Dolly off Sandy's hands but he point blankly refused, as Jimmy was leaving he said it had been a pleasure doing business and he was looking forward to their next deal. Sandy was so disillusioned with the state of this poor beast he thought this is the first and last deal we will be doing my friend, but it was a learning curve for Sandy and the lesson learnt was never do a blind deal in future because there are vultures out there waiting to clean your bones. Before bedding down for the night Sandy paid his new acquisition a visit, he was worried at the state she was in, she was in the stall next to Dolly but seemed to be having difficulty standing, Sandy had a medicine he was given by the vet so he decided to dose her with that, he had to smile when he noticed the young ones had a name plate above her stall they had named her Sally. Sandy had a sleepless night and was out of bed well before daylight he headed straight for the byre and was shocked to find the little heifer lying on her side and frothing at the mouth, he ran back to the house and roused Jim, between them they managed to turn her to a more comfortable position, they would need to get the vet but it was a bit early to send for him, Jim was a bit harder than Sandy and said they should get the vet now it would be too late after the coo wis deid, without more ado Jim was on his bike heading for the phone box at the shop, with-in half an hour the vet was diving into the yard, Sandy was full of apologies for calling the vet so early but he brushed him aside and said that was what he was paid for. Bob Michie had been the vet for many years and had known the Duncan boys all their lives he was a kindly man and his nature seemed to suit the job he did. He asked Sandy the details of his sick animal when he heard the name Jimmy The Swick he shook his head and said that man should be locked up he causes us no end of trouble with his underhand dealing but, "Sandy man I thought you wid hiv hid mair sense than get teen in wie the likes of him.

They entered the byre the heifer was still lying down she appeared very distressed; the vet began his examination one of the first problems that I can see is severe neglect which has led to under nourishment due to starvation, he got quite agitated as he waited for the thermometer to register her temperature, as he waited he had a good feel of her stomach, he stood back shaking his head, "Sandy this beast is in an awful state at the moment I have no idea what is causing the problem, I need to take some tests and get them to a laboratory for analysis I don't think its foot and mouth but it could be worse." Sandy was sent reeling once again as he stammered, " What, what dea yea mean worse Mr Michie"? " Did yea ever hear of anthrax"? Sandy shook his head, the vet continued, " If it is every beast for miles around could be wiped out, as for that slimy bugger Jimmy the Swick he should be hung". The vet returned to his car where he had a bundle of manuals with all the government rules and regulations in bold print and bearing the government seal of approval this indeed looked serious, Sandy was going to pieces, Mr Michie removed a fairly thick manual stamped across the cover in red ink the word ANTHRAX, he started to thumb through the pages until he came to the part governing the procedure of quarantine, he was reading and occasionally shaking his head, to the Duncan brothers it felt like hours before he spoke again. "Weel Sandy we have a big problem on our hands if this proves positive, all the symptoms are pointing at anthrax so I have to treat it as positive until proved different, first thing I have to do is put a restriction order on the croft that involves the police, first I am going to show you how to dose the beast this has to be done every two hours then I will go and speak to Dod Simpson, its his job to cordon off the entrance and post notices around the croft, in the mean time don't use any milk from either of your beasts until we get results", he went to the boot of his car and produced a large tin of disinfectant and instructed Sandy to set up foot baths at the gate so that anybody entering and leaving had to walk through them . Poor Sandy was devastated he said to his brother Jim "What a bloody mess I've made of things ," Jim put his arm around his brothers shoulder and assured him the whole family were in this and they would stick together and they would conquer this situation they found themselves in. After giving final instructions the vet took his leave twenty minutes later Dod Simpson was erecting the barriers and notices barring all unauthorised persons from entering the croft, later in the day Jim decided to walk as far as the gate but the bobby on duty shouted at him when he was fifty yards away not to come any further but if he looked in the bucket at the side of the road he would find mail and the daily paper, the bobby was a stranger so he was showing his authority and abiding by the rules. When Jim arrived back at the house he started to sort through the mail, he couldn't believe his eyes at the amount of notes from their neighbours encouraging them to keep the chin up and they were sure it would all work out for the best. This was a real moral booster as Sandy had expected a bit of a backlash from his neighbours for being so stupid. It was now four hours since the vet left time to dose the heifer for the second time; they were in for a pleasant surprise out of the blue she seemed to have taken a turn for the better. It was twelve hours since Bob Michie had first looked at the heifer, he had just arrived back it was supper time at Hillside he was asked if he would like to join them.

He was a bit unsure if he could spare the time to join the Duncan's for supper that was until he was told that they were having fresh herring and Tatties in their jackets a great favourite in that part of the world, Sandy told him the herring were freshly caught that day, one of his fisher friends had dropped off a box at the barrier. But before they would eat he wanted to look at the heifer, Sandy went with him and mentioned that he thought she looked a bit better the last time he had dosed her, they entered the byre the vet let out a breath as he said " Bye gosh boy that beast looks one hundred percent better than she did the last time I examined her", he took her temperature again and announced that it was still very high but they should keep dosing her every two hours through the night and he would access the situation in the morning. The kitchen smelled like a fish shop as Meg coated the fresh herring and then fried them, a huge pot of potatoes were boiling away merrily the aroma made the men feel hungry, it was obviously a favourite with Bob Michie as he scoffed three large herring and a few Tatties, as they ate the vet was running over the restrictions imposed on the movement of people and livestock, there were pages and pages of information nearly impossible to absorb everything they were supposed to , if anthrax was confirmed all the animals on the croft would have to be destroyed, the carcasses had to be burned and the remains buried in a pit six feet deep and covered with quick lime, as the gory details emerged Sandy was feeling numb it would be thirty-six hours before they would have confirmation one way or another, to try and put his mind at rest he asked Bob Michie if he had any idea what the out come would be. Bob Michie put his elbows on the table and cupped his chin in his hands he then looked the two young men straight in the eye and said. "Weel lads your heifer has all the symptoms associated with anthrax, but she is so badly malnourished that it could be a magnitude of things the encouraging part is that she has responded since morning, all we can do is keep dosing her through the night and pray that my diagnosis is incorrect, he shouted thanks to Meg for the wonderful supper she had provided then headed for the byre for one last look before going home, she was still lying on her side but here eyes were much clearer and she seemed more alert, he shook his head and wondered how anybody could allow an animals to suffer such agonies. As he drove off he shouted goodnight lads see you in the morning, he had had a long tiring day and was ready to jump into bed as he had a heavy workload to-morrow. Sandy looked at his watch it was nearing nine-o-clock fifteen hours since they had called Bob Michie, he watched as the vet stopped at the barrier and scrubbed his wheels and boots with disinfectant he looked at Jim and said " Being a vet is a worse job than we have".

The two brothers decided to have a walk as far as the barrier and were quite pleaded to see it was Dod Simpson who was on duty they went to with-in ten yards and Dod said, "yea better nae come ony closer boys jist incase", he asked if they enjoyed the herring then told them who had left them, he then went on to tell them who had all called at the barrier to wish them all the best, they spent about twenty minutes having a blether with Auld Dod Simpson this was probably the biggest bit of excitement he had ever experienced in his thirty years as a copper. He asked the lad's aboot the heifer and if they had plenty food, Sandy told him the only thing running short was milk.

They explained that they had been advised not to use old Dolly's milk until the root of their problem had been sorted out, Dod said he would see if any of the neighbours had a spare drop they could give, with that they bade each other good night and the lads headed for home. During the walk to the steading they decided they would take turns to look after the heifer, Jim volunteered to sit up until two am and administer the next dosage this would allow Sandy a decent sleep until it was his turn to dose the animal. Sandy was in a deep sleep when

Jim went to waken him, the animal was due its next dose at five am the little heifer had been fine at the last dose so Jim left his brother to sleep a while longer, Sandy woke with a start and looked over at Jim snoring his head off, he jumped out of bed it was quarter to five in a panic thinking he had overslept and missed dosing the heifer at the correct time he rushed through to the kitchen and there on the table was a note form Jim, Next dose at five am Sandy could have kissed his young brother for being so thoughtful he had near a full nights sleep and felt ready to tackle whatever the day would throw at him. He opened the byre door cautiously and peered round the corner, he felt quite emotional as he walked up the aisle between his animals, the little heifer was still lying down but there was some movement in her when Sandy approached. He dosed her once again then tended the rest of his beasts, as he worked away he had an awful thought at some point today he would find out what the future held for them, by nightfall his byre may be empty and his animals a heap of burned out cinders it was quite a shocking thought and any notion that Sandy had of enjoying a good breakfast suddenly disappeared, he turned away from the steading and headed down to-ward the barrier the young copper on duty was a school mate of Sandy so they had a good blether. The young copper was not enamoured with his stint of guard duty and told Sandy he would rather have been tucked up in bed next to the wife, but he hadn't long to go before Dod Simpson relieved him, Sandy offered him a flask of hot tea but he declined and looked anxiously towards the Police station to see if there was any movement but it was early he was on duty until six am he asked Sandy what the latest was on his sick beast but he couldn't tell him anything except that they should get conformation later in the day, the copper said he hoped it was favourable news as he didn't fancy many more nights of the boredom he had just endured, with that they parted company. Jim was sitting at the table when Sandy got back he offered his brother a cup of tea then got onto him for not wakening him to help with the animals. Sandy pointed out that once the animals were seen too they were at a loose end the waiting was beginning to get to him, he decided to walk the perimeter fences to make sure all the fences were intact, as he left he pointed out to Jim this could be the last time he needed to worry about fences depending on what Bob Michie had to say. Jim got a bit up tight and told him to get a grip and think positive he was sure everything would be ok and they would be back to normal by night fall Sandy said he wished he had his younger brothers confidence, Jim continued " Sandy there is only one thing I am just waiting to see and that is Lang Dod Wilson knocking the hell out of you for being to bloody stupid getting involved wie Jimmy The Swick" "Oh! Shit Sandy exclaimed I never thought about Dod but no doubt I will get my character" with that he headed up the hill and enjoyed the fresh morning air his dogs had a good run out and enjoyed the exercise. Sandy was starting to get nervy he was really up tight as he made his way home.

Around nine am the vet arrived Sandy met him in the yard he asked how the beast was looking this morning, Sandy told him she was still very weak and ill looking but at least she had survived another night. They reached the byre just as Meg was leaving with the milk from old Dolly the vet asked if she would put it in a container and he would take it away and get it analysed just to make sure there was no nasties in it, and still refrain from using it until told otherwise. Bob had a look at the heifer and again carried out a thorough examination all the time he had his head cocked to one side as though he was listening for some thing, he completed his checks and looked at Sandy she seems to have improved a little bit more since my last visit her lungs and chest seem to have cleared up immensely its all down to what the test labs tell us now we have gone as far as we can. "When I get home I'll phone the Lab and gie them a gee up yea ken fit like the office Walla's are never in a hurry".

Jim was at a loose end time was dragging a bit the waiting for answers was starting to stretch the nerves, Sandy was like a wild cat as he prowled about finding it difficult to focus on anything in particular, eventually Jim had a wander down to the barrier to see if there was any mail at least the daily paper would have something in it to pass the time, he just left the perimeter of the yard when he noticed it was Dod Simpson on duty he was jumping about and waving his arms frantically in the air. As Jim got near the barrier Simpson was shouting are you Hillies buggers deaf I have been shouting for over twenty minutes trying to attract somebody's attention but none of you paid any heed, " The vet was on the phone and ask me to pass on the message that your beast has been given the all clear as far as a contagious disease goes, but we are nae allowed to take the barrier doon till he gets back." Jim could feel a shudder run down his spine what a relief especially for Sandy he had been going out of his mind with worry not only for their own livestock, but everybody in the glen would have been affected, Dod

Simpson kept Jim inside the barrier and told him he was there until Bob Michie said differently, Jim thought it was appropriate to give him a bit of cheek now that the pressure was off, " Man you're a fussy auld bugger Dod just hand me the mail and I'll go hame and leave you in peace" As he reached the house he met Sandy, he passed on the message from the vet, Sandy gave a sigh of relief as he felt the weight lifted off his young shoulders. As Jim scanned through the mail he shouted there was card from Willie, Meg made a grab for it and was disappointed once again about the lack of information, Bob Michie arrived and tried to console Meg by pointing out Willie must be in a sensitive area and they didn't want the Germans to get any clues what was going on. Over a cup of tea Bob Michie tried to explain the problems with the heifer all the tests at the lab were negative, the main problem seemed to lie in the fact that she had never had proper food a bad case of neglect whether it was intentional or lack of knowledge will never be known, but I want to keep the restrictions on until the week-end just to make sure we haven't missed anything. It was a relieved pair of laddies that accompanied the vet to the byre, they decided to try and get the heifer on her feet, she was no problem to lift as she was probably slightly heavier than the collie dog. The vet had another urgent call to make he wrote out a list of instructions on the after care of the animal and the medicine she would require he told the boys to keep an eye on her and he would be back on Saturday morning, he would then decide if the barrier could be removed.

Sandy decided he would better let the bobby know the full story so he walked down to the barrier, as soon as he was with-in ten yards Dod Simpson was exercising his authority and stopped him in his tracks, Sandy assured him everything was ok, he told the old bobby, " The vet said it was ok to get close to the bobby but don't kiss the ugly auld bugger yea dinna ken whit he might be carrying" the two of them had a good laugh and Dod remarked man Sandy its good to see you managing a laugh yea hid me fair worried aboot you this last week or so. Sandy replied, " Dod I hid a lot tae be worried aboot if that beast had had anthrax it would have wiped out the livelihood of all the people in this glen how dea yea think I would have felt then, it disna bear thinking aboot." "Oh by the way your pal Jimmy the Swick is in the nick he wis arrested last night, he will be away for a while, as well as the dishonesty charges, they found out he never registered for call up so he shouldn't bother anybody else for some time to come."

Saturday felt like a lifetime in arriving Sandy's patience was at a premium, they had their hands full nursing the heifer back to full health it looked like it would be a long slow process, he was right thankful he had kept hold of auld Dolly she would supply milk for a while yet, in the mean time they had to keep the croft going, they still had the potato crop to harvest yet, it would be busy in the run up to winter and of course they still had the threshing mill in the next couple of weeks. At last it was Saturday another few hours of apprehension as they awaited the vets arrival. Just on eleven Bob Michie arrived he was waving a piece of paper, it was a clearance notice lifting all the restrictions Sandy breathed a sigh of relief now they may be able to get back to normal. Before leaving the vet had another thorough examination of the heifer he was quite satisfied she was on the road to recovery but she would require medication for a while yet and good nourishing food plenty black treacle if you can get it would be the answer. As he was leaving he said our friend the dealer will be out of circulation for some time to come he is in the nick, Sandy told him the bobby had let them know the latest happenings with that Bob Michie took his leave saying he would call back in about a weeks time.

It was now heading for nineteen forty three, the war was still going full blast, the effects of the rationing was grim, the minister announced at Kirk on Sunday that the death toll and men reported missing from the surrounding district was now twelve four are believed to Prisoners of War, the circumstances of the other eight have still to be confirmed. The community had banded together once again to lay on a Christmas treat for the bairns and adults, with a party and then a concert dance arranged, it was getting harder to get ingredients to bake cakes etc but somehow they had managed to persuade the Commanding Officer at the Mansion house to donate some sugar and other ingredients so that some fancy goodies would be available. The night of the party everybody let their hair down and all had a great time they finished at quarter to twelve so that the hall would be cleared before they entered the Sabbath.

The lead up to Hogmanay proved to be real winter weather with heavy snow storms but it was seasonal even though it caused mass disruption, the locals were used to it so it was a case of batten down the hatches and sit tight, only young Tommy believed in Santa the twins were ten so they had been non believers for some time now although they still hung up a stocking just to enhance the youngsters beliefs.

Tommy was due to start school at Easter so a lot of his gifts were school orientated Meg had managed to a quire a blackboard with a clock face on one side, he could now learn to tell the time and start writing, he got a new pullover and some socks all in preparation for his first day at school. The New Years day dinner that year was a turkey Meg had managed to conjure up the ingredients for a Clootie dumplin and a trifle so there was the usual feast war or no war. As usual there was a tendency to over indulge and apart from Tommy who was still playing around with his gifts the rest were lounging around trying to get rid of the discomfort caused by being greedy. Sandy was just drifting off to sleep when there was a loud knock at the door, over the racket the dogs were making somebody was shouting was anybody at hame, it was Big Will Watson doing his first footing rounds and no doubt walking off his over indulgence, they all wished each other a guid new year Will removed his heavy overcoat and commented about the depth of snow over five feet in some places, according to the mannie on the wireless there was more to come. Will stayed and had supper with the Duncan's he didn't have any family himself so he regarded the Duncan bairns as his own, he left at around eight pm, Sandy walked a bit of the road with him then turned back, there was a bit of a gale getting up he was glad when he got in the house and settled down for the night, Jim was busy doing a jigsaw puzzle so Sandy sat beside him at the table and helped to fit some pieces, at around ten o-clock he decided to pay his animals a visit before going to bed, it had been a long day Tommy had been up in the middle of the night looking for his stocking anxious to find out if Santa had been. As he stepped out of the back door he was overwhelmed with the blizzard that was now blowing, very fine powdery snow he could hardly breathe and he had difficulty finding the steading completely disorientated as he only had about twenty yards to walk he soon bumped into the wall and felt his way along until he came to the door, he quickly entered the stable lit the hurricane lamp, his horses were peaceful chewing away at the hay and whinnying away when they saw Sandy everything quiet apart from the odd rat scurrying along the rafters, the cattle were the same some of them lying down but all very peaceful, the young Heifer was on her feet she was looking well again, he decided to take the lamp back to the house as the blizzard was still raging in the short time since he had first crossed the yard his foot prints had been obliterated but with the light of the lamp he found his way back ok but he was thankful he didn't have to go far, this type of weather was dangerous. Next morning he was up at his usual time he looked out the window but could see nothing, Meg was in the kitchen first that morning and had the kettle boiling so he had a cup of tea before facing the elements, he told her about the blizzard last night and offered to milk the cow for her as he presumed it would be difficult getting to the byre. Jim arrived looking a bit dishevelled Sandy told him to have a cup of tea and he would get things started he tried to open the back door it eventually gave way with a struggle.

In his nineteen years Sandy had never experienced anything like what confronted him, there was a solid wall of snow he tried to push a brush handle through it to test the depth, he was in the length of the brush head and it still never gave way. He had no other means of getting out other then to start shovelling the snow, he had to take it back into the wash house and after digging for twenty minutes and possibly eight feet he finally broke through, the snow was nearly up to the guttering which meant it was around twelve feet high, eventually Jim joined him and between them the dug a path to the steading although it was very cold the two brothers were soaked in sweat by the time they had finished. It was well past feeding time and the hungry beasts were letting them know that this was not good enough, it took six weeks for the snow to disappear not a lot could be done about the croft and the timber control was at a stand still, the war was still going full tilt nearly every country in the world involved, Auld Spencer kept the Home Guard on their toes with his usual enthusiasm. It was a great relief when the birds started singing, there were buds on the trees and daffodils everywhere it was spring at last. Willies usual monthly field card arrived still no words as to his whereabouts, but on his latest card in very faint writing was a message (see you soon) the postie must have had a good read because when he handed Meg the card that morning he said, " I think Willie man be due hame there's a very faint message at the bottom of his caird this month". Meg flew at him "Yea ken fit yea are Jock Mitchell, yir jist a nosey auld bugger yea hiv nae business reading ither fowks mail". Jock wis taken aback by Megs unusual outburst but replied " Yea ken this Meggie Duncan half the fowk in this glen canna read or write so I hiv to read their letters to them so there yea go". In true womanly fashion she had to have the last word and stated she didn't come into that category. As she turned to enter the house she heard her name called it was Jock Mitchell having another go at her before he left, " Gwa back tae yir bed and try comin oot the ither side maybe it will mak yea a bit mair pleasant to fowk" he roared with laughter as he headed back down the farm track and his next delivery. Meg was desperate to closely examine Willie's card and try and find a clue if he really was on his way home, she waited until she was indoors before she attempted to scrutinise the card more closely, she certainly didn't want to give Jock Mitchell the satisfaction that he had seen it first. The work on the croft was in full swing Sandy and Jim were back working for the timber control it was getting real busy again, Sandy was hoping Jim would not get his call up papers till after the harvest was finished but that was just a selfish thought, it would be difficult keeping the croft and the timber going on his own even with the help of younger sister Mary she was now twelve but lacked the strength of a male, but she was a trier. The one piece of good news was that the dealer Jimmy The Swick had been up in court and was sentenced to three months and to add to his misery he had to join the army on his release from the nick, he was also banned from keeping animals for ten years. Meg kept going back to Willies field card trying to find a clue on it or to make sense of the clue faintly written along the bottom but try as she may she was none the wiser when she finally gave up. Betty was great at corresponding with a letter at least every week Meg would reply right away, Betty was getting on great and enjoying her training, she was homesick occasionally but nothing she couldn't handle.

Chapter Ten

BETTY HAD NO WORD OF GETTING home for a weekend, she had fairly long hours and it was nose to the grindstone all day long according to her letters. Meg kept up her feud with Jock Mitchell, inwardly she enjoyed it as it was a bit of a distraction from the humdrum life on the croft, she also knew that she couldn't fall out with the old postie all together as he was very obliging if they needed anything from the town. It was Saturday evening Sandy had spent the time with Will Watson listening to the Scottish Dance Music on the wireless after having a cup of tea with Will and his wife, Sandy headed for home it was just coming up to ten o-clock a lovely moonlight night he had the collie dog with him and it kept running ahead then doubling back makin sure the master was still coming, they reached the steading and decided to have look before bedding down for the night, everything was in order so he didn't hang about patted a couple of his beloved animals on the rump extinguished the hurricane lamp and headed for the house. Meg was knitting a sock, Jim reading a cowboy book the rest were in bed, he was offered a cup of tea but declined as he had just had one at the Blacksmiths. He was about to bid the others goodnight when a hell of a commotion started with somebody hammering the back door the dogs were going mental, Sandy made his way to the door giving the dogs a nudge with his foot trying to quieten them down he shouted through the closed door, " Whose there"? The reply that came back said, "Open the bloody door and yea'll ken fa's here." Sandy would recognise that voice anywhere he threw the door open and said " Willie far the hell did yea come from at this time of nicht" Before Willie could answer he was lying on his back with his sister Meg on top of him with the impact of her hitting him he had lost his balance and land flat out, his army kit strewn all around them. Willie was rubbing his hip as Sandy helped the two of them to their feet. Willie exclaimed Meg I hiv jist spent four months dodging live bullets and never received an injury like you hiv jist inflicted," with that he caught his beloved twin sister and gave her a huge hug, they proceeded to the living room and were chattering away each anxious to find out how things were, their mother shouted from the bedroom wondering what all the fuss was about but when told Willie was hame she looked rather puzzled her mind was beginning to deteriorate, Meg soon had the frying pan on the fire and before too long Willie was tucking into a fry up assisted by Jim who was always ready to eat. Willie had been on the road for thirty hours he said travel was terrible with trains being delayed and having to be re-routed he went on to describe the bomb damage to all the major cities like you could travel up a street to-day with houses both sides come back to-morrow and the whole street flattened, Jim asked about people being killed, Willie told him there were hundreds killed and maimed every night he told them unless you see it its hard to visualise. It turned out Willie was stationed in the south east of England not far from the French coast in fact he told them that at night time you could see the flashes from the guns light up the sky, he didn't say much about his job except that they kept law and order just like a civvy bobby, Meg got onto him about not sending an address but he explained that he was in a very sensitive area, if they mentioned where their mail would be confiscated as all correspondence was censored. The four of them blethered into the sma oors discussing various topics and bringing Willie up-to-date with what was going on in the glen.

Jim was all ears when Willie talked about what he did in the Military Police, Jim asked how he managed to get in Willie replied, "Right place at the right time we had no choice it was a case of you, you and you MPs but I have no regrets as it's very interesting, now good-night I am absolutely jiggered. Their late night blethering took its toll next morning, Sandy looked at his watch he was over an hour late the cattle would be bawling as it was long past breakfast time, they were better timekeepers than a watch as they knew exactly when their feed was due. Willie of course the cause of their late night was still snoring his head off as was young Jim, he waited long enough for the kettle to boil, he grabbed a quick cup of tea before heading for the steading, as he was leaving the house he met Meg with the milk pails she had done her bit, as they passed she said "Aye its aboot time I'm near driven mental wie the racket that beasts are makin", Sandy was feeling a bit groggy for the want of sleep so he just grunted and kept going he didn't feel like an argument this early in the day, a few neeps later and you could have heard a pin drop. Back in the kitchen Meg was preparing breakfast everybody was up except Willie, he was still feeling the effects of his epic journey ; his sister gave him V.I.P treatment with breakfast in bed. Willie volunteered to stay at home with his mother while the rest were in the Kirk he said he had been forced to attend every Sunday since being called up so he would give today a miss. After lunch it was decided they would have a walk down through the village, many of the villagers stopped and asked Willie how army life was suiting him when he told them ok and mentioned he was a Redcap it raised a few eyebrows. Willie was due to leave on the Friday he was due to be posted when he got back destination unknown but he promised Meg he would do his best to communicate if at all possible, Dr Findlay had to be at the station for the early train so he offered Willie a lift, he was quite impressed with the young Miss Findlay the doctors daughter, if he had known she was at home and maybe at a loose end things might have developed, but he enjoyed her company as far as Aberdeen, where they parted company, Willie then went looking for his three companions, when they got back to camp the strong possibility was that they would be split up you were never sure with the Army. A fortnight later they got a card from Willie saying he was being shipped abroad possibly to Italy the big push to get rid of the Germans was about to take place with landings at Sicily, right away the Duncan family had the school atlas out trying to find out where Sicily was, the older ones had heard of it during geography lessons at school. The harvesting of the hay was in full swing once again, Betty managed to get a few days at home otherwise it was the usual humdrum existence plenty hard work and very little reward. From a selfish point of view Sandy was still hoping Jim would be at home till the hay was over but his brown envelope was expected any day now. Auld Spencer the laird was sure there was something big in the offing as the troop movement and manoeuvres were being intensified according to the old fellow he was sure the bubble was about to burst, he was not for telling which bubble. The weather was holding out nicely every hay field in the glen was a hive of activity as the crofters and farmers struggled to get the harvest over as long as the sun shone, another couple of days would see Sandy complete he had a good crop with well matured hay plenty to sustain his animals all winter.

It was just before the dinner break the little post van was chugging up the hill, as he stopped beside the house Jock Mitchell was out waving an envelope and shouting Jims name, Jim came running down from the field anxious to find out his fate. Just as he accepted the brown envelope his sister Meg appeared, Jock Mitchell turned to her and said, "Aye they've got young Jim at last". Meg totally ignored him and looking at her brother she said, " Dinna bother opening it Jim jist ask that nosy bugger Jock Mitchell nae doot he already kens what's inside it." With that she summoned Jim to follow her indoors leaving auld Jock standing with his mouth open wondering what news Jim had received but Meg was too cute for him, he had to leave non the wiser when Jim would have to go all he could tell his customers was that he had received his call up papers as he gossiped his way round the district. Jim like elder brother Willie had his first train journey the day he went for his medical to Aberdeen, the sheer size of the city was an eye opener and then of course the trams it was all mind boggling, he had to endure the same humiliation as Willie did, in the examination room he was shown his cubicle told to strip everything off, he asked the guys next door if that meant his drawers as well his neighbour nodded meekly and proceeded to undress. The Duncan family had had a very modest up brining they were never allowed to enter the living area of the house unless they were suitably attired it was always implemented that what was below the waist was private used for passing unwanted body waste and fluids not to be flashed around in front of other people and certainly not to be grabbed in front of a room full of strangers, in later years when they got married it could be used as a means of reproduction so what Jim was about to go through was sheer humiliation. He was told to face the cubicle and bend over while the doctor had a look at his duke of argyles he was feeling quite distressed he had never experienced anything like it before but worse was to come when he was told to stand up and face the front, the doctors hand shot out and grabbed his dangly bits and told him to cough he near fainted, this was terrible and the fact there was an audience of about twenty didn't help matters, the relief he felt when told to get his bottom half dressed was overwhelming, he then had a series of injections before getting fully dressed, he was told to go home and they would be in touch, before catching the train he managed to have a cup of tea with his sister Betty before heading for home. Back at Hillies they were all keen to find out what was happening, Jim really didn't have a clue except that he would receive instructions by post and he would have to take it from there all he knew was that he was passed fit A1 and he would be getting involved in the war shortly. By the end of the week Jim had his orders, report to the Bridge Of Don Barracks where he would become a Gordon Highlander to arrive as early as possible on the Monday morning. Meg made a huge lunch on the Sunday and they had a quiet afternoon it was a worry wondering what would happen to Jim he was only seventeen and a half, and defiantly not as mature as Willie had been Meg was glad he was only going as far as Aberdeen and Betty was there if he needed any help. Sandy now knew what hard work was, having to keep the croft going and his job at the timber control, Mary was an excellent help to him and could use her own initiative to get things going when Sandy was at work. Tommy was a bit of a let down showing no interest in the croft and being a proper spoiled little nuisance at times he caused Sandy a lot of grief at times, he also caused friction between Sandy and Meg.

With Jim now gone the house was getting very quiet, Sandy found life quite boring at times, as the only male company he had was Tommy and sadly the two of them just didn't have a very brotherly relationship, Meg would take Tommy's side and kept telling Sandy he was jist a bairn and allowances had to be made, but Sandy felt Meg was too liberal with him and he showed no respect for either of them, frequently when Sandy just about had enough he would take off and spend some time with Will Watson, but Will's company could be tedious at times as he was going through difficult times business wise, but life had to go on and you just had to make the best of things. Meg received a great boost with a letter from her sister Betty she had managed to get ten days holiday due to start this coming week-end, that really cheered them up no end so it was all systems go as she prepared for the arrival of their guest. The news from Jim was not so pleasant he had completed his basic training and was due to be posted abroad at the moment he was not too sure where to but it could be anywhere in the world . Sandy had been busy the harvest was over, just the potatoes and the threshing mill of the major items to be completed then they would wind down for the winter. Betty arrived late on the Friday evening she had managed to buy a few goodies the big problem was getting ration coupons you could have the money but if you had no coupons you were sunk. Once everybody had gone to bed the two sisters settled down to have a good old chinwag, Betty reached into her case and pulled out a little package and handed it to her sister adding just a special little present for you Meg, she quickly removed the package and in her hand was a pair of nylon stockings, Meg had never seen anything like it before Betty had to tell her to be careful as they were easily torn, Meg was over the moon she had never seen material as sheer as what she was holding in her hands she felt real overcome with emotion, her next question was where Betty had acquired them, she told her big sister to hold on to her chair tightly and she began to explain, " Meg I have been seeing a lad from Canada for a good while now he flies aero- planes back and forth between America, Canada and Britain he is stationed at Dyce Aerodrome so we usually manage to meet once a week depending on our shift pattern, his name is Walter, Walt to his friends." Meg was all ears as Betty rambled on about life in Aberdeen and what Walt and her get up to when they get time off, she explained he was off farming stock and his folks had a huge wheat farm in Manitoba. Eventually Meg noticed it was way past bedtime so she had a final look at her mother and the two of them parted company and headed for bed. Next morning Sandy had booked the Tattie howkin squad to lift his Tatties so at seven-o-clock the yard was alive with about a dozen youngsters all armed with their own personal bucket and dressed ready for a day's hard graft. It was well into the afternoon before the Tattie lifting was complete, as the youngsters lined up for their pay there was a lot of banter and leg pulling it was always a happy time of year and it also taught the young ones that to have money you needed to work they would receive about twenty five pence for there efforts but they would have anything from two to four weeks work so at the end of month they would have earned about six pounds an absolute fortune in those far off days, with the money they would have to buy clothes if they could find clothing coupons. Betty's week at home soon passed and she was on her way back to the city, Meg had her usual tearful goodbye as Betty pulled away from the house.

Meg had many sleepless night's as she worried about her brothers, Willie's whereabouts were unknown and Jim was on a troopship bound for the far east it was very stressful not knowing if they were dead or alive but she was assured that if they were dead the War Department would have informed them but this advice did nothing to ease the worry. Meg also had the added worry of her mother she was so poorly that Meg feared she would have to go into hospital it was hard work keeping everything going, she had the help of the twins who were very willing helpers but Sandy needed Mary to help around the croft when he was busy but life had to go on. The end of the year was closing in fast the Glen people always tried to liven life up and this year was no different the concert party were in rehearsals, Sandy and Will Watson were going over their music almost nightly and Meg was involved with baking etc for the kids school party. The Army guys at the Mansion house had agreed to do a stint at the concert and their Jazz band would be there by popular demand so it was all heading for an enjoyable evening. As was usual at this time of year they had a fall of snow probably about an inch deep, it gave a very seasonal appearance to the countryside. Concert day arrived and kicked off at three pm with the kids party Will Watson in the guise of Santa pulled on a sledge by a couple of goats the kids thought this was hilarious as the goats looked nothing like reindeer but it was all done in good spirit as usual the kids had a whale of a time this was an area Will Watson excelled in, keeping the kids amused, the sad part for him was that he had no family of his own. The kids party over and a lot of work had to be carried out before the concert could go ahead but the team spirit of the Glen folks soon had the place spik and span and over eighty chairs laid out to seat the audience. Sandy and Will always played a medley of tunes as the curtain went up this year was no different, as they waited Sandy picked up a programme and just after the interval he read item number six The Lairds Special Surprise, he turned to Will and asked what that was all aboot, Will shook his head but said " Yea ken fit like Spencer is he probably has a troop of strippers or something like that, yea nivver ken fit oor laird is up tae." Bob Paterson was the M.C he gave the musicians the thumbs up and as they struck the first chord Frankie Smith who was operating the curtain opened it up, Sandy was quite taken aback with the crowd it was way above the eighty chairs they had laid out but it would be good for the funds. The interval arrived and every male in the place lit up their fags and some of the ladies as well at one point it looked like there was a thick fog in the hall. The interval over and the curtain was pulled back, standing in the middle of the stage in all his glory was the Rt Hon Spencer Tracy Major (retd), " Ladies and Gentlemen boys and girls the moment you have all been waiting for my special surprise, as you are aware I try my best to bring you something special every year well this year I have excelled in my efforts, I am sure you are all aware that we have Polish soldiers stationed at the Mansion house, they are here to train with our own British troops, among these fine soldiers there is a Polish Dance Troup and with much persuasion I managed to get them here to-nite, they are about to perform the most amazing routine ever witnessed in this area please put your hands together for the amazing Polish Dancers". As the applause reached a crescendo eight young men in National Dress somersaulted their way onto the small stage Auld Spencer was correct the locals were gob smacked.

For the next twenty minutes these lads did very near the impossible as they danced and twisted around the stage and not one of them fell or even stumbled the feats they performed were just breathtaking, at the end of the show they got a standing ovation what a performance. Sandy and Will Watson were next on stage they gave a twenty-minute session of jigs and reels before the Mansion House Jazz Band relieved them. As they left the stage Will said to his young mate, " I think I'll go outside and get a bit of fresh air", Sandy said he would come with him, when they reached the front entrance of the hall, they were a bit taken aback when they spotted Dod Simpson the bobby and surrounding him were six Military Policemen. Will asked auld Simpson what was going on he replied " Were keeping an eye on the Poles they seemingly make some sort of hooch from Tatties once they get a fill of it they are fighting mad and they are pretty tough buggers when they're drunk, and wouldn't think twice of using a knife if the odds were against them, did you notice anything funny going on in the hall"? Both Sandy and Will shook their heads. Then Will ever the joker said " Come to think of it to carry out some of the manoeuvres the Polish Dancers carried out on the stage yea wid need tae be half fill oh something how any man in his richt senses managed the performance they did is jist beyond comprehension but they didn't look drunk tae me." With that the two musicians retreated to the hall to carry on the entertainment. As usual the night ended at quarter to twelve and the Glen folk headed for home it had been a wonderful night everybody fully enjoyed themselves and the Polish Lads never put a foot wrong, Sandy was on his own as he walked up the road there was a good covering of snow but he could still see the set of footprints left by Meg and the younger ones, they had left for home earlier, Mrs Morrison had looked after his mother so Meg didn't want to take advantage by staying until the end anyhow Tommy and the twins were starting to get tired. It was a lovely moonlit night even with four to six inches of snow it was just perfect for a walk Sandy could see for miles as he wandered along at his leisure he wondered if Willie and Jim would be seeing the same moon as he was even although he had no idea where they were, anyhow it would be Hogmanay in seven days time it would be very quiet this year without his brothers and sister Betty the family was shrinking every year, but most families in the Glen were in the same boat as soon as the sons were old enough they were called up, to get an exemption was getting harder the longer the war progressed, Sandy had a round of his beasts before retiring to bed he was quite tired, the time spent playing his music was quite tiring. Hogmanay day arrived the Concert and Dance was history but it had lifted the gloom for one night. Meg had fattened up a goose for New Years Day once again she asked Sandy to give her a hand with the plucking between the two of them they soon had the fowl naked, as Sandy held it up for singeing he remarked on how heavy it was and that they would be eating goose for the first month of the year, they had a good laugh about it, "Mind you Willie and Jim would have eaten half the bird between them if they were here" he realised he had trod on a raw nerve when Meg burst into tears and howled her eyes out for a good ten minutes, after she dried the tears even though she didn't tell Sandy she felt as though a burden had been removed from her shoulders, there is no doubt a good greet works, Two and a half hours to go before the New Year arrived everything thing in hand just the presents for Tommy and the twin's stockings then she could relax.

The hands on Sandy's watch pointed to eleven forty nine eleven minutes until the new year, Will Watson had managed to procure a half bottle of whisky from one of his Black Market sources he had poured a couple of drams in an old medicine bottle and given it too Sandy so that Meg and him could toast the New Year. He was on his way to get glasses when all of a sudden there as aloud hammering on the back door " Who the hell can that be", he said to Meg in between shouting at the dogs to be quiet, he made his way to the door and shouted " Whose there"? The voice at the other side shouted back " A friend open up" Sandy edged the door open and was confronted by a huge guy in some sort of uniform Sandy was speechless but his visitor said " Hiya Sandy I am Walter and I have brought your young sister along to bring in the New Year, with that Betty appeared at his side and was soon smothering her brother with hugs and kisses before long Meg had joined in, the four of them slithered about on the icy ground what a lovely start to the new year, Meg thought to herself it was not all doom and gloom there was the occasional ray of light. It was still a couple of minutes away from midnight, Walter produced a couple of bottles of Canadian Club from his bag and poured four drams. As the big grandfather clock struck midnight Walter ask if he could ask a question before they drank the toast. " Sandy as you are the head of this household would you grant me permission to marry your lovely sister, we got engaged a couple of hours ago and would like to get married later on" Sandy was flabbergasted he had never been asked such an awkward question in his life so he turned to Meg and said "Fit div yea think" " Of coorse we winna mind Walter what I've seen of yea I think yea wid mak a grand brither in law" with that settled they drank a toast in fact by the time they went to bed they had drank many toasts and traded stories about their back grounds, Sandy was fair taken with Betty's choice of suitor as he had a great knowledge of farming. Eventually around four am they retired to bed Sandy being the worse of the ware, he had probably had more booze to night than the rest of his entire life, he flopped on to his bed lying face down, but with-in minutes it was like he was on a merry-go-round the bed spinning out of control he felt awful with-in the next five minutes he made a dash for the skylight and just had his head out into the cool night air when whoosh a projectile of vomit shot about four feet from his mouth followed seconds later by another not so ferocious bout, from then on it was painful retching and nothing happening, he was just about to go back to bed when he felt something tugging his shirt tail looking down he let out a wail when he saw young Tommy looking up from the dark and asking "Hey Sandy wid yea like tae see whit Santa brocht me"? Sandy felt awful but if there was an inconvenient moment to view presents it was right now he tried humouring little Tommy and managed to get him to go and rouse the twins before flopping back on his bed feeling bloody awful. He regained conciseness from his drunken stupor while it was still dark he opened one eye, but quickly closed it again as it felt as if it was full of sand, his head was throbbing and his mouth felt foul, to crown it all his teeth were chattering with the cold he had no recollection how he got to bed or what time. Eventually he pulled himself up moaning and groaning about how awful he felt, looking towards the skylight he could just make out it was wide open no much bloody wonder it was so cold, still quite inebriated he left his bed to close the open sky light scratching his head wondering why it had been opened.

Once out of bed Sandy thought he better check the time with much squinting of his eyes his brain engaged and he discovered it was nearly seven-o-clock his poor cattle would be starving. Feeling a bit flustered that his beasts were being neglected Sandy started to get dressed but found it was no easy task when you were under the control of the demon drink after a couple of attempts to get his trousers on standing up he gave up and sitting on the edge of the bed eventually managed to get dressed. He staggered his unsteady way to the kitchen and was quite surprised to see the twins and Tommy sitting at the table fully dressed and Meg hovering about preparing things for the New Year Dinner. Well she scolded Sandy, "Fit time a day dea yea call this"? Sandy shook his head and said he was sorry but he had just over indulged with Walter last night, " Its nae every nicht ane oh yir sisters get engaged", he tried drinking a cup of tea but started to retch again it was real painful he gave up and started heading for the steading when Mary asked where he was going, to feed the cattle he replied, Mary told him nae tae bather as they had already been done and the best thing he could dea was go back tae his bed for a while. He couldn't wait to get back up the stairs it was the best suggestion he had heard in years, before lying down he had a look out of the skylight this set him off retching once again as her viewed the remains of his regurgitated supper splattered all over the roof of the house, but it was an answer as to why the skylight had been wide open this morning, Sandy slept soundly until midday, although he had been tipsy before on a few occasions this was the worst he had ever experienced. When he appeared down stairs for the second time that morning all the family were round the table the young ones were having a great time with Walter as he told them tales of Canada, he asked Sandy if he would like a hair of the dog, shaking his head he made a dash for the back door and had another session of painful retching. Meg said she would leave the dinner until three pm that would give the hung over members time to recover Sandy eventually managed a cup of tea and by dinnertime he was ready to eat. After dinner they lazed about and later on they had a few neighbours call by, Will Watson had his fiddle, Sandy was now back to full capacity again so they had a good singsong, Walter seemed to have a never ending stock of Canadian Club which he kept handing round, but there was no way he could persuade Sandy to have another mouthful. Walter and Betty were leaving first thing in the morning he wanted to get back to Aberdeen in daylight he was used to driving in the snow but the roads could close in very quickly in the N.E. of Scotland so he didn't want to take any chances. Next morning Sandy was back to his usual self up at five am and had his animals seen to before seven, he was just settling down to have his brose when Walter appeared, Sandy asked if he fancied a bowl, Walter said he had never heard of brose before so yes he would try some, using his best culinary skills Sandy made his future brother-in-law a bowl of oatmeal brose smothered it with the best cream in the milk house and told him to stick in, Walter was smacking his lips together when Meg arrived back from milking, she asked what he would like for his breakfast, he told her Sandy had just made him the most wonderful bowl of Scottish brose and he would not require anything else,(Meg shook her head at Sandy she thought brose was beneath her guest she intended giving him eggs trust Sandy). They left mid morning with Betty saying they would be back to discuss the wedding arrangements in a few weeks time.

It was near on six months since Jim had been called up, the folks at Hillies had no idea where he was, after basic training he was sent abroad to the Far East, Meg spent many sleepless nights worrying about her younger brother especially with the tales of the brutality dished out by the Japanese troops mind you some of it was so brutal it was hard to believe it was possible to be true. Then out of the blue a letter arrived from Jim it was posted in Australia, when told Sandy said "What the hell's he deein in Australia" Meg explained " It appears that he had his left arm badly wounded in Burma and he was sent to a hospital in Australia to get it repaired, he is no longer fit to hold a gun so he has been given a job in a huge Military Stores Depot he is still in the army and it looks like he may be there until the war's finishes when ever that may be." Shortly after that she had a card from Willie he was now a full corporal and he was back in Britain and was trying hard to get a few days leave, he would be in touch, as usual it was very brief. So life went on it would soon be time for the threshing mill again this always brought bad memories for Sandy as he tried to work out how many years since his fathers untimely death, his meetings with Lang Dod had dwindled to once a year but he was always available if Sandy needed him, he was fairly pulled over the coals for his stupid purchase of the sick heifer but apart from that they got on fine.

One Sunday afternoon at the beginning of March the peace and quiet of the Glen was broken as the old steam engine pulling the threshing mill appeared over the horizon, she was belching smoke and steam as she crested the hill, but apart from the clanking of the wheels and chains she was relativity quiet, she had an easier passage as she descended the hill, at the cross roads she wheeled into Frankie Smiths place and the operators got to work setting everything up for an early start on the Monday, much and all as Sandy loved the old steam engine she sent a shudder down his spine , but he was looking forward to his week at the mill it would be his turn on the Tuesday which meant an evening in the company of the mill operators where he would catch up with the gossip from the last six months. Meg finally received confirmation from Willie he would be home on a forty-eight hour pass at the weekend. The days threshing at Frankie Smiths went without a hitch as usual there was plenty banter and bye mid afternoon the mill was being dismantled ready for the move to Hillies the crofters went home to catch up on some work, to-morrow they would all turn up at Sandy's place for his days threshing. He got stuck into his chores when he got home he was anxious to get finished early so that he could enjoy a long evening with the two old operators whom he had known since he could walk. Six-o-clock prompt and the Duncan's were seated round the table waiting for their guests to arrive but of course they had a lot of scrubbing to do to remove the grime and oil that covered them from head to toe, the old steamer was not the cleanest of machinery to work around, they didn't have long to wait when the two old worthies arrived looking like they had been recently polished, they sat down and waited for Meg and the twins to dish out the grub. Jimmy Burr had known Meg since her nappy days, he always had a bit of a tare with her asking about her love life and when the wedding would be, but she let it go over her head and totally ignored him as the meal progress the topic turned to Lang Dod Wilson Sandy's ex boss.

Chapter Eleven

JIMMY BURR ASKED SANDY IF HE had been invited to the wedding, "Fit weddin"? Asked Sandy "Oh yea hinna heard" replied Jimmy, "Weel Lang Dod married the Land Girl at the week-end he had to it was a shot gun job, there's mair to Lang Dod than meets the eye". First question Sandy asked was "Fit aboot Lizzie I'll bet she was delighted wie that arrangement". "Oh Lizzie up and left about a month ago as soon as she heard the young dame was expectin tae the Lang fellow she was gone her nose wid have fair been oot of joint as she always fancied herself as the mistress of Burnies. The next bombshell for Sandy was to be told that this would be the last time the steam engine would be powering the threshing mill, the Steam Engine and the two operators were being put out to grass after this season and in November there would only be one operator and he would use a new Allis Chalmers tractor, Eck Davidson's words were ringing in Sandy's ears, when he said "Sandy this new fangled tractors will cost jobs". The two steam engine operators Jimmy Burr and Jimmy Black were both over seventy so it was well past time to retire it would need a young fit fellow to carry out the one man operation. It was into the sma hoors before they had discussed everybody in the glen so after countless cups of tea they decided it was time to get some shuteye. Sandy never had any problem with falling a sleep but before he dozed off he ran his mind over the work load for to-morrow, the threshing would take most of the day and then by the time he had tidied up and filled the mattresses with fresh chaff he would have plenty to keep him occupied. Next morning crack of dawn it was still pitch dark as he crossed the yard heading for the byre he could see a hurricane lamp at the steam engine as the twosome fired her up ready for the seven am start, they would probably have already spent an hour cleaning out the tubes and greasing and oiling the moving parts the old steam engine was hard work. As Sandy moved towards the kitchen to have his breakfast he was joined by the two operators, they continued to elaborate on the stories started the evening before, at three minutes to seven the steam whistle broke the silence of the glen they were ready to go to work all the neighbours were at their appointed work place, another hard days graft to be executed. It was also a busy day for the females as the workmen required a decent three course meal at dinner time it was no mean feat preparing food for fifteen hungry men but her trusty friend Bella Morrison was there to help and the twins were roped in as well. As soon as they were all seated Meg started to dish out the broth, they were like a cage full of monkeys all chattering at the same time, eventually somebody brought up the subject of Lang Dod and his new young wife, after the usual banter about a man of his age and a girl just tuned twenty, one comment was " Aye he wis a gie decrepit looking bugger before she got a hold of him, a strong young filly like her winna dea his stature any good" and so it went on each observation getting worse than the last. "Lang Dod is a fly bugger I ken there's a story gan jist noo that the government are allowing Prisoners Of War out of the internment camps to help oot on the fairms, ken fit? Lang Dod is the first in the district to get one. "Aye! The Lang fellows nae as green as he's cabbage looking". Sandy had a look around the table at all those present and was amazed to notice he was the youngest there the rest were all over forty and some as old as seventy this war and the instigator Herr Hitler had a lot to answer for. By four-o-clock the mill was ready to move to the next croft.

The shrill blast of the steam whistle was heard for the last time as the engine pulled out of the farmyard at Hillside, with-in two weeks she would be gone for ever, this was called advancement and new technology for Sandy it was a sad ending to a friendship that had lasted all his short life, this modern way of life was supposed to make the standard of living better for all. Soon the first POW's made their presence felt with the arrival of Italians they were employed by the timber control. They were kept under guard in an area by themselves, Sandy was intrigued with the red diamond patches on their uniforms and mentioned it to his mate Will Watson, Will was well versed on everything that was happening and he told Sandy, " That's a target to aim at if the bugger's try to run awa ". " Is that nae a bit drastic"? Sandy asked, "Drastic! Drastic" Will spluttered "I think it wid be ower bloody good for them, it could be one of them that shot poor Spider Morrison and he defiantly didn't deserve that", "Ok point taken but I still think that going tit for tat is nae the wye tae end the war", Will's final words were you try telling Shelia and Davie Morrison that, they sat in silence for a couple of minutes then changed the subject. The weather was clearing up nicely and the ground would soon be dry enough to start the ploughing it was getting near the busy time again, Sandy could envisage six hard weeks ahead but it was what he was trained for and was well prepared for it. Tragedy hit the glen once again when the Lairds son Adrian was killed in action he had crashed somewhere over Holland and was unable to bale out before he hit the ground, the papers and the radio were full of stories about the war being over before the autumn, people were beginning to wonder how many more of the young men would be killed before it came to a conclusion. Sunday morning and as usual the Kirk was full to capacity, Jim Kerr once again had the unpleasant task of offering up a prayer for young Adrian he had been built in the same mould as his father Spencer a bit of a mad man, the locals described them as being a bit Hallyrackit not an inch of fear in them, Adrian was the heir to the estate but they would never know what kind of Laird he would have made, another young life wiped out so that the rest of us could enjoy living in a free world, as Sandy and Will made their way home after the service the topic of conversation was about Auld Spencer. Will started it off by saying how shattered the old fellow looked, of course Adrian was the apple of his eye he had started to groom him to take over the Estate when the war broke out and everything was put on the back burner, I have never seen him look so down as he was to-day normally he is trying his best to keep every bodies spirits up but his own are rock bottom at the moment. Jock Mitchell the postie arrived at the back door at Hillies just as Meg was making for the wash line with her first basket full ready to hang out to dry, it was right up Jocks street he loved to get Meg going although he didn't always come out on top. "Fit like the day Meggie"? Jock enquired, "Fa wid like tae ken"? Meg retorted, " bye the way she continued its only my close friend that have the privilege of calling me Meggie you don't come into that category, its Miss Duncan tae the likes of you". Jock had taken the bait and lost the plot, " Meg Duncan yea are the most unpleasant crabbit bitch I have the misfortune to have to speak to in the whole glen and the day I have to call you Miss Duncan yea can rin tae hell" as he thrust the mail into her hand he said, " Ane oh the letters is frae yir sister Betty in Aberdeen".

Meg stood staring at him he was starting to squirm when she asked, "are yea nae gan tae tell me whit she's sayin". Jock new he had been beaten again and jumped into his little van with much crashing of gears he roared down the road no doubt to stick his nose into somebody else's business. His nosiness soon got him into more trouble again involving the Duncan family, Betty and Meg tried to keep the forth coming marriage under wraps until everything was settled, Meg was burdened with sorting things out at the Hillies end while Betty got on with organising her dress etc in Aberdeen. The date had been agreed it was the middle Saturday in August that would give them a couple of weeks before Walter was due to return to Canada and demob. It was very difficult to keep in touch except by letter, to telephone was a bit of a chore you see there were very few private phones most of the ordinary people had to use the Red Public phone box, if the sisters wanted to speak by phone they would have to write a letter giving a time for the other sister to be waiting at the phone box nearest home in Megs case the box was a mile from the house, when she would arrive at the appointed time the chances that somebody else was phoning were very good so she would have to wait while they made their call it could be pouring rain and there was no shelter, on the other hand the phone at the Aberdeen end could be busy and Betty would have to wait her turn so it could be awkward doing something so simple as making a phone call. It was sometimes much more convenient just to sit down and write, when the wedding plans were at an early stage the sisters were corresponding on a daily basis, this aroused Jock Mitchell's suspicions, what could be so important that they needed to write daily, one thing he better not broach the subject with Meg or Sandy as he was libel to get his head in his hands, what about the twins they were nearing school leaving age maybe they would enlighten him but when he got the opportunity to ask the girls he was told, " Bugger off and mind your own bloody business" obviously they had been prompted to tell him nothing, (and what language from twa young quines he thought). Jock's nose was really getting the better of him when he struck on an idea Will Watson, he would ken he was as thick as thieves wie the Duncan's, he would make an excuse to enter the smiddy and speak tae Will. His opportunity arose when he had to get a signature from the big man, Jock Mitchell was not the most popular man in the glen so he didn't get many cuttings from Big Will he signed for his package and then picked up his hammer to continue with his job when Jock struck. " Hi Will dea yea ken if everything is ok at Hillies" Will stopped mid blow and said as far as he was aware everything was fine, and did Jock have a reason for his enquiry. "Weel it's like this Meg and Betty have been writing one another everyday for the past month I jist wondered if there wis anything wrong." "Not as far as I am aware" replied the Blacksmith, Jock wasn't happy with the answer and continued his probing. His next statement proved to be the wrong subject to involve Will Watson in, "Betty winna be in the Pudden Club wid she knocking about wie that big yank it could be possible". Jock knew he had gone too far when Will Watson drew himself up to his full six foot six and let out a bellow like a raging bull, he strode across to the now quivering postie, bent over until they were eye ball to eyeball then let rip Jock could feel the hot air and spittle hit his face he knew he had hit a raw nerve.

"Don't you ever discuss any of my friends again Jock Mitchell and further more don't enter my yard, deliver my mail at the house from now on.

" Further more if I get any inkling that you have discussed any of the glen folks during your line of duty as our postman I will personally go into town and talk to your Post Master about your behaviour that should cost you your job, now before I turn violent get aff my premises. Jock was quivering as he made his escape that had been a close call; he was slithering on the loose gravel as he scurried towards his little van. Will was real pleased with his warning and was sure Jock Mitchell had got the message. Betty's plans were that they would be married in August have a few days honeymoon and then they would fly to Canada early September, that would mean they would be settled in their new home before the winter arrived, Meg was very emotional she kept wondering if she would ever see her sister again after she emigrated. Another bombshell was dropped on her when Peg one of the twins announced that she was hoping to get a placement in Aberdeen as she also wanted to be a nurse, soon there would only be herself and Sandy and of course Tommy had still a few years left in school. Mary was still a great asset to Sandy and as she got older and stronger she was able to work as well as any man but Mary also had the wanderlust and dropped a bigger bombshell when she said she wanted to join the army thankfully she would have another two years at least before she was old enough by then it was hoped the war would be over. It looked like things were beginning to happen up at the Mansion house more and more troops were arriving and they were running around the moors shooting and blowing up things the noise could be horrendous at times. Betty managed to get a thirty six hour pass this was a great help as she had managed to scrounge and scrape some ingredients for her wedding cake, Walter had also managed to acquire some much needed rations. Willie managed to send a rare letter he was unable to say where he was except it was in the south of England and said that they were going through a very rigorous training programme and that he would probably be unable to make contact for some time he also said that his chances of being at home for the wedding was very remote. Jim had no hope of being home for the wedding, he did manage to send mail now and again but as was usual there was always a censor's stamp and any dodgy word would be crossed out the joys of being at war. Will Watson arrived at the house one evening and told Sandy he had a great bargain for him when Sandy asked what it was Will told him he could acquire a wireless for about three pounds, one of the army boys at the Mansion said it was surplus to requirements, Sandy was dead keen to have it until Will told him he would need to keep it hidden for a few weeks just in case anybody missed it, Sandy was a bit nervous about it until Will pointed out that if he didn't have it somebody else would jump at the chance and it would be gone. After a bit of serious mind searching he decided to take a chance, it turned out to be a big clumsy Military Affair with the War Department stamped on it, but it was a beauty as far as reception went and could pick up any country worldwide, Sandy made up a wooden cabinet to hold his newly acquired wireless, if any strangers arrived at the door they just close up the cabinet and it blended in with the rest of the furniture. The wireless was a great addition to the Duncan's possessions, what a difference it made to their lives one major asset was that they could get up-to-date news bulletins and then all the entertainment stations it was a real boon to their lives and it was never missed, or at least nobody ever enquired about it.

Betty's wedding was all systems go for August everything was in hand, Sandy would have the barn cleaned out and they would have a dance in the evening, Will Watson one of the invited guests would help with the music he also said he was able to purchase some booze so everything was shaping up nicely. Everybody was talking about how they hoped the war would soon end, Auld Spencer was sure that all the activity at the Mansion House was preparing the troops for an offensive in the summer but of course it was all hush, hush and the security around the moor was very tight you were only allowed though if you had permission. The locals were getting a bit fed up with the Military traffic when you had tank transporters and huge lorries on the sixteen foot wide roads nobody else could move and then the security was tightened up with road blocks all over the place what ever was about to happen it looked real serious. Auld Spencer still had the same enthusiasm for the Home Guard as he had when it started unfortunately the turn out of locals at times was rather disappointing but if the weather was good they had to take advantage of every daylight hour available, Spencer always tried to make people think he was well up to speed with what was happening world wide but when questioned about the activity at the Mansion house he didn't have an answer.

It was the beginning of May the crofters were all busy getting ready to harvest the hay it would be ripe in about a week. Suddenly early one morning all hell broke loose as the Military started to leave the Mansion House the vehicles were nose to tail all sorts of lorries, cars, tanks, motorbikes and even buses loaded with soldiers it was none stop for about four hours; they were heading for an unknown destination. (Years later it was reviled that this convoy was part of an elaborate hoax to try and have the Germans believe that the nineteen forty-four invasion was about to happen in Norway). Down in the south of England Willie Duncan now a full corporal in the Military Police had been involved in manoeuvres simulating an invasion, on the third of June they were under curfew stuck in a tented camp some where near Portsmouth the M.Ps had their hands full keeping law and order as tempers became frayed, on the fourth of June they were on red alert ready to move out, after many hours fully kitted out they were stood down this also added to the tension imagine hundreds of teen age boys all herded together with no room to swing a cat the waiting was hellish. Then late afternoon they were marched to the docks at Portsmouth and loaded on to ships this must be it the real thing at last. They left the harbour about five in the evening and steamed across the channel in the company of thousands of other ships, the weather was quite rough and many of the guys started to be seasick before long the decks were awash with vomit the stench was overpowering, as they neared the French coast they were aware that some sort of battle was taking place with the noise of explosions and the flashes lighting up the night sky, an officer came round and told them that when they were about a mile from the shore they would disembark from the ship onto landing craft, Willie had experience of this manoeuvre and certainly didn't look forward to it with the craft bucking around on the rough sea it would be no picnic

Chapter Twelve

THE DIN FROM THE SHORE WAS getting louder, the officer in charge announced that they would disembark in five minutes time some of the really bad cases of seasickness had to drag themselves up onto the deck feeling terrible, one of Willies duties was to make sure everything was done in an orderly fashion and count the men clambering over the side into the landing craft as soon as he had his quota he leapt over the side and they cast off, they were bobbing around like a cork, before long they were up to their knees in vomit and oily water, further more they had no idea what would happen when the ramp on the landing craft was lowered. The adrenalin was pumping hard although Willie was quite unafraid the emotions on some of the other fellows faces showed they were terrified some were shivering either from fear or cold, the seasickness was also taking a terrible toll on the lads not the ideal preparation when you are about to go into battle. Willie was in the second row of men ready to disembark as soon as the ramp was lowered he was worried that the ones behind would surge forward and the would end up in a heap at the bottom of the ramp which would be submerged in water no telling how deep it might be, no doubt the Naval guys in charge of the landing craft would want them off as quickly as possible so that they could get to hell out of the way of the enemy guns. Getting near the shore the bullet started to hit the ramp ping! ping! ping! The sound of the ricocheting bullets caused the adrenalin to pump even harder still Willie felt quite calm in fact he had a little smile to himself as he thought, now I know how Gary Cooper feels when he is pinned down behind a rock and the Indians are shooting at him. Suddenly the guy who was measuring the depth of water started to read out the depths he was using a rope with a lead weight on the end they were in under a fathom of water the officer in charge of the disembarking shouted at the men to stand by. The ramp seemed painfully slow as it began to fall away from the landing craft what greeted the lads as they slithered their way down the ramp was scenes of carnage bodies and body parts floating about everywhere, Willie who was six feet three was up to his shoulders in water some of the smaller guys would never have survived once they were over the head the weight of the gear they were carrying would have kept them down under, what a horrible end to months and months of real hard training to get shot would have been bad enough but this was unthinkable. Willie plodded steadily on there were men getting killed and wounded all round him but as if by a miracle for as many as were killed thousands survived, now on the beach Willie managed to find cover behind a disabled tank he decided to rest for a couple of minutes but before long it started to get overcrowded as more and more guys dived for cover, as soon as there was a bit of a lull in the shelling Willie made a dive and crouching down managed to run to the breakwater if everything had gone to plan he should be near the French village of Arromanches he knew from photographs that it had a rocky shore and was similar to his home village of Covie. Willie was looking forward to his next birthday, which would be his nineteenth; he had never in his wildest dreams imagined that he would have to witness such carnage. During his short sortie into Italy he had travelled by landing craft but it had no bearing on what he had come through that day the sixth of June nineteen forty four as darkness fell Willie got down on his knees and thanked God for looking after him.

Back home in Banffshire news of the invasion of Normandy was headlines on the radio, the folks lucky enough to own one sat listening to the bulletins for most of the day. Folks like the Duncan's who had relations in the forces were worried sick when the news of the casualties started to filter though, of course Meg was up to high doh worrying about her twin brother until Sandy got fed up with her wailing and pointed out she was making all sorts of statements about Willie and they didn't even know if he was in Normandy. Near the middle of July Betty managed home for another short visit this would be her final visit before the wedding everything was in order, she had her wedding dress almost complete the twins were being the bridesmaids although they didn't have fancy dresses they would just wear their Sunday best, it was most certain that neither Willie or Jim would mange home a bit of a blow but this is what war was all about, disrupting peoples lives, Betty would have to leave on the first train on Monday but she had handed in her notice at the hospital and would be home for good the second week in August that was until she was married then in September it was off to a new life in Canada with her husband. The news from Normandy was a bit alarming as the Germans had proved much more stubborn an enemy than was first anticipated, there was no word from Willie but on the other hand they hadn't received a telegram from the War department to say he was killed or wounded so they could only assume he was ok. Sandy was all prepared for the harvest he had the barn empty for the wedding dance and he had tidied up the yard so that it would look a bit respectable. The troops had gone from the Mansion house and auld Spencer was given it back but he had problems it needed a lot of renovation and he didn't have the money so he had a bit of dilemma on his hands.

The day of the wedding was fast approaching everything was in order Walter's sister and her friend who were also in the Canadian Air Force and were stationed at Prestwick had managed to obtain leave passes so that they could attend the wedding, they arrived at Hillies on the Friday, Betty had been home for over a week she had everything in hand, Will Watson had arranged the transport from Hillies to the Kirk but being Will he said it was a secret, Sandy had no idea either but kidded Betty on saying " Yea canna trust that man Watson he might arrive up here wie a wheel barrow yea ken how he operates nothing is ever serious." Walter and his Canadian best man were staying with Will so they would already know what form of transport the bride would arrive in, the ladies from the W.R I. had volunteered to decorate the church with flowers it was a great honour for them as there had been no weddings in the Glen since the war started so they were always keen to practice their flower arranging skills. In order that auld Peg could witness her daughter getting married Will Watson had managed once again to obtain a wheel chair for the day. The wedding was scheduled for two pm Will said he would be at Hillies at one thirty, Betty was getting anxious no sign of the big fellow and no idea what the mode of transport would be, suddenly one of the twins shouted here comes Will Watson wie a horse and cairt, Betty imagined a huge Clydesdale pullin an old dung cart.

She let out a squeal and rushed over to the window what a relief when she spotted the blacksmith coming up the road, he was sitting in the driving seat of a lovely old gig pulled by a beautiful white pony, Will looked the part dressed in top hat and tails, when he arrived at the kitchen door Betty rushed out and gave him an enormous hug. The bride her two bridesmaids and Meg the chief bridesmaid piled in and arrived at the church with time to spare. Sandy was waiting at the church door it was his duty to give his sister away. Walter looked resplendent in his dress uniform as he stood at the alter waiting to receive his new bride from his soon to be brother in law. The service went without a hitch there were tears shed but it soon turned to laughter, about four pm the Duncan family and their four Canadian guests sat down to a lovely dinner some of Megs neighbours had taken over and the wedding party were waited on hand and foot some how the Canadians had managed to procure a couple of bottles of champagne so that the happy couple could be toasted in style. Around seven pm the neighbours started to arrive so that they could get the dance under way before long the old barn was jumping the Canadian's were in their glory as they tried out all the old Scottish dances that were still popular, there were not many wall flowers if there were a shortage of men the women would dance with each other just to make sure they were not left out of the fun, one or two people had managed to get a small amount of booze mostly whisky and sherry but there was never enough to cause any mayhem of course the war kept all the luxury goods in short supply, but everybody had a good time even although it was a fairly dry affair. One good thing in Sandy's favour was the fact that there were quite a few musicians among the Glen fowk so it meant that Sandy's and Will could join the dancers, it turned out to be a grand evening and come eleven forty five the dancers were reluctant to call a halt to their enjoyment but the rules of the Glen was that the Sabbath started at Midnight on Saturday although it was a very old understanding it was always adhered to, so the last dance was started at eleven thirty and the final chord was played fifteen minutes later the newly weds were carried shoulder high from the barn to the back door, Sandy then returned to the barn to make sure there were no smouldering cigarettes left lying about, Meg was busy making a cup of tea before they all retired to bed. Of course Betty and Walter had to strip their bed before they could get into it some kind person or persons had made the bed in such away it was impossible to get under the blankets but all in the days fun.

The following morning was just a normal day for Sandy auld claes and tackity beets as he headed for the stable to feed his animals, all his chores done he was sitting having a cup of tea around half six when Meg appeared she looked rather unkempt, as she lifted the tea pot Sandy knew it was better to keep quiet until his sister was ready to speak, finally he said, "How would you like to have a long lie I'll milk the coo for yea this morning,"?, Meg put her arm round his neck gave him a hug as she picked up her cup of tea and made for the door leading to her bedroom, he realised that the past forty eight hour had been hectic for her and further more she would have a house full for the next few days. Sandy finished the milking and fed the hens on returning to the house the two Canadian Girls were sitting having a fag and a cup of tea they asked him if he would care to join them.

The two girls Jenny and Betsy were full of praise about yesterdays proceedings they thought the wedding was a beautiful ceremony, then the dance they had never experienced anything like it, the dancing was a whole new ball game to them, although they did have dances in Canada like the Canadian Barn Dance which they were surprised was so popular in Scotland. During the conversation with Sandy they brought up the tragedy of the crashed Canadian bomber and asked if Sandy could show them the site. He told them that he would take great pleasure in taking them up to the top of the hill where the crash happened after they had been given some breakfast. Meg made her second entrance just on eight-o-clock she looked in much better shape and asked what everybody would like for breakfast the vote taken was overwhelmingly for boiled eggs, so boiled eggs it was. Next to appear was the new bride looking rather dishevelled, maybe this was how a day old bride was supposed to look, she grabbed a couple of cups filled them with tea before disappearing back through the lobby to her room she shouted that Walter and her were having a long lie.

Jimmy the best man who had slept at Will Watson's arrived just on nine-o-clock the girls told him about the visit to the crash site which he was keen to join as he had known two of the lads who had been killed. It was a wonderful summer morning as the party set off for the top of the hill the Canadians were over awed by the beauty of the countryside, at the crash site there was nothing to be seen somebody had erected a wooden cross you could see the area of different coloured grass where the original had been burned but if you didn't know the story it would go unnoticed, the girls had a camera with which they took some photos promising Sandy they would send him copies if they came out. Sandy continued round his perimeter fence passed the quarry where he told them the story of how lucky the tinks had been, having moved the day before the crash and how a wheel had landed right on top of their camp site. Back at Hillies everybody had surfaced Walter was sorry he had missed the pilgrimage to the crash site but pointed out that he had already been at it on his last visit. Meg was busy getting her mother ready for church Jim Kerr had made a request that as many of the family as possible would be welcome to attend the service, they still had Will Watson's wheelchair so it was a good opportunity to take their frail mother to church so it turned out the whole wedding party would attend, by the time they arrived the Kirk was fairly full, Jim Kerr met them at the door and accompanied the newly weds up the isle to the front row the whole congregation stood until the Duncan Family were seated, Sandy felt his friends had done them a great honour which was greatly appreciated. After the Kirk service a quick bite to eat and most of the party set off for a tour round by the village of Covie the Canadians were awe struck when the looked over the brow of the hill and saw this wonderful little cluster of houses plus the most delightful little harbour all nestling at the foot of the cliffs, late afternoon they were back at the croft Sandy did his usual Sunday afternoon party piece and had a nap much to Megs annoyance when she got him alone she told him he was bloody well ignorant lying snoring his head off and them with guests in the house. In the evening the twins who were fascinated with the Canadian Girls because they had lipstick and wore nylon stockings something they had never seen around the Glen so they stayed close to them hoping they may leave a lipstick behind.

The Canadian party were leaving on the first train in the morning Walter who had his car with him had promised to run them to the station the train left around seven am, the whole Duncan family were up early to wave the girls goodbye and also Walters friend Jim he was going on the same train, the girls said before they left that they would like to come back and spend a week on the croft if that was ok, Meg assured them all they needed to do was let her know when they would be arriving.

Over in France Willie was still in the thick of things he had managed to escape unscathed but the carnage all around him would be in his memory for ever it was sad to see so many young men killed and maimed, one thing that stood out in his mind and this was maybe because of his farming back ground but fields of beautiful cattle and horses lying dead some of them with horrendous injuries poor beasts they didn't deserve to end up the way they did, it was hard to say whether the ones that remained alive were better off than the dead ones because the living ones were terrified, as soon as they heard aeroplanes they flew into a panic. He was not really involved in front line fighting but you had to be alert especially when handling prisoners many were quite prepared to commit suicide and kill as many British as possible then the next ones were quite happy to be prisoners rather than risk being killed in action. Willie was hoping that soon he would be able to send some word home to his family and let them know he was safe and well. The fierce fighting was around the town of Caen the Germans were resisting and defending very well it was holding up the advance, to soften the enemy up it was decided to launch a huge bombing raid, this was another memory Willie had that would probably never leave him on the second week in July just before dawn the first wave of bombers flew overhead it was estimated that there were one thousand planes and some of them managed to make three journeys the town of Caen was virtually flattened but it allowed the British to advance towards their goal Pegasus Bridge.

Life reverted back to near normal at Hillies, Betty and Walter were having a week honeymooning then he would have to return to his base at Dyce, Betty would stay at Hillies until she received word that she was on her way to Canada Walter was trying to wangle it so that they could fly together not easy but there was ways and means. It was harvest time again a hard time for Sandy as he was still obliged to work in the Timber Control although he was allowed days off to attend his croft. The last week of August and Walter managed to get a message to Hillside saying he would be paying a visit the following week-end Betty was over the moon it was over three weeks since their last contact, the job Walter did ferrying aircraft across the Atlantic was not nearly so dangerous now that the German Air force was needed full time in Europe. Walter arrived late on the Friday evening he said it was getting harder to obtain petrol coupons, Sandy told him he may be able to obtain a few he was allowed so many for the petrol he needed for his little engine that worked his small threshing mill he never used it but he used to take the coupons as somebody always had a use for them. Walter was the bearer of gifts for everyone of the family and he was especially popular with his young twin-sisters-in law, his own sister Jenny had told him the girls were desperate to own a tube of lipstick so you can imagine how popular he was when he presented them each with a compact set complete with powder puff etc.

Tommy was presented with a mechanno set all the way from America he was probably the only boy in Scotland to have one but it was something that kept him amused for years to come. Meg got a compact set and some nylon stockings and Sandy was given fags and some booze. Betty was just happy to be reunited with her man and very happy with the news that he was due for demob in two weeks time and they would to fly from Prestwick the second week in September. Not everybody had the same happy feeling Meg was sure she would never see her sister again, one reason was that they never had enough money to visit anywhere their existence was from hand to mouth all the time but you never know things may get better. At the Kirk the following Sunday Jim Kerr was running through the world wide crises as he usually did and at the end he announced that this week was not all doom and gloom due to a technical hitch the threshing mill would still be powered by the old steam engine as the fancy new tractor had developed some sort of problems the smiles on the faces of his congregation showed a great affection for the old girl, but it also allowed them to have one final get together with the two old operators Jimmy Burr and Jimmy Black. The minister went on to say that one or two people had intimated that they would like to honour the old guys for the fine sterling job they had done over the years so they were going to convene a meeting in the village hall on Tuesday evening at eight pm to try and thrash out a way to say thanks to this two fine servants to the community. Tuesday evening and the popularity of the two retiring Steam Engine Operators shone through with the turn out of Glen folks every household in the place was represented in some cases two or three Generations were present, on the platform sat the committee Chaired by Bob Paterson the headmaster, he called them to order and proceeded to explain the reason for the meeting he then asked if anybody had any suggestions as to how they could lay on an evening to entertain the old guys some suggested a dance but it was pointed out that they were both over seventy and dancing would no longer be one of their strong points. As suggestions were bandied back and forth the audience were asked if anybody could suggest a suitable gift, somebody suggested a collection , Auld Doug Imirie a shepherd from the top of the glen said that he made fancy walking sticks with carvings done out of horn as a handle he had two ready now and he would be willing to let them have them , next on offer was from Will Watson one of his hobbies was making weather vanes he could conjure up a couple before the presentation evening the last offer came from Lang Dod he said he would donate a bag of Golden Wonder Tatties to each of them, it was decided that that would be ample, so they returned to the entertainment, the best

110

suggestion being again from Lang Dod Wilson his idea would be to hold a Bothy Nicht with any local performers willing to donate their skill at singing telling stories feats of strength anything entertaining, this idea was unanimously accepted. The participants were asked to leave their names with the secretary, and state what their showbiz skill was, this would enable the committee to produce a programme of events for the evening, the W.R.I. volunteered there services to provide tea and what ever the rationing allowed, they would have some eats and it would be helpful if anybody could donate any baking ingredients, sugar, flour, baking powder and fruit. So it was agreed that a good old Bothy Nicht would be the order of the nicht, fingers crossed that the old boys would be staying overnight.

Four pm on the first Sunday in November and the peace was shattered for the final time as the Auld Steam Engine breasted the hill about a mile from the crossroads, it was music to the Glen Folk they would have their barns and lofts filled with winter feed for their animals and of course this visit was extra special because it was definatly the last time a steam engine would be present in the Glen unless there was roadwork's to be carried out they still used steam rollers so they were not totally extinct yet. Normally the two operators stayed at the croft of Davie and Shelia Morrison on the Saturday but they have been known to take their bikes and cycle home for the week-end after finishing threshing mid-day, this move had to be knocked on the head at all costs as the surprise party was well and truly organised for the following Saturday evening. The sight of the threshing mill brought great apprehension to the Duncan family and opened up the old wounds of their fathers death as the years were passing bye it did get easier but the sound of the sheaves going through the drum always brought a shiver down Sandy's spine, the one job at the mill he would never carry out was feeding the drum, the job his father was doing the day of his accident, it was never confirmed what caused the accident but there were suggestions such as Sandy Senior had taken a dizzy turn was the main theory, he could have had a loose belt or a torn sleeve on his jacket which could easily have got caught in the teeth of the drum but there was no concrete confirmation other than that it was an unfortunate fatal accident. Although the accident had blighted the lives of the Duncan's Sandy enjoyed his fortnight at the mill it was the twice yearly get together of his friends and neighbours the banter and leg pulling went on everyday and of course all the gossip was brought

111

up to-date, who was courting who, who was pregnant and who was to blame just some of the subjects discussed. On the middle Saturday of the fortnight the big farm belonging to the Bremner family usually needed a day and a half to complete their work, it would be finished at half eleven and the mill would then move to Davie Morison's croft set up and be ready for Monday morning. Shelia shouted to the two auld guys to come and get a cup of tea shortly after they arrived, Jimmy Burr arrived at the door he was leaning heavily on his walking stick, Shelia asked him what was wrong, "Ach its that bloody sciatica, my hip is giving me gip, I think I'll need to go hame and get some mair pain killers av run oot oh the dammed things" Shelia was near floored when he said he was going hame and quickly thought up an excuse to stop him, " Jimmy yea will dee yir hip mair hairm than guid biking all that distance we hiv a bottle of codeine in the hoose yea can use them" she was relieved when he agreed that he would be better to rest so she gave him the bottle and a cup of tea he went to have a lie down in their works caravan, she was quite thankful she had offered him a cup of tea in the first place otherwise he would probably be gone, the next problem was to persuade him to come to the village hall in the evening. After a good dose of codeine and a sleep Auld Jimmy was in fine fettle when he wakened he headed for the Morrison house where Shelia had the dinner ready, she was juggling the problem of getting the two-auld guys to the Village hall without giving the game away, suddenly she remembered that Jimmy Burr was very fond of bairns although he never had any of his own, the music teacher had formed the kids into a choir especially for the nights party they were to be the first to perform.

Shelia was as honest as the day was long, but occasionally you have to tell a little white lie just as she did to make sure the two victims attended their presentation party, she told them that the bairns from the Glen were going to be singing in the village hall at seven thirty, so instead of sitting around the hoose why not join the Morrison's and listen to the bairns in song. Jimmy Black was quite keen but Auld Burr started to moan aboot his damned sciatica. Davie Morrison pointed out that they may never have another chance of a night together because when the Steam Mill finishes the two operators would have very few opportunities to visit the Glen in the near future, with much persuasion he was finally railroaded into going the final bait being there may be a dram going. The Morrison's were expected at the hall at seven thirty the rest of the audience would already be seated waiting for the grand entrance of the guests of honour, they would enter by the back door which led directly onto the stage. Jimmy Burr had difficulty climbing the four steps and moaned and cursed at every step wanting to know why they couldn't enter by the front door but his complaining was totally ignored. The stage curtain was closed, on the dimly lit platform the only thing they could make out was a table and half-a-dozen chairs, four of the chairs were occupied by the head honcho's of the committee, Lang Dod, Spencer Tracy, Rev Jim Kerr and Dr Findlay. The two old guys were shown to the two remaining seats. Bob Paterson the chairman appeared and said " Jimmy and Jimmy have you any idea why you're here "? the two old guys shook their heads looking rather mesmerised, Bob Paterson continued. " Well in view of your thirty plus years of loyal service to the Crofting community of this Glen, we decided that you deserve a little show of our appreciation so if you both stand up for a couple of minutes we will begin". The two of them stood up looking at each other in amazement, Bob Paterson nodded to Davie Fraser who was in charge of the stage curtain, it began to slide open the hall was full to capacity, the two old mill operators received a standing ovation which lasted for a good couple of minutes, Jimmy Burr and Jimmy Black had never ever been treated like this before and were quite emotionally moved. The community committee took over and Lang Dod gave one of his very humorous speeches as he recalled many of the memorable incidents that had happened over the years, he also reminded the audience that most of the incidents were funny but there were ones that brought grief it was not always fun and games. Now for the presentation he called up The Rt Hon Spencer Tracy to do the honours, they each received a hand carved shepherds crook, a weather vane and a wallet containing fifteen pounds equivalent to at least six months wages. Jimmy Burr being the senior man returned a vote of thanks to everybody present, the time spent in the Glen over the many years had been a pleasure, many of the folks in the hall that evening weren't even born when the two mill operators started their twice yearly visits with the threshing mill now they were adults bringing up families of their own with a sigh he said " how the years have passed" he said a final thanks before sitting down. As soon as the presentation was over the hall was cleared and the Celeidh got under way, the Bairns choir was the first on stage their singing went down a treat especially the sing song for the final ten minutes and everybody joined in.

With the formalities over the two auld guys were allowed to join their friends the Morrison's and enjoy the nights proceedings which kicked off with the bairns choir singing a medley of Robbie Burns songs, next was Lang Dod Wilson with his rendition of some of the popular Bothy ballads, The Mucking O Geordies Byre, The Barn Yards O Delgaty and by special request from Jimmy Burr Drumdelgie, in between times Will and Sandy supplied some music, they had just completed some dance music when Will leaned over to Sandy and asked if he knew the tune to the song the Crookit Bawbee, Sandy said he kind of knew it but why, well said Will, "Beldie Smart always wants to sing it accompanied by Alick her loon, yea never heard a racket like it, it always reminds me of a lump of wood gan through a circular saw" Sandy burst into fits of hysterical laughter but had to pull himself together as Beldie got ready to flex her vocal chords. Half way through the evening the ladies from the WRI supplied a wonderful treat of tea and home baking and somehow they managed to get enough ingredients to bake a cake their way of honouring the special guests. Jimmy Burr was persuaded to get up on stage and play a selection of tunes on his mouth organ and to end a wonderful evening, they had a bit of a sing song with some of the popular songs of the times, everybody agreed it was a fitting tribute to a couple of very conscientious old men.

Monday morning the retirement doo was history, dead on the dot of seven am the peace and tranquillity of the Glen was shattered by the shrill whistle of the steam engine, then with a great thrust of power she burst into life ready for another hard days work, the crofters were already at their work stations ready to feed this hungry brute of a lump of steel. Apart from a short break for a cup of tea the engine never really stopped until half eleven then she shut down for an hour and a half, after dinner there was a lot of cheerful banter, some of the men lay down in the straw and had forty winks, with another blast on the steam whistle at one pm they were ready for another three to four hours of quite hard graft every function was done by hand so carrying the two hundred weight bags of barley up the stairs to the loft was no mean feat. But there was always plenty leg pulling and pranks so the time passed fairly quickly, it would be a different croft each day until Saturday by then they were at the last farm in the Glen they had enough work for a day and a half which meant the mill would finish around midday Saturday and the operators would then head for home, but this Saturday would be different because there would be no shouting see you next year boys, there would be no next year for the wonderful old Steamer because as a working machine she was now to become redundant, over taken by modern technology at the cost of at least one job. It was a real nostalgic journey for the threshing mill as she trundled down the glen making her way to the main road, nearly every resident was at the roadside waving goodbye not only to the Mill but to Jimmy Burr and Jimmy Black, as she disappeared over the brow of the hill the old whistle could be heard for the last time and the end of an era. The next piece of excitement to hit the Glen was the very next Saturday when the local ploughing match would take place, it was to be held at the Bremner Farm, once again they had a very good entry with the horses still holding their own two dozen pairs but there were now over a dozen tractors.

The ploughing match was the highlight of the crofting calendar and was an event eagerly looked forward to each year, the competition was keen and every precaution was taken to try and win the event. Many of the older men were very cynical towards the new fangled tractor and boasted that you needed a special skill to plough competitively with a pair of horse so there were some fierce arguments as to the advantages and disadvantages, this year did nothing to enhance the tractors versatility, the ground at Bremners was quite boggy and the early tractors were very heavy so this meant that on the boggy ground the tractors were being out gunned by the trusty old horse, there was a lot of cursing and head scratching every time a tractor floundered on the wet ground, allowing the cynics a field day as they shouted I told you they were bloody useless, well it was early days. The ploughing match overall was a great success and the usual journeymen won the top prizes, then in the evening the dance was always an enjoyable occasion, the next event would be the New Year.

Although Meg and Jock Mitchell were always at war with each other she was always watching for him coming up the farm track, she knew that if he was on their track he would have mail for them, it was just three weeks from the end of the year and there was Jock's little red van, she waited until he knocked on the door they exchanged unpleasantries and he handed over the mail she let out a shriek causing Jock to very nearly need a change of underwear, When he regained his composure he said, " Dear me Meg fits wrang wie yea" Oh nothing to concern you Jock Mitchell" and with that she whirled on her heel and left him standing on the door step cursing his luck, she had got a letter that caused great excitement and he had been unable to find out what it was all about. Inside the kitchen Meg ripped open the letter she knew the handwriting it was from her beloved brother Willie, wow! What a surprise she had given up hope ages ago partly blaming Willie for not bothering to write, but unless you were involved in front line fighting how were they to know the rules and regulations governing correspondence. One of Willies mates had been wounded and was being shipped home for treatment, Willie took the opportunity to get a letter home his mate posted it for him when he arrived in the UK this was one of the reasons Jock Mitchell hadn't a clue where it came from and no doubt he didn't recognise Willie's hand writing his letter hadn't been censored so he was at liberty too tell them where he was and what was going on, Meg was delighted and even more so when Willie pointed out that although things could be dicey at times he was behind the front line and so far had escaped unscathed.

A couple of weeks before the New Year it had started to snow it was causing disruption on the roads, the yearly concert was held and everybody had an enjoyable evening away from the usual hum drum life they were used to, both Betty and Jim managed to get letters home so Meg was quite pleased with her lot, Tommy finally confessed that he no longer believed there was a Santa Claus but hoped he would still get some presents just as normal, how the family were growing up. Hogmanay arrived with very little fuss, New Years Day dinner was a cockerel, after the dinner Sandy spread himself out on the couch and had a nice snooze, later in the evening Will Watson and a few neighbours paid a visit, some body had managed to procure a half bottle of whisky and a bottle of Port so they had a wee dram just to welcome a New Year.

They also toasted an end to the war the longer it lasted the harder it was becoming to survive, the rationing was really biting hard maybe in this remote part of the world where they had always been more or less self-sufficient the rationing was maybe just catching up. Into the first week of the year and the weather was getting worse the blizzards were a daily occurrence and the snow was at least four feet deep. Things were getting desperate in the house as they were running out of basic goods, in days gone bye the crofter women would stock the place up with enough provisions to last at least three months, but you needed ration coupons for everything you bought now so even if the goods were available you were only entitled to buy what ever your coupons allowed so it was a tricky situation especially for snow bound country folks. Sandy happened to bump into his neighbour Frankie Smith, he was bemoaning the fact that the wife was running short of rations and asked Sandy if he fancied walking into town next day they could take a sledge each and if they managed to get any rations they would load the sledge and pull it behind them easier than filling bags and then having to humph them home, Sandy thought what a good idea so they decided to leave next morning at around ten it was at least four miles so if they gave themselves two hours walking time each way they could be there and back before late afternoon, as Sandy walked away he shouted to Frankie am going to take some eggs, butter and cheese with me, there's a good chance the fishers will be willing to barter some fish for the fresh dairy products, so they both agreed that this was their plan of attack. Next morning after the cattle and horses were seen to the sledges were packed with dairy products and just on ten am the twosome set off suitably clad and pulling a four foot long sledge apiece. It was hard going over the fairly deep snow and by the time they reached town it was well over their anticipated time of two hours, the first move was to head for the harbour area to the fishing village part of town and see if they could exchange their goods for some fish products, this didn't take long as the local fisher people had been without fresh dairy products for the past six weeks so as soon as word spread they were flocking round offering all sorts of fish, kippers, smoked mackerel, dried haddock, dried ling and as many salt herring as they could load on the sledge, Sandy was sorry he didn't have a lot more to give but promised they would be back next week if the snow persisted. Back up town and they went round the town buying up what was available and what they had coupons for, all in all they had done extremely well and the sledges were fairly well laden, now another something that Sandy hadn't allowed for was the steep trek from the town to the top of the hill until you reached the flat, it was about a mile of twisted road and one in four in some places pulling the sledge which was now quite heavy up the gradient of the hill was extremely hard work and the winter clothing soon had the pair of them soaked in sweat the time was passing them bye at a fair rate of knots this was worrying them, from the top of the hill it was fairly remote for a couple of miles until you started to arrive on the outskirts of the glen in other words there was very little shelter although the weather had been perfect up until now darkness was beginning to creep in and the sky was clouding over Sandy reckoned they still had about three miles to go before they were home. As they trudged on the wind started to rise and that meant the powdered snow would soon start drifting off the fields nothing to get alarmed about yet but they were keen to get home.

Chapter Thirteen

Sandy and Frankie had lived in the Glen all their lives and blizzards were a yearly occurrence some years worse than others, normally when the blizzards would start to whip up the two guys had been close to home so the most they would ever have had to suffer was the whiteout conditions, they would have been less than a quarter of an hour from home, but to-day it was more of a crisis as they were in no man's land barely half way home, it is getting dark and they are now encountering blizzard conditions and no shelter available for a good while yet, to cap it all pulling the sledges up the hill had caused them to sweat so they were beginning to cool down it was alarming but they had experienced this type of weather before, so it was heads down and batter on. It was difficult to see where you were going and also very difficult to breath due to the powdered snow it was now pitch dark what a bloody predicament to be in, Sandy remembered the observers hut was some where close by but when in whiteout conditions everything looks the same so they kept plodding on they couldn't afford to stop and they were completely lost, Sandy shouted to his mate we will have to keep going were bound to land somewhere soon, they had no idea how long they had been walking and it was so bad they couldn't even check the watch to see what time it was, Sandy had a notion to abandon the sledges but he had no idea where he was and they needed the rations on board the sledges at home so head down and keep plodding, cold wet hungry and very, very tired they stumbled on for another while until eventually Sandy who was leading stumbled into a drystane dyke on one side the snow was level with the top but on the leeward side there was very little snow so they got behind the dyke they would rest for a few minutes but because of the cold sweaty under clothes they couldn't stay for too long, Sandy suggested they follow the dyke at least it was more sheltered than what they had been facing up until now he asked Frankie if he was still ok to pull the sledge he nodded yes and gave the thumbs up so they set off again and stumbled there way along behind the dyke, they had probably gone about a quarter of a mile when they came upon a gate opening, Sandy crouched behind the pillar and tried to picture where they might be but they were completely lost and possibly owe their lives to this drystane dyke. As Sandy crouched behind the pillar he was peering into the gloom and as if by a miracle there was a slight lull in the storm he was sure he spotted a building not too far away even if it was an old barn or shed he was sure if they got shelter they would be fine. Forcing his eyes to focus where he thought the building was Sandy asked Frankie if he had seen it he shook his head but also peered in the direction Sandy was looking and yes he thought he saw it as well. Sandy had a ball of twine in his pocket he had used it to tie the rations to the sledge so he told Frankie to hold one end of the twine and he would walk in the direction of the building and see what he could find by using the twine he would make his way back to where Frankie was with the sledges behind the dyke. Sandy didn't go very far when he came face to face with a solid wall further along was a window then a small porch he still hadn't a clue where he was but at least they would get shelter, Sandy banged on the door and the racket from inside with barking dogs and somebody shouting at them to shut up was like music to his ears their worries were over, the door eventually swung open it must have been swollen with the damp as the bottoms seemed to jam on the concrete base.

Peering out of the gloom was a weel kent face Jimmy Lindsay (theTink),Sandy could have kissed him what a relief, Jimmy asked "What the hell are yea dein oot on a nicht like this"? his wife shouted from out of the gloom who is it, Jimmy answered " Its Sandy Hillies and he's in a gie state yea better come in" Sandy explained that Frankie Smith was also with him and held up the bit string, Jimmy said he would get a hurricane lamp and shine it so that they could see what they were doing. Bye the time Sandy got back to Frankie he was sitting shivering from the cold, Sandy got him on his feet and the two of them staggered towards the cottage door where Jimmy guided them with his paraffin lamp. The Lindsay home was like a menagerie with bairns, dogs, cats and one of the boys was sitting stroking a ferret, the rafters of the house were hung with drying rabbit skins and there was also a roe deer skin hung up to dry one less for old Spencer, you could hardly see across the room for the reek of the fire Sandy's eyes were stinging the minute he entered the place, but at least they were out of danger he was sure they couldn't have held out much longer in the blizzard and Frankie who was a good bit older than Sandy was on his last legs. Jimmy soon had a cup of tea ready for them and he also offered a glass of his home made fire water with the assurance that it would warm them up it was made from the sap of the Birch Tree and although quite easy to drink the effects were almost instant, the two crofter lads felt quite tipsy with the one glass but it fairly thawed them out. Next on the agenda was some food Jimmy's wife Netty had a pot on the open fire she also had an infant on her hip, Jimmy explained that they were about to eat but things were very scarce the wife had just used the last bit of fish and they were having hairy Tatties (Hairy tatties are mashed tatties with dried salted Ling mixed through them) the two men were starving so they were quite pleased to join the Lindsay's at the table, the hairy tatties went down a treat although the house and its residents were pretty grubby. Sandy had a look out the door about midnight and it was still fairly stormy, in their struggle to get where they were they by passed Hillies by about a mile and a half and Jimmy Lindsay's house was in the complete wrong direction from where they wanted to be so Sandy asked if they could kip down for the night, it was no bother to Jimmy and his family they could have a chair each side of the fire, Netty would supply a couple of blankets, Sandy and Frankie were soon dosing off to sleep in the warm living room but soon found out they had intruders in the shape of fleas, they didn't sleep very well as the fleas needed a lot of scratching, Sandy thought to himself that bloody Lindsay clan must be immune to the little buggers. Sandy was wide awake at his usual time of five am he needed the lavatory but the Lindsay sanitation left a lot to be desired, at night it was an open bucket placed just inside the back door in the porch used by both male and female, Sandy was far too modest to expose himself to such a barbaric situation so he forced his way out the door and made for the shelter of the drystane dyke to relieve himself he heard a scrambling behind him and Frankie exclaimed that he was bursting. Sandy had a grope around to see where the sledges were and felt a shudder run through his body when he discovered the sledges buried under two feet of snow he began to realise just how lucky they had been, if they hadn't stumbled on the Lindsay hovel things might have turned out differently, it was still quite dark although there was a full moon and it was as bright as day, they decided to hang on for another hour they didn't relish a repeat of last night.

Before too long the Lindsay household was alive, Sandy compared it to a menagerie with bairns and animals all shouting and barking at the same time, there was a queue for the bucket at the back door this was causing agro as the participants danced from one foot on to the other. The proper toilet i.e. six by four shed with bucket was at least twenty yards from the house so it was nigh impossible for bairns to plough through four feet of snow to reach the wretched place the convenience of the back door bucket would be appreciated until the weather improved. By quarter to eight Sandy was straining at the bit to get going he could just imagine the state the family would be in wondering if he had survived the night they had rescued the sledges and after thanking Jimmy and Netty Lindsay they set off telling Jimmy to get himself over to Hillies and Frankie's place at Northfield and they would get stocked up with some rations and fresh milk. They had endured the most uncomfortable of nights but were so grateful to the Lindsay's who were as poor as church mice but still helped friends when in need, a deed that the two men would never forget and they would continue to give the Lindsay's what ever they could for many years to come, Sandy asked Frankie how he was feeling he replied ok but he was still itching where the fleas had bitten, he then asked Sandy if he had spotted the rats in the rafters Frankie's description was that they looked as big as Rabbits. They had landed about a mile and a half off course in the blizzard so it was about forty five minutes walk back to Hillies about halfway home they were met by a party of rather irate neighbours led by Dod Simpson he was ranting and raving at the two men and telling them how bloody irresponsible they had been, Sandy held up his hands and agreed but also pointed out it could have happened to anybody they were sorry for any inconvenience they had caused, Dod Simpson asked where they had sheltered all night, when Sandy told him he stepped back and exclaimed "It's a bloody wonder yea weren't eaten alive wie fleches (fleas) they tell me the place is jumping" " Oh aye they had a field nicht getting stuck into Frankie and me but fir aw that Jimmy Lindsay has a heart of gold". Sandy next had to face the wrath of his sister Meg she was near hysterical when he got home, he didn't tell her just how lucky they had been but tried to calm her down by explaining how quickly the blizzard caught up wie them, when told they slept the night in Jimmy Lindsay's hoose he was made to go and change his clothes and examine the ones he took off for fleches. Within a day the blizzard scenario was history, Jimmy Lindsay took Sandy at his word and appeared pulling an empty sledge Meg made up a box of groceries including milk, eggs, butter and homemade cheese, he also asked if it would be possible to get some tatties as he was having a job obtaining any, after he had gone Sandy remarked that Jimmy had used the wrong word instead of obtaining he should have said stealing, he was well known for his night time raids on the Tattie fields around the glen, normally if it was only a few for the pot he was ignored. The winter weather lasted for a few more weeks causing everything to be behind schedule. The war was still progressing but the Allies were having a struggle against a very strong German Army, it was announced that Eisenhower was to take over the duties of the Supreme Commander of the Allied Expeditionary Force, it looked like things were hotting up anyhow people were fed up of the war and all the nasties associated with it rationing for a start.

Chapter Fourteen

THE SEVERE WINTER SOON TURNED TO spring and everything was going full swing the planting of crops was in progress, Meg received another letter from her brother Willie in it he said they were getting ready to cross the River Rhine he was well and still remained unscathed he also intimated that the rumours were that the war would be over before the summer arrived, unfortunately there was no forwarding address so Meg was unable to reply. Sandy was listening to the midday news on his wireless when it was announced that the war was over in Europe and the Germans had surrendered. Next day the headlines in the papers were. 7th May 1945 Eisenhower Accepts Unconditional Surrender Of All German Forces at his headquarters in Rheims. Britain went mad with street parties and wild scenes all over the country even in the Glen the residents were out in the farmyards blasting off shot guns and shouting and cheering hopefully life should improve maybe not immediately but with time who knows. Meg was hoping her two brothers would be home shortly it was over two years since Jim left home and it must have been the same for Willie, There was good news for some, young Roddy Tracy was home and so was Tam Scott both had been prisoners for close on five years, there was no need to put up the black out screens now so yes improvements were beginning to shine through. Through out the country welcome home parties were being organised and the Glen folks were not going to be left out so the normal hall committee were summonsed to a meeting and preliminary plans drawn up for the welcome home bash, as was normal Bob Paterson was elected Chairman of the committee and a date was set for the sixth of June nearly a month away and also the anniversary of the Normandy campaign, it would be adequate time to get things going. Back at Hillies Meg was keeping a vigil as she waited for her daily post delivery but she had no luck Sandy tried to explain that the war in the far east was still going on and Jim was involved with that so she may have to wait for a while yet as for Willie he was a Military policeman and no doubt they would be in big demand until the aftermath of the war was sorted out so neither of them may be home for quite some time this didn't deter Meg she was still waiting for her deadly enemy Jock Mitchell to appear daily. Of the twenty young men called up to fight in the war five had been killed in action three were wounded and four had been prisoners of war, the POWs were home the two Duncan boys were still abroad and the remainder were arriving home in dribs and drabs, so there should be quite a turn out for the welcome home bash. The programme was set out, the first item was to parade the returning heroes followed by a children's fancy dress parade the rest of the afternoon would be taken up with games and of course there were some stalls such as tombola and a raffle, then in the evening they were going to have concert similar to the night they had at the Steam Mill fellows retirement doo where local talent would go on stage and perform along with the locals there was also a few Polish soldiers in a camp in the area, the day would end with a couple of hours dancing it should be an enjoyable break after the excitement of the war finishing. The 6th of June arrived and it turned out to be just perfect Auld Spencer in his full uniform got the proceedings under way the weather stayed good so everybody enjoyed themselves.

As usual Sandy and Will Watson provided the music for the dancers the impromptu concert had been a scream and would have gone on for hours but a halt had to be called at nine-o-clock to allow time for some dancing. From the stage the musicians had a great view of the dance hall and Sandy and Will were amazed at how many of the men appeared to be quite drunk this was not a normal trend as it was near impossible to buy booze with the rationing and what not, so it was quite a spectacle, the Poles started to get a bit rowdy and it looked like it could turn nasty so Dod Simpson was sent for and he soon had it under control the Poles seemed to respect the figure of a man in uniform, and everything got back to normal, this was not the normal run of the mill way things happened in this Scottish back water, the evening ended at quarter to twelve and everybody made their way home peacefully. The following week the hall committee called a meeting to discuss the outcome of the welcome home day the hall coffers had received a boost, but the dark cloud on the horizon was the matter of the nasty incident that happened at the dance, it was difficult to establish who was to blame until Jim Kerr pointed out that he would blame excessive amounts of alcohol, Bob Paterson added his comments and was adamant that this

sort of behaviour must be stamped out immediately otherwise it would
become the norm, if only they could pin point the culprits they could
be suspended from entering the hall but it was so unexpected that
nobody realised what was happening until it was over, but they would
ensure that Dod Simpson would be in attendance in future until thing;
settled down. There was more doom and gloom for the Duncan's i
never seemed to be far away Sandy was told the Timber Control peopl
would no longer require him and he was on a months notice, a bit of
blow although he had hated the job in the early days he had got used t
it and also the small wage he was paid subsidised the income from th
croft so he would feel the pinch and there was no other employment ;
hand, even his old boss Lang Dod was employing German Prisone
because they were cheaper than local labour so things were lookir
bleak. The twins had left school at the summer and were lucky th
had started work straight away in the new egg grading station that h;
opened in town they were able to cycle as the weather was favoural
at the moment but in the winter they would need to bus, it was or
a temporary measure for the two of them as they had their minds
on better careers than egg packers. Peg was going to follow sister Be
into nursing and as soon as she was seventeen she would be starti
her training in Aberdeen, Mary was determined she was joining
services and could hardly wait for her brother Willie coming ho
so that she could pick his brains about the best unit to join she di
fancy nursing but was sure there were other units where females w
employed. The summer wore on and the autumn was with them
crops were being gathered the farming community were busy, Sa
had managed to get a few days work at the harvest other wise he fo
his time dragging he had his own croft up to date so he let pec
know he was available for any odd jobs he was surprised at the amc
on offer like repairing fences etc it wasn't full time but it filled in
time and he earned a bit of much needed cash. It was nearing the
of the year again and the threshing mill was due she should arriv
the week-end, Sandy happened to look towards Frankie Smiths (
late afternoon and there stood the threshing mill alone, she had arr
silently the old Steam Engine was well and truly gone.

The war in the Far East was also over it seemed to end with le
a hullabaloo than the European war maybe because the European
was on the doorstep where as the Far East was far away and virt
unheard of in this part of the world. Meg had word from Jim he

125

on his way home but with the way transport was he didn't have a positive date, all Meg needed now was to hear from Willie and find out when he would manage home all she could do was keep up her vigil watching for the postman to arrive. Jim arrived at Southampton the first week in December it would take him a couple of days to get home he had to report to Woolmanhill Barracks on his way home but he would get in contact when nearer home if possible, if not expect me when you see me were his final words, finally Meg could rest easy and she even forgave Jock Mitchell when he shouted "Yea should be pleased the day Meg here's a letter fae Willie". Meg grabbed it and left poor Jock standing with his mouth open as he turned to leave he was heard muttering "That's aw the bloody thanks yea get for being civil, ignorant bitch that she is." With that he slammed the little van into gear and shot off to his next customer. Meg was shaking with emotion as she tore open Willie's envelope, she let out a squeal " Hey mother your son Willies a sergeant noo look at that she said pointing to the address 22839094 Sergeant William Duncan Royal Military Police B.F.P.O. Box 10 Berlin Germany" does that nae mak yea real prood. Sandy appeared she went through the whole scenario again and as she read on she held a commentary so that they could all hear what Willie had written and the exciting bit was he was coming home for a months leave almost certain to be at Hillies for Hogmanay, he told Meg he was looking forward to a decent New Years dinner, Meg had tears running down her face over come with emotion imagine both her brothers here for New Year is was just unimaginable. The annual concert and the bairns party had been a huge success this year as there seemed to be more goodies available, Santa was no longer a visitor to Hillies as Tommy had grown past that stage of his life although Meg was ecstatic about her brothers coming home she didn't have her worries to seek, her mother had been very unwell the doctor thought she was suffering mini strokes and advised Meg that she would be better off in hospital but Meg being Meg resisted all moves to shift her mother and struggled on with her sometimes getting by on a couple of hours sleep, her twin sisters even although they were now working full time still shared a lot of the work getting stuck in after they had their supper. Christmas Day passed without much notice then on the twenty seventh a telegram from Jim, he would be home some time to-morrow. Next day around midday Tommy came rushing into the kitchen, Meg, Meg there's a mannie coming up the road and he's weerin a funeral hat (trilby often worn at funerals), Meg rushed to the back door and exclaimed " that's nae a mannie that's

oor brother Jim"! with that she took off running and when the two met she near knocked poor Jim over, before long Meg was doing her normal party trick howling her eyes oot by now the remainder of the family were around Jim hugging and kissing him what a thrill, he had changed still not twenty years old but he was a man and he looked a real smasher with his funeral hat. Meg was doing the usual broody hen bit fussing over her young brother wanting to cook some food for him, he eventually reminded her he had only travelled from Aberdeen and he had breakfast before he left. Jim's first port of call was his mothers bedroom he had a tear in his eye when he saw her condition.

It was getting near mid night, twenty minutes and they would be into a new year Meg was up to high doh nae sign of Willie she was busy getting things prepared for to-morrow but at the back of her mind she was worrying incase something had happened to her beloved twin Willie. Then the back door was near staved in as it was hammered and somebody shouting is there anybody in. Mary was first at the door and flung it open what a sight her big brother in full military uniform complete with his red cap and best of all proudly displaying his sergeants stripes, it was like a rugby scrum as they all piled in hugging and kissing suddenly there was a barrage of shotguns along with the church bells ushering in the New Year, Jim had already opened a bottle of whisky and poured a dram for the grown ups well its not every year they will have a reunion like this just a pity Betty was missing, it was near three am when they finally managed to get to bed Sandy was a bit under the weather and reminded his brothers that the cattle would need seeing to shortly. Sandy woke to a brand new year feeling hellish he was not accustomed to heavy drinking sessions so one over the eight made him feel rather ill, he dragged himself out of bed and was having a cup of tea when young Mary entered the kitchen and announced that he could go back to bed if he wanted as she had everything under control her brother Willie had given a hand, Sandy gave her a big hug grunted and headed back to bed vowing that he would never pour another drink over his throat but haven't we all said that then found out we had only been kidding. Around nine-o-clock Sandy surfaced for the second time feeling much better that his original attempt at getting up, Tommy had scored as both his brothers had brought him presents and he was busy assembling them. Sandy had his usual breakfast of brose it seemed to help clear the alcohol from his system he then went for a walk to the top of the hill a great head clearing exercise. The glen was silent not a soul to be seen but no doubt Will Watson would call in the afternoon along with other neighbours some of them would be Willie and Jims pals anxious to see them as it was quite some time since their last get to gether. When he returned from his walk the kitchen was a hive of activity as the lassies went about preparing the dinner the aroma was very tempting and Sandy was looking forward to his New Years Day dinner, this year it was a huge cockerel stuffed with oatmeal and onions, the other two brothers were in the sitting room having a good blether, Jim had been demobbed but their was still the verdict on his wounded wrist to be addressed, he was slightly disabled in as much that he was unable to lift any heavy weights this could be a draw back when he went looking for work, he dropped a bit of a-bomb shell when he told the other two that he was planning returning to Australia where he was involved with a lassie from New Zealand. But what could they do, this war had disrupted peoples lives and just how many would move to different parts of the world remained to be seen, of course Jim came in for a bit of leg pulling about this Kiwi girl, was there going to be a wedding was one question, Willie said he would be quite keen to be best man and a trip to New Zealand would just be grand, Jim said that there was no final plans but he would see how things turned out when he got back there in a few weeks. It was then Willies turn to tell of his intentions well Willie was doing ok he was getting up the promotion ladder fairly quickly and for the near future he was going to stay in the forces, he pointed out that there was lot of exciting stuff about to happen like the trial of the Nazi Hierarchy in Nuremberg.

Jim agreed that that could lead to real drama and could see Willies point it was also history that may never again be repeated so why not be part of it, anyhow Willie pointed out that he would have regular leave cycles now that the hostilities were over, with a sly wink at Sandy he said to Jim mind and give me plenty warning when the weddings due. Meg was in her element as she served dinner only one of the family missing sister Betty and of course their mother was unable to sit at the table she had really deteriorated over the past few weeks but Meg was determined she was not going into hospital even though it was a real burden trying to get bed linen washed and dried with the wintry weather. It was a cheery family gathering that sat down to enjoy their New Year dinner Meg wasn't aware of her brothers intentions yet Sandy was hoping they would break the news to her after the festivities were past. After dinner as the females cleared up, Sandy performed his favourite party piece by falling a sleep and snoring his head off, they left him in piece for nearly two hours until the banging on the back door would have wakened the people in the cemetery, right away Meg said that that would be Will Watson as he was a big noisy brute, Sandy was unceremoniously wakened as being the host he was supposed to welcome his guests, a dram was poured for the big fellow and he had his usual tare with the lassies before settling down at the fireside to have a crack with the Duncan boys he was full of questions asking first Willie about his exploits in Europe and then Jim about his exploits in the Far East, they were soon joined by other neighbours and before long the musical instrument were produced and a real good going Celeidh was in progress, the Duncan's house was always a popular venue on New Years day. By nine-o-clock most of the visitors had left for home, the next day was back to work so the festivities were short lived, later that evening with time wearing on the future of the two brothers was brought up, Meg was a bit saddened to hear that they would be moving on especially Jim as he seemed to have his mind set on settling down in either Australia or New Zealand, Meg had read about these countries in her school books and she remembered the men who discovered them were away from home for years so she imagined that it would take Jim about a year to travel back there, he pointed out that a ship took about six weeks and if you were to fly possibly thirty six hours so he assured her it wasn't that far. Willie on the other hand could be home in about thirty hours that was overland but he also mentioned the fact that flying would soon be the favoured method of travel and from Germany to Britain it could be done in just over an hour so things didn't look all that bleak. It was another late night and nearing two am when they finally all headed for bed Meg lay for ages and worried about the break up of the family but it was happening all over especially the young men they had seen another side to life because of the war, some had met their future wives and settled down in her home area so it was disturbing, also at the back of her mind were her twins sisters who seemed determined to leave home as soon as they were old enough but could she blame them there was nothing in the Glen for young people if you managed to get a job the wages were little better than slave labour. As she lay thinking she suddenly thought about herself and Sandy they both worked from day light to dark, they didn't draw wages the income from the croft just couldn't sustain two people drawing a wage so they just used the cheque book when payment was required, an existence really, so who could blame the young people.

Willies leave was soon over and he had to get ready to travel back to his depot in Berlin, Jim had made arrangements to travel to Australia at the beginning of March, and life for the rest of the Duncan's just kept going Betty wrote a letter every two weeks so it was something to look forward to she had managed to get a job in the local hospital so life was going fine for her. Then out of the blue more heart ache for Meg and the whole family their mother suffered a severe stroke and passed away, Meg was beside herself with grief her mother had been her life's work as she had tended her for the past eight years, it was a blessing she had passed away as she was getting to a vegetative state who really needed specialist nursing but Meg was possessive and had refused to allow her mother out of the house anyhow it was over for her now. Telegrams were hastily arranged for Betty and Willie, they would hold the funeral arrangements until they had replies back just incase they may be able to attend. As Willie had just returned to his station he was unable to obtain leave at such short notice and Betty was unable to make the necessary travel arrangements as things were rather slower to happen in days gone by so it was decided that the funeral would have to take place with the family members who were available. As was normal for that part of the world the funeral was arranged for the Saturday at one pm, maybe the reason for this was that people only worked half day Saturday so they didn't really need time off, but any how Peg Duncan was laid to rest beside her husband Sandy who had preceded her nine years earlier, there was a huge turn out, she was buried from home which was the norm, it was the second time that Sandy had stood at the head of his parents coffin. After the burial there was tea and sandwich's at Hillies so all those who wanted to join the family headed back to the house it was pretty well jam packed but many of the friends just paid their respects and left until it was only people like Will Watson who were close friends and neighbours that were left, Meg was still in a bit of a state and was seen to be weeping quite a lot even though her friends did their best to comfort her. Next day the family were able to have a full compliment at the Kirk, Jim Kerr welcomed them and then based his ceremony on the loss of a loved one especially a mother after the service they congregated at the grave side before heading back home where they had a lunch and seeing it was a good day Sandy invited them to have stroll into Covie, Meg decided that she would have a couple of hours in her bed as her sleep had been sadly disrupted over the past few days. Soon everything was back to near normal, if there was a problem it was young Tommy he had spent many hours of his time in the company of his mother he was taking her death very badly in as much as he was being rather difficult, this was causing a rift between Sandy and Meg, Sandy's cure would be to give him a bloody good hiding where as Meg pampered him, if Sandy spoke to him rather harshly he would threaten to tell Meg, so there was a rift between them, Sandy happened to bump into Dr Findlay one day and mentioned the young fellows behaviour, Dr Findlay asked Sandy to be patient and he was sure Tommy would settle down, he explained that even though Meg and him had brought Tommy up he still had bonding with his mother, no doubt he resented loosing her and resented even more being told by Sandy what to do as after and all they were brothers and brothers often had differences of opinion. Sandy had great faith in the good Doctor well he had known him all his life and he was well thought of in the Glen so Sandy knuckled down and tried to go along with the young fellow.

Sandy had a build up of items that he felt he would like to discuss with Lang Dod there was a new subsidy being paid out by the government which he didn't totally understand and one or two other things that expert advice might help to solve. One of Sandy's pet hates was using the phone, to get to one he had to walk to the post office at the cross roads, then he had to work out what he had to do to make his call on reading the instructions for the umpteenth time he finally dialled Lang Dod's number his worst fears were realised when he heard the female voice on the other end, "Burnside, Betsy speaking" Sandy was speechless for a couple of seconds, he had never really spoken to the new Mistress at Burnies he finally stammered out that it was Sandy Duncan from Hillies and would it be possible to speak to Mr Wilson, " Just hold the line and I'll see if George is free" Sandy gave grin to himself and exclaimed George indeed never associated Lang Dod as being a George very posh . The voice at the other end was the familiar voice of his mentor," Aye Sandy min fit like and how can I be of assistance"? Sandy explained his needs and Lang Dod asked if Saturday one thirty would be ok, it was agreed and Sandy said he would be there sharp.

Saturday one-o-clock and Sandy mounted his bike it would take about twenty minutes to get to Burnies so he set off in his pocket was the list of things he wanted to discuss. He arrived at the back door at Burnies with time to spare, apprehensively he knocked and immediately went into shy mode as he confronted a beautiful young woman the likes he had never set eyes on before, she was a very confident sort of person and soon had Sandy at ease, " Hi Sandy we meet at last I have heard lots about you and all good stuff, just follow me George is waiting for you." Sandy again had a smirk at the mention of George, Lang Dod never ever looked like a George and he hadn't changed over the years.

He was sitting puffin away at his pipe but laid it in the ash tray as he stood to welcome Sandy, with that a young child burst out crying " Oh that's the young laird of Burnside he must be ready for his dinner". With that Betsy closed the door and left them to it. Sandy first asked about the new subsidy that was being paid out to encourage farmers to grow more crops Dod explained it, if you were in the habit of growing one acre of tatties they have agreed that if you double that they will pay you a sum of money to subsidise what the extra has cost you but I have called for a meeting of the local crofters and farmers in the hall so that it can be discussed and then everybody should know what route to go, he then went on to advise Sandy to make use of the moor land attached to his croft pointing out that again there was subsidy for using rough grazing the documents have not been circulated yet but when they are we shall set a date for the meeting. Sandy had one more item he wanted clarification on, Sandy's horses were getting on a bit they were well into their teens working them in the timber had taken a lot out of them so they would need replacing with-in the next two years what did the big fellow advise. Well Sandy with-in two years horses will be extinct as far as farm work goes the tractor is replacing them weekly. Ferguson have come out with a small model ideal for the smaller farmer I am not sure of the price but that's the line you should go along jist ask Will Watson how many horses he is shoeing in a month and he'll tell you very few. Sandy was getting ready to leave when Betsy opened the door she was holding a young toddler in her arms as soon as he saw his father he wanted to get to him.

Lang Dod, Betsy and little George came to the door to see Sandy off as he looked at them the thought went through his mind that Dod looked more like the lassies father than her husband the randy auld bugger. As he was passing the Bothy door he pushed it open and could see bodies lying asleep snoring their heads off he was about to creep out again when the one in his old bed stirred and said "Fa's at"? Next minute Eck Davidson sat bolt up right, " Sandy yea bugger what a bloody fleg (fright) yea gave me, fit are yea dein here"? Sandy explained that he had a meeting wie Lang Dod, Eck said he hoped he didn't call him that in front of Betsy as she liked to call him George, " The little man sitting in the other bed was saying very little until Eck introduced him, " This man here is Hans he's our new orra man (odd job man) a German POW disna speak very good English bit we manage to get bye his Doric is getting better aw the time, Eck told Hans who Sandy was then they got on to the subject of the new mistress Eck asked Sandy what he thought of her, Sandy thought she was a bit of all right a bit young for Dod but yes he was impressed, " Well said Eck when Lang Dod's nae fit tae look efter her I'm going to step in and take over from him" Hans who had been sitting saying nothing shook his head and said "There's nae a quine safe aboot here from you randy Scots buggers" this had Eck and Sandy in fits of laughter. Sandy took his leave before Eck got any more daft notions in his head, before he left he asked Eck to bring Hans over to Hillies one evening so they could have bit a blether, Eck looked in amazement at Sandy " Peer buggers nae allowed oot efter its dark he's released under licence and has to report tae Dod Simpson every Saturday for at least six months its nae fair because he's a grand lad and it wasn't his fault there wis a war" with that Sandy left for home.

Meg was beginning to get over her mothers death, it looked like she had come to terms with it, but for Sandy there was still a dark cloud on the horizon his young brother Tommy he was getting to be a right handful and he refused point blank to help around the croft, he was causing major disruptions between Sandy and Meg, the hurtful part for Sandy was that Meg always took the young fellows side and even when she must have known he was in the wrong she backed him to the hilt, on lots of occasions Sandy would clear out and either cycle or walk for miles the Duncan's were not used to this sort of behaviour.

Jim finally managed to get his life sorted out and emigrated to New Zealand first port of call was Australia where he was to meet up with his girlfriend Tina, her father had a farm so it would be no bother for Jim to find employment when he finally got there, it was a very tearful Meg that waived her younger brother goodbye. The Duncan family was shrinking Megs next dread was the twin's in about a years time they too were about to flee the nest it would be down to only three of them left and what would Tommy do when he was old enough, none of the young ones seemed to want to work at crofting any more it was hard work with little reward. Even the threshing mill that had recently been in the Glen was no longer a novelty, the new tractor driven machine just didn't produce the same thrill that people got watching all the well oiled working parts of a steam engine, the operator didn't have the same go in him as his predecessors for a start he went home every night so all the crofters saw of him was the few hours when he was operating the mill, the tractor going at full rev's was noisy so it was nigh impossible to hold a conversation with the young man so he remained a virtual stranger.

The meeting in the village hall was arranged the idea was to discuss the forth-coming subsidy payment that the government were about to announce there were one or two payments available but it depended on where you resided. It must have been an important meeting as the hall was packed to capacity; there was a lot of banter going on among the neighbouring crofters, which was the norm when they got to gether. The learned ones were on stage that evening trying to explain the new government rules regarding the introduction of subsidies, sheep were favourite if you were paying rent for moor land grazing you just bought a couple of dozen sheep chased them onto the moor and left them their until winter, over winter you would have to subsidise their feed but all that was required was an extra few rows of neeps and a little extra oats, when you had the sheep for a year along came the government paid you some money, you could then sell them on and start again, they were also well warned that the inspectors would possibly carry out a head count so be wary and don't try to cheat. Next man to take the floor considered himself to be a bit of an expert in the art of growing potatoes, he explained that due to the world food shortage the government were encouraging food producers to grow extra food stuff, if they were willing to plant extra areas of ground the government would pay a subsidy, the description of what had to be done was a long winded explanation by the expert Bob Kidd, Bob was one of the Glen elder statesmen, liked giving his advice although it was often ridiculed behind his back, any how he told them how to claim the government payment by filling in a form and posting to the address at the top of the page. His final part of the speech was to emphasise how easy it would be to cheat by saying they had planted more than they actually did, " My friends don't be tempted as the government have inspectors who swoop on an area and measure up the acreage if you are found to be cheating woe betide you", with that the meeting was closed. Sandy bought twenty-five sheep the idea was to fatten them up and sell them at the spring sales next year, he also planted one and a half extra acres of potatoes. Just before the potato harvest Sandy had a visit from a well-dressed man who introduced himself as a Ministry Of Agriculture Inspector, he would like to see the potato crop and he would be doing some measurements, Sandy had no problem with that and showed the man his crop he even held the end of the measuring tape, he left quite satisfied that everything was in order. Later that day he met up with his pal Will Watson who as usual was having a good laugh at somebody else's expense, Sandy asked what he was laughing at, Will reminded him of the meeting about the Government subsidies and the speech given by Bob Kidd about cheating, " Well Sandy there were twelve farms checked by the inspectors and the only one found to be cheating was the holier than thou Bob Kidd, no doubt he will be charged anyhow let him take it, there's always one rotten apple in the basket." That was about the only bit of excitement in the glen that year, the crops were all harvested and the dark evenings were upon them, the main attraction for the young ones was the cinema there was three different movies every week so the bus to town was always busy of an evening, then there was a youth club one night a week so the young ones had plenty to keep them occupied, the wireless was also a popular means of entertainment, with different people having their own special programme, this could cause arguments due to the choice of station's.

Chapter Fifteen

THE LABOUR PARTY CAME TO POWER in nineteen forty five, ousting the Churchill led wartime government, in nineteen forty seven they introduced a bill that was to revolutionise the Welfare State in the United Kingdom forever, people could not take in the changes implemented, especially health care, it was now to be given free, of course being human beings people are always greedy and soon the amount of waste was sad, as the years progressed the waste got worse. That same year was possibly one of the worst winters ever recorded. The first morning of the blizzards Sandy went to feed his animals, he had a job opening the back door, when he did manage to open it he was confronted with a wall of snow, luckily he had a shovel just inside the door so he started to dig, this meant taking the snow into the wash house and stacking it there until he had access to the outside eventually after about twenty minutes digging he reached the surface, the snow was up to the guttering of the house, it was twelve weeks before they saw black ground again, worse was to come when the snow melted there were severe floods all over the country, it was to be a costly winter for the farmers as their live stock was indoors much longer than normal that meant feed stuff was running short and had to be bought from the suppliers. The crofters had a difficult winter even the sheep that Sandy bought were beginning to cost him money before the winter finally disappeared, and they could get back to grazing on the moor it was such a fine profit margin that the least little hiccup plunged them into the red. Willie regularly kept in touch and he hoped he would soon get a leave but he was heavily involved in the Nazi War Criminal Trials in Nuremberg so it was difficult to get time off for a while at least. Betty seemed to be thriving in Canada and was expecting her first child shortly, a very exciting time for Meg how she wished she could be with her sister as she coped with her pregnancy so far from home, but according to her letters Walter's mother who was looking forward to having their first grandchild treated Betty like she was her own daughter so that was a blessing. Jim now working in New Zealand had been married for a few months none of his family could attend due to the distance, but according to his letters he had settled in fine, he had been awarded a small pension because of the disability sustained when he was wounded. The family seemed to be getting along fine, the next bit of sorrow for Meg would be in six months time when the twins would be old enough to pursue their chosen careers, Mary had decided to follow brother Willie and join the Military Police. Tommy was causing as much grief as ever he seemed to be in his element when his family were at each other's throat's caused by his unpleasant behaviour he would soon be in the higher grade at school so Sandy was hoping his behaviour would improve when Bob Paterson was keeping an eye on him. Things were beginning to change since the war ended there was still a wide range of goods rationed so there were times when the women had to make do and often mend garments that were ready for the rag bag but replacements were just not available and if they were you needed to have enough coupons and money to purchase them, life was a hard struggle but they had to keep going. The following year seemed to be some sort of revolution with big changes afoot.

The year of nineteen forty eight was the start of the demise of the crofting industry as a self contained means of earning a living, the first crofting family in the glen to throw in the towel so to speak were the Sutherland family there were ten of them Jock and Jessie the parents then four boys four girls they were all aged between eighteen and twenty eight at least six of them had been in the forces or doing work related to the war. The four boys had learned to operate bull dozers and mechanical diggers during their service two of them were at Normandy with the Royal Engineers. When they were demobbed there was no work at home so they put their newly learned skills to use and found jobs in the Highland's working on the big Hydro Construction sites the wages they could make in one week was about the same as the crofter could earn in eight weeks if he was lucky, Old Jock at the age of fifty two and listening to the wealth his boys were enjoying soon decided to give up the croft and join the lads, some of the lassies also managed to get jobs in the work camps, of the ten of the family seven were employed on the same site, Jock soon got established and was enjoying the same conditions as his sons, their earning power soon became evident as one by one they became the owner of a new car. Jock had made a deal with the laird to rent the croft house and the laird rented the ground out to one of his bigger tenant farmers so he was also on a nice little earner trust Auld Spencer to be at the forefront. In later years as Sandy looked back it was always in his mind that Jock Sutherland was the beginning of the end but fair play to the Sutherlands they seized their chance when it was available. But there were many more changes to come from then on, because of the war (blamed again) the human breeding programme had been disrupted a couple of the local girls had become pregnant to soldiers stationed in the district, but apart from that the birth-rate had declined over the six years the war was in progress this meant that some of the classes at the school had no pupils and the school role had dropped dramatically, when this happens the hierarchy see means of saving some money so they start swinging the axe, exactly what happened in the Glen. It felt like a whole generation of people had all become of age at the same time, Bob Paterson the head master was over retirement age he had stayed on because of the shortage of teachers due to the war, his mind was made up when the education authorities decided to re-grade the school this meant that they would only teach up to primary five the qualifying class, pupils would have to go to town to finish their education, this move maybe saved the Education Authorities money but it cost the families additional expense because the pupil would need a school uniform, some sort of lunch or maybe school meals which were about to be introduced, the local people caused a rumpus about loosing their secondary education but as usual when change is in the wind it fell on deaf ears. The next to go was the local bobby, Dod Simpson was retiring age so when he finished the police station was closed and all the policing was done from town another chapter closed, where would it all stop. For Sandy the biggest blow was when his good friend of many years announced that he too would be closing down and sadly would have to move on. Will Watson had been struggling for the past few years he just wasn't making any money one of his best earners was shoeing horses, sadly the horse population was on the wane, without horses he had no income so he had to take the bull by the horns and retire, Sandy was devastated even more so when he found out Will would be leaving the district.

He was absolutely devastated but then when he thought about it he himself was about to make his horses redundant and buy into the world of modern mechanics, so it was understandable that if Will didn't have any income naturally he would have to pack it all in, there was no call for his skill at joining hot metal with hammering or rivets, the modern method was arc welding and Will was much too old to take up the new skill of being able to weld so his only alternative was retirement. This was three stalwarts of the Glen who would no longer be taking an active part in the welfare of the people the sad part was that Will and Bob Paterson were the back bone of organising the various activities that took place they would be a hard act to follow all three of them were moving to various parts of the county so there was a certain sadness about their retirement. The fete held in honour of the lads returning from the war was now considered to be an annual gathering of the Glen folk so it was decided to dedicate this year's event to the honour of the three departing members of the community, a meeting at the Mansion House was convened without inviting the three guests of honour. Lang Dod Wilson was elected the new Chairman even though he strongly protested that he didn't have the time to get involved, it was finally agreed that after the fete a meeting would be called and a new committee elected. As soon as a date was agreed Meg had the writing pad out so she could let her brothers and sister know about the retirement and the date of the fete, she was sure neither Betty or Jim would manage but no doubt Willie would make an effort because of his close relationship with Will Watson. With-in days she had a reply from Willie and yes he would be doing his best to get leave for the event, the others would take a bit longer to reply.

The twins had their departure date Peg to the nursing and Mary to the army, Meg was beside herself what would she get to do once there was only Tommy, Sandy and herself, she was considering trying for a part time job, there was talk about school meals starting up after the school lost its higher grade status, they would need somebody for that so she was watching points it would suit her down to the ground a couple of hours a day. Tommy was still causing major disruption, Sandy had given up trying to reason with both Tommy and Meg she seemed to think that giving in to his demands was the solution, but the more she gave in the more he demanded, Sandy was totally disgusted, he kept quiet so as to avoid confrontation with his sister.

A meeting was held at the big house once a fortnight where the main topic of conversation was what sort of presentation should be given to the retiring parties. There was a big debate and many arguments before it was finally agreed that they would each receive a wallet containing a sum of money and a new set of gardening tools spade, fork, hoe and rake. The wives would receive a flower arrangement courtesy of the

W.R.I; this was the final decision on the presentation to take place at the end of the day, in the evening they planned to hold a night like they had when they presented the old steam engine operators with their retirement gifts a Bothy Nights concert then a couple of hours dancing everything was now in hand but they still had about twelve weeks until the event. During one of his days of feeling a bit depressed Sandy was reflecting on how life was changing, take the threshing mill its twice yearly arrival was looked forward to by everybody in the Glen then overnight it was changed completely.

Gone were the days when the threshing mill brought a kind of carnival atmosphere to the Glen, the long dark evenings enjoyed in the company of two men who had dedicated their lives to provided a service to others, for many years as well as threshing the crops they provided a news service as they carried stories from one part of the county to another, sadly that was all history never to be resurrected again. In their place was a piece of machinery that arrived almost silently, made a terrible racket as it ran at full blast during the threshing operation and in its four visits to the Glen had been operated by three different young men who as soon as the days threshing was over they mounted their motor bike and disappeared over the hill for home sometimes barely acknowledging they were providing a service, aye thought Sandy changes are defiantly a foot. He himself would have to ring the changes shortly in as much as the need for a new horse or on Lang Dod's advice a tractor, when he discussed what he was about to do with Will Watson, Will called him a bloody traitor explaining that every new tractor was another nail the blacksmiths coffin, Sandy felt a wee bit guilty for his mate but his one little croft would hardly have bankrupted the blacksmith, anyhow Sandy reminded him that he was so bloody old it was time he retired. Sandy received a message from the agricultural showroom letting him know they had a second hand tractor that would probably suit his needs, could he come and see it as soon as he possible as they were inundated with potential buyers (of course being salesmen they would). He caught the afternoon bus and was at the showroom for just on two pm, the tractor was a David Brown with a plough and another couple of implements one hundred and eighty pounds for the lot. Sandy was staggered he had never talked about this amount of money in his life before, nearly a years turn over on the croft, the salesmen were pressurising him for an answer. Sandy needed time to go and visit the bank it was up to them if he could have the money or not. As he approached the bank door he remembered that frosty faced old bitch Jeannie Robertson would be sitting at the reception desk so he gingerly opened the door and had the surprise of his life, sitting at the desk was a lovely very polite young lady she asked how she could help and had he an appointment. Sandy explained that he needed to speak to the Mr Watt the banker she explained that Mr Watt was tied up all day but she would see what could be done. She disappeared into another office on returning she told Sandy to go into the office and he would get seen to there, Sandy entered the office and there sitting behind the desk was Dracula's daughter Jean Robertson. " Well what can we do for you" she asked, Sandy was slow to rouse but he thought what an ignorant woman and its my money that keeps her in a job so he gave up the Mr nice guy right away and got stuck into her. " I want to see Hamish Watt to discuss my money," She asked, "What's it about"? Sandy replied rather curtly "Its private and confidential" bang that shut the old witch up. Her attitude changed right away and she said she would see what she could do. She reappeared and said, " Mr Duncan, Mr Watt is tied up all day but his assistant Mr Fraser is available now if that would suit you." Sandy told her that would be fine and stood up and was shown where Davie Fraser's office was, Davie was ages with Jim Duncan he had been very clever at school but failed his medical for the services hence the reason he was in the Bank he was a Glen loon so Sandy was sure he would get sound advice.

First thing Davie did as soon as his client was seated was to order Jeannie to make a cup of tea, she obviously thought it was beneath her to carry out such a function as it was plain to see the contempt with which she placed the tray on the desk, just to keep her in her place Sandy repeated after Davie "Thank you Jeannie" if looks could have killed Sandy was blown away, Lang Dod had described her as being a frustrated old spinster in a very unsavoury statement Dod intimated that half an hour with a good strong man would set Jeannie up for life. Davie after enquiring about the Duncan family got down to business and after listening to Sandy's reason for needing a loan he had a quick scan at the figures on his bank statement, nodding his head he said the Bank would bank roll Sandy he could go ahead and buy his tractor but first he should check out the price the agricultural salesmen were asking for it. Sandy asked if he could use the phone and he called Lang Dod, the big fellow listened to Sandy then told him to lay down the phone and stay where he was. Ten minutes later the phone rang and the big fellow bellowed into his ear tell Davie Fraser you only need one hundred and sixty pound I just screwed them down twenty pounds for you he continued " Sandy you need to toughen up and show a ruthless streak when dealing with these bloody salesmen if you have a go at them they always find a means of knocking a few pounds off so really they didn't need to charge you that in the first place, bloody rogues the whole lot of them good luck wie yir tractor", with that he laid the phone down. As Sandy was getting ready to leave Davie told him his father was having the same trouble with his horses they were getting on a bit, but Davie's father was older than Sandy and he didn't fancy getting into tractors so he may be interested in buying your good younger horse I'll have a word with him over the week-end. Sandy was floating on air as he headed back to the show room he was met by the head salesman who was all over him even apologising at the price quoted and if he had known he was related to Dod Wilson he would have knocked his discount off, but as a gesture of goodwill they have reduced the price by twenty pounds he never mentioned the phone call from Lang Dod and intimated they had taken the initiative in reducing the price (typical salesman), anyhow Sandy left the saleroom with the promise the tractor would be delivered next morning before ten am. The arrival of Sandy's tractor caused a bit of a stir in the Glen and he had many neighbours visiting, some very interested and some down right nosey but the Duncan's made them all very welcome and Sandy was willing to share any information that would help, the older men were unwilling to change there way of life but the ones in Sandy's generation were all for stepping into the future. One of the visitors was Old Davie Fraser his son had told him about Sandy's horse being available so after a bit of bartering Davie bought the ten year old mare the deal was settled at forty five pounds this helped Sandy offset the price of his tractor, the other horse old Robbie had been in the family for around twenty years he had slowed up a bit but would be handy in an emergency, Sandy could just hear Lang Dod when he discovered the old horse was still at Hillies. " Sandy an extra mouth to feed and he is done get rid of him he is costing money and giving nothing in return we cant survive being charitable" but Sandy couldn't find it in his heart to part with the old fellow and so he remained as a passenger for some time to come. What Sandy did find out once he had mastered the tractor he had time on his hands and wished he could get a job or else more land.

Time was moving on the arrangements for the fete were all in place the three retirees were still unaware of the presentation, even though they were on the original committee, when a meeting was held to discuss their fate it was held in private at the Mansion House or else at Burnside, all that was needed now was somebody to present their gifts. The presenter of Will Watson's gifts was solved by a letter which had been delivered at Hillside, Meg had received it from her brother Willie he had managed to get fourteen days leave and it coincided with the date of the fete, Sandy got hold of Lang Dod and Spencer and suggested that Willie would present Will's gift they all thought that was a wonderful idea, to add more joy for Meg Willie had a girlfriend she was Swedish and he wanted to bring her home to meet the family. Meg was all for this as she wanted to see her brothers settled with their own families, the other puzzling thing on his address before his name he had C/ Sgt, Meg was flummoxed she thought maybe the C was a misprint, she waited until she was at the Kirk on Sunday and she asked Jim Kerr what it meant, more joy when Jim explained it meant that Willie was now Colour Sergeant Duncan, how proud Meg was of her twin brother and his achievements. Sandy was called to a meeting at Burnside to discuss some of the fete arrangements, he had some personal problems to discuss with Lang Dod so he contacted him and made arrangements to have an hour with him before the rest of the committee arrived, he parked his bike beside the kitchen door and knocked expecting the lovely Betsy to answer, but he was taken a back when the door was opened by another female whom he instantly recognised, she was Mary Morrison an old class mate from school, when asked what she was doing at Burnies Mary told him she was working for Betsy as she was pregnant for the third time in less than three years, the Lang fellow was fair having mass production from Betsy he was a great fellow for keeping wall charts for his animals i.e. when they were due to have a calf one of the local worthies enquired one day if he kept a wall chart for Betsy. Sandy was shown through to the big mans study as usual he was stretched out in his chair puffing away at the St Bruno in his pipe, he rose up and shook Sandy by the hand, " Well Sandy your one of us now I hear, a member of the age of modern technology." The two of them chatted away until the rest of the committee arrived it was still six weeks until the fete, all three of the retirees were keen gardeners so it was appropriate that they should receive a new set of gardening tools the old shepherd from up the Glen had kindly donated a hand made crook for each, so along with a wallet of notes it was decided that this should be adequate in the way of a retrial gift. Willie Duncan would be called upon to present Will Watson and his wife who would receive a floral display courtesy of the WRI, it would be quite a gesture to get Willies Swedish girl friend to present the flowers, Bob Paterson would be presented with his gifts from Dr Findlay's daughter Isobel and Dr Findlay to present the flowers to Mrs Paterson, Isobel Findlay had newly graduated as a Doctor, finally Dod Simpson the bobby, there was a big debate as to who would make the presentation, the most obvious choice was Auld Spencer the two of them had been in the Glen most of their lives and it would also boost Spencer's ego he always liked to be in the front line, with everybody in agreement the meeting was brought to a close, Jim Kerr offered Sandy a lift home, but it was a lovely evening and Sandy was quite happy to cycle home he could have a good look at other people crops and cattle along the way.

He shouted his goodbyes to Betsy and Mary Morrison as he left, he had one more port of call on his way out, the chaumer (Bothy), he tapped at the door then pushed it open, sitting reading a book was Hans the P.O.W he looked up and was so pleased to see Sandy, he told him to sit down, Sandy asked where Eck was " Oh he's awa visiting his sister he asked me to go but its awful place for flechs you end up scratching all night so I stay here" Sandy had a grin to himself he was well acquainted with Jimmy the tink's flechs, picking up Hans's book he read the title Hans explained it helped with his English if he read plenty books, Sandy had a laugh to himself and said to Hans " I see Eck hasn't got you reading the dandy and beano yet"" Hans shaking his head and laughing no I think my English stretches beyond the bairns comics but Eck seems to enjoy them." Hans continued to speak and had Sandy flabbergasted when he asked if he would be best man at his wedding, Sandy was again in shock when he asked who the lucky lady was, stammering a little bit Hans said it was " Mary the quine that worked in the kitchen", "Oh yea kept that very quiet, how long have you been going the gither"? Asked Sandy, " Well over a year noo" replied Hans. The next question was when is the wedding, Hans went on to explain that Mr Wilson had given him a cottar hoose and he was doing it up so it would possibly be the spring time before it is ready, he also told Sandy it was Mr Wilson's idea to ask him to be best man he went on to tell Sandy Mr Wilson thought the sun shone out of his backside and he had a lot of time for the Duncan family. Sandy agreed to help Hans out when the time came he then asked about Mary's brothers didn't Hans want one of them to be his best man but no he wanted someone of his own choice, so that was settled Sandy said his goodbyes and headed for home it was an enjoyable journey taking him just on the hour.

For as good as Meg had been bringing up her brothers and sisters and organising the running of the house, at times she would get in a panic which was totally unnecessary, her latest stushie was the forthcoming visit of her brothers Swedish girlfriend, Meg had never spoken to anybody outside her native Glen except her sister Betty's Canadian husband and his relations. When Sandy got on to her she pointed out that the Canadians spoke more or less like themselves but this girl would speak a lingo that only she could understand, Sandy was shaking his head in frustration, Willie man be able to speak tae her so we can speak tae Willie and he can tell her fit the hell were saying. He was about to leave when she again mounted her high horse and ripped into Sandy about the state of the Lavvy, " Wie aw the holes in the Lavvy you would be as weel squattin doon in the middle of the park the wind that blaws through it at times you would think the wa's were made fae netting wire yea'll need tae dea something about that before Willie gets here, Sandy baled out before his workload was further increased, he made his way to where the Lavvy was situated basically it was a four by four shed straddled across a burn when there was plenty water around it was possibly as hygienic as it could be but given to drought and you had the most disgusting haven for breeding blue bottles imaginable, really what was needed was a new sheddie well that was Sandy's summing up of the situation, thinking to himself the Duncan family had used this form of sanitation for over ten years noo and this was the first complaint, and with the open end over the burn there was always a good breeze so you weren't bothered with smell and nobody dallied too long especially on the frosty mornings but he would build a new one.

Chapter Sixteen

AULD SPENCER HAD TAKEN A BACK seat from running the Estate, Roddy his surviving son had taken over the reins, he was a very outgoing young man and very soon he had started to modernise things around the place, like Dod Wilson he was now using tractors on the home farm the horses in the Glen were getting less every year. The first crofting family in the Glen to own a car was the Sutherlands they were now the owners of a big grey Standard Vanguard car it seated six just ideal for the journey back and forth to the Hydro scheme at Cannich in Glen Affric. To keep Meg happy Sandy had spoken to the estate joiner and he had agreed to make a brand new Lavvy to be delivered and erected before the fete so that it was in place before Willies new Swedish girlfriend arrived. Jock Mitchell the postman had managed to get Meg to call a truce so they were now on talking terms but she still pulled some nasty tricks on him whenever she saw an opportunity. There would be big changes in the glen before the end of this year as soon as the school closed for the summer holidays it would loose its higher-grade status that was also Bob Paterson's leaving date, Tommy was due to start in the first year so he was among the first batch to be bussed into town. Then the Police Station was also to be closed and any policing was to be done from town they now had either motor bikes or cars so they could be at the Glen with-in twenty minutes if required, then of course Will Watson's smiddy was to shut and Will was moving to the Turriff area, they were changes that Sandy could well have done with-out but it was all in the name of progress or so they said.

The big day of the fete was just a week away, Willie was due home on the Saturday evening the brand new Lavvy was in place straddling the burn, Sandy was kidding Meg on that it was her birthday present, when told she retorted " Huh! It's the very first birthday present you've ever given me surely you could have done better than an auld wooden (s**** h***e) so it was kept up as a joke Megs twenty fourth birthday present.

The tension was mounting, as time for Willie and his girl friend

Maria to arrive home approached, Meg was still apprehensive about how she would communicate with her Swedish visitor. All eyes were on the cross roads as the time of the bus's arrival was reached and there was Willie resplendent in his army uniform with his colour sergeant insignia on the sleeve, there was a rush of Duncan's as they all headed down the road to meet Willie and Maria Tommy being the youngest was away ahead and the first to get a hug from big brother Willie the rest met half way and a rugby scrum developed as they hugged each other and had their first introduction to Maria, Meg was relieved to hear her speaking perfect English although for a couple of days she did have problems understanding the Doric words but she was accepted into the family especially the Twins who were intrigued with the latest fashions, lipsticks and perfume that she had brought as gifts, Sandy got a one pound tin of pipe tobacco and some spirits. Tommy as usual was not forgotten and Willie had bought him a watch, which was an unusual present for a boy, Tommy was sure nobody else in the Glen had one so he couldn't wait for Sunday to come so that he could show it off at the Kirk. They finally got to bed in the wee sma hours as there were lots of things to catch up on, Willie was delighted that he had been chosen to present Will Watson with his retirement gift, but he was sworn to secrecy until next Saturday.

Sandy was sitting at his morning cup of tea, he was feeling a bit groggy the late night and a few whiskies had upset his rhythm, the lobby door opened and a rather tousled Willie appeared asking for an old shirt and trousers so that he could give Sandy a hand, Sandy was delighted and said he would milk the cow too and save Meg having to get up, with that she arrived looking worse the wear, when told to go back to bed she gave her brothers a big hug and disappeared back to her bed room. An hour and a half later the two men arrived back in the house just as Meg made her second appearance of the day she boiled the kettle and made some fresh tea. By nine-o-clock the whole family had congregated in the kitchen, Meg said she would fry some breakfast so that they could eat before going to the Kirk, Maria said she had had a wonderful sleep and the family tried to explain that was because the mattress was filled with fresh chaff twice yearly, chaff was a difficult one to explain as most mattress's were filled with horse hair or flock, anyhow she had enjoyed her nights sleep.

Jim Kerr gave his usual heart warming ceremony and welcomed Willie and his girlfriend into their congregation, after the service

Willie was inundated with people wanting to shake his hand, big Will Watson had a few words to say to him especially about his smashing looking lady friend, the family paid a visit to the family grave before heading home for a cup of tea, Willie had a discussion with his brother about the possibility of hiring a car, Sandy didn't drive so he had no idea about car hiring even though he held a licence. Willie decided he would get the bus into town on Monday. He could show Maria a bit of the country side if he had wheels as he put it, he told Sandy that in his line of work as an M.P they had transport at their disposal all the time. Willie and Maria were up early to get the first bus into town they went at the same time as the twins who were going to work. Just before dinner time Willie came wheeling up the croft road driving a Standard ten car he managed to hire it for the week with the option of a second week if he so wished he was right in his element as he was now free to go where he wanted without depending on buses. Willie and Maria spent the rest of the week having day trips all over the country side they even persuaded Meg to accompany them as far as Elgin, this was a thrill for her as it was the first time she had been so far from home, before the end of their leave she asked if they could maybe manage as far as Aberdeen she was dying to see what it looked like.

The first week of Willies leave soon went in and the Saturday of the fete was upon them before they knew it. Starting time was eleven am, everybody had prayed the weather would be favourable, their prayers were answered when it turned out to be a wonderful sunny day, as an added bonus to the days proceedings Roddy Tracy the young Laird had managed to persuade one of his ex army pals who had been a Pipe Major and now trained youngsters, to turn up with his Junior pipe band what a spectacle they were as they marched along the main road into the park, the retirees were getting a right Royal send off. The first few hours was taken up with preliminary races and one of the fiercest competitions was the tug-of-war there were ten teams entered and the day would finish with the best two teams in the final. Mid afternoon and everybody was called in front of the platform to listen to Lang Dod Wilson. He started off by calling the three men about to retire to join him on the platform along with their wives he spoke for about ten minutes telling people about the wonderful servants they had been to the Glen after a round of applause he looked around.

After spotting Willie Duncan he called him up to join the others he introduced Willie and Maria to the crowd then he picked up the retrial gifts and Willie presented them to a rather embarrassed Mr Watson, Maria presented Mrs Watson with her display of flowers. Isobel Findlay along with her father did the honours for Bob and Mrs Paterson; finally there was never a show without punch in the form of Auld Spencer Tracy he had more or less elected himself as the presenter of gifts to P.C Dod Simpson but first Spencer had to give his spiel it lasted twice as long as any of the rest but then somebody commented he is bloody nuisance but his heart is in the right place. That was the presentations over and time to get on with the games the tug-of-war was in full swing and they had reached the semi final stages all eyes were on the contestants finally they were down to two teams the Lairds Loonies and Lang Dod's Dumplins' the final was scheduled for half past four just in time for a five-o-clock finish. Bill Findlay had been the doctor in the Glen for over forty years many of those present he had help bring into the world along with his now retired midwife Ma Morrison as he surveyed the healthy young people in front of him he felt proud of his achievements, the fete to-day had been the best since the war disrupted everything, in his young student days he had been quite a successful athlete specialising in cross country running he had set quite a few records which as far as he was aware still stood to this day. This year he had managed to resurrect two of his favourite sports, the hill race, which was ran over a distance of five miles up past Hillies to the top of the hill round the monument where the Canadian bomber had crashed. He was thrilled to see Willie Duncan come first as Willie was one of the babies he delivered twenty four years ago, in his capacity as sports umpire he had handicapped Willie because he was an active sports man in the Army but even his five minute handicap it didn't deter him. He still had about twenty minutes to go before the grand final of the tug-of- war, the two teams in the final were fierce rivals since before the war, it was as if a cup final was about to take place, this was the only event to split the crofting community Dod's Dumplins representing the west side and the Lairds Loonies from the east side it was all out war. As Bill Findlay killed time he sat and reflected on the days proceedings how sad he was to see the break up of the backbone of the community with the retirement of his two colleagues between them they had served the Glen for over one hundred years, he reflected on his own future his daughter Isobel was now qualified as a doctor their plans were that she would join her father in his practice and after a year he would hand over the reigns and retire so that he could have some time at his hobbies his favourite being golf. He wanted out of the medical profession, in just one year of NHS he could see a trend setting in, people who never called a doctor when they had to pay were now regularly turning up at his surgery and in many cases all they needed to do was break wind and they would be right as rain. Then there was the mountain of paper work form filling etc very soon they would need a clerkess to keep it all in order at the moment his wife was keeping it going but she needed help and this proved to be a distraction from his medical work. He also had to keep a large stock of drugs as there was no chemist handy, the administration to keep track of all the dispensed drugs was a job on its own, Isobel had been trained in the ways the NHS operated so she was better equipped than her father, so another vertebrae in the backbone of the Glen would also disappear soon.

Bill Findlay had been day dreaming although all his thoughts would become reality in the not too distant future, he jerked back to his duties and on checking his watch he noted that it was twenty past four ten minutes to the TOW final, he called over the loud speaker that it was time for the gladiators to take their places, they all had their regulation TOW uniforms on i.e. bib and brace dungarees and tackity boots. Will Watson at sixteen stone was the anchor on the Dumplins side and Dod Simpson at about the same weight was anchor on the Loonies side. The crowd split into two sections already shouting encouragement to their respective favourites at approximately twenty eight minutes past four Bill Findlay grabbed the centre marker and shouted " Take the strain" the two teams dug in and when the marker in Bill's hand was even with the line on the ground he shouted "Heave" and stepped back this was the cue for Lang Dod on one side and Roddy Tracy on the other to shout encouragement to their respective teams "Dig, dig, dig, heave, heave, heave" they were dead locked not an inch was given the longer it lasted the bigger the frenzy erupted from the crowd, then an avalanche of bodies slithered over the markers as Roddy,s Loonies succumbed to the might of Dod's Dumplins a two minute break and they were called into line again, line up the markers " Heave " and away they go again. The deadlock lasted about the same length of time and the line began to waver, but Roddy,s guys proved they were no duds and the score was one, one, the competition was hotting up the hands were French Chalked the heels dug in and Bill Findlay called "heave" for the final time, the determination on the faces proved how critical this pull was, nobody wanted to loose, but there has to be one looser and after much grunting and pulling and bellowing Dod's Dumplins were pulled over the marker and the Lairds Loonies were crowned champions, there was loud applause first for the losers and then when the captain of the winning team held the trophy a loft the applause was rapturous. Within minutes of the final of the TOW the field was deserted as the people made their way home, most would return for the Bothy Nicht concert and the dance, this type of evening had proved a winner before and there was no need to rehearse, and even if lines were fluffed it added to the humour and enjoyment, for Will Watson after his celebrity status in the afternoon it was back to auld claes and porridge as his services as a musician were required during the singing and later on the dancing, there was a wide range of artistes offering their services so they had to keep it going so that they would be ready for the dancing at nine-o-clock, everybody had done their party piece and there still was twenty minutes to go Will said there was time for one more singer he heard a shout from the back it was his old pal Beldie Smart, he turned to Sandy and said " Get ready for a bloody awful rendition of the Crookit Baw Bee" Sandy replied " Its yir ain bloody fault you said there was time for one more" " Aye ah ken that, bit if I hid kent it wis her I would have called a halt early never mind here goes." It was time to start the dancing by the time Beldie and her boy had screeched their way through the Crookit Baw Bee. Sandy had time to pay his family a visit before the dance started he asked Maria how she was enjoying her day she replied it had just been wonderful and she had enjoyed herself. A new kind of an annoyance had started to rear its ugly head, the consumption of alcohol, it was more plentiful since the war finished and quite a few of the younger men were getting quite drunk and making a nuisance of themselves once again.

The problem would be discussed at the next meeting some of the committee were sure it had already been highlighted but had been allowed to carry on, after to-nights problems it would need to be addressed. They could not allow the youth of the day to spoil things for the good residents of the Glen running amok swearing, urinating and vomiting all over the place it needed to be stamped on right away. The rest of the weekend passed without any excitement, Willie kept the hired car till Thursday and as promised he was taking Meg and Maria through to Aberdeen for the day, Sandy was invited but he was so busy he declined the offer, he wasn't very keen on leaving the croft unattended anyhow.

Meg was as excited as a kid with a new toy it would be the first time in her twenty four years she would be able to leave the Glen, the farthest she had ventured before was into town occasionally to the pictures, all her shopping was done from the mobile shops that visited the area some of them still horse drawn affairs. Her clothing was bought from the drapers van which visited monthly, but his fashions were way behind the times and Meg dressed in clothes that were obsolete even her under wear was huge bloomers with elastic above the knee and the top was elasticated just below her bust, she was always chastising her younger sisters because she thought their choice of lingerie was far to flimsy, but reality hit home that Monday morning she was hanging out the washing, Maria had some underwear that needed laundered so Meg told her just put it in the linen basket, as she picked up garments to peg them on the line she picked up a pair of Maria's flimsies, next was a pair of her own she pegged them and much to her disgust when they filled with wind they looked like a barrage balloon, she hastily removed them she would dry them in the house, she could just hear Jock Mitchell's grotty remarks if he saw them. Meg's teenage years had been a life of slave labour although she was free to do as she pleased; from the age of thirteen until the death of her mother she had worked a fourteen and maybe sixteen-hour day and never received a pay packet in all that years, her education was cut short although she never complained it had been hard work, work from morning till night seven days a week the only money she received was from selling farm produce, eggs, butter and cheese quite often the money she received went towards paying for the house keeping so she never really had money available, if she had a big payout Sandy would write a cheque and cover it with that, mind you Sandy never paid himself a wage either so it was a pretty frugal existence. Maria was pretty shocked when she saw just how behind the times they were especially with sanitation etc, in Sweden they were much more advanced but then they hadn't had a war to contend with maybe that was the difference. Meg had checked her purse she would need money to spend in Aberdeen, she didn't have a great deal so she asked Sandy for some he managed to scrape five pounds together that was after raking through all the pockets. Meg felt like lady muck as she was chauffeured along the road to Aberdeen she was quite amazed that the journey only lasted over an hour , they found a place to park the car and then set off to Union Street, Meg had often heard of Woollies but when she saw the shear size of it she was flabbergasted, in all her memories of reading about it Woollies far out weighed her expectations, she had spent over an hour just going round the place, when Maria told her there were other shops just as big if she would like to see the likes of Markies and Essolment and Macintosh's shops, they had a job removing Meg from Woollies.

Willie arrived back from Aberdeen late afternoon both Meg and Maria were laden down with their spoils from the days shopping, Meg had even been tempted in M&S to take a giant leap forward and buy herself two pairs of flimsy undergarments she was apprehensive about them as they didn't have elastic in the legs but to be upsides with everybody else she would give them a go. It had been her first full day shopping and it had taken its toll she was absolutely shattered and was glad of a cup of tea and to get her feet up for half an hour, then she would have to don her working claes and get the supper ready, no rest for the wicked, but she was full of her visit to the Granite City and vowed she would make the same trip again soon. Before she went to bed and in her bedroom alone she spread out her purchases on the bed along side a pair of her passion killer bloomers and was amazed to see that there was about seventy five percent more cloth in the old ones as there was in the new flimsy's so how could they justify charging twice as much for the small ones as they did for her much bigger ones and there was no elastic in the legs of the flimsy's, one thing was for sure there was no way she would wear the flimsy's at six-o-clock in the morning in the middle of winter when crossing the yard to milk the cow the thought made her shiver. Willie and Maria had to leave on Friday so their holiday would soon be over Meg had fair taken to Willies girl and found her a very down to earth person she was an interpreter in Germany working in the Swedish Embassy, very clever she could speak four different languages. The other two members of the family Betty in Canada now had two bairns and Jim and Tina in New Zealand were expecting their first shortly. On the Friday it was an early rise for everybody as the two visitors had to catch the early train for Aberdeen they still had to travel to London in order to get to Germany, there was much weeping and wailing as they took their leave, with Megs words ringing in their ears to heesht yea back. With all the excitement over life settled down to its normal drab dreary pattern, Sandy was trying to fathom out what he would do to pass his evenings when his big pal Will moved on the time of his flitting was getting close. Bob Paterson was gone and the new head teacher would be in place before the new term started there would only be two teachers and they would be assisted by a music teacher, art teacher and physical training teacher, they were allocated periods on a fortnightly basis so life would go on, Dod Simpson would also be on the move shortly so life in the Glen was about to have a complete change, for better or worse was still to be experienced. The new head teacher arrived she was a Miss Tocher aged about forty and from near the city of Aberdeen she had been teaching for eighteen years but this was her first time in charge she seemed a very go-ahead person. Tommy was still causing grief at home with his temper and tantrums, he would soon be on his way to the High School, Sandy hoped that the big boys and the teachers their might manage to knock some sense into him. Now that the community was three members of the committee short it was decided to call an open meeting to elect a new committee, there was a big turn out of people, this sort of meeting was always well supported. Dod Wilson acted as Chairman for the evening. Previously it had been predominantly an all male committee but there were moves afoot to include the ladies. Names of those interested were asked for, they would require nine, this number was achieved without any problem.

The numbers were equal six men and six women that was three more than required so a vote had to be taken to eliminate the excess numbers, once reduced to nine a chair person had to be nominated they were down to a short leet of three, they were Betsy Wilson, Roddy Tracy and the new head mistress, a further vote was taken and Betsy Wilson was elected, Lang Dod's final words as Chairman was "It Looks like I will be doing more than my share of baby sitting fae noo on." Well Betsy had three young bairns all under school age. The committee set a date for their first meeting and proposed a vote of thanks for all the out going members who had served the Glen well over the years. Of course auld Spencer had to give his usual spiel before the meeting ended but then he was entitled to he had been on the committee for over twenty years, he was now over eighty and was beginning to look rather frail. At the first committee meeting Betsy Wilson stamped her authority as Chairperson, she had a folder with all the points she wished to address and had fairly researched every point. The first she brought up was the excessive drinking at the dance after the fete, she asked for any suggestions on how to nip this in the bud before it got out of hand, one very strong point was to bar the offenders from entering the hall some wanted to give them a caution first but Betsy was adamant that they should post notices around the Glen telling the offenders that they are not welcome in the hall if they are drunk end

154

of story, she showed how strong willed she was by getting her own way, her next point was something for the young people of the Glen to do and take up their attention she suggested a youth club, she herself had been a keen badminton player when she was younger so she was quite capable of coaching if need be, Sandy who was one of the newly elected committee was very impressed by the young Mrs Wilson she knew what road she was on. As this was the tenth anniversary of the Christmas concert it was decided to have a special evening Miss Tocher the new head mistress was interested in becoming involved as she was into the arts, the meeting was closed and the conclusion was that it had been very successful. The youth club was set up and with-in a month was active, they still needed to get some equipment and the word was that they would receive a grant to pay for it so things were looking up.

Sandy's hopes that his young brother would get a short sharp lesson when he moved to the High School proved to be unfounded if Tommy changed any it was for worse he was even more awkward and cheeky than he had ever been, Sandy had often to restrain himself fearing that if he broke loose he would commit murder, after one severe spat Tommy retorted that he just couldn't wait to get to hell away from this awful placed he was sick of being hounded by his brother and sisters, you carry on like you were my mother and father but your nae he screamed at a distraught Sandy, Sandy in disgust replied " Yea may rue the day" then took off with his dogs for a bit of piece and quiet up by the quarry, also out for a walk was Hans the POW from Burnies he sat down with Sandy and the two of them talked for about an hour Hans thought his marriage would be in the spring he was getting on with the renovations to the cottage, but after a day working you didn't get a lot done Sandy asked if he needed a hand but Hans said there was a lot of joinery work and it needed time and patience to get it done. They bade each other goodbye, Sandy headed for home hoping that things had cooled down the continual bickering was getting him down.

Chapter Seventeen

SANDY WAS UP AND ABOUT EARLY he was getting ready for the threshing mill it was due the following week, once it had passed they were getting close to the end of the year again. As he pottered about the stack yard his mind wandered back to some of the outstanding moments when the old steam engine would arrive, the new fangled one did nothing for Sandy but the old one used to bring a bit of excitement about the Glen while it was here for its two week duration, it was quite early morning when something caught Sandy's eye, it was Bill Findlay's car going pretty fast towards the head of the glen obviously somebody in trouble. Shortly after that Bill Kerr the minister also going fairly fast, headed up the glen and finally fifteen minutes later the new police car from the town was flying up the road, surely there has been an accident. Sandy never gave it any more thought until about an hour later Jock Mitchell the postie pulled up in the yard, Sandy was about to ask what all the excitement was up the Glen, Jock near to tears and shaking his head told him the Laird had keeled over and was deed, once he hit the ground he never moved again, Sandy was shocked the Laird was the oldest man in the glen eighty six years of age he had been a resident before anybody else what a shock. It was easy seen that Jock was also shocked so Sandy invited him in for a cup of tea before he continued on his round. Auld Spencer had been a figure of ridicule he did many stupid but funny things and was good for a laugh, but his heart was in the right place and he looked after his tenants, he would be a hard act to follow. The news spread like wild fire, this was another vertebra removed from the backbone of the Glen four of them in one year it was beyond comprehension. There was an air of sadness over the Glen the passing of the Laird was being felt far and wide, but it was accepted that young Roddy would fill his fathers footsteps he was a smashing guy and very approachable he had been brought up with the crofting families so he was treated as one of the boys. At the Kirk on Sunday Jim Kerr based his ceremony on the passing of the Rt Hon

Spencer Tracy, he also announced the funeral arrangements, it was to take place at the Mansion House on Wednesday at midday everybody was invited to attend. On the Wednesday the Glen folks started to congregate at eleven thirty the Lairds coffin draped in a Union Jack was laying in the front hall, seeing it was a decent sort of day the service would be conducted on the driveway in front of the house, after the public service the coffin would be driven to the family mausoleum where Spencer would join his deceased family this part was to be private. He had arranged his own funeral so being who he was it had to be extra special, a coach pulled up just behind the house and soon the sound of pipes could be heard, minutes later a full pipe band appeared, they marched up and down in front of the house until it was time for the service. The coffin was wheeled out followed by the family, the glen folks crowded round and Jim Kerr preached a wonderful service, forty five minutes later Spencer's faithful old pony Polly was led round in front of the coffin she was fully saddled and the old fellows boots were in the stirrups facing behind, then a pair of Clydesdales pulling a flat cart drew up along side the coffin six estate workers lifted it on board, before departing a lone piper played the Flowers Of The Forest, the Pipe Band struck up the Black Bear and Auld Spencer began his final journey, somebody remarked its easy seen he planned it.

The funeral over the Glen Folks dispersed, as they walked down the glen loads of Spencer stories would be told many of them had different incidents they could recall when Spencer made a boo, boo, but it never fazed him he would laugh at himself and possibly say it will be ok next time. No doubt the solicitors would be busy getting all his affairs in order it would be an opportunity to line their pockets, as it was a big estate to administer.

Over the next few weeks there was little excitement the twins flew the nest, Peg to the nursing and Mary at last had her wish granted when she was accepted into the Army, as soon as she could she volunteered for the Royal Military Police just like big brother Willie, she hoped eventually to join him in Germany. Tommy still continued to cause grief between Sandy and Meg, although Meg knew Tommy was at fault she always took his side, it grieved her to fall out with her elder brother. A New year was about to start it was quiet at Hillies on New Years Day there was only three people at the lunch Meg commented that it was hardly worth dirtying the pots, there were very few visitors, and the twins didn't get home, Willie had gone to Sweden to visit Maria's people and of course one of their regular first footers Will Watson was no longer in the Glen. It was about the most miserable start to a year Sandy could remember apart from his wireless it was a pretty drab time. When Will Watson left he caused the Glen folks problems he was the only person in the area who could charge the wet accumulators needed to supply power to the wireless, Sandy couldn't be bothered having to get somebody to take his accumulators to a garage in town to be charged, so he took the bull by the horns and purchased a brand new wireless, this only required a dry accumulator which was disposable when it was finished you just dumped it(maybe the start of a very wasteful life). Life was just chugging along fine for Sandy since he got his tractor he could do things in half the time the horses needed so he managed to get a bit more time to himself even although he was also carrying out part time work for others, Meg also had a part time job it didn't pay a lot but every little helped. The face of the Glen was about to be transformed when the old smiddy was bought over by an agricultural engineering company, they built a new work shop and installed fuel pumps courtesy of the Shell Oil Company so things were starting to look up, Will's little workshop was retained complete with forge so that any horse shoes could be done by a visiting farrier. Next to be sold off was the old Police Station it was being transformed into a hotel restaurant and bar, people were beginning to talk, with all these buildings being sold had young Roddy an ulterior motive. Sandy was hearing strange rumblings from the village of Covie, some body had told him that an American evangelist (he had to ask what that was) had started to convert the villagers to the Brethren Gospel and if you didn't become a member they would have nothing to do with you, curious to find out what was going on he set off for Covie on the Saturday evening, he took the dogs for company. As he entered the village he met some women they were dressed in black from head to toe he knew them by sight, he passed the time of day and was taken aback when he got no answer, he noted that people seemed to scurry up the close when he approached, Sandy was scratching his head what was going on, thinking back over the last few weeks he noticed that very few fisher folks had been up to Hillies for eggs.

Sandy was quite taken aback, what was going on the Duncan family had always been on friendly terms with the Fisher folks of Covie, had they been offended in any way not as far as Sandy was aware. Two of the lassies he passed had attended school and were in the same class as Sandy, they were frequent visitors to Hillies and were good for a laugh many times their banter was very near the bone, he was nearing the far end of the village where he would turn left and head up the hill the dogs were having the time of their lives as they sniffed and scurried along the narrow street. Suddenly he was jogged out of his daydream, " Hi Sandy Hillies fit like min?" it was an old school pal Fred West nicknamed (Freddy Shounders) the two shook hands, Sandy asked what was happening and told Freddy about the snub he just received. There were tears in Freddy's eyes as he explained the situation in his home village, "Am sure you've heard aboot the Yanks that arrived in the village six weeks ago and persuaded the folk in Covie to abandon their Protestant Religious Belief's and convert to the Close Brethren belief's". " Well Sandy you can hardly believe this but over ninety percent of the fowk were like sheep, lamb's tae the slaughter, they jist abandoned everything and followed the Americans, now they spend every spare minute in the gospel hall singing hymn's nae like the ones we learned bit eens the Yanks made up themselves". " If yea dinna follow them your classed as unclean and the believers winna speak tae yea, am fair broken heartet, aw my faimly jined, noo naebody speaks tae ma, I even hiv tae ate ma grub alene. Yea ken we own oor ain boat,? my uncle and my father are partners well they've given me an ultimatum if I dinna jine the Brethren I winna hae a job, tell me Sandy fit kinna fowk wid dea that tae their ain?". " Hale families are split down the middle its heart breakin bit I'm damned if I'll change for them, infact av jist applied tae jine the Merchant Navy hopefully I'll be off in a couple of weeks time and its doubtful if I'll ever be back". Sandy was full of sympathy for his friend and really felt sorry for him, it was awful that a handful of fanatics could cause so much disruption in one small village. Sandy agreed with his pal and told him not to be bullied into something he didn't believe in, having to join the Navy was a bit drastic but if he thought that was the right thing to do why not.

Sandy had been away from the croft for over two hours, he had just time to feed the cattle before it would be time for his own supper he called in the house to let Meg know he was back. As soon as she heard him at the door she was through to confront him " Lang Dod Wilson wis here aboot twenty minutes ago, he said to tell you there was an extraordinary meeting being held in the Hall to-morrow evening at seven thirty, it's in all the Glen Fowks interest to be there, he said there wis a problem with the Lairds' will and things were'na looking too clever." Sandy had a scratch at the side of his head and asked " Whit can be wrang wie the will that wid involve people like us, michty me aw that should be sorted oot wie his legal folks, trust Auld Spencer tae get things wrang." It would be twenty four hours before the meeting surely somebody wid ken fits geen wrang, probably Jock Mitchell wid be the best bet he aye seemed tae ken aw thing that wis going on.

Next morning Sandy hung around the steading waiting for Jock's wee red van as soon as he pulled up in the yard Sandy made his way over and asked what Jock had for them the day, " Nothing very interesting replied Jock but nae doot you've heard aboot the big meeting the nicht" " Aye ah hiv that replied Sandy bit naebody seems tae ken fit its aboot something aboot Auld Spencer's Will", " So am hearin replied Jock bit its affa hush, hush naebody seems tae ken fits going on bit nae doot we'll hear aw aboot it the nicht" with that he started his engine and shouted " Nae doot we'll see yea the nicht

The tragedy now was that according to the records Adrian was still the heir to the estate he had been single when he was killed so he had no heir, and with this situation the estate was now liable for death duties, Roddy was lucky his share being the home farm, it was legally signed over to him at birth so it was a real bag of worms, Auld Spencer's legacy would be with them for a long time yet. The Estate was eventually turned over to a Trust Company as there was not enough money to pay death duties but it was government coffers so it would have to be paid one way or another as one local commented (auld Spencer's wasn't such a smart old bugger after all). The Trustees just didn't like parting with money so the first thing they wanted to do was divide everything up and sell it off as job lots, they had no problem selling off the larger farms as the tenants could well afford it, but it was a different kettle of fish when it came to the seventy acre crofts with no electric light and no sanitation, most had water but that was it. The meeting had been called to let the crofters know what was taking place. They invited Roddy Tracy along and Lang Dod both men were educated and clued up on what was about to happen, what the trustees hadn't bargained for was the fact that Auld Tracy had been very generous to his tenants and given them a lease hold of twenty five years, this meant that the likes of Sandy Duncan still had over fifteen years to go before his lease ran out they also had a fixed yearly rent increase so it was a difficult situation for all concerned. The meeting turned out to be a rowdy affair and at times it got heated some men wanted to vent their anger on Roddy the young Laird but it was pointed out that it was out of his hands, it was an over sight on the part of his father, some of the crofters had fairly large families and they were really worried that they might land on the street if there crofts were taken away, but Dod Wilson assured them that, that could not happen, but they were then advised to go and see their solicitor and make him aware of the situation. The meeting dispersed and there were small groups debating the issue for ages, the next move was up to the trustees, in Sandy's case he had nearly finished paying for his tractor but he was reluctant to go back in the red by buying the croft. He made an appointment to see his solicitor, it had been a few years since he last had a meeting with Davie Still, he aged quite a bit but business must be booming the office had been modernised and transformed, and there was an army of people moving about or sitting at desks. Davie greeted Sandy like a long lost brother he called for a pot of tea, then they got down to business Davie was well aware of the situation as he had been prompted by others, but he assured Sandy he had no need to worry as his lease was water tight for the next fifteen years, Sandy asked for his thoughts on buying Hillside, Davies's advice was to find out what they were asking for it then come back and see him in the mean time he would get a surveyor to have a look at it so that he would be prepared for Sandy's next visit.

Sandy did as he was told and sat tight, he didn't have long to wait before he received the official letter enquiring if would be interested in purchasing the small holding known as Hillside, as usual there was no word of price just the bait tempting him to get involved, back at the solicitors Davie Smart advised Sandy to reply stating that he would need to find out what price they were expecting , this he did and of course the price was ridiculous, his solicitors advice was to forget about it until they were more realistic.

Sandy flatly refused to get involved in buying the croft and opted to carry on paying rent the rest of the crofters followed suit but the big boys like Dod Wilson bought their places with the assurance that they would have electricity and improved sanitation in place in the very near future. The smiddy was being transformed and would soon be operational as an Agricultural Engineering Works and Showroom it would also bring fuel pumps which were badly needed now that people were buying motor cars, planning permission was being sought to start work on the police station soon to become the local hostelry, were all these changes going to improve the way of life the Glen folk were used to, as Sandy said " It may improve our way of life but at what cost, they were also moaning about the younger generation and their drink habit and now they were giving permission to build a place that sells the very stuff everybody is against it jist doesn't make sense". One bit of progress that seemed to make life better was the newly founded Youth Club it was very well supported and Betsy Wilson's badminton classes were in big demand to such an extent they had to devise a time table so that everybody interested would get a game, it wasn't only youths that attended some of them could be classed as in the twilight years of their youth but it was a great achievement to get the youngsters interested. Sandy didn't have to look far for problems although he was a quiet living sincere man like everybody else he had a cross to bear his was in the shape of his younger brother Tommy, he had now been attending the High School for over a year all that was in his head was to leave school and get as far away from Sandy as possible. Sandy received a recorded delivery letter, as it had the name of the sender on the receipt Jock Mitchell could tell exactly who it was from, " Aye Sandy a letter from the skeewl for you, maybe your Tommy is Dux and they are keeping it a secret" Sandy signed for it and Jock hung around his nose was really bothering him, Sandy could see he was anxious to find out what the contents were so he deliberately half opened it then turned on his heel and made for the house leaving the nosey Jock standing with his mouth open. Meg asked what was in the letter and Sandy explained that he hadn't opened it as Jock Mitchell was desperate to find out the contents he remarked, " He gets more nosey the older he gets but I told him damn all it would be round the glen like wild fire." Sandy had a bit of shock when he read the letter it appears that Tommy had been giving the teachers a hard time his behaviour was disgraceful and there was a really serious incident that the Headmaster needed to discuss with his parent or guardian. Sandy scratched his head and asked Meg what he could have done that was deemed serious enough for the headmaster to require a talk with Sandy, they made an appointment for the next day at ten-o-clock, Meg and Sandy decided not to say anything until after Sandy had met Mr Gill next morning. He did ask Tommy if anything exciting had happened at school during the last few days but he was in one of his sullen moods and was unprepared to hold any sort of discussion. Sandy woke early he had endured a restless night as he tried to fathom out what his kid brother could have done to upset the headmaster, he wanted to discuss with Tommy what had happened but it would possibly have ended up with a shouting match then grief between Meg and him so he bit the bullet, got himself rather tiredly out of bed and got stuck in to caring for his animals at least they caused no hassle as long as they were fed on time.

He decided to be at the school about quarter to ten and start off on the correct footing he would use his old bike otherwise he would be restricted to having to work to a time schedule something Sandy detested. Meg tried to reassure him that there may be nothing wrong and to try and go there with a positive frame of mind. Sandy parked his bike along side the pupils bike shed he had ten minutes to spare so he had a puff at his pipe as he strolled towards the main entrance, as he pushed the door open he was accosted by a man in a navy blue suit with a cheese cutter hat on his head printed in bold yellow letters on the hat was the word HEAD JANITOR, Sandy had never seen a janitor before. The janitor asked if he could help, Sandy told him his mission and was shown along the corridor the janitor opened the door and announced a Mr Duncan for you head master, the head master came to the door held his hand out for Sandy to shake then welcomed him in and told him to be seated. Ronald Gill had been a teacher all his working life starting at the bottom and working his way up until he reached the dizzy height of head master so he had a wide experience of handling bairns. Mr Duncan I'm sorry we have never met previously but our school is a very busy place and even more so since they started closing down the small country schools, I was well acquaint with Bob Paterson your recently retired head master from the Glen school. Well before Bob retired he gave me a run down on all the pupils who were being transferred to us and he explained their strong points and also their weak points, family background etcetera, I see by the report on Thomas Duncan that you are his elder brother and also his guardian, Sandy nodded, Bob also explained why this unfortunate circumstances came about, but he was also full of praise for you and your sister how you both rallied round and kept the family home and the croft going, so even if we have never met due to Bob Paterson's meticulous report I feel I know the Duncan family already, he asked Sandy if he would like some tea and proceeded to make a phone call requesting tea for two. " Now to get down to the reason I asked you to come to the school, it concerns Thomas he has been a handful to say the least a boy who has no interest in learning he is disruptive and cheeky our younger teachers find him very stressful because when Thomas decides to perform there are a few others who egg him on and sadly he ends up being branded the sinner all the time, no matter what discipline we dish out it makes no difference in fact the more severe the discipline the worse he gets. His attendance at school is appalling but it seams that either you or your sister condone his absences because he is always covered by a note, with that he produced a bundle of written notes all giving a reason for Tommy being absent from school, Sandy was livid and humiliated he spread the notes in front of him and picked out three that had been genuinely written and signed by his sister Meg. Sandy was in turmoil as he stammered and tried to explain his brother's behaviour but what could he say he explained that he had changed when his mother died that he had been very spoiled by the elder members of the family but he had no excuse for his behaviour. Ronnie Gill felt sorry for the young man sitting in front of him he was trying to soften the blow but it was difficult from his point of view his staff had a difficult enough job without having to pander to the Thomas Duncan's of this world, it was a difficult conversation to carry on, but worse was still to come, Ron Gill cleared his throat.

The next point Mr Duncan is probably out with the school jurisdiction but for me it is the straw that broke the camels back, because the complaint was channelled through us as it was during school hours we were forced to act. As you probably saw on your way here there is a small Bakers shop, for years now they have sold goodies to the pupils of this school, but sadly they are on the verge of banning our pupils because of the amount of theft that occurs during the lunch break, it appears that the pupils fill the shop to capacity and while the three assistants are busy the pupils are filling their pockets from the trays, some days half of the profits of the shop disappear. One day last week the owner of the shop heard some one enter and when she appeared from the back shop Thomas Duncan was filling his pockets there were no other customers in the shop but about half-a-dozen boys watching through the window they started clapping and cheering when the old lady appeared, Thomas then bought a sausage roll. Sandy felt as though he had been steamrolled what a disgrace to be caught stealing was just something he never bargained for he was speechless what was he going to do. Ronnie gave him a couple of minutes before he continued, the people who own the shop were swithering about calling the police in, they are really distraught about the whole business and don't really want to be responsible for youths ending up with criminal records before they leave school, theft is a stigma that never leaves you, Sandy was well aware of this and felt absolutely washed out. Ronnie Gill proceeded, Mr Duncan my school committee have discussed this problem and we could expel your brother, but we try to give our young people the best chance they can get in life so we decided to issue a severe reprimand to Thomas Duncan and a few of his cronies, along with the reprimand they are forbidden to enter the bakers shop and this is a final warning if anything similar occurs during the time they have left in school I'm afraid we will take drastic action. I think your young brother needs to have the stark reality of his ways laid in front of him and explain that he is on his way to spending life in borstal. Sandy was close to tears how could Tommy be so bloody stupid he was heading for leaving school totally uneducated. Ronnie Gill had no more to say on the matter except that he was sorry he had to bring Sandy into this, Bob Paterson had given the Duncan family a pedigree second to none he was sure Sandy had done his best and he hoped he would be able to convince his younger brother that he was on a slippery slope with that he stood up shook Sandy's hand and promised he would keep in touch, Sandy thanked him profusely and apologised for the umpteenth time and promised he would do his very best, with that he said goodbye. Outside the school Sandy had to lean against the wall for a few minutes he had never had to suffer such a humiliating half hour in his life at the moment if he could get hold of Tommy he would strangle him. He stood about for a few minutes until he was fully composed then tried to get his senses sorted out where should he start. First he decided to pay the bakers a visit where he would offer to pay for what Tommy stole, he swung his leg over the crossbar and slowly pedalled to the small shop. He entered and an elderly woman appeared, she asked what he wanted thinking he was another customer. Sandy was real embarrassed he asked if he could speak to the owner, the old lady said she and her husband were the owners and her husband was busy baking. Sandy took a deep breath and explained who he was and he was here to pay for what his brother had stolen.

Mrs Slater the shop owner could see Sandy was quite young and very distressed so she offered him a cup of tea which he gladly accepted, she showed him the way through to her living room and asked what he had in his tea, he was very grateful but this was adding to his embarrassment. He could hear her filling the kettle then presumed that she used gas to boil it he noted that the lighting in the room was by gas, she stuck her head round the door and said she would give her husband Willie a shout as it was near his break time, Sandy felt a slight panic course through his body, what if Willie Slater was six foot six and weighed about eighteen stone it was possible he may knock the daylights out of five foot eight Sandy. He could hear feet shuffling along the corridor and his imagination of Willie Slater was way out Willie was about five seven he was quite stooped over probably due to his years leaning over the mixing basins in the bake house he also had quite severe breathing problems again due to his choice of employment and years of breathing in dust off the flour. He held out his hand for Sandy to shake, he had a real firm welcoming sort of shake, this made Sandy feel a lot more comfortable. Jean appeared with a teapot and a plate of newly baked scones, she made a bit of a palaver by asking Sandy if he preferred the milk in first or last, then sat down and they had a blether, it was obvious to Sandy that Jean had told her husband why Sandy was there. Willie started off by talking about the modern bairns about how cheeky they were and the stealing of his wares in the bakery he estimated that some weeks they were having four or five-dozen items stolen, in a small bakery that was a big percentage of their profits to combat the problem they now only allow four bairns in the shop at any one time, " Yea see Sandy we need their business to survive if we stopped serving the bairns our business would go bust, but if any kid had no money and was hungry all they needed to do was ask Jean or myself and we would gladly give them a bag of food to keep them going so why do they need to steal from us."? Sandy shook his head and said he had no idea but he was sure it wasn't a money problem he felt they were doing it for some sort of dare, which was the case the day his brother was caught. He finished his tea and as Willie prepared to go back to work Sandy really hit a raw nerve he offered to pay for the goods Tommy had stolen, Willie near blew a fuse stating he would do no such thing it was good enough of him to come and apologise, with that Sandy left and headed for home he still had the problem of having to tackle Tommy about his wrong doing especially the stealing no doubt it would be all over the Glen by now. How Sandy wished he had Will Watson or Bob Paterson to ask for advice or even Dod Simpson would have put the frighteners on Tommy if he had still been the local Bobby. Sandy decided to put his trust in the Minister Jim Kerr he knew the Duncan family from birth and he was a wise sort of man so Sandy would ask his advice. He was in predicament did he tell Meg why he had been called to the school or would he talk to the minister first his head was in turmoil as he debated his next move. As he walked up the path to the manse door he was very apprehensive and was really glad when Jim Kerr stuck his head round the door. Jim was knocking on a bit probably close to retiring so he had plenty of experience with young folk problems, he showed Sandy into his study and listened while Sandy poured his heart out about the problems Tommy was causing the family.

Jim Kerr listened thoughtfully and allowed Sandy to continue until he had exhausted his story, the minister then sat silent for a couple of minutes while he weighed up the situation, he was aware that Tommy had been brought up in a family environment with no father and his mother more or less unable to participate in his welfare he had been close to his mother and spent many hours at her bedside and then suddenly she was taken from him it was bound to play havoc in his young life, Jim reminded Sandy that in no way was he sticking up for Tommy entirely but going over the points that may have triggered off his behavioural problems. Jim Kerr wondered if he could maybe have a word with the young fellow and try and point out the error of his ways, he also told Sandy to try and involve himself in Tommy's life a bit more it was a difficult situation but one that Jim was sure could be resolved, he also advised Sandy to sit down with Meg and tell her what had happened at the school she had a right to know what was going on.

The only way was to take the bull by the horns and that is exactly what Sandy did after leaving the minister he went home and told Meg they needed to have a chat, he explained what had happened at the school and the bakers shop he also told her he had talked to the minister. For once Meg showed real concern for Sandy as the gravity of Tommy's behaviour finally sank in when he told her how close the headmaster had been in getting the police involved Meg burst into tears, they were both at a loss what to do, Meg thought that she would be better to tackle Tommy as he listened to her better than he did with Sandy. So it was left to Meg to find an opportune moment to tackle her young brother about his wayward behaviour, the opportunity arose one evening when Sandy was attending a meeting and Meg and Tommy were alone she told him they were aware of his behaviour at school and about the theft from the bakery at first Tommy took up his usual defensive stance but when it was explained that the stealing from the old couple in the bakery was threatening their lively hood he started to pay head. He explained to Meg that on the occasion he was caught he had been dared by others, the idea was to steal a roll and not get caught they carried out this sort of ploy regularly, Tommy said he was genuinely sorry for what he had done and he would not be so stupid again, he was also keen to find out what Sandy had to say about it, Meg told him Sandy was quite upset especially the fact that the police were very nearly involved that gave young Thomas more food for thought. Between Meg and himself it was decided that Tommy should visit Willie and Jean Slater at the bakery and apologise for the stress he had caused them, Meg told him that Sandy had offered to pay for the stolen goods but they had refused payment so she decided to make up a parcel with some fresh eggs butter and cheese when he went to apologise he could give them the present, he decided that would be a good idea. Sandy had stayed well clear and allowed Meg to handle the situation, Tommy had never brought the subject up but Meg kept him informed about what they had decided, Sandy was well pleased with the outcome and thought that Tommy had started to behave a bit better. The following week Sandy got quite a surprise when on the Sunday Tommy left for the Kirk ahead of him and Meg he thought this was a turn up for the books, normally it was a struggle to get him to go at all, it turned out that Jim Kerr had managed to have a talk with young Tom and even persuaded him to take over the job of pumping the bellows behind the church organ.

Sandy felt as though they had made a break through with the young fellow but his joy was short lived as Tommy was as awkward as ever, totally refusing to get involved around the croft but he expected to be given money on a regular basis, Sandy also suspected that he was not adverse to helping himself if the opportunity arose, his time at school was nearing an end then what.

On the crofting front they were still at loggerheads with the Estate Trustees they had now passed on all the repair work to the individual crofter so any expenses incurred on repairs they had to stand good them selves, the trustees had a gun at the crofters heads as they threatened to re-value every croft, this could incur an expensive court battle so really they were between the devil and the deep sea. The number of crofters still active had dropped to eleven that was four gone since Sandy took over around ten years ago, it could even get worse as a company from England were actively recruiting people to relocate to Corby in Northamptonshire with a company called Stewart and Lloyds a huge Steelworks the promise was steady work forty hours per week and a new modern house, the people from the north east were flocking down there and rumour had it that two of the Glen crofters were in the throws of joining the exodus, it made life more difficult for the remaining few.

Another crisis hit the world when it was announced that Britain and the United States were once again at war the rumour mongers and scare mongers had a field day as they envisaged that this was the start of WW3. The Press headlines stated that war had broken out in Korea, the Glen folks discussing world affairs would say " Korea far the hell's that" out would come the school Atlas and they would hunt for Korea only to find it was an insignificant little island not far from Japan. Insignificant it may have looked but over the next three years it would be world news, as the fighting intensified British soldiers once again became cannon fodder, fighting some body else's cause. It didn't take long before the casualty lists started to appear in the press. This war was to last three years and there were quite a few never returned. Sandy was dealt another blow when talking to his near neighbour Frankie Smith, Frankie told him that he had received word from his brother in Corby that there would be another recruitment drive just shortly and he was seriously thinking of taking the plunge. Frankie had four of a family all midway through their education, Frankie asked Sandy what did he think they could do in the way of employment around the Glen, Sandy shook his head and said nothing there was no work even the bigger farms were cutting back, mechanisation was helping the big farmer not the workers as every new tractor means anything up to three less jobs, Frankie continued "Sandy if I stay put as soon as my bairns leave the school they will have to leave hame to find work, just look at the Sutherlands their hame for aboot thirty six hours every second week, I just dinna want my family broken up like that, but if I move to Corby they will all get jobs there even the wife will get employment nae bother" Frankie continued " If you think of the wages six of us will be taking into the hoose then compare what we earn off the croft knocking our pans in here there is nae comparison and another thing you only work an eight oor day, here some days its nearer eighteen oors and often seven days a week." " Na, Na Sandy I have had enough of it, sixteen years since I took over this place and nothing to show for it."

Sandy was quite distressed after his conversation with Frankie he was a wonderful neighbour and nothing was ever a bother, it was getting serious but maybe Frankie was just having a rant and when he cooled down he would just carry on as normal, but there was also word that Davie Fraser was about to give up as well, Davie was not in the best of health, none of his family were interested in the croft so he had to struggle on by himself if the two of them went that would leave nine of the original fifteen and the Estate Trustees would not re-let the croft they wanted rid of them so they would be sold off no doubt one of the big guys would get first offer. If there were any moves it would be next year as the November term was only weeks away so there was no time to give up the croft before that date. But there was more world wide drama to happen before this year finished it was announced that King George the sixth had passed away he had been in poor health, and finally he succumbed to his illness there was quite a problem as the new Queen was abroad visiting in Africa so she had to be brought home and all the pomp and ceremony planned before the funeral, the Wireless broadcast nothing else and all the programmes were cancelled for a couple of days, finally the King was laid to rest his funeral service was broadcast over the wireless so people sat with their ears glued to their sets and listened to this historic occasion. Finally that year on the fourteenth of December Tommy was old enough to leave school, what was going to happen now, he had never discussed his plans about a job and things had reached a point where Sandy no longer asked what was going on. The day after he left school Tommy set off on his bike around ten-o-clock, when Sandy went to the house for his dinner Meg told him that his young brother was off after a job with some woodcutter, she also had a go at Sandy about the hostilities between the two brothers, as usual she thought it was Sandy's fault, but he pointed out that every time he tried to speak to Tommy he got the most insolent of answers and he added if he would only tell him why he may manage to sort things out. Tommy got the job he went after and was starting on the Monday morning but he would be moving out and staying a in bothy, Sandy had a little chuckle to himself and thought, Aye he'll ken whit side his breeds buttered on noo, this could be interesting, of course Meg had to have a session of weeping and wailing where as Sandy had mixed feelings and considering his other two brothers had left home and were doing fine he was sure Tommy would do the same, furthermore the atmosphere should be a bit more pleasant.

The Hogmanay came and went, Tommy didn't turn up for his New Years dinner, this caused a bit of unpleasantness between Sandy and Meg as she still took the younger brothers side, Sandy had no recollection of doing anything that could have upset his brother he had tried to instil some discipline into him but never with a heavy hand so where had he gone wrong and in Megs eyes still going wrong. Sandy decided after dinner to go and first foot some of his neighbours the Morrison's always had a crowd in so he made his way there, he had a couple of drams then made his way to the Sutherlands they were all home from the Hydro. It was easy seen the wealth that family were enjoying, everything in the house was new there were at least four cars in the yard there were grand children there and they had toys Sandy had never set eyes on before, the old man tried to convince Sandy that working the croft was slave labour and he could get him a job up North just say the word and I'll get you fixed up.

Chapter Eightteen

S ANDY WAS TEMPTED BUT HE HAD no idea what life beyond the glen was like so he declined the offer and continued in slavery for the unforeseeable future. He arrived home early evening feeling rather tipsy, he switched the wireless on and promptly feel asleep, Meg was moaning when he awoke around ten-o-clock about the racket he made snoring, Sandy got up from the chair and headed towards the byre for a check on his beasts before bedtime.

Early in the New Year a committee meeting was held in the village hall this was to be a big year of celebration as the new Queen was having her coronation in June. The committee after much debate decided to have a Fete along the lines of past years where everybody seemed to enjoy themselves and in the evening they would have the same sort of Bothy nicht concert. Sandy was asked if he could provide the music he said he would contact Will Watson and see if he would come back and play for the night. The highlight of the afternoon would be the final of the tug-of-war and this year a new trophy would be awarded the Coronation Cup. Lang Dod immediately volunteered to provide the cup this was accepted as it cut down on the village funds so it was promptly christened the Lang Dod Coronation trophy, the committee would meet fortnightly to make sure things were well organised before the big day. To add a bit of spice to the day it was decided that there would be an adult fancy dress parade right behind the bairns one.

The Glen was going through a transformation that would bring it into the twentieth century the new estate trustees had appointed Roddy Tracy as a sort of liaison manager between the farming community and themselves they were based in London and were really only interested in the shooting and fishing rights of the estate so if they could dispose of the bricks and mortar they would. Roddy's job was to oversee the running of the estate; between the home farm and his new appointment he was a very busy man. One of his first tasks was to call a meeting and explain to the tenants what was about to happen, again he asked if anyone was interested in buying the croft they were leasing but again there were no takers. Roddy called the meeting to order sitting beside him was Dod Wilson and on his other side was a representative from the trustees the consensus of opinion was that the bugger wie the fancy suit on him had never done a days work in his life but then it was agreed that most likely he was a pen pusher from London. The first thing on the agenda was that permission had been given to go ahead and start installing the new plumbing system in the glen this meant that every house in the Glen would have a full sanitary system complete with a bathroom which included toilet wash hand basin and bath, the second item was the installation of electricity the hydro board were about to start running power to every house and business in the Glen it was hoped that all this modernisation would be complete before winter set in. The fellow with the suit stood up and for the first time during the meeting he spoke, first he introduced himself as being an accountant for the estate trustees and it was his job to point out what all this was going to cost. He continued " Gentlemen this is a huge project and as I am sure you are aware big projects cost big amounts of money.

"So our company are looking to you people to help find some of the funding", there was a lot of booing and stamping of feet and shouts of " far the hell dea yea expect us tae get the money fay"? The accountant held up his hand and asked to be allowed to finish, " gentlemen there are three methods of payment first a cheque for the full amount of one hundred and twenty five pounds or two instalments to be paid with your rent immediately installation is complete the third is for us to increase your rent by twelve percent per annum". This caused uproar there was shouting and heckling and near riot among the usually docile crofters they were not a happy bunch, the suit continued after he got peace and quiet again. " There is another alternative we can install all these facilities up to the door of your croft and terminate them there but think of your dear wives would you be a popular fellow watching your wife carrying water or using one of these cumbersome hand pumps when, by turning on a tap she had instant water, I think your life could become pretty miserable" he then asked if there were any questions one of the main ones was how long did they get to make up their minds the answer they got was one week, the meeting would be reconvened one week from today, the suit got up and left leaving Lang Dod Wilson and Roddy Tracy to try and convince the crofters they needed to take advantage of this offer now as things would only go up in price. Dod Wilson stood up and asked for hush he began to speak everybody listened when the Big man spoke. " Gentlemen I don't really need to be here to-day you see I already have a bathroom installed, have had for a couple of years now paid for the lot my self and let me tell you it cost a lot more than what you are being asked to pay. It came to the point where I could no longer expect my wife and bairns to run to the bottom of the garden and use the most primitive system of sanitation imaginable, every time I went near the place the bucket was always full to the top and swarms of blue bottles everywhere it was bloody disgusting. For your money you are also getting the electricity installed I have still to pay for that as we use a generator at the moment. But if you allow them to increase your rent the majority of you would be paying an additional pound a month. Not a lot for the luxury you are going to enjoy. As is normal you can never get one hundred percent agreement there is always one awkward disruptive person and at the meeting it was Albie, Albert Grant he was unique in as much as he was an only child the majority of crofting families had between six and twelve bairns, Albie, s parents had him his father had died when Albie was about fourteen so between him and his mother they carried on the croft, the mother doing most of the graft, he was getting on for forty when the war started unmarried and was waited on hand and foot by his mother, it was envisaged that Albie would remain a bachelor for the rest of his life, then Victoria came on the scene she was a huge land army girl as strong as any man, it was said she could lift two fifty six pound weights above her head and hold them for five minutes, anyhow Victoria was working for the Bremner family who were neighbours to Albie and his mother, Victoria befriended Mrs Grant and spent a lot of her spare time helping out around the croft. Suddenly it was announced that Albie and Victoria were about to get married it had been all hush, hush but the weddin g went ahead and Vicki became Mrs Albie Grant but the mystery didn't end their because a few months later a young Grant was born the calendars were produced and the dates worked out and it was nudge, nudge, wink, wink bad boy Albie.

For the next six years Vikki produced a bairn every year somebody stated Albie was bound to be good at something and he seemed to have found his vocation producing bairns Now Albie was the butt of many jokes in the Glen and it was said he was the tightest man that breath was ever put into, the other men would say Albie, s as tight as a puddocks (frog) erse, when it came to parting with cash he put up a strong fight. He was busy stating his case about how he had a job making ends meet and there was no way he could possibly afford to start installing fancy bathrooms and any how he had used a pail all his life and it hadn't done him any harm. Lang Dod was usually a sympathetic sort of man but Albie was getting under his skin, here was a man who had everything handed to him on a plate, he had a wife who worked her fingers to the bone as well as looking after six young bairns and three of them possibly still needing nappies and he was reneging on making life easier for her, he was a selfish fat lazy bugger time for Lang Dod to let rip. "Albie Grant!! I just canna believe whit I am hearing you have a fine hard working wife, the mother of your bairns works her fingers to the bone and you, you miserable bugger would begrudge her the means to make her life a wee bit easier, if any man in the Glen should be all for this huge step forward it should be you shame on you man". Albie was completely caught off guard and he could feel the blood rising as his face got redder by the minute maybe he had been a bit out spoken but he hadn't had time to think maybe the big fellow was right he should be backing the scheme. The meeting was closed and it was agreed that there would be answers in a week's time; Roddy told them that they would have to sign a form agreeing or disagreeing with what ever decision they come to, as soon as the men started to move Albie Grant got hold of big Dod and apologised for being as he said himself a pain in the arse, " But Geordie yae ken me I aye need an argument before I can agree wie other folks and can yea picture big Vikki if I went hame and telt her I had rejected the installation on the bathroom my life would be over so forget I ever said a word", with that they shook hands still friends. Sandy and Meg had a major discussion regarding the bathroom, Meg pointed out that she felt it an embarrassment having to show people like Maria Willie's girl friend to an old stinking shed in the garden and also it must have been quite embarrassing having to pee in a potty during the night all these points were discussed and then the installation of the electricity what changes that would make to their lives, ok it would cost money but surely they were entitled to make life easier if the means were available, so Sandy was convinced that they would go ahead and have it done what about paying for it. They kicked it about for quite some time and finally the option of paying two instalments seemed the most favourable.

Meg had busy contacting the family members who were rather scattered around the globe trying to get them home for the Coronation celebrations both Betty and Jim had young bairns and a lot of miles to travel but she had better luck with the other three, Peg was overdue some time off from her job as a trainee nurse so she would be home for two weeks. Willie and Mary both Military Police personnel were on duty in London for the weekend but had both managed to get some timeoff starting the Monday after the big celebration, Willie said every MP in the British Army would be on duty that weekend and no doubt they would be kept busy. So at least Meg had something to look forward to.

Sandy had managed to persuade Will Watson to come and play at the dance he was going to stay the weekend at Hillside so it should be some celebration. There was a lot of planning and the committee were busy but they had some great organisers especially Betsey Wilson she could get everything going like clockwork and she wasn't slow at putting Lang Dod in his place if he stepped out of line. There were going to be some major changes at the November term another three of the older residents were ready to retire, it was always a sad occasion when the elders of the Glen decided to call it a day. Jock Mitchell the postie was due to retire he was going to remain in the glen, Jim Kerr the minister was going, another part of the community backbone he was moving into a new house in the town and finally Dr Findlay he was also moving his daughter Isobel had taken over the practice but there was word she was moving and going into practice in the town not an ideal situation for the glen folks but according to N.H.S rules there was not enough patients to warrant a full time doctor, the locals put up a bit of a fight and finally got an agreement that there would be a surgery three evenings a week and finally Frankie Smith confirmed that he would be moving to Corby, he had a job ready to start in the new year so the Glen was shrinking yearly. Sandy went straight to the estate and enquired about the possibility of taking over Frankie's land but the only way he could have it was to buy it and anyhow they already had an offer, Sandy could see the writing on the wall it was easy seen the crofters were a dying breed in this part of the world but all he could do was soldier on. Finalisation of the programme took place at a meeting in the middle of May there was large entries for all the events but way ahead of everything else was the Tug-Of War because it was Coronation day they had made it an open event and they were overwhelmed with entries, it was a time consuming event so they had to restrict entries to eighteen teams making sure that the locals were all accepted, it would be on going most of the day so a small team was picked to ensure the smooth running of that one event. Since Tommy had decided that living in a Bothy was better than the comforts of home they rarely saw him when he did call home he always made sure Sandy would be out Meg would make up a box of goodies for him and he always assured her he was doing ok, he never ever discussed his beef with his elder brother and when Meg tried to broach the subject he just clammed up.

The agreement to carry out the work to install power and water was signed and sealed and work was due to start the week after the Coronation bash they hoped to have most of the houses connected by the New Year all the people in the Glen had agreed they wanted the services although there were still moans about having to pay towards it. Coronation Day didn't take long to come round after a lot of hard work and long hours by the committee and volunteers the field was ready well ahead of schedule the judges and umpires were all ready to keep things moving, they were lucky and the weather was favourable, the first item on the programme was the Fancy Dress parade, there was a wonderful entry, the over all first prize went to a brother and sister who were dressed as the Bisto Kids everybody was thanked for their effort. Another highlight and an annual event was the Hill Race about five miles and then of course the Tug-of-War the most supported event on the programme it had to be started early due to the amount of teams who wanted to take part.

The final was due to take place at four thirty so the semi finals were ongoing from quarter to four; it was a hard fought contest and the final two teams were eventually achieved, one being last years winners Lang Dod's Dumplins versus The Tartan Terrors they were a team from up the Inverness area they wore Tartan Trews when competing, they travelled all over the country competing this was their first time on the east coast so they were dead keen to win, they had brought a good few supporters with them so it should be quite a keen contest. Both sets of supporters were getting worked up into near frenzy this was being treated like an international cup final insults were being traded, Lang Dods team had one or two changes this year Will Watson place as anchor had been taken by Hans the Jerry he was quite small but chunky Sandy was still their along with Eck Davidson it was all set for a show of strength. Bill Findlay in his capacity as umpire was looking at his watch; this would probably be his last time as an official. Fifteen minutes to go and he called the teams to start getting ready there was a cloud of French

177

chalk over the teams as they chalked there hands, to spice things up it was decided to have five pulls instead of the usual three, Lang Dod was already well hyped up jumping around like an excited school boy, his team was his pride and joy if they could pull it off what a boost for the district, Betsy called over to him " George calm yirsel doon wie dinna want you having a heart attack". The Tartan Terrors looked good in their Seaforth Tartan Trews this was an indicator that they may have been ex Seaforth Highlanders so this would make them quite fit men, both teams looked fairly even weight wise around one hundred and fifty stone. Bill Findlay called the teams to get ready with much grunting and digging in of tackity boot heels they started to take the strain Bill Findlay measured the markers just to make sure everything was fair and in order, then he told them to take the strain holding the centre marker until it was in line with the line on the ground he held for about thirty seconds before letting go and shout heave. This prompted the two-team captains to start their ritual of jumping about and encouraging their men to pull, heave, dig, heave, and dig! They were at fever pitch as the two teams held steady not an inch was given for what must have been two minutes then with one mighty heave the Dumplins started to buckle, one nothing to the Terrors the excitement was unbearable. Set up again and the same ritual was repeated again the Terrors pulled the Dumplins; Lang Dod was near demented as they set up for the third pull it was quite a short pull probably thirty seconds the cheering was tremendous when the Dumplins pulled one back two, one, another cloud of French chalk descended on the crowd as the lads chalked their hand for the fourth pull it was do or die for the Dumplins. Take the strain pull shouted Bill Findlay and the captains were laying into their charges the Terrors were determined to finish it but they were so even it was unbelievable finally one had to give and Dods Dumplins managed to square the match the crowd went bananas they had never witnessed a contest like it before, Bill Findlay decided to give the contestants a five minute breather before the fifth and final pull. One or two of the lads needed refreshments as they were loosing gallons of sweat, the hands were rechalked their positions were taken up, Bill Findlay had the centre marker in one hand the other hand held above his head get ready heave! The gladiators were in full flight as they tried to pull each other over the line.

Bill Findlay had to be on his toes as the markers drifted back and forth coming perilously close on either side, they held steady for at least three to four minutes finally something had to give and Dods Dumplins managed to pull the Terrors over the marker the victors were mobbed by their supporters they had never witnessed such a close run contest before in the Glen. Immediately the Terrors captain congratulated Lang Dod and invited him and his team up to Cawdor to take part in a tug-of-war contest courtesy of the Young Farmers. As the captain Lang Dod lifted the Coronation Cup and gave a little speech in praise of his team and finally said a word about how sporting the loser's had been. The dance in the evening was well attended but again was slightly blighted by the fact that a few of the young men were drunk and to the extreme in some cases, Meg had been speaking to her young brother and was sure she got a smell off booze off him this was a real worry as he was just over fifteen and a half, she kept it to herself as she didn't want Sandy going off in a tangent about it, the evening soon passed and the last dance was played in time to clear the hall before midnight, Sandy, Will Watson, Mrs Watson, Meg and Peg walked home together it was a lovely summer night not properly dark and soon daylight would be appearing but the Coronation bash had been a very enjoyable day. Will was staying over the weekend he was hoping to be able to see Willie before departing for home; Sandy and Will had a great day on the Sunday visiting all the old haunts this was after they had all attended the Kirk, Jim Kerr was getting very frail and he spoke of his impending retirement he had spent thirty years in the Glen he would be sadly missed, he also said a word for his fellow retirees, Dr Bill Findlay and postman Jock Mitchell between the three of them they had clocked up one hundred years of service carrying out their various occupations. Monday would see the arrival of Willie, Maria and Mary, Meg was up to high doh as she fussed about making up beds and trying to keep conversation with Bell Watson, she had been very busy all week-end especially on Saturday at the Coronation bash where she was on the WRI tea stall Willie came flying into the yard at quarter to twelve on the Monday he had hired a car in Aberdeen it was a Standard Vanguard with seating for six people. As he and his passengers got out of the car Meg nearly suffocated them as she hugged and kissed and howled her eyes out she was so overcome it was some time since Willie had been home, Mary had been seven months away without a break, she looked a real smasher in her army uniform and of course Maria was the usual Swedish cracker. Willie spread his arms out and told them what a relief to get out of London it has been a mad house for the past couple of weeks he told the assembled company they didn't know they were living with all the fresh air, peace and quiet they were getting for free. Himself and Will gave each other a huge hug and then sat down and started to reminisce, Will said that he and Bell would need to get the next bus home as it was hours until the late one, Willie told them not to be daft he would drive them home and just sit where they were until he had something to eat he assured them it was no bother.

Willie and Sandy drove the Watson's home to Turriff around eight-o-clock in the evening they got so engrossed in each others lives and stories before they realised it, it was supper time so Meg insisted they wait and eat before they left for home, Willie handed Will a bottle of duty free whisky as he dropped them off outside their house, they were invited in but Willie declined he had very little sleep over the past couple of days so he was desperate to get home for some rest. But it was late before the Duncan family got to bed they sat and talked into the sma hours, of course there was drink in the house courtesy of Willies duty free, next morning would be a different kettle of fish. With a vehicle at their disposal it was decided that they would do as much touring as possible, Peg was due back at her nursing on the Wednesday so it was decided that they would all head for Aberdeen and the girls could have a day shopping, Meg gave a whoop of delight her last trip had been a while back. Sandy was restricted about getting away as he had animals to see to and he was still managing to get some casual work he didn't like turning it down as there were plenty others ready to take over. Willie put his foot down and told his brother that come the week-end the two of them would get up early get the chores done and Sandy could join them on days out both Saturday and Sunday. On the Saturday they were ready to hit the road it was decided to have a drive up the coast so that they could view the Highlands getting there in time to have lunch somewhere, this was a first for Sandy he had never been so far away from the croft in his life, he was fairly fascinated by the huge fields through Morayshire and Nairn and then of course the magnificent view of the Black Isle and west over the Craig Dunain hills it was breathtaking. They parked in Inverness and found a restaurant serving lunches Sandy was over awed with the magnificent old buildings that formed the High street and it was teeming with people somebody mentioned it being Saturday all the country folks were in town. After lunch they had a wander around in through Woollies and back to where they parked the car. Willie asked where they should go for the afternoon they had a bit of a confab and it was decided to head home through by Grantown, Tomintoul, Dufftown and then back to Banff, they stopped off on the way and eventually landed in Banff about five-o-clock. Willie invited them all to come to the chipper and they would have a fish supper in the little café, they thought it an excellent idea especially Meg a whole day without cooking what luxury. After they had eaten Mary decided it would be just about right to go to the pub and have a couple of pints before they went home Sandy was looking at his watch but he was told the only thing to do when they got home was to milk the coo. Sandy and Meg were the real country bumpkins when they entered the Lounge Bar they had no idea what to do as they had never been in a pub before so they felt rather awkward, but they soon got into the swing of things, the men had a couple of pints while the ladies had sherry that was except Mary who insisted in having a pint along with the blokes, much to Megs amazement she thought it very unlady like but said nothing, as they headed for home they all agreed it had been a lovely day out, Mary and Willie got stuck in and helped Sandy with the bits and pieces he had to complete before his day was over they finally settled down and had a drink and a blether before going to bed. The leave soon came to an end and Willie, Mary and Maria had to return to their respective places o f work. As usual Meg bade them a tearful goodbye.

All was quiet once again the farming people were getting geared up for the harvest busy times were ahead, especially for Sandy as he was in demand helping out with harvest at various places a chance to earn a few extra shillings, there were some additional events taking place this autumn, Frankie Smith would be having a roup (sale) he intended to sell everything and start afresh when he moved to Corby, Davie Morrison likewise he never got the option to hand his croft down to any of the family, the Trustees stepped in and offered to sell them the croft otherwise it would go on the open market and that is exactly what happened one of the big farmers bought it and would use the buildings to shelter livestock, Sandy was quite shocked as the more crofters that gave up the more expensive it became for the ones that were left, less people to share the transport cost's etc. But this was progress, since the war the population of the Glen had almost halved, where it was once a desirable place to stay it was now getting very distant. The old police station was soon to open as a hotel and the old Smiddy now an agricultural engineering works had just installed fuel pumps and had permission to open a shop selling newspapers etc, the post office was due to shut as it was seemingly uneconomical to keep it running the mail would be delivered from the main post office in town Jock Mitchell would retire in November.

Sandy was busy at the top end of the hill one fine day middle of June he had given up keeping sheep so he was tidying up some fencing when he spotted a huge fancy coach driving up the croft road, immediately he thought to himself that the driver had taken a wrong turn but there was nothing Sandy could do he was too far away he watched to see the outcome the driver pulled up in the yard, next thing he saw was Meg speaking to the driver and pointing up the hill the driver had a look at the farm track that led to the top fields he then went back to his coach and people started to disembark, Sandy could tell by the look of them that they were not locals as most were in light coloured clothes and wore sun glasses, they started to walk up the hill, a curious Sandy started to walk down to meet them. They met about halfway and shouted hallo at each other the coach driver stepped forward and explained, his passengers were Canadians they had been doing a tour of France visiting battlefields and cemeteries where they had relatives buried, they were here to see the crash site and small memorial where the Canadian Bomber had crashed during the war. The parents of two of the crew were here and relatives of some others they were over the moon that Sandy had witnessed the crash and he could relate how the Glen people had tried in vain to pull the crew from the wreckage, they spent about an hour taking pictures of the site, of Sandy and just everything that moved. Sandy walked them back to the coach there were thirty five of them some quite elderly, when they reached the croft house Meg came to the door and asked if any of them would like a cup of tea, she had thirty six takers somebody asked was she sure it was not too much bother. Meg replied " Naw, Naw its jist like a big day at the thrashing mull", her scones got short shrift it was a good job she was always prepared. The Canadians were still applauding the Duncan's well after the coach was on its way they had really appreciated what had been done for them and no doubt it enhanced the Scots peoples standing in the eyes of the Canadians they were on their way to Prestwick and flying home, no doubt with a mind full of tales about a wonderful adventure.

Some time in the middle of July Sandy received a letter from his friend Will Watson in Turriff, in it Will pointed out that Turriff Agricultural show was due in about three weeks time, in the evening there was a special treat, at the evening dance in the marquee in as much as Jimmy Shand was providing the music and a guest appearance by Will Starr, could Sandy manage through it would be great to hear Shand live and to hear and see Will Starr was just out of this world. He would discuss it with Meg before making up his mind, all the animals were in the fields all Meg would need to do was milk the cow and she was so docile that would be no problem, Meg was quite agreeable her brother had never been away from the croft overnight in his life so here was an opportunity to have a break. Sandy replied that same day saying he would contact Will nearer the time and make arrangements about his arrival time this was something to look forward to and break the monotony of work. The men installing the power and the bathrooms were hard at work but it was hard physical work all done by hand, so they looked like they may be falling behind a bad spell of weather would really hinder them, it looked like it would be the following spring before completion. Sandy still managed to attend the pictures on a fairly regular basis sometimes both he and Meg would go and as a treat after the pictures they would have a fish supper eaten from a news paper (lovely) at the moment some of the films going the rounds were breath taking The Greatest Show On Earth, and Annie Get Your Gun with the gorgeous Doris Day, in some cases these films were so popular that people had to queue to get tickets to get in. The rest of the year had quite a few highlights coming up, there was the two roups both scheduled for the second week in November, the threshing mill was due but it was only here for eight days now as there were less places needing work done, the ploughing match was organised so there would never be a dull moment, along with all that they had the Christmas concert and the WRI had arranged a bus trip for a days shopping in Aberdeen so all this would keep them busy till the end of the year. So life in rural Banff-shire just trundled on they were moving to-wards the twenty first century more than half way there, Sandy had been running the croft at Hillies for the past fifteen years and money wise things hadn't improved a great deal he had finished paying for his tractor, but soon he would have to pay the first instalment to the Estate Trustees for the installation of the bathroom and electric connection, then the real expense would start no doubt the women would be requiring all the labour saving devices that go along with the power of electricity so it was never ending Sandy had less in the bank than there was when he succeeded his father. They had a lot less trouble than some of the crofters who had families many of them had problems where the daughters would get pregnant, this would result in a shot gun wedding everything kept hush, hush, either that or the girl would be secreted away and hidden until the baby was born then her mother would bring it up, years later the bairn would find out that their older sister was in fact their mother but it was a taboo subject although it was quite common. Sandy was looking forward to Turra Show day he had been working a lot of hours lately and he felt quite tired so twenty four hours away would leave him rested and refreshed, The new hotel in the old police station was advertising that they would be open for the New Year serving food, booze and had a few bedrooms to let.

The morning of the Turra Show Sandy was up with the lark he had a few chores to complete before he left he didn't want his sister having to put herself out doing jobs that were too heavy for her so he got everything in order before heading for the kitchen for breakfast, there was a great feeling of excitement about him he sat and relaxed over a cup of tea and a sook at his pipe, that reminded him that he had better take a packet of fags as it wasn't always convenient to blast pipe smoke all over the place, he still had a few packs of Willies duty free, he laid a couple on the sideboard to be picked up on his way out. Meg returned from the milking and remarked on the wonderful morning and how good it was to hear the skylarks twittering away and the blackbirds as they scurried back and forth to the hedge obviously they had nests full of young. Sandy started to get ready he would be wearing his sports jacket and flannels the black shoes were gleaming in their highly polished state, he left in time to catch the school bus eventually he should arrive in Turra for about eleven-o-clock Will would be waiting for him. On the way to town he had to endure quite a bit of cheek and comments from the teenage scholars, he very rarely used this bus but he was thinking that the behaviour was a lot different from his last journey, his first reaction was, some the older boys could have done with a good kick up the erse that would knock the bloody impudence out of them, he knew some of their parents and was sure they wouldn't be allowed to carry on like this at home , he was glad it was only about a twenty minute journey although quite a few of the pupils were polite and shouted cheerio when they left the bus one or two left a lot to be desired. He had to change buses and catch the Aberdeen service, it was about forty minutes but much more civilised as there was no youngsters on this service. By the time they reached Turra the bus was packed they had stopped at nearly every house and road end on the route some of the farming folks Sandy recognised from various other times they had met, but you could tell by the dress that they were all heading for a day out, probably their yearly treat. At the bus stop in the square the familiar six foot six frame of Big Will Watson was standing erect waiting to greet his young pal, he shook Sandy by the hand and asked if he had enjoyed his journey, Sandy said he had except for the cheek and impudence he had to endure on the school bus, their behaviour was appalling. Will decided they would be better to go up to his house and drop off Sandy's overnight bag and say hallo to Bell they might even manage a cup of tea it was early enough yet the show didn't really get going till afternoon but there was plenty for them to have a walk round and examine, the most up-to-date tractors and implements and of course the live stock, it would need a good bit of time to see all that, so it looked like a busy day ahead of them. After being shown where he would be sleeping and a cup of tea to wash down Bell Watson's home baked scone the two mates set off to the show ground, Bell said she would be down later as she hoped to meet up with some of the members of the WRI she asked Sandy if the Glen women were coming through but he had no idea Meg hadn't mentioned it. At the show ground quite a few people were already there, there was so much to view that it was hard to say where to start but the nearest to the gate was the live stock so they wandered round the pens, the judging was already in full swing, Sandy was overawed with the amount of cattle and the condition they were in it was amazing, there were plenty horses still being shown, the love of both Sandy and Wills lives they could have spent all day there.

Sandy was amazed at the number of people he knew the whole of the Glen must have taken the day off, they spent a further hour or so looking at the tractors and machinery, Sandy intimated that the stuff on show was for the big rich farmers the likes of him couldn't afford such luxuries. They finally arrived at the arts and craft tented area they would have a wander round and see where the various items came from, at the WRI tent one of the tables had items laid out from the Glen WRI Sandy had a look at some of the names and was surprised to see his sister Meg had won first prize for a decorated cake, he turned to Will and said "Very sneaky I never even saw her bake it" with that Betsy Wilson appeared she gave Sandy and Will a big hug and commented on Megs success as a baker, she told the men that George was in the showground somewhere she then asked Sandy if Meg was with him he told her no that she was at home, Sandy noticed a sort of smirk come over her face but she said nothing, as they were leaving she told them to come back later and have cup of tea with them. The parade of animals was due to start at two pm so the two some had ringside seats well in advance of the time it was a smashing day and up till then had been most enjoyable Sandy was enjoying his day out especially in the company of Big Will he was a very humorous man, as the parade finished they were both beginning to feel the heat and were quite thirsty so they decided to go back to the WRI tent and see if Betsy was still offering that cup of tea. Sandy was first to enter and was near bowled over when the first person he spotted was sister Meg, "Fit the hell are yea dein here"? He asked. "The very same as you she replied" "Bit I thought you were at hame looking efter the place" he said. She bent forward and put her mouth close to his ear and said " Sandy if I had said I was coming here you would have stayed at hame fit is there to steal aff the croft tell me, so jist you enjoy your break, am getting a lift hame we Valerie Tracy the young Lairds wife so I'll be hame in plenty time to milk the auld coo dinna worry aboot it" Sandy was left in no doubt that it was better if he said no more and got on with enjoying the rest of the show one item he was desperate to view was the final of the tug-of-war. The final turned out to be some contest pulled between a team of Gordon Highlander sojers and a team of young farmers from the Huntly area, Sandy mentioned to big Will it was a wonder Lang Dod didn't enter a team he would need to have a word wie him. After the tugging was over the two of them headed for Wills house where Bell would have some food ready they intended to be back at the Marquee in time for the dance music starting, after supper they set off but did a detour and went to the Commercial Hotel and had a couple of drams just to put them in the mood, the tent was huge Sandy was over awed by the sheer size the stage was empty apart from the musical instruments, the only one missing was the maestro Jimmy Shand's accordion, of course Will had to make a wise crack and said " They tell me he never tak's it aff and even sleeps wie it on." Dead on quarter-to-nine the whole place went silent as the spot light was trained on the stage the musicians trooped on took their places and waited as the man himself appeared to a rapturous standing ovation, Sandy couldn't believe he was such a small frail looking man and as bald as a coot. Within minutes they were playing Sandy was mesmerised he knew every tune they played and tapped his foot in time as his hero played tune after tune, then at ten-o-clock the music stopped and the compare spoke, he announced that the band would be having a break but a very special guest was here.

Ladies and Gentlemen we spare no expense on Turra Show Day to bring you nothing but the best, you have just heard the best Scottish Dance Band and now we bring you the best Button Key Accordion player in the world put your hand together for the one and only Will Starr, the drums rolled and the spotlight shone on the man himself dressed in full Highland Regalia he bounded onto the stage to a standing ovation, he bowed to the audience and waited while the Jimmy Shand band left for their break. He then hit the buttons and thrilled the dancers with a display of wizardry that only he could perform, The High Level Hornpipe, The Mist Covered Mountains and a host of others Sandy and Will Watson were thrilled he sounded even better than he did on the radio, he played for twenty minutes non-stop, then the Shand Band joined him and both Jimmy Shand and Will played duets on the box, finally Jimmy Shand asked Will Starr if he would join him playing his latest hit the Bluebell Polka what music, real entertainment. Finally for his last number he played probably his greatest hit the Jacqueline Waltz the dancers were going mental shouting for more, but he was holding up his hands and pointing as though they were painful, after and all he had given his all for fully an hour. The two friends were just thrilled Sandy had never enjoyed an evening so much and to be able to sit within twenty feet of his accordion hero's was just something he never ever dreamed of, it had been a long tiring day now near eleven-o-clock so they decided to head for home, Sandy needed to catch the first bus in the morning he had plenty work ahead of him when he got home, he went straight to bed and slept soundly until his usual time of five am that was just perfect he would be able to catch the quarter to seven bus and he should be home by ten am.

The summer passed without much excitement the family were doing well in their chosen fields of life, Willie would soon have spent ten years in Germany he had promised to try and get leave so that he would be home for Frankie Smiths roup, he also announced that Maria and him were planning getting engaged so their was the possibilities of another wedding in the Duncan family, their only fear was that it would take place in Sweden after and all it was Maria's home country. Both Jim and Betty had two bairns each but still no word of them coming home they had also been away for fifteen years, Meg missed them terribly. Mary was doing well in the army she was waiting to be promoted to full corporal and trying hard to get posted along with Willie, Peg was progressing well at the nursing and Tommy well nobody ever quite knew what he was up to he was a strange character very deep, his brother Sandy who had contributed to his upbringing was treated like public enemy number one the galling bit about it was Tommy would never discuss what the problem was, although Sandy had kept a tight reign on him he never dealt with him harshly just tried to bring him up as their parents would have done, on the other hand Meg spoiled him something rotten as did his twin sisters so they maybe undid what Sandy had tried to achieve. Lang Dod called for a committee meeting in the hall he wanted to find out what they could do in the way of a Christmas Party this year maybe try something different. There was a pantomime in Aberdeen maybe they could arrange a trip for the kids just a change away from the usual fare they produced, it was decided that enquiries would be made as to cost etc, the next on the agenda was an invite for the a tug-of-war team to attend a tournament up at Cawdor near Inverness.

Due to the short notice given by the Cawdor organisers the invitation had to be declined, it was the wrong time of year for the Glen people as they were very busy with harvesting so, a reply was sent thanking them for the invite but they would be better prepared next time. About two weeks after the Turriff Show Sandy was busy tidying around the croft when he noticed a police car driving up the farm track, he was always wary of the town Bobbies, as they never called unless they had police business to discuss. The car pulled up along side Sandy, the younger of the two in the car got out and asked if this was the home of the Duncan's of Hillside, Sandy nodded and said it was the young Bobby continued, " We wid like to speak to Thomas Duncan" " Oh said Sandy he's nae here he hardly ever bides here now-a-days" The Bobby continued " Well this is where he gave as his home address the night he was charged" Again Sandy exclaimed, "Oh! Fit wis he charged wie?" " Well he has a few charges against him drunk and disorderly, breach of the peace and using foul language to a police officer ". This sent Sandy reeling the last thing he wanted was involvement with the police he explained that Tommy stayed in a Bothy about three miles away. The policeman said he knew where it was and he also added that Tommy would be in bother because he was underage and shouldn't be drinking alcohol the Bobby said it was a fair charge sheet and he could expect the book to be thrown at him. As the policeman prepared to leave he said to Sandy " If I was you I would have word with your young brother about the company he keeps, they are a bad lot never out of trouble there's five of them and at least one of them is in court every week the same carry on all the time they get drunk pick on somebody and then a fight starts but one of these days they will pick on somebody that will dish out a right bloody hiding to them. With that the policemen left, Sandy was in shock his biggest problem was that the neighbours had seen the Bobbies car so word would soon get oot that young Tommy Hillies was up in coort, what a disgrace on the family, Sandy's stomach was churning as he entered the house to relay to sister Meg what the police had just told him and dash he had forgotten to ask what date the coort was not that he was that desperate to know, the way he felt he could strangle that young bugger Tommy he was the bane of Sandy's life. When Sandy explained to Meg why the police had called she had a session of weeping and wailing as she contemplated the idea of her young brother in jail, Sandy tried to pacify her by saying that as it was Tommy's first offence he would more than likely get away with a fine but he was running on thin ice as the sheriffs were talking about clamping down on under age drinkers and people causing disruption to law abiding citizens but they would just have to wait and see. Tommy's court appearance didn't take long to come round, he called in past Hillies to get a clean white shirt and his suit, Meg gave him a piece of her mind but felt it was doing no good, he did ask what Sandy was saying about it, Meg let him know Sandy was not pleased about it especially as the court case would be plastered all over the papers and he felt that was a disgrace, Tommy continued his devil may care attitude and his comment was, "Whits done is done and I'll just have to take whits coming to me." With that he left to catch the bus into town, Meg shouted after him to let her know how he got on she was up to high doh and real worried, but she seemed to be the only one.

Tommy and his four mates had a fairly arrogant stagger about them as they entered the Courthouse they were laughing and joking as they waited their turn to appear in front of the sheriff. The two youngest ones Tommy and his pal were called first. The police sergeant called them and lead the way into the court the old sheriff was seated in a sort of pulpit slightly higher than everybody else there were four other people sitting at a desk. The sheriff glared at them over his half moon glasses, their names were read out and they were identified, the sheriff then studied a sheet of paper in front of him he raised his head and looking at the two youths started to speak. " Mr Duncan and Mr Reid you are appearing in front of me to-day on very serious charges, five in total but you both seemed to think its a huge joke, this is according to the Court officer who has just told me that your behaviour in the waiting area is abominable laughing and joking and being very rude to the receptionist, Gentlemen do you think that this court appearance is some sort of joke" Both answered rather sheepishly "No Sir". The old sheriff was in no mood for joking and he laid down the law, he left both young men in no doubts that if they appeared in front of him again he would make sure there would be no third appearance. He told them that in view of the five charges against them he would be applying the maximum sentence he was allowed to give and that was to fine them both ten pounds, Tommy was in a bit of a sweat that was very nearly a month's wages the alternative was twenty one days in custody the fine had to be paid with-in twenty four hours, Tommy started to plead with the sheriff that he would find it difficult to get the money in twenty four hours and could he possibly extend the time for another day, the old sheriff had a word with one of his staff and reluctantly agreed to extend the time for an extra day. As Tommy left the courthouse the arrogant swagger had been knocked out of him he had to find Ten Pounds with-in forty eight hours considering his wages were less than four pounds a week and out of that he had to buy food, it looked like hard times ahead his mate was in the same boat at the moment between them they had just over ten shillings (50p). The other three men got even stiffer sentences as they were fined fifteen pounds each the sheriff held them responsible for leading the younger ones a stray and encouraging them to drink alcohol they were over eighteen so the underage drinking didn't apply, it would be a few weeks before any of them would be able to afford another drink. Tommy decided to go home to Hillside he would be a day short in his wages this week so times looked even bleaker, he walked up the croft road rather sheepishly hoping his brother Sandy wasn't at home, everything looked quiet as he opened the door and crept in Meg didn't hear him enter so she let out a squeal when she realised she was not alone, " Tommy she scolded yea nearly made me jump oot oh ma skin, creepin in on me like that". Tommy shrugged his shoulders and said sorry, she then anxiously asked how he got on in court so he told her, then asked if Sandy was at home, she told him Sandy was away working for Lang Dod and wouldn't be home till supper time, she then asked if he was hungry as usual Tommy was starving so Meg heated some soup for him he soon wolfed down two helpings and some slices of bread.

Tommy was near to tears as he poured his heart out to his sister, he had to find Ten Pounds with-in forty-eight hours or he would be arrested and sent to the jile for twenty one days, he was beside himself with worry about finding the money and also what Sandy would have to say about it. Meg asked how much money he had; he said he could possibly find four pounds. Meg didn't want to give the impression that she was a soft touch so she made him sweat a bit, he asked her what Sandy would say if he asked him for the money, Meg exclaimed Tommy I wid hate to tell you what Sandy would say he is suffering enough as it is, he has hardly slept for the past week worrying about you. Meg disappeared to her bed room and when she returned she had six pounds in her hand she handed the money to Tommy and told him she wanted it back with-in a month as it was savings for her next trip to Aberdeen she hastily added that she hoped that this would be a lesson to him and that she never again would need to pay money to take him out of a hole he had dug for himself, he had a tear running down his cheek as he gave his sister a hug and thanked her. He caught the next bus back to town so that he could pay his fine he didn't want to have another day off work. Sandy arrived home from work, Meg told him how Tommy had got on in the court but she never let dab that she had help pay the fine the less Sandy knew at the moment the better.

Jockie Mitchell the post had only weeks to go before retirement but his gossip mechanism was in good working order and there was plenty to gossip about that morning, the headlines of the daily paper told the story of Tommy Duncan and his cronies and how the sheriff had thrown the book at them. Sheriff applies maximum sentence on young teen age drunken hooligans, Jockie was having a field day and could hardly contain himself as he neared Hillies he was hoping that Meg would collect the mail, what an opportunity this would be to wind her up. As he pulled up in the Hillside yard he was disappointed to see Sandy striding over to the van, but it didn't matter Sandy would do fine. " Aye a bet you Hillies fowk are feelin important the day its nae everyday yea get the headlines oh the papers." Sandy asked what he was talking about, Jockie held up the paper making sure Sandy would get a good look at the headline. SHERIFF IMPOSES MAXIMUM SENTENCE ON YOUNG TEENAGE DRUNKEN HOOLIGANS. Sandy grabbed the paper from the gloating postman and with his face very nearly touching his tormentor told him to get his van and himself as far away from Hillies as he could as he Sandy would not be responsible for his actions as the van sped away he shouted, "thankfully we wont have to put up wie yae much longer yea bloody auld sweetie wife" , Sandy was stamping his foot with rage he had never been so humiliated in his life and when he read the article in the paper it did not amuse him that Tommy had given Hillside as his home address. He handed Meg the paper and told her to have a read he was sick and disgusted his young brother had let the whole family down and what got to Sandy more than anything he didn't seem to be unduly worried about it, as they discussed the incident Sandy pointed out that should Tommy land in any more bother he was libel to be sent to a borstal, he continued " But can you blame the sheriff ? it is his job to make sure decent law abiding citizens are allowed to go about their business without being pestered by young boys drunk and spewing all over the place its jist getting oot oh hand" .

Tommy and Sandy didn't cross paths until about six weeks after the court case, Sandy was working away in the shed when he heard to sound of a bike passing he popped his head out the door and was surprised to see his young brother, Tommy was taken a back he was hoping Sandy would be away working but no he would have to face the music, "Weel, weel yea div mind that this is your hame address, I don't suppose your here to apologise for the disgrace your sister and me have had to pit up wie because of your selfish child minded carry on, don't tell me your proud of your achievements", Tommy hung his head and said nothing while Sandy ranted on for a further five minutes and finally tried to point out the error of Tommy's ways. Tommy still said nothing finally Sandy asked if he could explain why he had such an ill will at him as he doesn't re-call ever doing any harm to him, as a parting shot he said, " In fact your sister Meg and Me have been dammed good tae yae but the thanks we are getting for it leaves a lot to be desired", with that he stamped off leaving Tommy standing, as Tommy entered the kitchen Meg was surprised to see him as she thought he should be working but he said he was going back to work but called in to give her the final instalment of the money she had lent him, she asked if he would stay for dinner but he declined saying that the mood Sandy was in it would be better if the two of them kept well apart, Meg burst into tears and grabbed Tommy in a bear hug, with tears streaming down her face she sobbed, " Tommy, Tommy whits geen wrang, Sandy and you just canna stand the sicht oh een an ither that's nae the wye families shid cairy oan can yea nae jist forget the past and try and agree wie ane anither". Tommy again remained silent he had no wish to bury the hatchet, Sandy and him could not agree and that was that. He handed Meg her money and was on his way she was still sobbing as he cleared the road end and headed back to his job in the forest. Sandy entered the house he could see Meg was upset and he braced himself for the onslaught he fully expected, if Tommy had told her about the blazing row they had just had, but no there was no mention of it just that he had, had a brief conversation with him but as usual he didn't get much cuttings.

The year was moving on all the harvest was successfully stored for the winter the first big highlight of the autumn was the Frankie Smith roup and the following week Davie Fraser's roup, Frankie told Sandy to take anything he wished from the croft, but apart from some bits and pieces there was nothing Frankie had any better than Sandy already had so he didn't take much but offered to help to set up the items for sale everything was going Frankie had half a dozen tea chests with some keep sakes and clothes other wise it was going under the hammer, Sandy was quite sad as he helped his good neighbour dispose of his worldly possessions, the two of them had been neighbours all their lives it would be a huge wrench and the house was to remain empty for the time being anyway. The Saturday of the roup arrived and there was quite a good turn out of people a lot of collectors were attending the roups and buying up all the antique items but they were only interested if it was knock down prices they didn't like spending, the sale went reasonably well the highest price was paid for the pair of horses he received just on one hundred pounds for them. It took precisely two and half-hours to dispose of Frankie's lifetime achievements and before the end of the day he would know how much it was worth.

Frankie had worked the croft for fifteen years he was now thirty-eight years of age, his final bank statement after all his debts had been paid was three hundred and twelve pounds, as he discussed it with Sandy he reminded him that when they got to Corby he would have to furnish a house and re-cloth the family as they were starting a new school, they also had the expense of transporting themselves and their possessions to Corby, so he expected to make a big hole in his bank account. On the plus side he had a job to start so they should be earning with-in a week of arriving. Meg had laid on a meal for the Smiths they had a long journey ahead of them but Jean Smith had made up food and flasks of hot tea for them to eat on the way. As Sandy and Meg stood waving goodbye to their ex neighbours they couldn't but help wondering who would go next the crofting population was down to nine, some of the croft houses had been taken over but the type of people who rented them weren't Glen Folks and just didn't have the same interests in what was going on around them.

The year was passing quickly it was halfway through November. Davie Fraser's roup was the next weekend it would follow the same trend as the Smiths did, Davie was retiring he was over seventy, the wife and him had managed to get a cottage on the outskirts of town, so it was another resident lost to the Glen his croft was gobbled up by the Bremner cartel and the house left empty, it was really a depressing time but this was all in the name of progress. The Estate Trustees informed Meg that Hillies would have its bathroom and electricity installed before Hogmanay. She received a letter from brother Willie telling them that Maria and him had more or less fixed a date for their forthcoming wedding it was around Easter and would be held in Stockholm Maria's home city he wanted as many of the family there as possible, Meg shook her head and thought he's nae asking for much. Mary was now stationed in Germany and was in Willie and Maria's company quite often, she had managed to get leave over Hogmanay so herself and Peg would be at home which was something for the Hillies ones to look forward to. They could also discuss Willie's forthcoming wedding, who would be able to attend etc, Meg was quite concerned as she had never been past Aberdeen before and was already apprehensive about the journey, but no point in worrying it was a few months away yet.

The next item on the agenda for that year was the retirement presentation, three more leading lights of the community were to disappear before the year was up, the arrangements had been made to hold an evening similar to the one held when the threshing mill operators retired it was decided to hold it, the first week in December. As usual it was a Saturday evening and they were assured of a big turn out. Jim Kerr had been the local minister for over thirty years he was a well loved man and a friend to the crofting community he would be a big loss, but his son also an ordained minister had been chosen to succeed his father. Young Jim was a son of the Glen he was ages with Jim Duncan and he had done his time at the front line during the war, his horizons reached far beyond the Glen he would settle in to where his father would vacate at the end of the year. Dr Bill Findlay was also going he had semi retired a year earlier but had worked with his daughter in an advisory capacity he too was calling it a day. The third was Jockie Wilson the postie he was over retiring age, so he was also hanging up his post bag.

Although often despised because he poked his nose into everybody else's business Jockie the post would be sadly missed, he delivered everybody's daily paper this was a favour not known to his bosses at headquarters, he was also very obliging if anybody needed a message from town Jockie would always help if possible. It was well known that Meg Duncan and Jockie had an ongoing feud, it was never very serious a lot of one-upmanship, one trying to out do the other but it had lasted for years although Jockie had offered to bury the hatchet, it was often the highlight of her day to have a tare with the postie. Betsy Wilson gave her spiel about how Jockie would be sadly missed and she added we have a special friend of Jockie's to present his retrial gifts; I am now calling on Miss Margaret Duncan to do the honours the place erupted, Meg nearly fainted it was the last thing on earth she expected, there was no get out, much and all as she hated the limelight she had to take part in the spirit of the evening, Jockie never had a better chance to give Meg a red face as she walked across the stage he grabbed hold of her and gave her a kiss right full smack on the lips the audience were going wild, finally to show there was no hard feelings they gave each other a huge hug after the presentation, the hall was cleared ready for the evening's entertainment as usual it was started off by Lang Dod giving his repertoire of the old Corn Kisters. Nine-o-clock and they were ready for the dancing this was mostly the old Scottish Dances, they seemed to get the crowd up on their feet young and old, once again the evening was slightly blighted by young men who were the worse of drink being a nuisance and of course vomiting around the outside of the hall it was becoming a bad habit but the committee were at a loss wondering how to tackle the root of the problem, worse was maybe just round the corner as the new hotel was supposed to open in time for Hogmanay so there would be instant alcohol on their door step shortly, what a thought. The end of the year was closing in fast four weeks away Meg would be busy getting everything in order for her sister's arrival, she had posted her parcels to Canada and New Zealand how she longed to see her nephews and nieces but at the moment it was not possible, Tommy would celebrate his seventeenth birthday on the fourteenth of December she would try and get in contact with him and see if he would come over for his dinner, she was hoping for miracles but she could only but try, she reminded Sandy about Tommy's birthday but she would have just as well not have bothered as all she got was a grunt, so she thought to herself one is as bad as the other. The residents committee decided that they would follow the same pattern as last year and take the kids on a day out to Aberdeen where they would see the pantomime it had been a popular choice last year so why not repeat it, some of the older folks were a bit upset as they looked forward to their yearly concert, well some of them fancied their selves as budding actors, but this was progress get rid of all the old fashioned ways of living and in with the new even though they were no better than what folks were used to, Meg was all for it she had been saving for ages and had a nice wee nest egg to spend on presents. Sandy had everything under control he had time on his hands as the casual work had dried up over the winter, he could have done with the cash as he had to pay the first instalment of his plumbing in May so every penny would be needed. His old buddy Will Watson had told him that he doubted if he would be back to supply music he was having problems with his hips and his back, sad fact the ageing process doesn't come alone.

Tommy's seventeenth was on the Sunday, on the Saturday evening along with a couple of work mates he decided to visit the Cinema in town, they watched the film starring Burt Lancaster and Deborah Kerr and left the picture house about quarter to eight the idea was that they would attend the dance in the town hall and get the last bus home. But as often happens one of the company had a good idea, seeing it was Tommy's birthday to-morrow why not go to the pub before going to the dance just a couple of drinks and that would be it. Tommy reminded them that he was underage and had already been in bother with the law, but the big boys assured him if he kept his head down nobody would bother him so easily led Tommy took their advice. In the pub one of the older boys aged over eighteen ordered the drinks, Tommy said he would only have a sweet stout, after his second one he was persuaded to have a short his mate told him to have a Cherry Brandy saying it was a wifies drink and would have little effect on him. It was his first try at Cherry Brandy and he liked the taste so the sweet stout was abandoned and he downed about half-a-dozen C.Bs, by now he was fleein and was just about to leave the pub when two huge men in diced caps stopped him and recognised him from his last escapade, Tommy looked round for his mates but they had legged it leaving Tommy at the mercy of the local constabulary, he was well and truly blootered so the coppers decided seeing he was alone and legless they had no other choice but lock him up for the night. It was still dark when Tommy came to life he peered around him but had no idea where he was, his head was bursting and he felt bloody awful he tried to stand up but he was still very much under the influence, suddenly he heard a rattling noise and could just make out the outline of a door suddenly there was a shaft of light shining through a slot like a letter box Tommy could just make out a pair of eyes, " Where am I"? He asked, the anonymous voice answered, "In the jile are yea aw richt"? "Aye nae very weel but aw richt" the voice then asked if he would like a cup of tea, Tommy eagerly accepted then looked at his watch it was quarter past six still dark and no sign of a light. The bloody jile he muttered, he had no recollection of getting here, he sat up on the bunk it was as hard as a concrete floor, suddenly the door opened and the cell was flooded with light his head and eyes were liking to burst, the policemen with the cup of tea was full of the joys of spring he had just started his shift so he was bright and breezy, he told Tommy he needed to get a mop and bucket of water and clean up the spewings he had left in the corridor and also the cell floor, Tommy had a close look and as sure as death his last meal before his inebriation was scattered over the floor, this was the last thing he needed to see as he started to retch again, the officer told him he would be required to give a statement later on as he was in no fit state to give one last night. Tommy asked when he would be able to go home he was severely shaken when told he would be appearing in court on Monday morning after that he would be free to go depending on his sentence, the copper added "Bearing in mind its nae yir first offence is it." Tommy shook his head disgusted with himself and answered No. He near leapt out of his skin as the bobby slammed the cell door the clanging near drove Tommy demented. He drank his tea and lay back on the bunk he was trying to fathom out what went wrong then he remembered his mate saying that Cherry Brandy was a wifies drink Tommy thought they must be hardy buggers to waken up feeling like he was after a night on the C.B.

Chapter Nineteen

TOMMY WAS SO ILL HE WAS coukin (retching) and nothing was coming up the stench in the little cell was overpowering along with the urine from the enamel chantey it was hard to stomach he was tossing and turning in the bunk trying to get comfortable when the door clanged open once again and a huge police sergeant entered, he looked at Tommy and asked if he was ok, Tommy groaned and said he wis nae bad the sergeant started to give him a bit of a lecture about how bloody stupid he had been. He told Tommy to get on his feet and get his mess from the night before cleaned up pointing out there was a bucket and a mop in the cupboard along the passage. Still trying to throw up Tommy cleaned up the passage and his cell he then had a wash and felt a lot better, he could hear movement in the other cells so he wasn't alone, he heard the Sergeant speaking to one of the other inmates they were on first name terms so he must have been a regular visitor, there was more clattering and banging this was caused by a middle aged woman with a trolley she was dishing up some breakfast, Tommy was beginning to feel a bit peckish so he ate a plate of nearly cold porridge and had another cup of tea, along with it he had his first fag of the day, this he had to ask for as all his belongings had been confiscated the night before. He lay back on his bunk and started to think of the predicament he was in no doubt they would throw the book at him in court and then he had to face his brother Sandy, he began to feel quite depressed and annoyed with himself for being so stupid he needed to get his act together, he had just finished paying his sister back the money for his last fine and here he was on the brink of receiving his second or so he hoped, the thought of having to go to jile was driving him crazy he looked at his watch it was exactly twelve minutes since he looked at it last time and worse than that it was only nine-o-clock how the time was dragging. About an hour later Tommy was called to the interview room, he had been unable togive a statement the previous evening due to his state of intoxication it was his sergeant friend along with a young constable, the old sergeant put Tommy at ease he was quite a fatherly sort of man, he asked Tommy if he wanted the police to inform his father and mother about his whereabouts, Tommy shook his head and with tears welling up in his eyes he explained that he was an orphan but his older brother and sister had brought him up he even explained that his brother Sandy and him hardly ever spoke they didn't seem to like each other, the officer asked what had gone wrong last night for Tommy to get in the state he was in, he explained that he had gone to the pictures with two older workmates and that they had suggested they go for a drink before going to the dance. The sergeant stated to speak, "Well Thomas I don't think much of your workmates, they filled you full of drink knowing full well you are underage and when they spotted the police approaching they baled out and left you, some mates would agree" Tommy nodded his head which was hanging in embarrassment. Now you are being charged with being drunk and incapable and also for drinking below the permitted age of eighteen, according to our records this is your second offence in the last six weeks, I'm afraid the Sheriff will take a dim view of this behaviour its hard to say how he will react. He then read out the charges and told Tommy he would remain in custody until to-morrow morning and he would appear in court at ten am, his final words were " Just pray you don't get the same sheriff as you had six weeks ago, a different one might take a different view.

With that over Tommy was returned to his cell the door was left open so he could move about if he wanted, later in the day somebody handed him a Sunday Post so that kept him reading for ages. Eventually he got fed up reading so he lay down and closed his eyes it was still at least an hour till midday he would be mental before to-morrow morning if this is what the jile is like he would rather give it a miss, with his eyes closed he began to think it was time to do some forward planning if he hung about here he would only end up in more trouble, that would be curtains as from tomorrow he would have two convictions against his name and who knows it could be borstal if the Sheriff decides that Tommy is playing silly buggers he would have to wait and see, but his mind was made up he would be moving on and he was going to keep it to himself. Later in the day a middle-aged woman brought him some food he was very grateful as his hangover was getting better and he was feeling peckish once again.

After a very boring day and night it was time to get ready for his court appearance, along with three others he was shown into the Black

Maria and driven to the town house where the court was held as he climbed the steps his heart was pounding, this was it make or break time. Tommy was third in line so it was longer to worry he would have preferred to go first and get it over with, the first middle aged guy was a habitual offender his forty second offence he was sentenced to twenty eight days custody, the second was a first offender fined five pounds he was only drunk and incapable but he was legal age. Thomas Duncan his name was called the adrenalin was pumping he felt giddy as he followed the court officer, as they entered the room his name was again announced so that all could hear. Tommy had a quick look at the bench and sighed with relief when he noticed that there was a different sheriff, here's hoping. He may have been different but he had all Tommy's particulars in front of him and laid into him in other words he threw the book at him, he was concerned that Tommy was treating his court appearances with contempt. Tommy apologised and said this latest misdemeanour had been a stupid mistake on his part he had been easily led astray but he should have known better. The sheriff hummed and hawed and consulted one of his minions and finally made up his mind. Thomas Duncan I had serious thoughts about sending you to borstal but I am blaming your thoughtless friends for getting you in the state you were in on Saturday evening and more so for running away like cowards when they saw the police approaching, so I will give you one final chance and will impose the maximum fine for a second conviction which is fifteen pounds you have twenty eight days to pay. Tommy said thank you sir and walked from the courtroom he was pretty shocked fifteen pounds would be hard to find even with twenty eight days grace. But he was determined to get out of the rat race he was living in and he made his way to the Labour Exchange, the young lady at the reception asked how she could help, Tommy explained that he was looking for a job, she asked if he was working as this would make a difference to what forms he would need to fill in. She told him to have seat and someone would be with him as soon as possible while waiting Tommy had a look at the situation vacant board there was hardly anything local but a few out with his home area so he started to browse, Corby seemed to be the big employer but it was all inside work Tommy didn't fancy that but the next one jumped out at him. Timber contractor requires experienced person to work in remote part of the Highlands that looked just perfect.

Ten minutes later his name was called and he was shown into a booth the young woman took out some forms and started to fill them in she asked Tommy if he had registered for his National Service which he hadn't so she said she would do that with him to-day, after the paper work was complete she asked what kind of job he was looking for and in which area, he pointed out the job in the Highlands on the vacancy board. She went to a filing cabinet and pulled out a folder and returned to her seat. She started to read the card and then read it out to Tommy " Men with forestry experience wanted to work in Achnashellach cutting dragging and loading timber, only experienced people need apply a fifty hour week is worked and there is Bothy accommodation provided" Tommy said that sounded fine but what were the wages? She turned the card and read what was in front of her at seventeen the wages are three shillings an hour (15 pence) over eighteen and it is three and thrupence (15.5p), he thought for a minute and worked it out, that was much better then he was getting, now his next question where is Achnashellach, the only thing she could tell him was that he needed to take the bus to Inverness and then the Kyle train to Achnashellach, that all sounded straight forward. The lady in the dole office said she had a phone number and she would give a ring, this turned out to be of not much use as it was an office in Inverness, but they gave her a phone number that Tommy could phone after six-o-clock in the evening so armed with this number he set off home to Hillies he would need to tell Meg of his week-end escapade before Sandy read all about it in tomorrows paper. As he expected Meg was totally knocked out with what he told her she was weeping and trying to find out why he was so stupid, one thing he was delighted about was that Sandy was away at work so the dust would have settled before he had to face him, Megs biggest worry was if he had enough money to pay his fine she offered to help but Tommy told her to hold off until he had a chance to work things out, he still had an ace up his sleeve if he got this other job he was sure he would manage to pay the fine before the twenty eight days were up. Tommy got away from Hillside as soon as he could and managed to work the afternoon his boss was a bit iffy about him missing the morning but he said he was feeling unwell, he was then reminded he wouldn't get paid for the morning, Tommy was hoping he got the job he was phoning about to-night then he would tell this miserable bugger where to stick his job just wait and see, the two workmates that had abandoned him on Saturday evening were very quiet probably feeling guilty. After he had his supper Tommy cycled to the nearest phone box it was about the second time in his life using a phone so he was far from confident. He put his money in the box and dialled the number given to him by the lady in the dole office he could hear it ringing then somebody picked up the receiver Tommy pressed button A and this voice said " Achnashellach Hotel how can I help"? Tommy started stammering and stuttering he said he thought he had dialled a wrong number the female at the other end asked what number he had dialled he told her and she said that this was the number he had dialled. She then asked who he wanted to speak to Tommy told her it was Mr Hugh Mackay the Timber Contractor "Oh yea mean Gimpy he's the only Timber man here". Next moment the side of Tommy's head nearly exploded as she bawled out Giimpee and in a normal tone said " He's on his way" Tommy could hear her tell the man its for you Gimpy.

" Hi Gimpy here wha's speakin" Tommy was very nervous as he explained who he was and why he was phoning, after giving his particulars and his experience working with a horse Gimpy asked how old he was, although Tommy had only celebrated his seventeenth birthday he thought it would sound better if he said he would be eighteen next birthday. Gimpy sounded ok on the phone but he did let Tommy know he hoped he was as experienced as he was telling him and also pointed out that Achnashellach was pretty remote Tommy assured him that the remoteness wouldn't bother him and he had been brought up in the country and had been around horses all his life. They made a deal; and Gimpy told Tommy to make his way to Achnashellach on the third of January and he would meet him at the hotel he said the train got in about five-o-clock. Tommy was on a high as he cycled back to his Bothy he had cracked it, he now had to tell his present boss that he would be finishing at the end of the month, but he was sure he would be told to go right away his boss was a very spiteful man, but Tommy would wait until the last minute to tell him as he needed another weeks wages the thought of this fine was weighing heavy on his mind. He suddenly struck on a plan if he didn't tell anybody where he was going he could delay paying the fine until he had the money, that's what he would do and anyhow he wasn't telling any lies as he had no forwarding address. Tommy gave in his notice and as he had predicted his boss was down right nasty and told Tommy just to take his belonging and go, this left Tommy in a bit of a predicament his only option was to eat humble pie and ask for ten days lodgings with his folks at Hillside. Meg was busy baking in the kitchen when Tommy appeared he crept up behind her causing her to near jump out of her skin, she asked what he was doing home at this time of day. He told her how he had been treated by his boss but Meg who had been in school with him said, " That's to be expected of him he was a big ignorant bugger when we were in school in fact I am surprised you managed to stick with him for so long but wait till I lay my tongue on him he'll ken all aboot it. Tommy said he's nae worth bothering aboot, he then broke the news about moving to the Heilans Meg was flabbergasted and as usual gave a display of her deep emotional feelings, Tommy pointed out that he would have to go sooner or later as his time for National Service was coming up shortly. Meg gathered herself together and put the kettle on, Tommy then asked what she thought Sandy would have to say about him being at home. Meg turned on her younger brother and told him, "Tommy whit ever you may think Hillies is your hame and until your eighteen Sandy and me are responsible for you, he will be more than delighted to see you have come hame but he is likely to have a go at you about that story that was in last weeks paper, Sandy was very hurt and upset about that so it may be in order for you to apologise to him for the embarrassment you caused us, as was usual Tommy went quiet. But secretly Meg was in her element she was having five of the family over the Hogmanay including herself and Sandy so it should be just like old times, she pointed this out to Tommy and she hoped he would join in the spirit of Hogmanay and try and show Sandy some respect because as far as she was concerned there had never been any visible reason for them to be at loggerheads. Mary and Peg would be arriving on the thirtieth but she had no idea what time. She had been very busy preparing beds and food and of course she had spent a day in Aberdeen with the bairns at the pantomime.

Although Sandy and Tommy weren't exactly bosom pals they seemed to be getting on a lot better than they had in the past, Tommy even giving his big brother a hand with the cattle. The thirtieth arrived and it was getting late there was quite a lot of snow about so maybe the girls would be delayed, suddenly there was bit of a commotion in the yard and a big car stopped just outside the back door, Meg had a look out and was taken aback to see her young sister Mary behind the steering wheel she called Sandy and Tommy and the five of them had bit of jig at the back door, Sandy commented on the car Mary said it was hired from a garage in Aberdeen and added, " Sandy this is the only way to travel now-a-days", they grabbed their luggage and all trooped inside, it was hard to get a word in edgeways as they all seemed to be talking at the same time. Meg soon had the kettle boiling and they all sat down to a cup of tea and some home baked scones, Mary then proceeded to tell them about Willies forthcoming wedding, they then had a discussion about who would be able to attend, Sandy counted himself out as he had the animals on the croft to tend too he also suggested that Meg should go after and all she was Willies twin sister, Tommy counted himself out as he said he would be unable to afford the trip, Mary and Peg were definatly going so at least there would be three sisters giving their brother moral support. It was into the early hours before the Duncan girls retired to their beds, over a glass of sherry they had put the world to rights, discussed many things that happened to them, of course Mary had the most exciting life of the three of them she loved staying in Germany and she spent much of her time off with big brother Willie he had an apartment in Berlin. Mary reminded them that their brother was an important chappie in the British Army being involved with the Russians, Americans and the French, Mary told them that Willie could speak French and German as good as any native. Meg had a wee touch of envy as she listened to the life her twin sisters were leading, it made hers feel like gloom and doom and with the decline in population in the Glen nothing really exciting ever happened, she had received a Christmas card from the Smith family in Corby they were doing well for themselves the ones who were old enough to work had jobs, Sandy and Meg just plodded on trying to scrape a living from the bleak landscape called Hillies. The new hotel had been opened for a week they were having a bit of a doo on the Saturday evening, Spud Thomson the owner had invited Sandy to come and play some music he said he would pay him for it but Sandy being Sandy told him seeing they were newly opened he would do it for nothing. So on Hogmanay night a new format was set for the Duncan's they all went to the pub, that was except Tommy he had made a pledge to himself that drink would never blight his life again, another deciding factor was lack of money he needed to pay fares and probably have a lying week at his new job so he had to be careful he still had three weeks to find the fifteen pounds for his fine. The new pub was heavin and quite few of the punters were under the weather before the nine-o-clock closing time Spud would have liked to keep open a while longer but he had a licence to think about. Sandy had mixed feeling about how he had spent his latest Hogmanay evening from what he could see many of the younger locals were drunk and it was doubtful if they would see in the New Year, this being the whole idea of staying up late on the thirty- first. Tommy had the kettle boiling for them when they got home so they had some tea while they awaited the bells.

Mary had brought some duty free booze home with her so she opened a bottle of whisky and one of brandy, they had a couple as they sat blethering, at the stroke of midnight the sound of shot guns being fired brought the family to the back door where they witnessed about half-a-dozen people blasting away, it lasted about ten minutes before it all went silent, by two am the last of the Duncan's had gone to bed, New years morning to Sandy was like the other three hundred and sixty four mornings of the year he had hungry cattle to feed.

Meg had her usual banquet prepared for the New Years dinner she had fattened up a turkey this year, Mary had brought home some crackers so they all finished up wearing daft hats with the slogans in German, after the meal Mary produced the brandy bottle and they had an after dinner drink. Sandy found this to be more of a sleeping draught than anything else, he was soon snoring his head off until Mary shook him awake and said they were going for a walk although reluctant he put his boots on and really enjoyed the fresh air. They just managed home from the walk before darkness fell, one of the girls suggested a game of cards, and Meg declined as she had supper to get ready so the other four had a game of whist waiting until suppertime. After supper Sandy was listening to the wireless when they heard a commotion at the back door, Peg went to the door and was delighted to see some of their old school pals they were here on a first footing mission she noticed there was strong smell of booze so they must have been drinking on the way, they piled into the house Meg produced glasses and Sandy opened a bottle of whisky, before too long Sandy was requested to get the box out and give them some music, four hours later the first footers left some of them slightly more worse of the wear than they had been on arrival, but there was no doubt they had cheered the place up.

On the third of January Tommy was up early packing his bits and pieces, Mary said she would drive him into town to catch the Inverness bus, Meg said she wanted to come as well so they set off the roads were not too clever as it had been snowing. They arrived in plenty time and as usual Meg was fussing about checking this and that she asked Tommy for an address which he truthfully couldn't give her as he didn't know himself, but promised faithfully he would let her know as soon as he could, just as he was about to board the bus Meg handed him an envelope and told him to put it in his pocket, she then grabbed hold of him and much to his embarrassment started to hug and kiss him at the same time howling her eyes out, he finally prised himself free gave Mary a hug and a kiss and boarded the bus before Meg got hold of him again, she was still waving as the bus disappeared round the corner at the end of the street, she then burst into a real heavy sobbing session wailing that she hoped he would be all right. Mary got her back in the car and told her straight that everyone of the family had left home at seventeen Willie and Jim to fight in a war all Tommy would be doing was working among trees just about a hundred miles away so what was all the fuss aboot. Meg was still sobbing as they drove along the road to Hillies she couldn't help herself Tommy had been with her since he was a toddler the rest of the family were older but Tommy was different he could be so easily led and did silly things. But Mary the hard case, full corporal Military Police told her sister that her young brother would have to get a grip and stand on his own two feet and if he was daft enough to get into bother hell mend him the problem with the young ones now-a-days they were mollycoddled.

Tommy was quite excited as the bus sped along the road he was now into unfamiliar territory the farthest he had been from home, Portsoy he had heard of it but had never been there before it was the same with all the little villages they passed through they all looked the same with a main street and small harbour so he settled down to enjoy the next three hours it would take to get to Inverness, he suddenly remembered the envelope his sister had handed him as he boarded the bus. He slit it open and near collapsed, inside a card nestled three five pound notes and a message when you get on your feet you can pay me back it was enough to pay his fine what a gem Meg could be at times he was quite emotional about it and a shudder ran through him as he wondered if he had made the right move, he folded the envelope and put it back in his pocket, he was off the hook but he was determined he would not send the money to the Sheriffs office until two days before it was due. Tommy settled down and was quite fascinated with the scenery he had just left the town of Buckie and was well into unfamiliar territory, soon he was admiring the huge flat fields of Morayshire what a contrast to the rugged rock strewn fields that Sandy tried to scrape a living from back in the Glen, there was quite a deep covering of snow so the fields all looked the same although he could tell by the length of the fences that the fields were huge flat areas. About an hour and a quarter later they pulled into the town of Elgin on the way in he had noticed Pinfield Army Barracks with an armed sentry at the gate he would soon get a taste of army life as he was due for call up later this year. They set off again and passed through various villages and towns like Forres and Aulderan on to Nairn still the fields were flat but due to the snow there was not much activity. Finally two and three quarter hours after leaving home he arrived in Inverness another mind boggling change had occurred to the landscape as Tommy viewed hills and mountains for the first time he was captivated, Inverness was surrounded by hills what a magnificent view. He got off the bus picked up his luggage and headed for the train station to find out the time of the train to Achnashellach, he had plenty time on his hands the train didn't leave until four fifteen, that would suit Tommy fine as his new boss said he would see him at the hotel at the back of five. Tommy went away exploring he was badly in need of something to eat so he found a chip shop and for 5/- (25p) he had a slap up feed of fish chips bread butter and tea he made it last as it was warmer than standing around the station he began to wonder if the man would be waiting for him when he arrived he was a little apprehensive, totally now in alien territory. The train held Tommy quite fascinated it was the first time he had been close to a steam train it was hissing and sizzling as it got ready for the journey to Kyle Of Lochalsh, exactly four fifteen the engine burst into life the train was quite busy with quite a lot of men carrying small suitcases some of them seemed to be quite drunk and very noisy luckily Tommy was in a carriage with an elderly couple and two teenage girls so apart from them chatting to each other it was quite peaceful, the biggest disappointment for Tommy was that it was pitch dark so he had no idea what the scenery looked like. The train halted at every station, at most of them more men boarded again all carrying small cases, after stopping at Dingwall the elderly man commented that the men with the cases were Hydro Workers going back after the week-end most likely they would be going on nightshift later in the evening.

At Garve station the old man was proved correct most of the men got off the train and disappeared along the platform, Tommy could just make out some buses in the car park no doubt waiting to transport the men to their work camps. Before long they had stopped at Achnasheen, next stop was the one Tommy was waiting for, they pulled into a small station and the guard shouted anybody for Achnashellach leave the train now, Tommy had a huge knot in his stomach as he got off the train into the chill evening it was quite frosty. He made his way to the hotel and entered he told the young lady at the desk he was here to meet a Mr Hugh Mackay " Is that Gimpy Mackay by any chance" " Aye that's what they call him I think" replied Tommy, " My names Wendy" she said extending her hand for Tommy to shake, " General Dogs Body about this place" she continued. " Gimpys' nae here at the moment but he will be shortly jist take a seat and wait in here its fine and warm will I get yea a cup of tea?" Tommy said that would be smashing and thanked her she seemed a real friendly sort. With-in ten minutes the door burst open and Tommy had no need to ask who entered the first sighting of Gimpy made Tommy think he would have been more aptly named if they had called him corkscrew he never seen a man so badly disabled in his life and still walking about. Gimpy shuffled over to where Tommy was standing and grabbed him by the hand he looked him over and said, " Grand to meet you Thomas I see you're a fine lump of a chiel did yea have a good journey" Tommy shook his hand firmly and said the journey had been ok. Hugh then said he was going into the bar for his daily medicine, which was a nip and a half pint he downed them in no time at all and motioned for Tommy to follow him, in the car park stood an old Ford van they piled aboard and drove about a mile mostly through a wooded area finally they came to a couple of wooden huts one was Tommy's Bothy the other was a make shift stable for a horse, Hugh told him to dump his case in the Bothy then he could come and meet the Gimpy family, he then explained that he had been in an accident many years ago and this was the reason for his physical shape. Now you ken why they call me Gimpy and as is the custom in the west coast if one of the family had a nickname quite often this was the name the whole family were referred to, so Hugh MacKay's family were called the Gympie's . With-in minutes they had arrived at a bigger Bothy it looked like it possibly had three or four rooms, as the old van drew to a halt the Bothy door burst open, he had a squad of kids hugging and kissing him like he had been away for days . He turned to Tommy and said "Thomas meet the young Gympie's" he started to rattle off their names and they all shouted simultaneously please to meet you Thomas. That formality over Hugh said to Tommy "Now Thomas come and meet the most important Gimpy of them all Martha the wife" Tommy was in for a further shock Martha turned out to be a huge woman about sixteen stone, she was wearing bib and brace dungarees and a tartan shirt, Hugh introduced her and Tommy had another shock as she grabbed him in a bear hug and nearly squeezed the breath from him, she told them all to be seated Tommy included, Hugh said grace and Martha proceeded to dish up plates of steaming hot broth. Tommy had never sat round a table like it in his life although the six Gimpy bairns were well disciplined they were noisy and all seemed to be talking at the same time. It took about an hour to get over the meal and Tommy was thankful for it, he didn't fancy having to cook for himself especially his first night.

After the meal the bairns were pestering Tommy to get involved in some of their games but Tommy was tired after his long journey and he had to be up early to feed the horse, Hugh said he would come along in the morning and show him where everything was, because of the light and the weather it was doubtful if they would get started much before eight am. Before he left the house Martha who spoke with a Caithness accent said Tommy could have his dinner with them every night if he wished, she would charge him one pound five shillings (£1.25) a week, Tommy accepted this offer with both hands he was sure he could survive the racket and to have his meal ready after a hard day in the forest was just ideal. He left the Gimpy circus early he was tired after his long trek plus he had an early start so he got his Bothy organised and had an early night he fell asleep thinking of the Gimpys he had never come across a crowd like them before but he was sure he had made the right move and they seemed genuine people. Next morning the alarm clock had him jumping out of bed, he got dressed and headed for the stable to feed the horse he heard the engine of Hugh's van coming along the drive he was true to his word and showed Tommy the ropes, Hugh asked if the Bothy was comfortable and if he had slept ok Tommy nodded and said "Aye it was fine" there had been a fresh snow fall through the night but they would still manage to work as soon as it was daylight. After the horse was organised fed and watered the two men left to get some breakfast before time to start. Tommy took to the tree dragging like a duck to water and his first day went in without any mishap, Hugh was delighted with his performance, it looked like it could be a happy partnership. Tommy was back in the stable when Hugh pulled up in the van he explained his routine, before his dinner he always had a nip and a half pint in the hotel before going home, he offered Tommy the chance to join him, but he refused pointing out that he was underage he was determined not to blot his copy book again. Tommy fed the horse gave it a groom he then went to the Bothy washed and changed, as he walked up to the door of the Gimpy residence Hugh pulled up behind him, the two of the were inundated with bairns as they rushed to welcome their father home, Tommy felt quite overwhelmed as he received the same welcome, even Martha between serving plates of soup managed to give the both of them a hug. It was the usual turmoil around the table until Hugh banged his hand, he said grace and told the family to show some respect while they were eating, the meal was eaten in virtual silence Tommy was amazed how disciplined and well behaved the bairns were. As it was only a week after Hogmanay the Gimpy bairns were still playing with gifts they had received so after dinner and the washing up complete they got round the table and played all sort of games till bedtime Tommy had never enjoyed an evening like this for many years. There was a squad of four men three plus Gimpy two of them felled the timber Tommy dragged it to the loading bank and Hugh cut into lengths he had the latest Swedish Power Saw which made it a one man operation if he landed in difficulties Tommy was on hand to help him shift the offending piece of timber. The weather was playing havoc and hampering them a bit but Tommy was delighted with his move and the way Hugh and Martha treated him was just out of this world, he posted his fifteen pounds to the sheriffs office at home making sure they would get it on the twenty-eighth day, now he had to save enough to pay Meg back what she had kindly loaned him.

Back at Hillies a week after Tommy left, the two girls Mary and Peg left to go back to their respective jobs, the three sisters had made arrangements for travelling to Willie's wedding Meg was quite excited about it as she would be able to fly for the first time, as usual she had a tearful farewell as her sisters departed, for her it was back to the loneliness of Hillies she was getting a bit fed up of the humdrum life she and Sandy had to lead, as she sat and felt sorry for herself she decided she was going to ring changes about the place she got out a piece of paper and a pencil and started to do some sums.

Sandy knew there was trouble afoot as soon as he saw the expressions on Megs face, " Well fit hiv I deen wrang that's nae pleasing yea" he asked, " Oh its nae fit eve deen its fit am gan tae dee fae noo oan," Sandy took his seat at the table and Meg started to lay out her plans for the future, she held up a page with figures on it, "Div yea ken fit ats aboot"? She said, Sandy shook his head well let me explain his sister continued. " I have just spent the last couple of oors working oot how much money we make aff the eggs butter and cheese and Sandy by the time we pay for feed and all the other non productive items associated with keeping hens makin butter and cheese I'm possibly working for about sixpence an oor (2.5p). The young ones don't want hame made butter or cheese and if the mobile shops take it they have to sell it that day or it goes off so we are possibly now producing these items at very near a loss" Sandy became interested at the word loss so he asked what's the alternative, Meg already had a part time job in the school where she helped out with the school dinners it was only five hours a week but it paid her around a pound a week, she now had the offer of another part time job cleaning the new pub again she would earn around a pound per week, " Just think Sandy that's over eight pound a month and only working twa oors a day". "I'm looking for a reaction from you fit div yea think"? As usual Sandy had a scratch at his head and a puff on his pipe and eventually agreed with what Meg was saying there was no use working at a loss, and taking into consideration the amount of time spent producing all these items she was dead right she was working for next to nothing, Meg pointed out that last year the profit they made was under forty pounds and she didn't receive a wage for what she did. So if everything was taken into consideration they were doing a service free of charge and as Meg bluntly put it she was not prepared to do so any longer she would keep enough hens so that they had a fresh supply themselves and she would still make enough butter and cheese for themselves and that would be it, Sandy had to agree with her they were practically running at a loss he had found the same problem with his few sheep, you needed a flock of over a hundred breeding ewe's to make a profit and that was a full time job for a few weeks at the lambing but Sandy didn't have the land to sustain that size of a flock, in the end he had to get rid of the twenty five sheep as they were not paying their way, thankfully he was still managing to get a fair amount of part time work, with that and what little he made on the croft he was managing to scratch a living but only just. At the May term that year another couple of the original crofters threw in the towel and left the Glen there were now only six actively carrying out the traditional crofting methods two still worked horses, they were elderly men and would never change their style.

Up in Achnashellach the weather had improved and Tommy was managing to get a full week in without interruptions, Hugh Gimpy was delighted with his young dragger and the two of them made a fine team, the family were over the moon with Tommy and made fun of his broad Doric accent, Martha was like a mother to him and treated him like he was her own. It was the first time he had felt like he was part of a real family, Hugh Gimpy had three loves in his life his wife and family, fishing and a drop whisky. Friday evening was whisky night he loved a couple of hours in the pub with his neighbours and would often arrive home worse the wear. Then his fishing some Saturdays the older bairns and himself would pile into the old van and head for Ullapool or maybe Gairloch where they would go sea fishing off the rocks or possibly hire a boat, Hugh had an old fish barrel at home where he would keep the fish cured in salt so that the family could have fish when ever they felt the need. One night as Tommy lay in his bed his mind turned to his life at Hillside, he started to compare his then life with the wonderful life he was now experiencing. Suddenly he started to have a guilt complex about the way he treated his brother Sandy and his sister Meg he felt terrible about his behaviour but there was no way they could have treated him the way Martha Gimpy and the family treated him. First he had never known his father he was killed when Tommy was very young, Sandy had to act as his surrogate father and what did poor Sandy know he had no family of his own he was very young and had no experience of how young people should be treated, Tommy felt that his treatment of his brother who had meant well was shameful, the only real parent he knew was his mother she had been poorly most of Tommy's life so Meg had tried to act as stand in mother but again she was young and childless and anyway Tommy was her brother so when she would give him a cuddle it was nothing like the cuddles his mam would give him. Then one morning there was a commotion in his mothers' bedroom Meg came running out screaming " Get the doctor quick". The doctor arrived shortly after but it was too late his beloved mother was dead, Tommy was heart broken and to make matter worse they put her in a long box and finally dropped her in a hole in the cemetery it was a lot for a ten-year-old bairn to handle, and with no mother instinct to take him and hold him close while he cried his eyes out, it took Tommy over six months before he got over the loss of his mother but he had to more or less over come that hurdle alone. From then on he showed an awkward streak making life difficult mainly for Sandy but also giving Meg a hard time when the mood came over him, but now when Martha gave him a hug it was like coming from a mother and of course Hugh treated him like he would one of his sons, Tommy fell asleep that night feeling very guilty but then when all this happened he was only a bairn as well. He made up his mind that once he got on his feet he would go home to Hillside and apologise to his brother and sister for his behaviour to-wards them. He had paid off his fine and was now saving to pay Meg back her fifteen pounds by the time he had paid for food fags and bits and bobs his pay was left rather depleted he also spent some of it on sweeties for the Gimpy bairns, but his life was much more settled and relaxed he was loving it. Finally after scrimping and saving for about six weeks he had enough money to send to Hillies, but he still had a mean streak and when he wrote the letter telling Meg he was ok and enjoying his job he didn't tell her his address.

Meg started her new job as cleaner in the new hotel she was fair enjoying it being in amongst company was great, many days at Hillies she would see nobody except for Sandy so even to have a blether with Spud Thomson's wife Sadie was brilliant. She enjoyed the hour she spent in the school as well and with the two jobs one after the other her mornings were taken up quite well. Meg had a mega highlight coming into her life just a few weeks away when she would have one of many firsts in her life, her first holiday and it was abroad and her first time in an aeroplane she was so excited she could hardly wait, the post was red hot between Berlin, Aberdeen and the Glen as the three sisters corresponded their plans for Willie's wedding. The day for Meg to depart the Glen soon arrived she travelled to Aberdeen on the train and was met at the station by sister Peg, they were travelling overnight to London then from Heathrow they were now flying direct to Gothenburg in Sweden where hopefully Mary would be waiting for them. They boarded the old steam train at twenty to eight and on the hour of eight with one mighty puff of steam from the two engines they were on their way, Meg checking for the umpteenth time that she had her passport, visa and other documents needed for the journey, the overnight journey wasn't too bad although Meg had dosed off quite a few times she didn't manage a sound sleep but she felt fine when the train pulled into Kings Cross just before eight am it had taken near on twelve hours. They found a ladies toilet and had a good wash before finding a place to have breakfast they had plenty time as their flight didn't take off until afternoon. After breakfast they had a wander round after depositing their luggage in the left luggage office, Meg was mesmerised with the amount of shops although the area was dirty and scruffy there was plenty to keep them amused, finally about midday they boarded a bus to take them to the airport, Meg could feel the adrenalin beginning to kick in she had often wondered what like it was to be in an aeroplane, she was about to find out shortly. The airport was the biggest building Meg had ever been in and everywhere she looked there was escalators so you didn't need to climb the stairs she felt quite overwhelmed. Peg was very accomplished at the travelling lark she had been to Germany to see Willie and Mary so she was well aware of the procedure. They were called to book in and then ushered to a waiting room where they were served coffee and biscuits; Meg felt a real toff being waited on hand and foot. The flight announcement was made and permission to board they joined the long queue of shuffling passengers waiting to be checked on board. Megs first impression of the inside of the plane was that it was like being in a bus, there were four lovely young Swedish girls fussing about helping people get seated. Finally after about twenty minutes the doors of the plane were closed the engines started to rev they were soon driving up to the end of the runway where they turned, the engines were revved and they were off the fastest Meg had ever travelled she felt utter panic until she felt the plane start to rise with-in minutes they were told to unfasten their safety belts. Meg had a peek out the port hole and near collapsed when she saw the height they were at, she closed her eyes and when she opened them again and looked out all she saw was a blanket of white cloud, the whole business was fascinating, Peg was already reading a magazine quite unconcerned with what was going on around her. Before too long the hostesses were on their way serving a meal this was shear luxury as far as Meg was concerned, she would need to do this more often.

Chapter Twenty

LESS THAN TWO HOURS LATER THEY were told to fasten their safety belts as they prepared to land. As they waited at the carousel to pick up their luggage they were happy to see Mary approach basically because up until that point they hadn't understood a word that was being said, even the English that some of the Swedes spoke was hard for Meg to figure out but then on the other hand it was pointless Meg trying to speak to them as I am sure the Doric speakers in Gothenburg were few and far between. Mary told them that Willie was waiting for them in the car park so as soon as they picked up their luggage they were on their way first to their hotel then they were invited to Maria's parents house for their supper. Meg was near to tears as she hugged her twin brother in the car park she felt rather overcome, but Willie as usual told her to stop being bloody stupid and to start enjoying her holiday she wiped away the tears and settled down to enjoy her stay in Sweden, as they drove through the city Meg was fascinated with the huge very clean buildings everywhere they looked, everything was spotless what a transformation to what they had seen in London, even the hotel was like a palace and they were waited on hand and foot, Meg was finding out how the other half lived. They still had a day to go sight seeing before the wedding so they spent it going round all the important sites and in the evening they were invited to a meal with Maria's brother and his family it was quite an awkward evening for Meg as she was the only one who didn't speak any other language than her own so she felt isolated at times, Maria's family all spoke different languages as could Mary, Peg was also fluent in French so she was able to join in the conversation, back in the hotel after the meal the girls had a long evening in front of them Willie had said he would meet them in the bar later so that they could have an hour or two together before his big day. Mary decided that they should try on their wedding clothes to make sure everything fitted, Meg reneged she was sure all hers was in order. Peg was the first to go on the walkway just like a mannequin parade she strutted up and down the room looking fabulous in her dress high heel shoes with matching handbag and tiny hat, Mary was going next she was unsure whether to go in her number one dress uniform or a dress but anyhow she would do her turn in the fashion parade, the bathroom door opened and Mary stepped out looking resplendent in her new outfit one thing in the twins favour they were still quite slim so they were easy to dress. Next it was Meg she was still protesting as she was railroaded into getting dressed, the bathroom door swung open and Meg shuffled through looking like Old Mother Riley, Mary near collapsed her sister was dressed as though she was going to the Kirk in the Glen there was no way she could attend the wedding dressed like a bag of tatties they would need to get her some fashionable clothes in the morning, thankfully they still had time on their hands Meg protested profusely, Mary told Willie of the problem and he told her regardless of cost get his sister into the modern world he didn't want the Duncan's to be the laughing stock of Sweden. The wedding would be quite a posh affair, Maria's family all held important posts in Sweden her father was a leading surgeon her mother had a degree in medicine as had her brother, Maria had a degree in languages and was employed by the diplomatic corps, so it was a wee bit up market from the last wedding in Hillies barn. Later that evening the Duncan family met for a drink Willies last night of freedom.

Next morning Meg was dragged kicking and screaming to the nearest ladies outfitters where she was given a complete make over hair, underwear, handbag and shoes she was protesting like the dickens saying she couldn't afford such luxuries and she went mad when told her brother Willie was picking up the tab. Back in the hotel they were looking through their purchases when Meg spotted the wide legged kami knickers, she went mental stating there was no way she would be wearing that things with no elastic in the legs the draught was bound to be unbearable but again she was overruled and told to get dressed so the lisle stocking were discarded for Nylons the old bloomers with elasticated legs were given the heave and replaced with a nice new pair of lacy French Kami knickers and then the dress which cost an arm and a leg transformed Meg into near model status she had to admit that she had looked awful in her own clothes, but then in the Glen the only magazine she ever saw was the peoples friend they were more interested in showing how to do cable stitch knitting then the latest fashions from Paris or Rome, but what she had was good enough when feeding the hens about the croft at Hillies. They were all seated in the Orthodox Church the service was to be in Swedish so it was pointless the Scots even looking at the sheet in front of them the only bit in English they understood was when Willie pledged to love, honour and obey. The meal was traditional Swedish fare very enjoyable with plenty champagne, the evening lasted until about midnight they were all invited to join the family on the Sunday for their regular church service. The newly weds would be there then they were leaving on a honeymoon that would take then round the word Willie was looking forward to seeing brother Jim in New Zealand and sister Betty in Canada and to finish up they would visit Hillies before returning to London where Willie was now stationed. On the Monday Meg and Peg flew back to London and Mary set off back to Berlin she was due leave shortly and was looking forward to getting home for a spell. Meg arrived home at Hillies just after midday they had travelled overnight from London, her visit to Sweden was the highlight of the year so far and she made a lot of mileage as she relayed her exploits to all and sundry before that week was over, Sandy was bloody well sick hearing about it but he grinned and bared it as it was his sisters first venture away from the Glen and yes she would have been excited about it. As soon as she had arrived home she searched the letters looking to see if Tommy had been in contact, she was wailing to Sandy that their young brother could be dead and nobody would have an address for him, Sandy looked at her and said, " Na, Na if that would be the case the bobbies would soon find oot far he came fae" Meg shook her head but remained silent that was just the sort answer she would expect out of laid back Sandy. The Sunday after she got back from Sweden Meg decided she would give the Glen folks something to talk about by wearing her wedding outfit, she turned a few heads as she took her usual pew some of them were delighted but the deadly sins of envy and jealousy raised their ugly heads, in one or two cases after the service the comments were flying, the nasty ones just out of earshot, "Meg Hillies must be trying to upstage the young lairds wife wi that oot fit", " She didn't buy that from J.D.Williams clubbie nor frae Humpy Danny the mobile draper and so the spite mongers went on. On the other hand the young laird's wife and Betsy Wilson were very complimentary and keen to know the fashion house that tailored such a lovely dress; it really does take all kinds.

Life in the Glen just ambled on there were now eight crofters actively crofting, they were all getting on a bit Sandy was the youngest at thirty-eight others were slightly older. The younger generation weren't interested they could get their money easier than working anything up to fifteen hours a day and unsure at the end of the day if any money had been earned, their earning power depended on the prices they were given in the market place and the weather played a big part Sandy didn't know any other kind of work so he was stuck with what he had, now that Meg had two jobs she was earning a bit and he was still managing to get casual work. But his potential for casual work received a mighty hammer blow that summer, his yearly day out over the past few years had been a day at Turra Show, if there was a good broadcasting band at the Marquee Dance in the evening he would stay over with Will and Bell Watson, but Will had taken a bit of a turn early on that year and was unable to accompany Sandy to the show so he went alone. He visited all the stalls of interest and stayed for ages looking at the livestock finally he ended up in the W.R.I tent where he knew Meg would be and he was sure of a cup of tea, he spent half-an-hour talking to neighbours from the Glen, by the time he had a look at the machinery it would be time for the parade to start he had plenty time so he just poked about looking at this and that being hounded by eager salesmen trying to flog him all sorts of machinery and plant all of it above Sandy's means. When he arrived at the Massy Harris stand he could just make out the figure of Lang Dod Wilson he had his son George with him he would soon leave school and no doubt be groomed to take over from his father, who was beginning to show a bit of wear and tear and walked with the aid of walking stick. He spotted Sandy and gave him a great welcome, Dod although a very kind considerate man was always full of enthusiasm about what he owned and what he had just bought, in other words he was a bit of a bum (in a nice sort of way) Sandy got the treatment right away " Sandy fu are yea dein min? Yir lookin weel cum heer and see fit I've jist boocht" Sandy followed the two Dods round the back of the huge tent as they reached a gleaming new machine the likes of which Sandy had never seen before, Dod stood with his hands splayed out asking Sandy whit he thought, Sandy asked whit it did, "Weel for start it dis awa wie four or five workmen its a baler" turning to his young son he continued "Sandy at the moment a field of hay needs about half-a-dozen men for about a month depending on the weather, see young George here he could harvest all the hay at Burnside on his own wie this machine and maybe somebody to build the stacks in the yard". Dod would never have done young Sandy Hillies any harm but he just dealt him a body blow that left him physically sick, the gathering of the hay always ensured Sandy of six weeks work and here was a machine that could do it all with one man he felt ill and made his excuse to leave the company at the first opportune moment, Sandy could feel the noose tightening all it would need was some sort of machinery to harvest the oats and barley and Sandy's chances of casual work would be at an end, for the first time in his life he felt slightly worried about the future so much so that he couldn't concentrate on the rest of the show, he decided to go home early first he had to call on Will Watson he was another source of worry as he had failed terribly since they had last met. Sandy was quite depressed as he made his way home; he felt his whole world was starting to collapse around him.

Tommy was still enjoying life working with Hugh Gimpy there was never a dull moment he often thought of Hillies and how he should pay them a visit just to give his sister peace of mind and make his peace with brother Sandy, but the longer he put it off the harder it became, then there was finance he never seemed to get out of the bit he got off to a bad start when he had to pay Meg back what he had borrowed from her. His wages were roughly seven pounds fifty a week, after tax and insurance he was left with under six pounds then he had to pay Martha dig money for his dinner, he had been persuaded to take out an insurance policy and finally he had bought himself a new outfit sports jacket and flannels, socks, shirt, tie underwear shoes this set him back over ten pounds but the travelling draper allowed him to pay it up monthly, after all that was taken into account Tommy was left with less than three pounds he always bought the Gimpy bairns sweeties on a Friday night and probably the biggest drain on his resources was the fact that he had found himself a girlfriend. She was an Orcadian girl a trainee cook at the hotel her name was Arlene, she was getting the lowest wage possible less than five pounds a month, so it landed with Tommy to supply the fags for most of the week but he was madly in love so he didn't mind one little bit.

The year was passing them bye Tommy was on cloud nine but suddenly he was brought back to earth with a clatter, he had just got home from work and was in the Bothy getting tidied up before dinner when the second oldest Gimpy boy burst through the door in his hand was a very official brown envelope with Her Majesty's Service stamped on the front Tommy's blood ran cold his call up papers he was almost sure. Deep down Tommy had kept thinking that if he kept his where abouts secret he would possibly avoid having to do his National Service but how wrong he was the establishment had been a step ahead, Hugh Gimpy pointed out that he paid Tommy's income tax and insurance stamp every week so through his National Insurance number it was possible to trace him, he would just have to grin and bear it. He had to make the journey to Inverness to register and have a medical examination; Arlene managed to get the day off to accompany him to the town it was just as well to make a day out of the situation. Tommy had a bit of a predicament, he had been advised to try and get into one of the support corps like the Royal Engineers, REME or the RASC where he could learn a skill that he could put to good use in civvy street, in the recruiting office he was given a form to fill in one of the questions was which unit or regiment would he prefer, Tommy filled it in stating First choice Royal Engineers second choice Royal Army Service Corps and third the Royal Mechanical Electrical Engineers the recruiting sergeant told him the only way he had any hope of being accepted for any of his choices was to sign on for three years which he did otherwise it was the Cameron Highlanders and shipped to Korea within twelve weeks, he didn't fancy that and at the end of his two years it would be back to the timber knocking his pan in for peanuts, no he would take his chance and try and learn a skill while he had the opportunity. Arlene was a bit miffed that he had signed up for three years but when it was explained that Tommy would be able to get better employment when he left the Army she calmed down and hauled him away to study the engagement rings after and all he would only be twenty one when he finished his service.

When Willie and Maria returned from their world tour honeymoon they had called in briefly at Hillside they had run out of time so only managed an overnight stay. Willie had promised Sandy that he would come back when the crops were ready and give him a hand to bring in his harvest. Meg had phoned as she now frequently did it was easier than writing letters, she told Willie they would be starting to harvest the following week, Willie said that they would be home the next week-end which would just be perfect Sandy would have all the crops cut and ready for leading home. Meg of course was in her element she would be able to fuss over Maria and spend some time with her on her own the men would be busy, Sandy was praying the weather would hold. It would be a busy week ahead as she had to help her brother with his harvest until Willie arrived home, if Sandy had to pay for hired help

220

he might as well throw in the towel his resources would not stretch to paying wages, so the two of them struggled on Meg would help with the binder, it was quite easy although the control handles were very stiff and required Sandy to help her occasionally. By the middle of the week everything was under control Sandy had all the stooking up to date the stack yard was cleared ready for this season's stock. Willie was due to arrive late Friday evening and about ten thirty he drove into the yard in his big black Mercedes nothing was done in small measures by Willie, after the hugging and kissing and back slapping the four of them sat down to have something to eat Sandy hated going to bed with a full stomach but this was an exception, after the meal they had a dram and Willie asked when the harvesting would commence he was flabbergasted when Sandy announced it would start at eight am to-morrow morning, Willie had hoped he would get a week-end to recover from his journey, " Aye yir a hard task master Sandy, bit I'll be ready when you are" with that sorted out they retired to bed. True to his word Willie was up and dressed at the same time as Sandy so they had breakfast and headed for the steading to get the days work under way, Sandy was chuffed to death he had a whole two weeks of his brothers company they would work away for a while then stop and have a breather and a blether putting things to rights, when Willie put the question to his brother about how the croft was working out Sandy was in a bit of a quandary did he tell Willie that it was a fight to survive or tell a lie and say everything was fine, he hesitated before answering, " Willie the way things are gan it is doubtful if we will survive another year it will just take one more financial disaster and the crofting in this Glen would be finished just look around us there are very few true Glen folk left when we moved here there were fifteen crofters and five big farms plus the Home Farm now there are seven crofters and rumour has it that three more are about to quit so things are looking far from good, as long as I could get casual work we could survive but that's gone and if this new fangled combine harvester appears next year that will be the end." Willie looked at his brother and felt sorry for him he had dedicated his life to bring up the family worked long hard hours and it looked like it was crashing down around him, " Look Sandy if its as bad as you say maybe now is the time to get out don't wait till it happens if you don't see anyway back start making a move now, the rest of the family all have good jobs so they are not interested in the croft, I am sure you could get a job if you moved nearer the town there is bound to be something you could turn your hand too, go for it min before your ower auld." Did Willie sow the seeds?

Meg and Maria had a great time while the men were working the two of them toured around in the car even managing a day in Aberdeen where they met up with Peg who managed to wangle a day off. Willie and Sandy had a great couple of weeks reminiscing about all the folks in the Glen some of them long gone, on the middle Saturday of the fortnight they finished at one pm and later on in the afternoon they piled into Willies Merc and drove to Turriff where they paid a visit to Will and Bell Watson, Will was just a shadow of his former self the stroke he had suffered had taken its toll, although Sandy had seen him less than a month ago he had gone down hill. Bell wanted them to stay for supper but they could see she had her hands full trying to cater for Big Will, he was quite cheery but finished, he would never be the same again, they said their goodbyes and headed to Mintlaw where they had high tea then a leisurely drive home, Willie parked the car at Hillies and they headed for the hotel for refreshments before they called it a day on the way up the hill Willie was asking who was all there as he didn't recognise many of them, Sandy shook his head and sadly told his brother he hardly knew any of them either. On the Sunday after the Kirk and lunch Sandy asked if they were interested in a walk down to the village of Covie Willie and Maria were keen but Meg decided she would give it a miss as she had some things to tend to. Sandy explained the religious situation and the fact that very few if anybody would acknowledge them, not only the religious business most of the little cottages were no longer inhabited by locals they were being sold off as Holiday Homes, as they skirted the brow of the cliff overlooking the sixty or so houses Willie could see where Sandy was coming from, in the little harbour instead of the old fishing cobbles that Willie remembered, were expensive looking yachts. As they strolled along the narrow street they could see that they had been spotted as the curtains were moving and nosey villagers was weighing up the intruders, they were near the far end of the village when they met the only person about, an old class mate from school he was overjoyed to meet the Hillies boys it must have been at least fifteen years since he last spoke to Willie, he lost Maria with-in seconds as his words were spewed out like they were coming from a machine gun, he had spoken to Sandy not so long ago but he told Willie how he was an outcast in his own village because he wouldn't knuckle down to the new religious masters, he was waiting to leave the village and join the Merchant Navy, with tears in his eyes he went on to explain that even his own brothers and sisters shunned him because according to them he was a none believer and therefore unclean. The two Duncan brothers and Maria felt quite moved by the story they had been told, Sandy went on to tell them that he was not alone quite a few families had been disrupted by the American evangelists who seemed to have the people eating out of their hands and would do what ever was asked of them. Sadly Willie and Maria's leave had come to an end and they would travel back on the Saturday, Willie had enjoyed his two weeks even although it had been hard work and he discovered muscles that had lain dormant for years, as for Maria she was fascinated with her sister-in law, Meg's ability to cook and bake, she could produce just about anything she even learned how milk was produced then turned into butter and cheese all good information for a townie. Willie had intimated that he was trying to get the whole family to come home next summer so that they could have get-together, as it was fifteen years since the break up of the family started so he was doing his best.

Tommy didn't have long to wait before his call up papers arrived with instructions to travel to Catterick Camp in Yorkshire, he had to call in at the recruiting office in Inverness and collect a travel warrant so it was an early start from Achnashellach, after a long tiring but exciting journey he arrived just before midnight it had been hard leaving Arlene she was howling her heart out as he departed, this was very upsetting for him but he promised to write as soon as he had an address. Tommy would do his ten weeks basic training before being posted to a training depot where he hoped he would learn to operate heavy plant, his ten weeks soon passed and his passing out parade came and went he didn't have any family present as it was too far to travel anyhow the folks at Hillies were unaware where he was as he had been a proper rascal and gave his home address as the Gimpy home in the North. He was given a week-end pass but the travelling time to go north would use up the forty-eight hours so instead he volunteered to do guard duty, on the Saturday evening nearing the end of his two hour stag he was looking forward to a hot cup of tea when he spotted headlights coming up the drive, it was a jeep he waived it down, the jeep halted and Tommy had a look inside they were on a fairly high alert, so he had to make sure no unauthorised persons got in the camp, the driver was a lance corporal in the RASC, he studied the drivers pass then went to the passengers side it was quite dark but he could make out it was a female in uniform she also had three stripes on her arm he was about to ask for her pass when she said, " Fancy seeing you here young Thomas Duncan" Tommy nearly filled his trousers and virtually went to pieces, it was his sister Mary what a shock, Tommy was a wreck but his big sister took it in her stride she said she would wait inside the guard room until he finished his stint, as the jeep pulled away Tommy was still trembling. Tommy's stint of guard duty ended they were dismissed and had four hours rest before the next stint, as he walked to the guardroom door he was apprehensive no doubt he would get some hassle having his sister arrive so unexpectedly and more so because she was a copper that should go down well. The orderly sergeant was waiting, " Ha Duncan we have a visitor waiting for you, your sister" putting his mouth close to Tommy's ear he whispered, " You never mentioned she was a snout (copper) I wonder why that was." Tommy could feel his face burning he could well have done without this. He was shown into the little office at the back of the guardroom and there was Mary his favourite sister looking resplendent in her Red Caps uniform and thee gleaming strips on her arm, she was drinking from a mug of tea and had another in front of her for Tommy they embraced in the middle of the room (Tommy hoping no body was watching he would never live this down). Mary explained that she was in Catterick as witness in a Court Martial trial she had flown in from Germany that evening and she would be there until the trial finished probably three days from Monday she asked Tommy if he had the day off on the Sunday which he had so they decided to meet up after lunch and head into the city Mary said she would try and wangle some transport, Tommy said he had one request she asked what that was and he said please wear civilian clothes, Mary burst out laughing " Why? Are you ashamed of me" "No it's just that I wouldn't get any peace if I was seen wandering about with a Military Cop." She left shouting see you tomorrow Tommy tried to look uninterested as he rejoined his guard companions.

Tommy received a message to meet his sister after church they would get some food in town so dressed in his civvies he made his way to the gate sitting outside was a little sports car, Tommy signed out and walked towards the vehicle he had to smile as he saw Mary dressed to kill complete with sunglasses, she told him to jump in, he asked where she stole the car, Mary explained that she often had to come to Catterick in her line of duty so she had quite a few friends who were

224

always willing to help her out, she went on to say she did the same for them when they visited Germany. They were soon bombing down the road it was Tommy's first run in a sports car and the first time he had travelled at eighty miles an hour. Mary told him she had the car for the day so they would find a restaurant have some lunch then decide what to do, she was full of questions about him being in the Army. She went on to say she had spoken to their sister Meg on Friday evening over the phone and she hadn't mentioned he had been called up, Tommy hung his head and told her he hadn't told the Hillies folks where he was and said he had more or less made his home in the Highlands. Mary asked her brother why, she had slowed down as they continued their conversation, Tommy didn't have a specific answer he said he had let them down badly and with two court appearances the shame for Sandy must have been awful, Mary got stuck into her young brother she tried to be civil about it and pointed out how unfair he was being especially to Meg, Sandy would probably get over it being a man but Meg who had brought Tommy up would be suffering although she would be keeping it to herself, Tommy felt quite ashamed. They found a place to eat and Mary kept up the conversation about Tommy's behaviour towards his family, she went on to tell him that Willie was trying to arrange a family get together for the following summer so she urged him to make his peace with Meg and Sandy as they would all expect him to be there. She went on to ask what he had been doing in the Highlands he told her all about meeting the Gimpys and finally how he had a girl friend Arlene, Tommy proudly showed his sister some photos of his girl Mary commented how pretty she looked. They finished their meal and decided to have a look around York during their tour of the city centre they noticed a picture house showing a film called the Robe, Mary asked if he fancied an evening at the flicks, it was ages since he last saw a movie so he agreed it would be a nice way to end the evening. On the way back to the camp Tommy explained to Mary he was being posted to his training depot some where around Salisbury Plain so he would probably be gone early morning they were being transported by road, Mary told him to make sure he made contact with Meg and Sandy also brother Willie who was working in London and he was looking to buy a house shortly, Tommy promised he would as soon as he got settled in his new camp, they parted company at the camp gate, it was to be a quite a while before they would meet again. True to his word Tommy sat down when he was settled in his new training camp and wrote a long letter to his sister Meg he also included Sandy in it, Meg must have sat down and written a reply and posted it the same day, she said she was over the moon to hear from him and was so pleased he had found himself a girlfriend and they were hoping he would bring her to Hillies when he got a leave, inside the envelope was three pounds incase he was short, Tommy's eyes filled with tears a thought ran through his mind what a bloody fool he had been the way he had treated his family.

After getting Megs letter Tommy felt really homesick he wanted to be with Arlene and now to visit Hillside and try and undo all the unpleasantness he had caused. The following week he was called to the camp post office there was a parcel for him, he near burst into tears when he opened it, Meg had baked a cake and filled a box of goodies he was overcome. He managed to get in touch with Willie who said he would drive up at the weekend and pay Tommy a visit, Tommy hastily wrote back and said he would be delighted to meet Willie but please on no account wear your Red Cap uniform. Willie was stationed in Aldershot and Tommy was at Warminster so they were not too far apart, when Willie arrived to pick Tommy up for their first meeting Maria had also come along, they decided to drive to Bath where they had an enjoyable day, Willie explained that he was trying to arrange a family re-union for the following summer as it would be fifteen years since Betty and him had left Hillies and Jim left a year later, Tommy thought it was a great idea. Willie told him he should transfer to the Military Police and make a career out of the Army, but Tommy wasn't keen he just wanted to get his three years over and get back to civvy street and a steady job he was getting on great, being brought up in the country was a great help in learning to operate the plant, the old dung loader was similar to the diggers and bull dozers he was working on. Tommy had been five months in the Army when he was given fourteen days leave, when he found out he contacted Arlene, as it was off season at the hotel she was able to get a week off so Tommy planned to travel to Achnashellach and stay with the Gimpys a few days then Arlene and him could travel to Hillies and stay with Meg and Sandy for the rest of his leave the only thing was that Arlene would have to travel back home by herself other wise Tommy would have to pay for his fare and at the moment every penny was prisoner as he saved to buy an engagement ring. He set off for home on a Friday it was a long hike to Achnashellach over twenty four hours the old steam train was a filthy uncomfortable means of travel but there was no other option and anyway the government was paying so why complain, Tommy felt quite rich as he had been given his subsistence money to help with his digs. He arrived at his destination mid morning on the Saturday he was knocked for six when he spotted the whole Gimpy clan waiting for him on the platform, old Hugh had waited in the van but the rest had him in a rugby scrum as they hugged and kissed him, then big Martha said welcome home son and nearly smothered him as she hugged him against her huge mammary's, as he raised his eyes he spotted Arlene she had just entered the little station, Tommy dropped everything and made a beeline for the love of his life they hugged for a few minutes when Martha said, "Come on you two or I'll hae tae throw a bucket of water ower yea" as they approached the old van Gimpy himself emerged and gave Tommy a big hug and welcomed him home. Tommy was over whelmed by the bairns, poor Arlene found herself getting a back seat as the young Gympie's swarmed over her man, Martha had a huge breakfast cooked in the oven she only had to fry eggs then they could eat. Tommy was inundated with questions about where he had been, the bairns all had a try on of his beret, soon the novelty of having him home wore off much to Arlene's relief she could at last get close to him, it would be short lived as she had lunch to prepare at the hotel just shortly, she would be unable to meet up with Tommy until after the dinners were over probably around nine-o-clock in the evening.

Old Hugh had intended doing some fishing so he asked Tommy if he was interested, he replied of course he was interested, as he had no opportunity to fish where he was stationed, after lunch the whole family plus Tommy piled into the old van and headed for the rocks around Gairloch and spent a wonderful afternoon relaxing and catching fish most of which were Pollock with the odd mackerel thrown in. During the course of the day Hugh asked Tommy if he fancied a few days work the following week, he was over the moon having the chance to earn a few extra bob (shillings) but first he would need to find out what Arlene was doing. She had agreed to forfeit her days off the following week as she was having a week's holiday so Tommy was able to work the whole week it was another fiver in the bank. The week with the Gimpys soon passed and on the Saturday amid weeping and wailing Tommy and Arlene left Achnashellach and headed for the East Coast and Tommy's home Glen, Arlene was quite apprehensive about meeting Tommy's relations maybe it wouldn't be too bad meeting his brother and sister instead of his father and mother, if Arlene was apprehensive she had no idea how Tommy felt he had knots in his stomach wondering what kind of reception Sandy would give him, Mary and Willie had assured him everything would be fine. After quite a long uneventful journey they stepped off the bus at the new hotel Tommy commented that it had opened just as he left home he also saw that the old Smiddy had been extended and along with the fuel pumps there was now a shop. They started the journey up the road to Hillies it was about six hundred yards, Tommy was trying to keep a conversation going but the nearer he got to the house the blood pressure was rising to such an extent he felt he was going to burst, but his worries were all unfounded as Meg shot out the back door and grabbed her young brother round the neck she near drowned him in a flood of tears, Tommy was trying to introduce Arlene who was standing rather embarrassed not knowing what to do, Sandy appeared and caught her by the hand mumbling " Yea must be Arlene pleased to meet you"? Meg had composed herself at last and Arlene had to endure a few moments of hugging and being welcomed into the Duncan family. While Meg and Arlene were getting acquainted Sandy put his arms around Tommy and said its good to have you back loon. Tommy felt quite emotional but maintained his composure after an all he was a sodjer. Sandy was busy at the hay on the croft so Tommy came in very handy, while helping out on the croft it gave Arlene and Meg time together, they were getting on great guns, Meg was delighted with Tommy's choice more so when she showed a lot of willing to help out even cooking the dinner one evening. Tommy and Arlene spent as much time together as was humanly possible but their week was soon at and end Arlene would have to leave on the first bus the next morning, Tommy travelled as far as the town with her and saw her on the bus for the north, as she boarded the bus she blew him a kiss and was still waving as the bus rounded the corner at the bottom of the street, he was quite emotional and felt really empty this little lady had him well and truly hooked, unfortunately he still had two and a half years military service to complete worse still he could be sent anywhere in the world the thought didn't bear thinking about. Back at Hillies Meg was full of praise and urged Tommy to make sure he kept hold of Arlene as her type were few and far between. To-morrow he would also have to leave he invited Meg and Sandy to go to the hotel for a drink seeing it was his last night, they were delighted.

Everything got back to normal and the laid back way of life in the Glen continued for Meg and Sandy, it was now possible to have a telephone installed in the house, Meg started to pester Sandy to get one, as he scratched his head and pretended not to hear her the thoughts going through his head was " Mair bloody expense", but it was only a matter of time soon every house in the Glen would be connected. At the moment Meg was in contact with most of the family except Jim in New Zealand there seemed to be a problem there but she regularly walked down to the cross roads and used the Red Box to chat to Betty, Willie, Peg and Arlene who had access to a phone in the hotel she worked in, she would phone them all and then go home and write a letter telling them the things she had forgotten when she phoned. Willie was busy trying to organise a date for the Duncan family re-union and eventually decided to have it the week of the local fete/games that way they would meet up with friends and neighbours from their school days it was nine months away so they had plenty time to get organised.

Tommy was counting the days till his next leave he was due two weeks off at Christmas and the New Year that was six weeks away he had volunteered to be a member of a stand by squad, they were paid and extra 2/- (10p) per day, the idea was that if they were needed anywhere in the world they could be moved at a moments notice the attraction was the 2/- a day more money towards the engagement ring, his spell of stand bye would finish at Christmas. Quite often Tommy and the rest of the standby crew would be called out to carry out an exercise the idea was to keep them on their toes, new guys would ask what's the standby crew, Tommy would explain that they would be the first to be rushed to a trouble spot should one occur, he had been in it for three months now and had never been asked to do anything other than exercise and of course the extra ten bob (50p) per week came in handy. But things can change overnight, even quicker than that and that is exactly what happened, the media were full of the problems on the Suez Canal the Egyptians were causing hassle and the word was that the British, French and Israelis were about to invade by dropping Paratroopers into Suez . The standby squad were told to muster in their billet and an officer would put them in the picture, their squad Captain breezed into the billet. " Well chaps I'm sure you are anxious to know what's going on, if you think back three months you may well remember volunteering as the standby squad, for that you were paid the princely sum of ten shilling per week", they all nodded yes. The captain continued, " Now its pay back time no doubt you will have heard the

Egyptians are playing silly buggers over the Suez Canal, we the Brits, French and Israelis need to go and teach them a lesson, as we speak we are probably dropping Para's on their territory, the Para's need back up support troops, that's where you volunteers come in, from here you will proceed to the Medical Room to receive your necessary inoculations, then to the stores for your lightweight clothing back here and start packing you fly out from Brize Norton at ten hundred hours tomorrow morning destination Malta, any questions?" he answered one or two then handed them over to the platoon corporal who marched them to the Medical room. Tommy didn't know whether to laugh or cry he was five weeks from going on leave he wondered how long this would last having said all that he was quite excited to be flying for the first time and also his trip abroad to Malta. "Wow"

The transport plane was huge much bigger than Tommy had imagined the engines revved up the pilot released the brakes and they were off what a sensation. They had six hours to think what lay ahead one worry for Tommy was the fact that he had a point three-o-three rifle as part of his kit it never occurred to him that he may have to shoot people when he signed on , some of the guys were real nervous, looking down on the Mediterranean was something Tommy never even dreamed of but there it was the Island of Malta it looked so peaceful, the sun was shining such tranquillity, but not too far away there were hostilities taking place with men shooting at each other the thought sent shivers down his spine, he wondered what their roll was going to be they weren't trained as front line troops but they would soon find out. Over the intercom they were told to fasten their seat belts as they were about to land, the plane was packed solid with men and equipment, the pilot started his decent and landed with hardly a bump after about a mile of runway they pulled up and the doors were pushed open, the searing heat that rushed into the plane made breathing rather laboured and soon the pale skinned young soldiers were pouring sweat, this could be hard work. They were transported to their accommodation it was a tented compound after allocation of a tent along with another five guys they were marched over to a marquee, and told to find seats, there were other guys there all from different Corps. After what seemed like ages a Lt Cornel and his entourage entered, on the huge board behind him was a map of the Suez Canal, there were arrows pointing all over the place and the names British, French, Israelis and Egyptians he explained what was going on, at the moment the men assembled

230

in front of him were on Red Alert ready to be rushed to Egypt when required. As of the following morning they would start training and practicing carrying out mock invasions, he looked for them to be in tiptop condition over the next few days. Fortunately for Tommy and his mates they were never needed, but they were there for the next six months and it was near Easter before they returned to the U.K, now a highly skilled back-up invasion force. Tommy had been promoted to Lance Corporal which gave him and extra sixpence a day (2.5p), he had set his sights on buying Arlene a fifteen pound engagement ring but he kept having to put it off as saving money out of his wages was quite difficult but he was getting there. Back at Hillside the New Year came and went not a lot of excitement the thrill of Hogmanay had gone, all the good old neighbours had gone, Sandy received word that Will Watson was very low and wasn't expected to pull through, he passed away the following March, Sandy, Meg and Peg attended his funeral and were amazed how few people were there as Big Will had been an immensely popular big fellow when he resided in the Glen. Willie had taken up a new job and now worked for the Special Investigation Branch of the Military Police he was often abroad in his new job. He was well ahead with the plans for the summer reunion Jim and Tina and the two kids were coming from New Zealand for six weeks the same as Walter and Betty and their two kids from Canada, the two families had decided to hire caravans which they could stay in and do some touring after the re-union bash was over. Tommy managed to get some leave after his return to the U.K. he told Arlene he wanted to get married and said they would get engaged the day of the re-union but they would keep it secret until then, she was over the moon.

Chapter Twenty One

Tommy had been promoted to full corporal and posted to a training depot, this suited him down to the ground, as he enjoyed passing on his skill to others and at the moment he was safe from getting posted abroad, it was all quiet in Egypt but now the EOKA terrorists were causing some grief in Cyprus and people were getting killed. He had booked his leave so that he would be home for two weeks in July during the re-union period; he was looking forward to that how enjoyable it would be to see the entire family together again. Arlene was going to try and get her parents to come over from Orkney so that they would be present for her engagement.

Sandy was busy getting everything in order for the big weekend he was also getting quite a bit of casual work so it was a busy time for all.

The re-union was scheduled to take place over the middle weekend of July, on the Saturday the Fete`/Come Highland games would take place, then in the evening the Duncan family were having a party a good old fashioned barn dance with plenty food and no doubt drinks this was the trend now-a-days. The first to arrive at Hillies the week before the doo was Jim, Tina and the bairns ten year old Billy and seven year old Alex, Jim had hired a camper van it was a new context for going on holiday but it suited people from abroad, they could come and go as they pleased, his arrival was a very emotional affair it was eleven years since he left home for good so Meg and Sandy were quite tearful when their young brother arrived, next to arrive in the yard at Hillies smiling and causing as much mayhem as usual was Mary driving a big Mercedes car she had picked up her twin sister Peg on the way it was also their first meeting with sister-in law Tina so there was much rejoicing and hugging and of course the two boys didn't miss out it was the first nephews they had seen, so believe me they were extra special. Two day's later Betty and Walter arrived from Canada with their two youngsters Walter fourteen and Liz twelve it was the first time the bairns had met their Hillside relatives, Walter had also hired a camper van he told them they were very popular in Canada and the States, Willie would be late he was abroad in the Far East but would be there before the week-end. Tommy had booked his rail warrant to go straight to Achnashellach where he was picking up Arlene and heading for Hillies, he spent a couple of days with Martha and Hugh Gimpy (his adopted parents). Tommy told them all about his family re-union and the big day of the Glen Highland Games, Arlene was only allowed one week off so they would travel down to Banff-shire on the Thursday so that she could be back to work for the following Friday, Tommy refused to show her the engagement ring saying she would see it on Saturday when he placed it on her finger, she had told her parents about the week-end but it was a long way to travel so they were undecided whether they would come or not. Eventually Willie arrived with Maria they pulled up in the yard and the car was mobbed by fellow Duncan's, before they stepped out into the summer sunshine Willie announced they had a big surprise, he got out and opened Maria's door when he helped her out the surprise was plain to see Maria was heavily pregnant the hugging and kissing went on for ages before they all calmed down again, Tommy and Arlene arrived on the last bus from town the family was now complete.

Arlene was over whelmed with the welcome the Duncan family afforded her she felt like a queen, and the fact that she was a fairly well qualified chef added to her popularity as she got stuck in and helped Meg getting food ready. After Meg had fed everybody she likened it to a thrashing mill day but she was in her element she loved having her family round her it was fifteen years since they all had a meal all together, all in all there were sixteen of them, Sandy said grace and Willie went out to the car and brought in a case of champagne, " Get the glesses oot Meg we hiv a bit of toasting tae dea here", by the time they finished the meal half the case of champers had gone. Willie and Tommy volunteered to do the washing up, Mary and Peg told Meg to go and sit down while they stacked away the crockery and made some coffee. Later on the men suggested they would go to the pub while the women caught up with the gossip this looked like being a whale of a weekend. On the Friday morning Sandy was up as usual at the back of five his head felt a bit fuzzy from the night before he was a bit unsure if the champers was such a good idea, he had just boiled the kettle when Mary came bounding through the door she was going for a run, as they sipped their tea and had a good blether the back door opened and the three young nephews and niece appeared, Mary had invited them to join her the evening before but didn't really expect them to take up her offer so early in the morning, but they were bright eyed and bushy tailed ready to go, next to appear was Tommy he asked Sandy for an old pair of breeks, so that he could lend a hand, Sandy was quite chuffed that he and Tommy had made their peace what a difference that had made, with Tommy's help they would soon get through the work so he decided that he would milk the cow and save sister Meg a chore she had plenty on her plate at the moment. Mary gave the youngsters some tea and toast before they set off she would probably go for a five mile jog, it was a lovely summer morning with birds singing and the sun just beginning to show, it was the first time the bairns had met their auntie Mary but they had gelled right away and thought she was just the bees knees, by the time they got back, Sandy and Tommy were back in the house and Meg was busying herself trying to get some breakfast ready, Sandy managed to muster the men into giving a hand at the playing field setting up the equipment needed for to-morrows fete, the ladies had decided to have a day out so shopping was the order of the day, they chose Fraserburgh for there day out, due to the busy fishing fleet, there was plenty money in the Broch so there were some decent shops. In the evening after Meg, helped by the other females managed to feed the extended family they settled down for a quiet evening to-morrow would be a hectic day, the foreign niece and nephews were moaning that there was no T.V the novelty of running about the croft was beginning to wear off. Sandy had a favourite past time something he had done for years that was to scan the Moray Firth with his powerful binoculars, the horizon was roughly thirty miles away maybe more on a clear day, starting in the east he could follow the horizon for possibly eighty miles, on a clear evening he could see the Pentland Hills, the most exciting view he ever witnessed was the Aircraft Carrier H.M.S. EAGLE in nineteen fifty she carried out part of her sea trials in the firth although you couldn't see her with the naked eye it was possible through binoculars, Sandy was kidding the young ones on, that the window was his T.V. the only problem was that picture never really changed.

Young Liz his Canadian niece was having a go looking through the binoculars, Sandy was watching the main road suddenly he exclaimed, " Bloody tinks!" Tommy asked what was up Sandy replied, " There's a tinkies van coming up the croft road nae doot they're lookin for the quarry, some times they camp there, usually they are quite harmless, their grannies and grand fathers used to come in the days of the horse and cairt noo they all hiv cars and vans" Tommy moved over to have a look, he let out a whoop " That's nae tinks that's Hughie the Gimp fae Achnashellach" he called to Arlene who was known as Lena (pet name) " Lena come and see Fa's coming up the road". Hugh pulled up at the door and soon the Gimpys, Tommy and Arlene were hugging and jumping about like they were long lost friends. There was Hugh, Martha and four of the bairns Arlene had told Martha their secret so they wanted to be present when the ring was presented, she classed Tommy and Arlene as part of her own family, Tommy got special treatment, Martha thought Tommy was the bee's knees, the feeling was mutual, when Martha hugged people it was like a mother hugging her young she was the only woman who reminded Tommy of how his mother would give him a hug, of course when she got his face squeezed against her huge tits it felt like he would suffocate, the hugging and kissing over the Gympie's and the rest of the Duncan's were introduced, Meg took to Martha instantly and found room in the house for them to have a cup of tea, Sandy was amazed that Hugh was able to drive, but it was obvious how he got the name Gimpy. Hugh asked Sandy if there was a spot they could set up a tent, they had all the gear in the trailer and would like to stay the weekend, they had a walk round the steading and Sandy told him to pick his spot he showed them where they could get water and there was toilet facilities at the back door of the house, Sandy said he would invite them to use the main bath room but there would probably be a waiting time of three to four hours, but Hugh was happy with what was available and told Sandy they were used to roughing it. Tommy was overjoyed that Martha and Hugh had made the trip he looked on them as family; it was turning out to be quite a weekend.

As usual Sandy was out of bed at the crack of dawn the best time of the day as far as he was concerned he looked towards the playing field and was quite impressed the way it was laid out for today's event it should be quite something, he hoped to meet many old friends who were to attend mainly because the Duncan family were holding a get-together, sadly one face missing would be Will Watson. Sandy had promised to supply the music in the evening although he had managed to get a couple of younger fellows to help him out it just wouldn't be the same without his big mate. He was also heavily involved in the

235

organising committee it was a struggle to keep folks interested with so many other diversions taking up peoples spare time, forming a committee was getting harder every event, the same people were in attendance all the time, if it wasn't for Betsy Wilson Lang Dods wife the Glen would be extinct she was the main stay along with Albie Grants wife Vicky, without those two it would all fall flat so Sandy felt duty bound to assist where ever possible as did his sister Meg. To give an idea of how the depopulation had affected the Glen, there were now only five active crofters, the rest had died, retired or up sticks and left, less than ten years ago at the local games there were four active tug-of-war teams that was about fifty young fit men.

Lang Dod who was approaching his eightieth birthday and walked with the aid of a stick he still took an active part in organising the sports part of the Fete, had to ask for volunteers to make up one team, Walter, Willie and Tommy offered their services the tug-of-war used to be the highlight of the games but sadly it had been overtaken by the Hill Race, this year there were almost ten members of the Duncan family entered to take part. Anyhow Sandy had made a pot of tea, no doubt Mary would be appearing shortly she never missed a morning training, as she breezed through the door bright as a button grabbed a cup and poured her self some tea, Sandy said he thought she would be resting in view of the forth coming Hill Race. "Na, Na I intend winning Sandy, they tell me Roddy Tracy has donated a special crystal Rose Bowl to be presented to the Hill Race Winner so my intentions are to be the owner of that bowl" with that the door burst open and the young ones were clambering all over their daft auntie Mary she was still a kid at heart. Sandy only had the milk cow to see to, his main source of income now was to buy about a dozen newly weaned calves and fatten them up over winter some times it paid very well but you were at the mercy of the market he had a few stirks but they were in the field so it was quite quiet around the steading he was busy milking the cow when he looked up and saw Hugh Gimpy coming hirpling along the byre, " Good morning Sandy is there anything I can do to help"? Sandy told him everything was under control but if he wanted a cup of tea just go over to the kitchen and help himself he would be over shortly. Hugh was sitting at the table when Meg arrived in her dressing gown, she asked if he wanted a bit toast he told her he was ok, Martha would be having breakfast whenever she got up, Meg commented that he was up early " Well I would probably still be in my pit but your sister Mary has all the bairns away for a run so I had to get them sorted oot, quarter tae five they were poking at me asking if it wis time tae get up". That young sister of min is nae wise imagine rinnin aboot the hills and it still the middle of the nicht". " Ach its great for the bairns Meg, Mary seems to hiv a wie wi them" with that Sandy appeared with the bucket three quarters full of milk, Hugh made a comment that many times he had drunk the hot milk straight from the coo, Sandy asked if he fancied a glass now, Hugh nodded his head and Sandy promptly filled a glass to the neck for their visitor, the Duncan's and the Gympie's had fair taken to one another.

Over the past few years the committee have been forced to put an entrance fee charge on everybody, every year it was getting more and more expensive to hold events like this so this year it was two shillings (10p) for adults and a shilling (5p) for bairns, Albie Grant was on the gate ready for the first arrivals at eleven-o-clock this was when all the preliminary events would take place the official opening was at one pm and was to be carried out by the Old minister Jim Kerr, then the fancy dress parade would form up behind the Pipe Band and the afternoon entertainment would begin, luckily it was a brilliant day a bit too hot if anything. Everything went like clockwork there were all sorts of sideshows and things to keep the young ones amused. There was an enormous crowd many people had returned when they heard all the Duncan family were home, Sandy was over the moon to see his old neighbour and school mate Frankie Smith, he told him about the doo at Hillies in the evening, Frankie was staying with his sister in town so he assured Sandy he would be there, there were loads of others, it was quite an emotional day.

The tug of war was scheduled to be completed at four pm in time for the main event, which was the Hill Race; the course distance was five miles, up past Hillies as far as the Canadian monument across the moor then down the main Glen road, because of the amount of youngsters and women taking part the committee chaired by Lang Dod decided it would only be fair to place a handicap on the runners especially this year with the Duncan Reunion Rose Bowl a much sought after prize. The girls were first off followed two minutes later by the boys followed by the ladies, there was a protest against Mary Duncan as she did cross country running in the Army, Mary being Mary and afraid of no one opted to start with the men alongside Willie and Tommy, she out stripped the whole lot of them and was leading as they rounded the

Canadian Memorial she was closely followed by her Canadian nephew Walter (jun) closely followed by Willie and Tommy so four Duncan's were in the lead as they neared the finishing line it was still neck and neck between Mary and Walter, they crossed the line in a dead heat. Lang Dod and Roddy Tracy had a bit of a confab and after much scratching of heads and gesticulating it was decided to award the bowl to Mary Duncan, Dod always one for a bit of banter decided that Mary won by a breast, she had a bit more sticking out than young Walter but to remind him of his close encounter with his Auntie they decided to award him a Shepherds' crook courtesy of the organising committee.

Just as the games were winding up Arlene had a pleasant surprise when her parents arrived her father had an appointment in Aberdeen on Monday afternoon so they decided at the last minute to come over on the Saturday and make a week-end of it, Tommy was hurriedly found and introduced to his future in-laws he in turn took them round his family, they had managed to book a room in the hotel for the week-end and yes they would come to the doo at Hillies later on, Alex and Lena Foubister were quite impressed with their daughters choice of boy friend and also his family they were very like the Orcadians in terms of friendliness. Sandy was quite concerned with the numbers attending the re-union bash in the evening it was lucky he had prepared the neep shed as well as the barn and even at that it would be pretty hectic but this may never happen again. Spud Thompson from the hotel had managed to get a special licence which allowed him to sell booze from a stall at the croft, the W.R.I ladies had donated all the baking from the fete so there was plenty food for anybody feeling hungry. Tommy got hold of Alex Foubister on his own and told him he intended to marry his daughter, he hoped Alex didn't have any objections, he shook his head and added " I wish you all the luck in the world and hope you get as many happy years as I have had with her mither" with that the two of them shook hands, Tommy was relieved he had got that off his chest, he told Arlene he had her father's blessing for them to get married and at nine-o-clock she would see her engagement ring. She begged Tommy not to make a spectacle of presenting it to her. He told her " Arlene I'm so happy I would make a spectacle of it to the world so be prepared". The people started to gather just before eight Spud was doing a roaring trade selling booze, Sandy and the other two younger lads were tuning up ready to start playing, the first half hour was pretty stale with very few dancers participating, Sandy left the two younger lads to play by themselves as he mingled with the crowd speaking to people he hadn't seen for years.

As Sandy wandered about two young fellows appeared at his side they were carrying Guitars, they told him whose grandsons they were and asked if they could play some rock-and-roll, Sandy asked " Fit the hell's that" the loons told him it was all the rage among the young ones American style music but getting very popular in Britain as well. Sandy was always interested in music and especially encouraged young people to get interested so he told the two boys to get ready and they could have half-an-hour to show how good they were. The two lads got on the small makeshift platform and were soon giving it big licks as soon as the music started the two Canadian cousins were on the floor jiving for all they were worth, soon Mary and Tommy joined them and before too long the place was heaving, Sandy watched in amazement he had vaguely heard of Rock-and Roll but this was the first time he had witnessed it being executed, one thing it would never catch on around this area as all the Town halls had signs up saying Strictly No Jiving or Jitterbugging, before long nearly everybody in the barn was having a go in Sandy's eyes it was standing in the one place shakkin yir erse aboot. It was well past nine-o-clock before the rock boys gave up there were shouts of more, more but, Tommy was desperate to take the stage and announce his engagement. He called for quiet while he made an important announcement, "Friends, Relations and anybody not included in those two words I would like to call on my girlfriend to join me up here because we have a secret we would like to share with you all". Arlene was blushing and shaking her fist as she joined her young man on the platform. Tommy continued, " Arlene and I have been going out together for over a year now and to-day I met her dad and mam for the first time, I asked Alex if he fancied me as a son in law and he thought that would be a splendid idea, so to let other guys know that Arlene is spoken for I am going to give her an engagement ring" he placed the ring on her finger then on one knee he asked her to marry him she said yes and the crowd erupted what a moving little episode and of course all the women were thrilled. When they went back to floor level they were inundated with people hugging and kissing and wishing them luck. The evening was wearing on, Maria who was due her baby in about two months decided to go to bed she was dog tired but first she had to give Tommy and Arlene a big kiss. Everybody wanted to buy Tommy a drink if he had accepted he would be on his back before long, he grabbed hold of Arlene and told her to disappear round the back of the building, he would join her as quick as he could she looked at him with a scowl and asked "Why"? but she did as requested and with-in five minutes Tommy was at her side, " Lets make ourselves scarce for a while" he grabbed her hand and started to walk towards the village, it was a lovely evening, they had been unable to be alone since they arrived at Hillies so they just carried on walking and soon they were overlooking the village of Covie, they sat on the cliff top for about half an hour talking about their future, their marriage and various other items, he looked at his watch, it was just about eleven they would need to return to the party it was due to finish at eleven forty five. Hand in hand they made their way back up the winding path it was fairly steep but it was a wonderful evening just perfect for young lovers having a stroll, Arlene was floating on air as they enjoyed each others company. The dancing was in full swing as they entered the yard there were three sets of eightsome reel dancers in the yard four in the barn and two in the neep shed.

Sandy didn't play the accordion very often these days so he was beginning to feel the effects of the evening his fingers were stiff, they still had half an hour before they were due to finish. The two laddies who played the rock and roll were still there so Sandy called them over and asked if they fancied another half hour, they were over the moon with the offer and with-in minutes were on the small platform giving it laldy the floor was packed with old and young as they performed all sorts of movements to the music, Sandy was sure this kind of music would one day be a big hit. Lang Dod came over and told Sandy he was ready to go home Betsy and the family were going to stay till the end but the big fellow who was eighty two next birthday had had enough. As he left he said to Sandy, "It's a good job it baid dry Sandy they wid hiv hid and affa job dancing amang the dubs" with that he burst oot laughing as he left. As Sandy had surveyed the floor from the platform he had spied many of his old neighbours it was quite emotional to see them all again many of them now old and infirm one man he had to talk to who was in a wheel chair being pushed by the most gorgeous young woman. was his old neighbour Jimmy Lindsay (Jimmy the Tink) he was nae Tink noo dressed like a city gent, Sandy approached and asked how he was he said he was fine except that his legs had gone he was now living in an old folks home and pointing to his companion he asked if Sandy recognised her, she was familiar but Sandy didn't recognise her, "

240

Its Sophie my second oldest daughter" " Of course it is, my Sophie the years have fair changed you and for the better I may add" she started to blush but said she would have recognised the Duncan family anywhere none of them had really changed. Jimmy caught Sandy by the hand and told him he wouldn't have missed this doo for anything as he continued he said " Sandy Hillies if it wisna for you and Saint Meg my bairns would never have survived many a day, all we had tae eat was oatmeal and tatties can you imagine porridge wie nae milk, the wife would bile nettles or kale even a neep, then make porridge wie the bree to give it some flavour, times were hard they dinna ken their living the day but even wie all the hardships I had ten bairns they are all scattered throughout the world and everyone of them has a good job, Sophie here is the Matron of a big hospital in Yorkshire she took time off to come up here and take me to Hillies for your reunion, another of my loons is a police inspector in the London Met thankfully none of them finished up a scrounging auld bugger like their father, poaching, scrounging and pinching the lairds pheasants, Sandy went on to ask about his brother-in-law Eck Davidson," Ach Eck bides wie his sister doon at Mintlaw I never really see much of him but he is dein aw richt as far as I ken but we are all over seventy noo so yir mair or less on the scrap heap at oor age they shook hands as Sandy left to make his way round one or two others who were not on the dance floor and really enjoyed renewing auld acquaintances, he had a quick look at his watch nearly eleven he was getting tired so he would let the twa loons hiv anither ten minutes before winding up the evening he had told the police they would shut down at eleven forty five. As Sandy started to play the final couple of dances he cast his eye around the old steading there were eight sets doing the eightsome reel that was sixty four dancers there were a few who didn't take part and more of the older ones had left for home, he figured out that there must have been around one hundred people taking part. Sandy started to play a Strip The Willow at twenty past eleven at twenty to twelve they were asking him to keep going but he refused the Sabbath was only quarter an oor awa and there was nae wie he wis gan to break into it, at eleven forty three the music stopped.

It was well past midnight before Sandy got rid of the last revellers drunk people could be a pain but everybody had behaved themselves, at last peace and quiet he sat down on a straw bale and lit his pipe he hadn't had a decent smoke all day, puffing away peacefully and his mind going over the days events, suddenly his few moments of peace were shattered when he heard footsteps peering into the darkness he was able to make out two people coming towards him as they got closer he recognised his younger twin sisters. Mary asked, " Fit are yea dein sitting oot here on yir ain" " Ach it was nice and quiet efter the stramash that went on the day, I wis jist havin a smoke afore I gang into the hoose, fit hiv you twa been up tae" he asked. The two of them started at the same time " We gave Martha a hand tae get Hugh back to their tent he wis as full as whelk, and what an awkward bugger he is tae cairy, they'll hiv some job getting him tae lie in a coffin." Sandy shook his head at his sister's remark trust Mary to come up with something so comical. Just as they were about to extinguish the barn light Tommy and Arlene appeared they had walked her parents back to the hotel saying they would see them in the Kirk in the morning, it was all quiet in the house Meg and Betty were having a cup of tea the rest were in bed, Mary grabbed the tea pot and asked if anybody else would like one, Sandy shook his head and said he was going to bed.

Rather groggily Sandy sat up in bed and looked at his clock michty me it was time to get up he felt as though he was newly in bed, but he had a beast in the byre needin fed and milked, he dragged himself out of the bed and toddled through to the kitchen and was quite surprised to see Mary sitting having a cup of tea she was dressed in her running gear and ready to go, "Aye Sandy fu are yae feelin this morning it looks like I'll be rinnin myself, nae sign of any life", but she was wrong soon she was joined by the youngsters all rarin to go. Sandy groaned as he put his cap on and headed for the byre at least the auld coo would be pleased to see him. After the milking and general tidying up Sandy headed back to the house and back to bed to many late nights were beginning to catch up on him, he had a couple of hours kip then got up and dressed for the Kirk.

Jim Kerr senior came out of retirement to help his son conduct this special service, for the first time in many years the Kirk was bursting at the seams, many of the people who had attended Hillies the previous evening made the effort to be in church, after a very nostalgic hour and a bit the Duncan family made their way to their parents grave and were joined by Jim Kerr who said a special prayer in memory of Sandy and Peg Duncan who lead a very tragic sort of life but they would have been proud to see the extended family they had left behind. There was quite a squad on the road to Hillies as well as the Duncan's and their off springs there was the Gimpys, Arlene's parents Alex and Lena, and other hangers on who just wanted to say hallo. Meg with the help of the other females especially Big Martha, had made a huge container of soup along with an array of sandwiches, again Meg referred to the assembled company as just like a big day at the thrashing mill nothing seemed to faze Meg she always seemed to be in control. Now came the hard bit as the first of the guests were ready to leave, Hugh and Martha would be on there way after the lunch they needed to be home that day as they had work to attend to on the Monday as usual Martha went round the company giving huge hugs, Tommy kept his head above her shoulder so as to avoid the suffocation treatment.

Meg had taken a great shine to Martha and told her and Hugh to make sure they came back for a weekend soon, Sandy stood shaking his head as the old rickety van and trailer set off on it hundred plus miles to Achnashellach, Hugh was some hardy character the horn was still honking as they disappeared over the brow of the hill. Sandy asked if anybody fancied a walk down to Covie, most of the men wanted to go and if Auntie Mary was going the young ones would also go. The women settled down to a cup of tea and a blether one of the topics was Maria's pregnancy, Meg told her that the old midwife who was now retired had told her at the fete on Saturday that she thought Maria was carrying twins, as twins ran in the Duncan family it could just be possible, Maria seemed to be unperturbed at the thought. Peg who had been very quiet but she was always overshadowed by her more powerful twin sister Mary, decided to drop her own bombshell she had applied for a nursing job in America it had been advertised in a Nursing Magazine, she would be based in a hospital in Houston Texas her interview was next week if she was accepted she would be away before the winter set in, Betty said that would be great she could fly up to Canada to visit her and Walter it was only a couple of hours by plane. Meg said nothing but in her mind she was thinking another one of the family abroad and there was one sure thing they would never be back, listening to her brothers and sisters the countries abroad had a far better standard of life than the British had, Peg went on to say she would be trebling her wages and there was accommodation supplied. Willie, Jim and Tommy along with Mary were taken aback with the lack of people going about in Covie occasionally they would spot a curtain moving as they were being spied on. Sandy explained the circumstances many of the sixty odd houses were now owned by holidaymakers, the ones that remained locally owned by the same people that had been in school with them were now members of the Close Brethren which meant they weren't allowed to speak to non believers, as they were half way along the single street three women dressed in black their heads shrouded in shawls passed them by, Mary recognised two of the women they had been in her class in school she shouted hallo but the greeting was in vain as she was totally ignored. Sandy shook his head and told how this American preacher had turned them against people they had known all their lives and even in families there were believers and non believers who didn't talk to each other infact they even eat at separate tables its bloody well disgusting. They continued their journey allowing the youngsters to have a while on the beach and the rocks before heading back up the hill to the croft; Willie announced that he had booked tables in the hotel so they would be dining out, Meg protested stating it would cost a fortune, Willie told her it would cost her and Sandy nothing it was the family treat for the two of them.

Monday morning and Peg, and Arlene's parents were leaving on the first bus, Tommy and Arlene walked Peg to the bus stop and the parents were already waiting for the bus to arrive they told Tommy to make sure he came over to Orkney as they had lots of relatives desperate to meet him, he promised he would when ever he got the chance. Tuesday the Canadians and New Zealanders were all packed up ready to start their tour of the country they would be gone for ten days Meg was offered the chance to accompany them but she had her work to consider so she declined the offer.

Thursday morning, Arlene was ready for off Tommy accompanied her into town where she got the Inverness bus it would be well into the day before she reached Achnashellach, it was hard leaving Tommy but their options were few and far between. Tommy would have leave at the end of the year and suggested they might manage to go over to Orkney but they had plenty time to get things organised they pulled each other apart just in time before the doors on the bus closed, the conductress commented on Arlene's engagement ring as she checked her ticket, " It must be brand new is it"? Arlene blushed as she nodded her head " Aye a thocht that wie the wye you were hinging on tae yir lad, when's the big day"? Arlene said her lad was in the army and still had over a year to go so they hadn't made any plans as yet.

Tommy left on the Friday morning he would spend the weekend with Willie and Maria before returning to his unit, Willie was in the throes of buying a house in St Albans, he had had a great notion to return North when he finished with the Army but after spending a week at Hillside he made his mind up that the good life was around London, he also stressed to Tommy that he felt sorry for their brother Sandy working that croft for peanuts, he had advised him to get out and find a job, but who would want an inexperienced forty year old that was the problem. On the Friday evening after his supper Sandy sat down on his favourite chair and soaked in the atmosphere, peace and quiet at last, he really loved having the family but the noise got to him at times, he puffed away on his pipe as he listened to a programme of Scottish Dance Music on his wireless, Meg was out at a Rural meeting so he had about three hours of total bliss. His mind wandered to events over the past couple of weeks the first thought was what it cost, Meg had to spend a fortune on food although the family had contributed; his second thought was some thing Jim had said during a conversation Jim had intimated that this would possibly be his only trip home as the cost was phenomenal, it would take him ten years to get over this trip financially, soon his kids would be attending college that was expensive in New Zealand, Sandy also had in his mind that this would be the last family gathering at Hillies he was really starting to struggle luckily he still had this years harvest, he was sure to get six weeks at Burnside where he would earn roughly sixty pounds, but Lang Dod was still hankering after a combine harvester if the price was right, if that happened Sandy's days of getting casual work at the harvest would be numbered. His peace was broken in the middle of the following week when the Canadians and the Kiwis arrived back they were staying another week before they dispersed and left for home, mind you Sandy loved Big Walters company he was good fun and he could talk the same lingo as Sandy, non stop farming, all their harvesting was done by combine it paid itself after about a couple of years so he insisted it was a good investment. Their week soon passed and on the Monday morning at the end of July the two families took their leave it was a very emotional tearful parting especially for Jim and Tina they were so far away it was hard to say when they would all meet up again. Walter and Betty were not so bad and air travel was improving all the time it was getting easier to get from Canada to Scotland every year.

245

Chapter Twenty Two

ARLENE WAS AS PROUD AS PUNCH of her engagement ring and showed it off as often as she could everybody commented how lovely it looked, real expensive looking some people remarked. It was almost a month since she had had her weeks holiday at Hillside, it had been a hectic week and she had felt a bit under the weather since she got back, she put it down to having had too much to drink something she was unused to, but she then suffered a malfunction in her reproductive system it was the end of the month and she had a no show, she looked at herself in the mirror and thought I canna be, she fell back on the bed and pounding the pillow she muttered " No, No, No me mother will kill me" as she sat alone her mind racing she thought back to some of the conversations with the older women in the kitchen, some of them had remarked that they were late so, as she was only hours overdue she would give it another day or so and see what happened, she wondered if she should contact Tommy but decided against it at the moment. Arlene waited three days and nothing happened the feeling of nausea every morning seemed to be getting worse, what now she needed to discuss he plight with somebody Big Martha seemed the best bet, Tommy called her the witch doctor because everybody asked Martha for advice be it Physical, Medical or Mental, she had a way about her and of course she was the mother of six bairns if she didn't know nobody would. As soon as Arlene finished her shift in the kitchen she headed for Martha's Bothy tapped on the door and walked in Martha was having an adult moment feet up reading the Peoples Friend she knew there was a problem as soon as she saw the distressed look on the youngsters face she also had a good idea what was wrong, Arlene burst into tears as Martha wrapped her arms around her " Whits up luvvie"? Martha asked in her most soothing of voices. Sobbing her heart out Arlene told her older companion what was wrong. Martha held her tight and told her in wasn't the end of the world she wasn't the first and she wouldn't be the last, Arlene wailed "

We only did it twice" Martha held her away and looked her in the eye and said " My darling girl there is only one way to avoid this happening and that was nae tae dea it at aw once or twice what does it matter the damage is done but don't you worry about it it'll come a richt jist wait and see" It took Martha all of twenty minutes to put the smile back on Arlene's face and convince her it wasn't the end of the world, she was a unique person with so many words to describe her such as kind, loving , considerate the list is endless she was definitely in the wrong niche of life and would have made a brilliant nurse but that is another story. She told Arlene to sit down while she made a cup of tea and over their tea and a fag they would work something out. To try and put the young girl at ease Martha decided to tell her about herself and the struggle life had been but as she said it all works out fine. "I was born and dragged up on a small holding in Caithness it was the most barren inhospitable place on earth we had nothing the only way my mother managed to cloth us was to spin her own wool and knit us clothes that was every garment we wore except our skirts which she made from any pieces of scrape cloth she could scrounge, we had very little food and often we ate what the animals ate i.e. neeps the only difference between oor neeps and the coo's neeps was that my mother boiled oors the coo's ate their raw, I attended school until I was fifteen there were nae jobs and nae transport to get to Wick or Thurso so I had to hang aboot at hame until I was seventeen".

" Div yea want me to go on Martha" asked " Oh aye am fascinated" " Well I managed to get to Thurso where they had a labour exchange and plenty jobs they tried me to go into service working all oors of the day for 5/- (25p) a week plus my keep but I didn't fancy that there were plenty other jobs in factories all over the country but I didn't fancy that either so I kept gan through the list, eventually two jobs jumped out at me one was to become a Land Girl the other was a Lumber Gill, the last one took my fancy working for the Forestry so that's was what I plumped for the wages was t 12/6 (52.5p) a week for forty five hours and we lived in a hostel full board. My first posting was Nethybridge, but I was only there a short time before they sent me to Lochaber to plant trees, one morning the foreman told me to stay by the Bothy they were expecting a lorry load of young trees and four of us had to help the driver unload. About an hour later the lorry arrived and this handsome chap wound down the window and asked where he was going to dump the trees we told him and he reversed into position, the drivers door was on the far side from where we were standing so we didn't see him get out but he seemed to be ages, I went round to see what was keeping him I near burst into tears when I saw this handsome man was severely disabled, it was difficult for him to stand on the hub of the wheel to get down on the ground, I looked away as he struggled not wanting to embarrass him, once he was on the ground he was fine and climbed on the back of the lorry and started to hand us the sacks full of sapling trees, he couldn't keep us all working so I jumped up and helped him. When we stopped for a breather he asked what us young lassies did with ourselves in this god-forsaken place. I asked his name and he told me it was Hugh Macleod but he was known as Hugh the Gimp because of his disability, this name didn't seem to bother him as he explained he had been disabled for eight years ever since his accident with a horse dragging timber. His next question was would I like to go to a dance in Spean Bridge the following Friday evening, I was thrilled and was beginning to take a shine to this cocky young fellow, he asked me how old I was which was eighteen he was twenty four, so I agreed to go with him but how would we get there, he told me just be ready at eight-o-clock outside the hostel and he would be there. I didn't tell the other girls but got myself dolled up with the meagre clothes I had available then sneaked out and met Hugh, he arrived in a Forestry van being driven by another fellow. Hugh didn't dance but we sat and listened to the music the place was packed with soldiers who seemed quite envious that Hugh had one of the few girls in the place while they sat around twirling their thumbs, many of them were drunk. " Anyhow to cut a long story short Hugh and I started courting, four months later I found myself in the same situation as you are in now pregnant no money no home, it was pointless going back to Caithness. We sat down and had a big discussion and decided we would best get married, Hugh managed to obtain a two roomed Bothy and we got the local minister to marry us and so we settled down to married life in the most Spartan conditions but we were in love so what more did we need. Six years ago we were up in this area fishing one week-end, Hugh met in with an old Forestry friend who said they were needing workers desperately and he knew where there was a three bedroom Bothy he was sure Hugh could get it, it was very basic but plenty room in it. So sixteen years and six bairns later this is our happy home we are still poor but happy."

Arlene felt totally relaxed Martha certainly had a way about her, now she asked what Arlene intended to do, " Yea think nine months is a lang time but believe me it will soon be upon you so you need to get cracking, have you told Tommy yet"? She shook her head. " Well that's the first thing you need to do so I suggest you get him to phone you it's much better than writing", " Then you need to see a doctor who will take care of any medical needs, what about your mam and dad? Arlene again burst into tears " Fit am aw gan tae say tae them"? She wailed. Again it was left to Martha to console her and try and convince her everything would be just fine, she hoped. Back in the hotel Arlene phoned Tommy's barracks she got hold of a clerk who promised he would get a message to Tommy to phone his fiancée that evening at nine-o-clock, she told him that Tommy knew the contact number. Arlene's brain was in turmoil as she fretted about how to approach her parents, Martha had said her mother would be over the moon once she realised she was going to become a granny, from the time she had contacted Tommy's headquarters until nine-o-clock seemed like a life time. She had been sitting by the phone since quarter to nine it was now ten past and no word she was getting impatient and at twenty past was about to go to her room when suddenly it burst into life she grabbed it and said " It that you Tommy" and was so pleaded when the voice at the other end said " Aye Lena fits up?" " Are you sittin doon?" " No I'm standing up in the phone box haddin the phone is there a problem" " Well I probably hiv a bigger one than you because I'm about five weeks pregnant", the phone went silent, then a voice at the other end said "Bloody hell that's a bit of a shock I'll need tae try and get hame. Oh gosh Lena I didn't mean that to happen I'm sorry", the tears were blinding Arlene as she felt so alone and abandoned, Tommy started to speak again, " Look quine I need to think things over and see what we need to dea, I'll phone back to-morrow night and let you know the plans" with that the phone call finished Arlene made her way to bed and cried herself to sleep. Tommy had to get the finger out he needed advice but who could he turn to, he confided in one of his mates who was already married he suggested the Tommy should go and talk to the Padre he was involved in welfare. The door at the end of the corridor had a nameplate saying Padre Capt Williams C of E, Tommy knocked and was told to come in, he had spoken to the Padre briefly once before so they were not well known to each other, he was a big gangly man very gentle when he spoke he stood up and shook hands and then asked Tommy what his name was once the formalities were over and he found out how far Tommy was from home he listened to his tale of woe of how his fiancée was pregnant and he would have to arrange getting married the Padre asked him some questions about how he felt about marriage, was he ready for it etc, he then advised Tommy to get an appointment with his company commander and see if he could get a forty eight hour pass, go home and see his girlfriend. At the same time he could make arrangements and set a date for his marriage he also told Tommy he could arrange to get a special licence which would speed up the process, Tommy asked if he could perform a ceremony if his girl was willing to come and live in England, the Padre said he would be delighted as he never had many opportunities to perform weddings mostly christenings and the odd funeral, Tommy thanked him and took his leave now to try and get to see his Company Commander....

The Company Commander granted Tommy an audience that morning just after company orders, he had requested a forty eight hour pass on compassionate grounds the Padre had already spoken to the C.C so he had the gist of the request. He told Tommy to be seated then gave him a short lecture about being a careless young man, he said he was aware from where Tommy came from and the length of time it would take to get there and back, Tommy explained that he would need to talk to his fiancée before he could settle a date for the pass she would need to get time off her work as well, the C.C said that would be ok as soon as he had a date get back in touch. It would be nine hours before he could speak to Arlene again but in the mean time he would work out a plan on how they would tackle things. Arlene must have had her hand on the phone it barely made one ring before she was speaking into it, she sounded anxious, Tommy told her his plans he could get a forty eight hour leave, could she get off Sunday and Monday and travel to Inverness and they could stay in bed and breakfast he would travel back on the overnight on Monday, she thought that would be all right but she would need to check with her boss, Tommy asked her to phone the barracks as soon as she found out, he would need to know the answer so that he could get things moving they said goodbye and settled down to another long night, this phone call business was hopeless. Tommy got the answer he was hoping for Arlene would meet him in Inverness on Saturday afternoon, would he phone her back that night to confirm the arrangements, Tommy made his request for a forty eight hour pass for the following Monday Tuesday. His plans were to travel to Inverness on the late train on Friday night he would arrive after midday Arlene should already have arrived so she would be waiting at the station.

Tommy had an uneventful journey and managed to sleep most of the way he arrived in Inverness at twelve thirty, his heart started to flutter when he spotted Arlene on the platform waiting for him. After a few passionate kisses and hugs they decided to find a bed and breakfast place so they could get rid of their small holdalls, where would they go neither of them were acquaint with Inverness so they asked a porter if he could point them towards a place to stay he suggested Castle Street it was a short walk from the train station and was clear of the town centre, with-in ten minutes they were deciding which door to approach as there were B&B either side of the street, one small white washed place had a vacancies sign in the window, as they approached the door Tommy whispered in Arlene's ear, "Am going to asked for a double room" this did nothing for her nerves but the door opened and a rather large West Coast woman asked how she could help, Tommy said they were looking for a double room for two nights, she held out her hand in welcome and introduced herself as Flora Matheson as she shook Arlene's hand she looked at the ring, she felt in her own hand, she held it up and praised the beauty of it before asking when the big day was, Arlene was blushing when she said that was the reason they were in Inverness to arrange their forth coming marriage. Tommy's plans were scuppered Flora was a professional it wasn't the first unmarried couple that had tried to use her guesthouse as a bawdyhouse; the shaking of the hands was a great leveller. "Right I'll show you the rooms I have available they are 7/6 (37.5p) per night each." She also made sure there would be no hanky panky by giving Tommy a room up stairs and Arlene was next door to her own.

They dropped their bags Tommy had a quick wash and they met in the hallway, might as well find some where so that they could talk it was a lovely day. They walked along by the river until they came to Cavell Gardens where the war memorial was sited there were plenty empty seats so they picked the most secluded one and sat down, Tommy asked if she had contacted her mother, she shook her head as her eyes filled with tears she said she wanted to get their plans sorted out first. Tommy asked if she had any ideas, she hadn't, really looking for him to take the lead, he said that if he had the money he would buy himself out of the army for a start but that would cost one hundred and thirty pounds so that was out of the question. He told her his plan, when he got back to his unit he would find out the rules governing marriage the padre would help him he would then contact Arlene to arrange a date she could then pack her job in and move down to where Tommy was stationed by that time he would have rented accommodation for them they would receive an allowance from the Army to help with rent etc. He asked Arlene what her thoughts were she said she knew her mother would be disappointed but she could see no alternative. They continued and had a walk round the Islands returning via the west side of the river just before they arrived at the Bridge they spotted an Italian Restaurant the Ness Café looking at the prices it looked quite good fish, chips, peas, tea, bread and butter 5/- (25p) each as it was about five-o-clock they decided to eat, after supper they carried on walking down the riverside until they reached the Palace Cinema on the billboards out side they were advertising the film From Here To Eternity, there had been great rave notices about this film so they decided to spend the evening at the flicks. It was after ten when they got back to Castle Street before saying good night to each other Arlene asked Tommy if he would like to go to Church with her in the morning he said yes, Arlene had noticed the lovely Cathedral across the river and decided that was where she would like to worship along with her future husband.

Sunday morning after a huge Scottish breakfast Tommy and Arlene set off about ten the Church service didn't start until eleven so they had a wander about trying to kill time. The service lasted for well over an hour, which saw them back on the street just on twelve thirty, they decided to get some Sunday papers and find a seat probably back at Cavell Gardens, for the next couple of hours they enjoyed the sunshine and read their papers. Tommy felt like a cup of coffee so they set off to find some where but it was like looking for a needle in a haystack there was nowhere open, he asked if there was anywhere he could get a pint but he should have known from his days in Achnashellach you had to be a bona fide traveller to qualify for a drink on a Sunday, Tommy asked a guy if it was possible to find a place so that he could buy a pint this fellow suggested the Northern Bar Tommy had quick look inside and turned and walked away it was virtually packed and held some really rough looking characters no place for a lady. They eventually found a café the Washington Soda Fountain they were able to buy coffee but it was quite noisy and seemed to be the meeting place for Inverness teenagers they drank their coffee and left. They trudged round the streets for the next couple of hours thankfully the weather was brilliant but as far as Tommy was concerned Inverness was the most boring place he had ever had the misfortune to have to spend time in, after managing to get high tea in the Columba Hotel they went to an evening church service there was nothing else.

They were back in the B&B around nine-o-clock, there was a small sitting room where they could sit and finalise their plans, they agreed that Tommy would get the ball rolling when ever he got back to his depot, they would both write Arlene's parents, they had to be told as soon as possible it was only fair to them. They were both in bed by quarter eleven Flora was hovering about making sure they remembered where their separate bedrooms were. Monday was just as exciting as the previous two days except for the fact that there were shops open, they spent a while going round Woollies Arnotts and F.A.Camerons an other hour was spent in the museum. Finally it was time for Arlene to catch her train back to Achnashellach. It was a very tearful parting, she reminded Tommy to get things moving as soon as he could. Tommy had five hours to wait his train didn't leave until eight pm. As he wandered around the streets he noticed another two picture houses both commenced showing movies at five pm great he would go to the flicks until half seven that would fill in the time for him. As he emerged from the La Scala Cinema it was now dark he made his way to the station and boarded the London train, the journey was quite uneventful and he would arrive in London around 8am. After a troubled night Tommy gathered his small travel bag and headed for the wash and brush up area he felt manky the old steam trains were dirty and the dirt added to the discomfort of travelling overnight, he thought of Arlene she would be busy preparing breakfast if they had any guests staying in the hotel probably fishers enjoying the lochs and rivers that were abundant in the north of Scotland. Feeling very much refreshed after having a shave and shower Tommy felt a new man he had eighteen hours before he was due back in his depot, looking at his watch it was getting near nine-o-clock he decided to phone his brother Willie the chances of him being at home were remote but you never know. Ring, Ring, Ring no answer, then life at the other end and a rather groggy voice spoke, he gave his home number then asked how he could help " A good feed o bacon and egg wid be fine" " Hi is that you Tommy fit the hell are yea dein on the phone this bloody early" " Well its like this I'm in Kings X station and I have a hale day to kill so I'll be there in just over an oor if that's a richt" " Great see you in an oor, bye" An hour and a quarter later Tommy knocked at his brothers door it was answered by a heavily pregnant Maria she gave him a huge hug and kiss, and in her heavily accented voice she said how pleased she was to see him.

Tommy hugged his sister-in-law and commented that she still had the bump; she nodded and said it should be gone next week. In the kitchen Willie was sitting in his dressing gown looking right miserable when Tommy asked what his problem was he told him he had just flown in from Japan he had done the return flight in five days so was absolutely shattered, he said he was going back to bed for a couple of hours but would be up in time to go for lunch possibly down to the nearest pub, Tommy blethered away to Maria and told her about his problem and that Arlene and him were getting married as soon as possible. Just after mid-day Willie made for the bathroom to shower, the three of them then went along to Willies local where they had lunch. Maria told Tommy he better give his brother his news, Tommy told Willie the whole scenario about having to bring the marriage forward and that he was getting things arranged down here as he would have difficulty with the residential laws governing marriage at home.

Willie shook his head "Tommy, Tommy if there is a wrang wye of dein things you're the man" he went on to ask what Arlene's parents were saying about it Tommy shook his head and said he hadn't told them yet. Willie then went on to say if Arlene wanted to come down here she could stay with them he also thought it would be good company for Maria. Tommy eventually sorted everything out and Arlene and him got married and started life in rented rooms, Maria had twin boys. Tommy was posted to Germany where he completed his army service, the Army pleaded with him to sign on but he had decided that with his skills as a bull dozer driver and digger driver financially he would be better off in civvy street. They settled down in Ross-shire where there was an abundance of employment, their first few years were spent in a caravan until such time as they got a house.

Back at Hillies life just passed them by, Peg had left for America to pursue her nursing career, by the November term of that year there were only three crofters left, Sandy's bank account was hovering back and forth from red to black and then it would go from black to red he was expecting a call from the banker any day. When he had stopped working his horses and bought a tractor, (he still had his old horse by the way even although Lang Dod always maintained that it was a waste of space and eating another profitable animals rations but he was Sandy's pet and no way would he hear any wrong about old Robbie) anyhow Sandy no longer needed to be in the stable as early as he used to be when working with horses so he had established a routine a few years previous where he got out of bed at twenty past five boiled the kettle, while that was happening he would have a quick wash, then settle down to a cup of tea and his first smoke of the day at five to six he would switch on his radio and listen to the weather forecast then the news, as he concentrated on what the news reader said that particular morning he near had a fit. Due to an out break of Foot and Mouth in Cumbria the government had placed a restriction on the movement of all cloven hoofed livestock, Sandy felt numb thankfully he had purchased his calves for fattening up over the winter but what if he couldn't sell them he would be sunk the money off the calves was his lifeline to survival if they didn't sell he had virtually no income, shaking his head he muttered to himself what the bloody hell next. It was heading to-wards the end of the year again Sandy was still worried about the outbreak of Foot and Mouth the government was saying it was under control but it would be better to hear it was over, he was getting very disillusioned with the croft they just seemed to lurch from one crisis to another. Meg decided that when the school broke up for the Christmas holiday she was going down to London to see Willie and Tommy and their wives she would book a sleeper and travel overnight, Sandy was a bit concerned at her going alone but Willie said he would meet her at King's X. Sandy and Meg had changed their lifestyle in as much as they only had a snack midday, in the evening at six-o-clock they would have dinner. To night was one of Sandy's favourite meals mince, tatties and mealie jimmie he was getting stuck in when Meg said " Dea yea want tae hear the latest" With his mouth full of food he nodded hid head, Meg continued " Dea yae ken fit Lang Dods getting for his eighty third birthday" Sandy shook his head and said " Fit" Meg shook her head and said " Betsy and the bairns are buying him a second hand combine".

Sandy near choked on his dinner as he spluttered a mouthful of mince and tatties flew across the table, Meg continued without realising the consequences of what she had just relayed to her brother, " The women at work were having a good laugh the combine is a Claas so somebody was asking if his first name would be Santa as in Santa Claus" Sandy wasn't hearing his sister as his mind was racing and wondering what the consequences for him would be, the Lang fellow was one of his best friends but every piece of modern technology that Dod Wilson purchased was another nail in Sandy's coffin. Sandy was in a very pensive mood all evening and continued through the night he hardly managed a wink of sleep, this year he had earned just under one hundred pounds from his six weeks harvest that money had kept his bank balance in the black without it he would be in dire straits things were looking grim and there was no diversifying he was stuck with what he had, his problem was that his business was too small, the other two surviving crofters had more or less full time jobs, Albie Grant worked for an agricultural contractor his job was a feast or famine hardly working at all then working round the clock to meet demand, Davie Morrison was a mechanic so he had a steady income the croft was only an extra and in Albie,s case Victoria was quite capable of running the croft on her own. Meg left on the eighteenth of December it was her first sortie in a sleeper and she wouldn't recommend it she had never felt so uncomfortable in her life and sleep eluded her for the whole twelve hours. Willie was his usual cheerful self as he hugged his twin sister there was a special bond between them, she was full of questions about the twins who were now two months old, he told her they were doing fine and also praised Arlene for the help she had given Maria over the first few weeks. Meg had her second tour of London as they drove through the centre past some of the famous places Buckingham Palace the Houses of Parliament etc but she was quite happy she was only passing through it was far too crowded for her liking. One thing she really enjoyed was the decorations they really brightened the place up, Willie and Meg had a great conversation bringing him up to date with what was going on in the Glen and who was doing what. An hour later they arrived at the house, Maria was up to her eyes with nappies, clothes and all the nick knacks required when feeding babies, she gave Meg a big hug and than handed her one of her latest Nephews one was Billy and one called after Maria's father was Heinz, when Sandy had first heard the names he was given a rebuke when he enquired if they had called one after a tin of beans. They were two healthy looking lads with an excellent pair of lungs, Maria handed Meg a feeding bottle while Willie made a cup of tea she was assured that after being fed there would be silence. Arlene and Tommy were coming to stay for Christmas then they were going to travel north with Meg on the twenty eighth heading for Orkney where they would celebrate Hogmanay with Arlene's parents they were all good friends after the initial shock of being told Arlene was pregnant but Tommy still felt a bit apprehensive about meeting his father-in –law. Maria was delighted she had two sisters-in-law staying for Christmas as the twins were a real handful but with Arlene being a chef and Meg being a first class cook she could concentrate on her babies. She did manage to add a little bit of Swedish to the proceedings just so that she would feel at home. The festivities went well it was a first for Meg and Arlene they had never celebrated Christmas before, Willie and Tommy babysat while the girls attended midnight mass.

Meg was in her element nursing the babies between herself and Arlene they gave Maria a good rest, but all good things come to an end far too quickly and soon Tommy, Arlene and Meg were chugging their way back to Scotland, they parted company at Aberdeen Station, she boarded the train for home and they continued their journey to Kirkwall, the idea was that they would spend a week with Arlene's parents then come back to Hillies for a few days with Meg and Sandy. Sandy was quite pleased to see his sister arrive back home he liked his own company up to a point but it was hard work looking after yourself and keeping a croft going he suddenly realised how invaluable his sister was and the amount of work she got through in a day. They were two days away from Hogmanay Meg had a lot to catch up on, she only had Sandy and herself to cater for but she would make sure they had a special New Years dinner as usual.

Hogmanay passed and you would never know anything had happened a few of the Glen people fired off shot guns at midnight Sandy and Meg had a dram or two then the phone started to ring as the family round the world called home to wish their oldest brother and sister a happy New Year how Sandy longed for his old pal Will Watson to burst through the door and strike up the fiddle but alas those days were well and truly gone. New years day and Sandy was in the byre just after six he told Meg to have a long lie he would milk the cow. He made his way back to the house there was a little snow on the ground and it was very frosty some folks would say it was seasonal but not nearly as severe as it used to be. New Years night Meg and Sandy had an invite to visit Albie and Victoria Grant they had just bought a T.V. more or less the first in the Glen the reception was very poor but they were promised there would be a booster fitted soon, Sandy and Meg arrived at seven thirty Victoria answered the door and called through to Albie that they had arrived he wished them a Happy New Year told Vicky to get them a drink then planked himself back in front of his Telly. It was a programme called Bonanza, cowboys, everybody in the house was glued to the little box with the flickering light Sandy and Meg were handed their drinks and offered a bit short bread, Vicky then sat down and stared at the box. As soon as that programme finished another one started if anybody tried to speak all you would hear was sh, sh, sh. Sandy was not enamoured if that was how it was with Television you could keep it, he remained silent for as long as was humanly possible then made an excuse to go home, he turned to Meg as they trudged through the snow and said, " There will never be a television in my house as lang as I'm livin." Tommy and Arlene arrived from Orkney, Sandy and Tommy had a belated celebration, Arlene's mother had sent over some of her home made cake so they enjoyed a good old chin wag while eating cake and drinking whisky, Sandy was still moaning about New Years Night, if only he could turn back the clock. Tommy and Arlene stayed three days before heading south, Tommy was taking up his new posting in Germany in the middle of the month, Arlene would stay with Willie and Maria until Tommy got quarters sorted out then she would join him, the baby was due in April so they had a decision to make would she come to Scotland so that it would be born a Jock or would she stay in Germany, then it would be hard to say what nationality it would be. After they left Sandy settled down to his usual routine, but at the back of his mind was the nagging problem of what the future held for him and also his sister Meg, there was strong rumours that the school was about to close.

Chapter Twenty Three

SANDY WAS BELEAGUERED WITH WORRIES DUE to the foot and mouth problem in England last year, nobody wanted to buy British beef although the Government had given the all clear the Europeans were against it so the price of British dairy products were in the laps of the gods, Sandy needed a good price for his calves and at the moment they were rock bottom. He suffered another disastrous blow that was to knock him for six, sitting at his breakfast early one morning the phone rang Meg was still in bed so he answered it himself, it was Hans the German P.O.W from Burnside he was real excited when he asked in his German/ Doric accent " Aye Sandy is that you min? Hans here."" Aye Hans yir early on the go this morning, fits a dea"? Stuttering over his words Hans continued " Its, Its Lang Dod he drappit deed this mornin, fin he tried tae get oot oh his bed, Betsy's in an affa state". Sandy was struck dumb his surrogate father gone and he hadn't spoken to him for weeks, he apologised to Hans as he said he would have to ring off and call back later he felt physically sick. Sandy felt weak another stalwart of the Glen gone how was he going to cope it had been a long time since he needed Lang Dod for guidance but occasionally he still talked to the Big man more or less for reassurance. The door of Megs bedroom opened and she looked at her brother and knew something was seriously wrong, " Fits a dea wie yea she asked and fa wis on the phone" Sandy shook his head and with his voice breaking he told her " It wis Hans fae Burnies Lang Dod drappit deed this morning" with that he buried his head and his hands and came close to bursting into tears, Meg put her arms round her brother and gave him a big hug, " Jist you sit there and have another cup of tea until you feel mair like yirsel, it hid tae happen some time Sandy I ken its sair at the time but it happens tae abody" with that she busied herself getting ready to milk the coo. Later on that day Sandy phoned Burnies to pass on his condolences, Young George answered the phone he asked Sandy if he would like to speak to his mother, Betsy and Sandy were great mates so it was fairly easy to talk to her she seemed quite composed and seemed to have got over the initial shock she told Sandy the big fellow had died in her arms at six-o-clock it only took seconds so it was quite painless, the funeral was arranged for one-o-clock Saturday and would Sandy be available to take a chord, he told her it would be a great honour for him to do so and with that they wrang off. Lang Dods funeral was typical for that part of the world it would take place on Saturday at one-o-clock the idea for this was that the farmers worked Saturday morning until midday, by having the funeral at one they wouldn't loose any working time speak about being tight.

The day before the funeral Meg had a phone call from Willie, he was coming North for Lang Dods funeral they would arrive late Friday evening, this call got Megs adrenaline going she would be able to spoil her twin nephews and of course have some time with her own twin brother and his wife, Tommy was in Germany, Mary in Japan, Jim in New Zealand, Betty in Canada and Peg in the States so there was little chance of any of the other Duncan family attending much to their sorrow as Lang Dod Wilson was as near to a father as they could get. Willie and Maria arrived, just before nine-o-clock in the evening the twins were sound asleep, Meg had a couple of cots ready for them so they were quickly undressed and night clothes put on and into bed hardly wakening.

The four adults sat and blethered until tiredness overtook them and they retired to bed, they had gone over some of the highlights that had occurred during Lang Dods life time, Meg had brought up the subject of the son that Lizzie Smith and Lang Dod had many years ago neither Lizzie or the boy had been heard of for many years, but they decided that it would put the cat among the pigeons if he turned up demanding his share of the will, Sandy added that he thought that the boy had been a teacher in London and that's where Lizzie went when she found out that the Lang fellow was having an affair wie Betsy the land girl. Sandy continued " Yea see Lang Dod was all for marrying Lizzie when he found oot she wis expecting but then his mither stepped in, she thought that because Lizzie wis jist a skivvie she wasn't good enough for her George so the rumour went that she paid Lizzie to sort the bairn oot herself, then when auld Mrs Wilson died Lizzie went back to keep hoose for Dod, people said they lived as man and wife but Dod wouldn't go against his mothers wishes even though she was dead and gone". Willie butted in " Aye the mither didn't think a skivvie was good enough for her precious son, have yae ever wondered what she would have thought when she found oot he had married the orra loon (odd job boy Betsy's job on the farm) she'd probably turned in her grave."

Saturday morning Sandy was up at his usual time, he was surprised to see Willie walk through the door in his dressing gown, Maria and him had just finished feeding the twins they were back sleeping so Willie decided to get up and have a cup of tea, he got a cup and the two brothers had a good chinwag as they supped their tea. Meg asked Willie if he would run her over to Burnside she was giving a hand with the catering, it was a traditional funeral so everybody was invited back to the farm for some eats. Back at Hillies Sandy had completed his chores around the croft and started to get himself ready, he would need to be early as he had the honour of being a pall bearer. Willie had to park the car outside the farmyard as room would be at a premium, as the two brothers walked towards the house Sandy had to smile to himself as they passed the new Dutch barn, standing inside the entrance was Lang Dods new toy his Combine Harvester and guess what he had never seen it working and had no chance of ever seeing it working now, Sandy explained to his brother why he had a grin on his face. Lang Dod Wilson's popularity shone through at his funeral the farm close was jam-packed. Sandy stood with the other pallbearers looking towards the assembled crowd he recognised many faces and even people who had left the area years ago, Frankie Smith, Eck Davidson (in a wheel chair), Jimmy Lindsay (the Tink) and many others. An hour later they were in the cemetery men only the women had stayed behind again sticking to tradition or so Sandy thought until his eye's wandered towards the gate and there stood a very frail old lady leaning heavily on a younger man, Sandy could recognise some thing about her and wracked his brain as he tried to put a name to her just as the coffin was being lowered into the ground he got it, Lizzie Smith dear me that was a turn up for the books. It set him thinking would she be there through love or hate knowing Lizzie it was probably the latter, the funeral service over everybody was making for the entrance gate Sandy spotted Lizzie sitting in a car he went over and had a few words she was well into her seventies, but very alert she asked Sandy how his family had fared.

Turning to the man sitting beside her she introduced her son Alistair, he had a strong resemblance to Dod Wilson, he shook hands with Sandy and said his mother had told him a lot about the folks in the Glen, neither of them mentioned the man who had just been buried. Back at Burnies there was quite a mob, the women had laid on a bit of a spread you were also offered a drink either whisky or sherry, Betsy looked rather sad but she had everything under control as she mingled among the mourners stopping for a word with Sandy and Willie. The Duncan brothers didn't stay long Willie wanted to make sure Maria was ok, Meg said she would get a lift home as she intended staying until the washing up was done. Maria was having the time of her life the twins were a sleep and she had managed to get her feet up for a couple of hours, a cup of tea and a bundle of Megs Peoples Friends had provided her with much needed rest.

Willie and Sandy decided to have some brother time in the pub that evening, over a couple of pints Sandy poured out his heart about how difficult it was to make ends meet on the croft and that he was staring bankruptcy in the face, he was due an update on his bank statement shortly and he was near having a nervous breakdown worrying about it. Willie looked his older brother square in the eye and told him " Sandy get out man you don't need to slave your guts oot any mair there's only you and Meg left here, so get yourself a job away from that slavery there is nae job noo-a-days where yae have tae work twenty four hours a day for the kind of money you get its nae worth it and the langer yea pit it aff the harder it'll be tae get a job, so tak the bull by the horns and get oot" Sandy was deep in thought and in his mind he was thinking I wish it was as easy as Willie was makin it. They left the pub at nine-o-clock which was the official closing time as they wandered up the hill they had a good old discussion about who was left in the glen, Sandy said he hardly ever saw any of his neighbours anymore and told Willie, " Yea could lie deed in the hoose for weeks and naebody wid miss yea that's fit its like noo-a-days. Willie and Maria left early next morning he was due to fly to Saudi on Monday evening so he wanted to be well rested before then. Another blow was received in the Glen when word was finally announced that the school would close at the summer holidays that would make Meg redundant from her two hour-a-day job her chances of getting another were pretty remote one or two women were employed at the mansion house mostly part time but those jobs were taken, things were looking grim. Sandy survived the May term by the skin of his teeth his bank balance had been saved by an upturn in the price he got for his calves, his next dilemma was how much work he would get over the hay and crop harvest he didn't hold out much hope and now with his mentor Lang Dod no longer around he was doubtful. He was heading for his forties in a couple of years time, soon the lease of the croft would be up he knew the options were to buy the place or move on, he shook his head at the hopeless situation he was heading for, Willie was right, now was the time to get out he would have a good think and start making a move shortly. He started to run through the changes that were about to happen, this was the last year the threshing mill would operate everybody was combine crazy, as of next year Sandy would need to hire a contractor to combine his crops they charged nearly twice as much as the traditional threshing mill, he would need to widen all his gates to allow access more expense it didn't bear thinking about.

To avoid causing Meg undue stress Sandy made an appointment to meet his banker, he used the public telephone beside the village hall. It had been quite some considerable time since he had occasion to speak to the bank, the voice on the other end sounded quite nice and helpful she asked Sandy what the appointment was about, he explained that he needed to discuss his account but made sure he avoided telling her that he was about to give up on the croft, if she was a bit of a gossip everybody in the Glen would soon find out. Sandy was told to report to the bank at two pm the following Tuesday that was over a week away they must be real busy. The stress of waiting for his appointment to arrive was getting to him he was frustrated and very short in the grain eventually Meg cornered him and asked what the hell was going on, after much stuttering and spluttering Sandy decided to come clean, Meg already knew that the income from the croft barely kept them afloat so it wasn't really a surprise when Sandy told her he was seeing the banker his main reason for the visit to the bank was to find out what his credit position was. Meg took it all in her stride she had never received a wage off the croft although Sandy always gave her enough to keep them going, he explained what Willie had said about getting out, she was in full agreement it was better to get out than to be pushed out.

As usual for an official appointment Sandy dressed in his best outfit, collar and tie and Sunday suit he was early at the bank, the young lady at reception told him to take a seat and he would be attended to shortly. As his eyes wandered around the place he could hardly believe the transformation that had taken place over the years. On his first visit with Lang Dod Wilson, there was only two women old Jeannie Roberson and a younger girl, everything was done by hand now there are type writers on every desk with young females working on them,

Jeanie was always dressed in a smart costume, the lassies working in the bank now were barely dressed at all their paps sticking out the top of their blouses and the skirts would not have looked out of place round their necks as there was little more cloth than you would get in a scarf it was enough to put a man wrang thought Sandy. The longer he had to wait the nerves in his stomach got worse and worse eventually the door to an office opened and out stepped Davie Fraser he shook hands with his departing client and turned to Sandy, " Aye, Aye Sandy fit like jist gang awa through" he said pointing to his office. He asked if Sandy would like tea or coffee then buzzed somebody on the phone and ordered two coffee's, when the door opened Sandy's eyes near popped out of his head this must be a record for the shortest skirt he had ever seen out of politeness he made no comment. "Thank you Gail" she smiled at Sandy on her way out. Davie had the Duncan folder in front of him looking at Sandy he asked how he could help, Sandy thought the best thing to do was come clean and tell Davie that things were terrible and getting worse by the day. Davie shook his head and told Sandy he was well aware of the crofters predicament as his father had started to experience it a few year ago but he was lucky in the fact that he had been ready to retire so he had no worries about finding work, he went on to say that the Bank were getting nervous about overdrafts as the means of paying them off were few and far between. He was aware that the modern technology was taking its toll on the crofters and Sandy was not alone in his predicament.

Davie Fraser was a very helpful man normally, but the problem before him was one the bank had no idea how to help, the whole thing was, we were now living in a changing world and people like Sandy Duncan who were set in their ways found change hard to get used to the bank had no easy solutions and lending money to a sinking ship would only lead to further problems and people like Sandy would end up with nothing, maybe in some cases homeless, Davie put the onus back on Sandy by asking what his plans were. " Well Davie and this is highly secret at the moment but I am seriously thinking of giving up the croft, I only have a couple of more years before the lease is up and the trustees will be wanting to sell Hillies how could I buy it,? my account is maybe in the red as it is so I have no chance". Davie scrutinised Sandy's file and nodding his head he confirmed that he was in the red. Davie's advice was for Sandy to contact the Labour Exchange see what they could do in the way of employment and take it from there, he pointed out that Sandy could still struggle on until he had had sorted things out, as the two of them shook hands he told Sandy to keep in touch and when he did, to ask for him personally. Sandy felt really down when he left the Bank he had never been in the Labour Exchange in his life and had no idea how to go about it. The last time he had such trauma on his hands he had Lang Dod for support, how he would have benefited from the Lang fellows advice right now. After walking for about ten minutes Sandy realised he was heading in the wrong direction instead of the Dole office he was heading out of town along the cliff top path the same route that Lang Dod and him had taken over twenty years ago when his father died, he decided to keep going and eventually arrived at the seats overlooking the bay he sat down his head in his hands and was lost in thought when suddenly he was jolted back to reality. "Aye Sandy Hillies fit are yea dein here, yir nae thinking oh jumpin ower the cliffs are yea"? "Bye the worried look on yir face yea hid me fair worried aboot yea." Sandy had to screw up his eyes as he tried to focus on the person who had conducted the verbal assault on him, " Michty me Freddie West ah thocht yea wir deed it's a lang time since we spoke tae ane anither", Freddie and Sandy had been in school together same class Freddie was from the village of Covie his father was a fisherman, the village was full of people with the surname West so they all had nicknames Freddie's family nickname was Shounders nobody had any idea what that meant but his grand patents had been Shounders so the name had been around for some time. Sandy was keen to find out what had happened to Freddie after he left school so he asked him all about it. " Well Sandy its like this you'll remember when the Brethren took over, most of the Covie folk were like sheep dein whit they wanted them to do, like attending meetings every evening well some of us reneged, me for one." " Well they broke oor family up my father, mither, brithers and sister all joined that left me an outcast, unclean as they put it so I was banished from the dinner table nae allowed tae take part in any family activities treated like a leper". "Well I put up wie it for say lang then reneged, when I was auld enough I joined the Merchant Navy and spent ten years travelling the world never going near Covie ever again, then I had some leave so I came North and met up wie a quine that wis at the school wie us, one thing led to another and we got married so I settled doon here, the story of my life till noo."

It was Sandy's turn to pour his heart out about the struggle and hardships he had faced in his life it had not been easy and now the biggest hurdle of the lot, Freddie listened to his friend nodding or shaking his head as Sandy rumbled on, at times Freddie would butt in and ask what happened to the rest of Sandy's siblings he was amazed at how far flung they were, world wide really. Their two lives sorted out up until the present the two of them settled down had a smoke and discussed various incidents and people they had grown up with some had passed on, others moved on it was one of the most relaxing couple of hours Sandy had experienced in a long time, finally after everybody and everything had been sorted out Freddie asked what Sandy's intentions were. Sandy shook his head and said he was unsure at the moment; firstly he had to get a job but that was very difficult as his skills were limited outside farming he also had to get a house and give up the croft as soon as possible other wise the bailiffs would declare him bankrupt. As the conversation continued Sandy asked his friend what he did for a living, " Well when I left the Navy I had nae idea whit to do in civvy street I didn't fancy the fishing so I signed on the dole six weeks after that I was walking along the main street and I bumped into a man who we both ken very well and I bet yea dinna ken fa am speakin aboot" Sandy shook his head but he was all ears, " Mind on big saft Cliffy Paterson the heid maisters son" Sandy nodded , " Well I got speakin tae Cliffy he asked me whit I was working at and when I telt him I wis idle he more or less offered me a job, yea see Cliffy's a big shot wie the County Cooncil, I started as a labourer then got on as a trainee gardener noo I hiv a squad of my ain four of us wie look after the cemeteries and parks for a twenty mile radius of the toon, its nae a bad job the pey is nae the best but I look after ither fowks gairdens and the extra few pound I mak keeps me in fags and beer." "Wid yea fancy a job wie the Cooncil, its steady work sure oh yir wages every week and nae affa hard caed jist a steady weeks work is ah they ask for." Sandy was interested ok but what were his chances he asked Freddie how he should go aboot applying, " Well Sandy yea ken Big Cliffy the twa of yea were brocht up the gither so go and have a word wie him and see fits dein, they like middle aged kind oh lads fa they can depend on. Sandy and Freddie parted company and Sandy headed back into town he was apprehensive about approaching Cliff Paterson and even felt a bit of guilt when he remembered back the bullying and mickey taking that Cliff had to endure while at school he was overweight a brilliant scholar, but useless at everything else, if the boys were playing football Cliff was always the goalie and even then he was pathetic but he ended up dux of the school and went on to University. As he walked back into town in his head he was trying to think what he would say but first he had to get an interview with Mr Paterson. He entered the Council Buildings and was confronted as usual by a female sitting at a desk, Sandy was sure he recognised her but she never let on if they were acquainted or not. She was quite abrupt as she asked how she could help, when Sandy said he would like an interview with Mr Paterson he felt she did her best to put him off, in desperation he said it was a very important personal matter, she relented and said she would find out if it were possible, she then took his particulars and revealed her identity to Sandy she was a sister of Davie Fraser the banker but far too young for Sandy to remember her, it felt like hours before she returned and said he would be seen in half-an-hour.

Sandy's nerves were as tight as a bowstring even although he new Cliff Paterson like he was a brother he was still up tight not so much about meeting Cliff but in as much as he was making a major decision and he had nobody left to advise him. He had never had to get himself a job before and had no idea how other people worked away from farming, the farmers all seemed to have a set way of working so it was easy to fit in but how did the council work and would they have any vacancies for a virtually middle aged inexperienced man. He decided to pass the half-hour by going for a walk round the square it would maybe calm him down a bit, he could well do without the disruption he was about to create all be it out with his control. Five minutes to go he returned to the office the lassie behind the desk told him just to go through Mr Paterson was ready for him, he knocked at the door with the brass name plate Mr C G Paterson a voice from with-in called out come in, Sandy opened the door and was confronted by a man mountain all twenty plus stones of him there was no mistaking Big Cliffy. He held out his hand and greeted Sandy with the words " Michty me Sandy it wis a surprise when the secretary said yea wid like a word wie me the last time we met was at the Hillies family reunion and that man be aboot three years ago" " Aye its ah that" as they shook hands Sandy could feel the big saft doughy palms of Cliff's hands he had never done a days hard graft in his life so his hands were as saft as the day the midwife washed them for the first time. Sandy was told to take a seat and was offered a cup of tea or coffee with apologies he couldn't offer him anything stronger. Sandy settled for tea Cliff picked up his phone and ordered a pot of tea and some biscuits that done he looked up at Sandy and asked what he could do to help him. Sandy explained his situation how he was near bankrupt in the croft and anyhow his lease was up in two years time so he would have to make a move, then he told Cliff about his meeting wie Freddie Shounders and he advised him to call in past the office in the off chance there may be vacancies. Cliff asked what Sandy intended doing aboot a house, Sandy said he would have to get his name on the housing list as him and Meg would be homeless when the croft went up for sale. Cliff rubbed his ample chin and looked Sandy straight in the eye " Sandy Hillies this could jist be your lucky day, the Council have just bought four new street sweepers one for the toon here and the others scattered around the district the idea is that we sweep the streets early in the morning before there's any traffic aboot so its an early start would you be interested in that, " Sandy felt really excited at the prospect oh! Aye that wid jist be up my street tractor driving is my only skill noo-a-days". Cliff went on to say he couldn't promise Sandy the job definitely as there was a labour officer who dealt with the hiring and firing, Sandy would have to fill in an application form and attend an interview, he had no problem with that and asked where he would get the application form. Before he left Cliff Paterson's office they had agreed that Sandy would keep the information to himself and would carry on at Hillside until the November term by that time the vacancy with the Council would be filled Cliff promised he would give Sandy a character reference, all he needed to do now was convince the Employee Relations Officer that he was the man for the job as Cliff said it's the way you sell yourself, this is s very responsible position and the equipment is costing the Council an arm and a leg, as they shook hands Cliff wished his old school chum the best of luck.

At the reception desk Sandy asked if he could have an application form, he decided to fill it in and submit it before going home. He had been away from home for nearly nine hours Meg was up to high doh when he finally appeared , he was full of the joys of spring his first try for a job and he was in with a good shout. Things in the Glen were pretty quiet about the only activity taking place in the village hall was the WRI they met once a week the Young Farmers met with similar frequency and occasionally there was a Friday night dance, the problem being there was so many other attractions taking place the few teenagers still in the glen would hire transport and head for one of the bigger more popular dance halls so small community halls like the one in the Glen tended to be neglected. Sandy had a bit of luck when he managed to secure a month employment helping to build a huge Dutch barn at Burnside; it was strange the first time he went there after Lang Dod's funeral but like everything else you get used to it. Although Young George was the farmer it was easily seen that Betsy had her finger on the pulse and would soon let her son know if she disagreed with his methods. There were some changes in the Duncan family that year Betty and Walter were still well settled on their farm in Canada their family were now through collage and working they kept promising to come over for a holiday but it never seems to materialise. Jim seemed to be getting along nicely in New Zealand his bairns were now teenagers no word of them coming home to Scotland in the near future. Peg was now well established in America her nursing career was going very well she had acquired a boyfriend who also worked in the same hospital in medicine. Tommy was still in Germany he would be finished in the Army later that year and would settle back in Ross-shire where there was plenty work Arlene was fine and now a nursing mother. Mary enjoying life to the full still in Japan she would be there for another year then home her future still undecided. Willie spending most of his time in the Middle East working through the British Army but mostly with Arabs, his twenty five years service would be complete next year, he could stay on but things in the forces were not as good as they used to be leaving a lot of veterans very disillusioned, anyhow that's how it was with the Duncan family as they survived the sixties. A month had passed since Sandy handed in his application form at the council offices and he had heard no word, out of character for Sandy but he decided to phone and find out what was happening. The secretary who answered the phone was very pleasant and helpful she explained to Sandy that there had been a delay in the new equipment being ordered so that had a knock on effect all down the line but she could assure him he would get a letter shortly asking him to attend an interview. Sandy was enjoying the company of the Burnside lads and it was good to be in touch with Hans but like everybody else he was getting on in years and he confided in Sandy about his thoughts on retirement, he was hoping he would last out another four years at least but he was having problems with an old war wound that affected his left leg, the floor of the Dutch barn was hard work and required a lot of concrete but with the four of them working and having a good banter back and forth the time soon flew in, the main structure was being built by a specialist firm who would take over when the floor was laid, Sandy asked the erection foreman if there was any labouring work available, he was delighted when offered three weeks more or less as handyman working where required.

A builder's labourer was a whole new field for Sandy although he had always done any repairs on the croft he had never seriously worked on a building site as a means of making his living but he was enjoying it, it was also a means of subsidising the income from the croft, with the Dutch barn being built at Burnies there would be no need for stacking the hay or straw as it could all be stored inside this also meant there would be no need for hired hands during the harvest the regular squad of the Wilson's and Hans could manage the lot by themselves. Sandy was on his last week employed on the building site but he had plenty to do at home his place was neglected over the last few weeks but he would soon catch up. When he arrived home on his final Friday evening Meg told him there was a very officious looking letter from the council for him, he lifted it from the table studied the front then the back before he opened it, he shouted to his sister, " Hey Meg its telling me to attend an interview a week on Monday, bring your driving licence and be prepared to have a medical, Sandy was shaking with emotion here was another step towards giving up the croft, he felt sad at the very thought, it had been his home for well over thirty years he was not really looking forward to giving it up. The next week soon passed, it does if your busy, before he knew it he was getting ready for his interview, ten-o-clock in the Council buildings he would need to catch the school bus it was pretty packed as of Easter all the Glen bairns travelled to the town, the Glen no longer boasted a school. Sandy was of mixed feelings as he waited for the bus he wondered how he would adapt to a new way of life and more so how he would take to working for a boss he was well aware Lang Dod Wilson had been his boss but that was different he knew Lang Dod and Dod was a man of the Glen where everybody used to know everybody else so his mind was full of pitfalls that may never materialise. Sandy was glad he wasn't the bus driver he had never seen such unruly bairns in all his life the noise was deafening and the cheek along with quite colourful language was something the Duncan's were never allowed to use, as he left the bus Sandy commented to the bus driver about the behaviour of his passengers, the driver replied " Am thankful I only hiv tae pit up wie them for half an oor twice a day imagine the teachers havin six or seven oors of the buggers." Sandy had time to kill so he decided to have a walk around the harbour, the boats were all gone it was Monday morning so they would have sailed after midnight on Sunday, he loved the smell of the sea especially around the sandy area in the harbour it had its own special smell, along the pier was a sort of pill box built during the war he stuck his head inside but quickly with drew as the stench of pish just about choked him, he shook his head as he walked away this although unsightly was a piece of history and some lazy thoughtless people were using it as a latrine, the way folk lived now-a-days seemed to be deteriorating he had noticed that younger folk seemed to be less mannerly than they used to be especially in his young day, his mother and father would soon clip them round the ear if they showed any sign of rudeness or bad manners but it seemed to be being eroded from society. Sandy looked at his watch, time seemed to be dragging he still had nearly an hour before he was required, further along the quay an old man was repairing nets, Sandy stopped to pass the time of day, as they talked and found out each others back ground the old man remembered when Sandy's father had his accident he used to get casual work in the Glen but that was many years ago, they parted company and Sandy made his way back.

He was still in plenty time when he entered the Council Offices the young lady at the desk was getting more familiar as she greeted him by his Christian name, everything seemed so informal but it did nothing for Sandy nervous system. He wandered around the corridor looking at photo's of former civic heads and of course there were some local views, his mind was a blank as his nerves got tighter and tighter the nearer the big hand got to ten-o-clock. Suddenly he was brought back to reality as his name was called formal this time, " Mr Duncan, Mr Taylor will see you now" as Sandy made his way along the corridor he passed another man obviously he had just been interviewed they nodded in acknowledgement. Near the end of the corridor the brass nameplate read Mr E Taylor Employment Manager, Sandy was near fainting as he knocked on the door, a voice from the other side called for him to come in, as he entered a huge man arose from behind the desk and shook his hand introducing himself as Ernie Taylor he looked a big tough customer probably six foot three inches tall and weighing around fifteen stone well built but not fat, Ernie had been all through the war one of Lord Lovats Commandos so not a man to get on the wrong side of. His hand shake was firm and solid he had Sandy's application form in front of him which he had obviously studied he also had a written reference from big Cliff Paterson, Sandy felt really at ease with big Ernie he was so easy to talk to, you would hardly think

it was an interview for a job as he studied Cliffs letter he said to Sandy
" I see you started work as a loon wie Lang Dod Wilson, I knew Dod
very well a perfect gentleman if ever there was one. The interview lasted
forty minutes, Ernie told Sandy he should know before the end of the
week if he had been successful, Sandy then asked how he would go
about applying for a house he explained to Ernie that if he got the job
he would need to move, the big fellow explained where he would need
to go but told Sandy to hold off till the week-end telling him that if
he was a key worker it would give him more clout, Sandy thanked him
and left feeling quite pleased with himself, Big Ernie emphasised that
the new machinery they were about to receive was very costly and it
was imperative that maintenance was of a high priority. Sandy assured
him that he owned his own tractor and he was well aware that neglect
could be a costly business, Ernie pointed out and possibly showed his
aggressive side that when working for a boss neglect of the equipment
you were responsible for could lead you to loosing your job, this was a
threat that Sandy didn't really need because if he got the job he would
treat all the equipment he was responsible for as if it were his own. As
Sandy left the office he had no idea if he had been successful or not Big
Ernie was a deep dour sort of man who gave nothing away, on the way
out he picked up a housing application form. He ran through his day
with Meg and told her it would be the end of the week at least before
he knew what was happening, in the evening they sat down and filled
in the housing form including sister Mary as an occupant as she used
Hillies as her home address and anyhow it may help to get a bigger
house if there were three of them. Meg had been forewarned that her
job at the school would cease at the Easter holiday, all the bairns would
be bussed to town leaving another gap in the community, she had no
chance of getting any other work locally, but she had been told that the
Social Works Department were always looking for home help people
so she decided to look them up one day soon.

Friday morning Sandy was on tenterhooks as he waited for the
postie to arrive as usual when you are waiting for something it seems to
be running late, eventually Sandy spotted the little red van he was just
passing the old Smiddy, Sandy had a nostalgic moment when he thought
back to his old mate Will Watson, what would he have thought of
Sandy's intentions of deserting the Glen, he could just hear him saying
" Aye Sandy yea are jist like aw the bloody rest deserting the sinking
ship" of course it would be tongue in cheek as Will would be well aware

of the predicament facing the crofters, wasn't it modern technology that had sounded the death knell for himself, of course he was lucky in so much as he was ready to retire so he didn't have the added worry of starting a new career like Sandy was about to embark on if the awaited letter had favourable information in it. The nearer the wee red van got the harder the adrenaline pumped through Sandy's veins by the time the postie was in the yard he was near at bursting point. " The postie wound down the window and handed Sandy a bundle of mail if it had still been Jock Mitchell he would have been able to tell Sandy who they were all from, he hastily thanked the postie and turned and headed for the house halfway there he spotted an envelope marked Council Offices private and confidential this must be it, his heart was racing as he tore it open, the contents caused him to feel weak and faint. Mr Alexander Duncan this letter is to confirm that you have been successful in your application for the position of Street Sweeping Operator, Sandy let out a whoop as he read on he was requested to attend an interview with Mr Ernest Taylor Employee Relations Officer, Mr Dennis Clark Operations Manager and Derek Wylie Cleansing Foreman at ten am on the following Monday, Sandy felt elated things were beginning to look brighter he hoped to unburden himself from the croft with-in the next six months. It was a long week and he thought the Monday of his meeting would never arrive but it did, he travelled to town on the school bus the chaos was as bad as ever he was quite glad he didn't own any of them they were cheeky young buggers and a good skelp around the lug wouldn't have gone amiss. As usual he had to hang around for a good hour so he decided to have a walk to a garage who dealt in motor cycles he would need transport as soon as he started his new job he hoped to find that out to-day, the man who owned the garage was very helpful and showed Sandy a motor bike and side car it was for sale at one hundred and ten pounds, he also pointed out that he could arrange hire purchase if necessary, Sandy was quite keen the combination would be handy as he could transport odds and ends where a bike on its own may not be so handy. He asked the owner of the garage if he would hold the bike until he attended his meeting then he would have a better idea of how things were going to happen, he said he would hold it for two hours but felt quite confident that Sandy would buy it, in the mean time he was going to give it a check over. There was a spring in Sandy's step as he headed back to the council offices for the first time in a long time he felt he was getting somewhere. As usual he was well ahead of his appointment time, the young lady at reception told him to go along to the waiting room where he could have a cup of tea, this would help him relax he still felt very nervous at facing the three council officials even though Sandy had played his accordion in front of fairly large amounts of people he was still a very shy unassuming person so meetings of this kind were an ordeal.

The last five minutes till ten-o-clock seemed like an hour and Sandy's nerves were getting tighter by the second, one of his favourite western songs was called High Noon sung by a an American Tex Ritter, as he waited one of the lines of that song kept coming into his head it was<Look at that big hand moving on nearing High Noon about a man facing the hangman's noose> Sandy felt as though he could identify with the poor fellow about to be hanged, he was brought back to reality when Big Ernie Taylor shouted " We're ready for yea noo Sandy". Ernie introduced Sandy to the two colleagues seated behind the desk, they all shook hands and welcomed Sandy on board, Derek Wylie was the roads foremen and he would be the man that Sandy would be mostly in contact with, he would be working a forty five hour week that was five eight hours and five on Saturday he would be paid an enhanced rate for Saturday and any time over his eight hours would also be paid at overtime rates he would be entitled to fourteen days paid leave in the summer four public holidays and two days off at Christmas and the New Year, he was expected to start work a week on Monday and his hours were six am until two pm Monday till Friday and Saturday was six am until eleven am. Sandy was asked if he had any comments to make but he had none he was quite happy with his lot, it was explained that he would have an instructor with him the first week until he got into the swing of things, with that the meeting broke up. His first port of call was back at the garage where he finalised the deal for the motorcycle combination, although his licence covered all types of vehicles he had very little experience motor bike wise except for his time working with Eck Davidson many years ago, Eck used to let him have a shot so he was familiar with the basics. As he was driving out of town he spotted his friend Freddie West and stopped to have a chat and also to thank Fred for putting him in the direction of the Council, when he told Fred he had got the job driving the tractor Fred looked at him and said " You lucky devil Sandy I ken a dozen lads that would have given their right arm for that job but fair play to you and good luck, I'll see you in the yard next week then". With that Sandy was on his way he was now free to hand in his notice of intent regards giving up the croft he would have to stick it out for another seven months as it was too close to the November term to quit right away and furthermore he had to find a house. Meg was delighted for her brother and couldn't wait to get her first hurl in the sidecar. Sandy was glad it was autumn time there wasn't a great deal to do about the croft he still had the threshing mill coming in November this was to be the final visit now that most farmers were using the combine harvester the old style thrashing mill was about to become redundant just like its predecessor the steam engine another sad chapter in the life of a crofter. Sandy had a horrible thought he would need to ask his new boss for a day off, or maybe he could mange with a few hours off somebody would start things off for him the problem being there wasn't a great deal of neighbours to pick and choose from now-a-days.

Monday morning and Sandy was to achieve a few firsts that morning one he would have to travel four miles to get to work, he would also need a thermos flask and some sandwiches and he was going to spend a day working away from the farm it was quite an exciting prospect. The journey to the council yard was quite uneventful the breeze was exhilarating as it rushed past his face at least he would be refreshed and cobweb free when he got there.

Chapter Twenty Four

Derek Wylie was just unlocking the gates when Sandy arrived he parked the combination and headed for the offices, Derek shook his hand and welcomed him aboard it was just after half past five so they would manage a cup of tea before starting. The equipment Sandy was about to use was brand new a lot of responsibility but that was the reason he had been trusted with the job his reliability, the fact that he had owned equipment for the past thirty plus years and understood the need to look after such machinery. The foreman ran over the different levers on the sweeper but had no need to lecture Sandy on the operation of the tractor, so fully instructed on the theoretical side of the operation it was now time to be practical and start work, Sandy found it straight forward up one side of the street and down the other straight away he could see one bug bear that was parked cars, not that there were many that early in the morning, but where there was an obstruction he had to dismount from the tractor and use hand equipment to gather up any cartons or wrappers thrown away instead of being put in the bins provided for such waste, it was also part of Sandy's remit to empty the small bins attached to the lampposts etc, he had two and a half hours to clear the town centre but that was reasonable time, Derek stayed with him until he finished the main street, he was quite satisfied they had chosen the right man for the job and Sandy didn't need to be watched he knew what he was doing, before he left he gave Sandy one bit of advice to make sure he didn't damage any parked cars as some of the owners would try and claim a new car even for the least little scratch, Sandy assured his boss he would be ultra careful. He was amazed at how many people actually started work in a town as early as six am, milk delivery drivers, postmen, scaffies like himself, cleaners and men in white overalls obviously bakers and no doubt chefs as they entered the hotels, so it was quite an eye opener most of them nodded to Sandy in acknowledgement. He found the time passed fairly quickly and it was soon after one pm time for him to return to the yard he had to get his equipment ready for the next morning, all in all he was quite pleased the way things had gone, at a few minutes past two he was on his motor bike ready for home. In two weeks time he would have to send in a written termination of his lease of Hillies, it was playing on his mind a bit, much and all as he was moving on it would still be quite a wrench leaving his beloved croft, his home for the past thirty two years, but it should have been expected, the rot in the crofting industry set in about fifteen years ago and the Glen had been in decline ever since, only the crofting side, the big farmers like Burnside and Westerton were flourishing but you needed to be their size to make a yearly profit, he wondered who would get Hillside the five main players would be outbidding each other in order to seize Sandy's seventy acres of fairly poor quality land. Meg had a field day phoning the family to let them know the latest and of course the fact that they would have to leave Hillies in six months was upper most in the conversation, Sandy would listen to her and shake his head and wonder what the cost was to phone Canada, America, New Zealand and Germany when he mentioned it she always pointed out that she waited until the cheap rate was available in the evening, they would often have an argument Sandy's theory was that because his sister thought it was a cheap rate she blethered for much longer than she would have done at the dear rate therefore probably costing more than if she had phoned through the day.

Sandy and Meg sat at the dinner table two weeks before the November term and between them they drafted a letter of termination of their lease of Hillside, Sandy was quite emotional about the whole business and after two or three attempts they finally decided the letter looked official, Meg who was a beautiful writer hand wrote the letter in copperplate hand writing all neat and efficient looking, it was addressed to the trustees office at the Mansion house. Sandy thought it would be appropriate to hand it to Roddy Tracy as he was estate manager, he had always been a great help to the crofters in the Glen so it would only be right that Sandy should let him know what his plans were, he would visit Roddy on the twenty seventh the day before the term. He got a great welcome when he arrived at the home farm, Roddy was a chip off the old block and had many of his fathers mannerisms he commiserated with Sandy on having to give up the croft but fully understood that crofting was no longer viable, he discussed the possibility of Sandy purchasing the croft house and steading but the financial implications would be beyond Sandy's reach, they went on to discuss the demise of the Glen and how that very soon there would be no native Glen people left, he asked Sandy about accommodation when he gave up the croft, he explained that he was in for a house from the council and was quite confident he would be rehoused before the May term. He spent nearly two hours with Roddy and his wife they had a great old blether and discussed many subjects, he was keen to find out how the family were progressing especially Mary, Roddy and her had been very close at one time even although Roddy was quite a few years older. It was now two weeks since Sandy had started work with the council on Friday he would receive his first pay packet, his hourly rate was 4s/6p (42.5p) after deductions he was left with £8/ 16s the best wage he had ever been paid in his life he was quite chuffed as he headed for home, he decided to stop at a shop and get his sister a box of chocolates, she was nearly bowled over as this was the fist time Sandy had ever been so generous.

There were quite a few happenings with-in the Duncan family that autumn/winter, Sandy had decided to take a gamble and rear another dozen calves a final throw of the dice if you like it was a fifty/fifty gamble he could do with some extra cash if the calves sold well he would win but if not he would be a loser but then that's what gambling was all about, Meg would have to help with the morning feeding but she was quite willing to do her share. Tommy Duncan would have completed his three years service in the Army, they had pleaded with him to stay on even promoting him to the rank of sergeant but Tommy had made up his mind and had even purchased a Mobile home, it was sited in Ross-shire he intended to put his army training to good use and had found employment with a plant hire company with his wages and lodging allowances he was going to be twice as well off as he would be in the forces. Willie had almost completed thirty years service he was talking about retiring and starting up a business of his own supplying body guards to who ever would require them he spent much of the last ten years in the Middle East doing that type of work for the British and Arab dignitaries so he knew what was required he intended coming home to Hillies for Christmas and the New Year, the best news as far as Meg was concerned was that Mary would be home for the festivities her tour of duty in Japan finished in the middle of December, she had visited the other members of the family over the past couple of years.

It looked like the final year at Hillies could be a memorable one it was a few weeks away from the New Year but Meg had already started the preparations, Sandy was his usual worrying self the fact that they would be homeless in less than six months kept the worry cells in his brain active, he had settled into his job well but still missed the daily routine of the croft, as he went around the centre of the town at the back of six in the morning his fellow early morning colleagues got to know him and soon they were on first names terms as they exchanged pleasantries briefly each morning. He was still kept fairly busy at home with his calves and the other few beasts he still had to look after he intended to keep them until the spring it was hard to envisage life without the bellowing of cattle but life was all about going forward and change.

Mary arrived home on the fourteenth of December she had been away for almost two years, she had many great tales about life in Japan and how many proposals of marriage she had from various wealthy Japanese gentlemen but she turned them down Sandy said it was jist as weel as he didn't know how he would have taken to slanty eyed nieces and nephews. Mary also brought them up-to-date with the family in New Zealand and Betty's family in Canada, Peg had flown up to visit as well, she met her twin sisters boyfriend and was impressed, Mary hinted that they may have to pay a visit in the near future as a wedding was possible. On the twentieth of December the family were in for another big surprise they received a telegram from the States telling them that Peg and her fiancée were arriving on the twenty fourth and intended staying for a week it turned out that this trip was an engagement present from her future in-laws they were ranchers in Idaho. Meg was near at breaking point the excitement was getting too much for her to bear apart from Jim and Betty the whole family would be spending the New Year together at Hillies, she would be pushed for room but Sandy would have to sleep on a shackie doon in the sitting room that would free up his room, Peg and Mary and her would sleep in the big bedroom, Willie and Maria would use Sandy's room Tommy and Arlene and their two bairns would use the third up stairs bedroom and Buck, Pegs fiancée could use the small downstairs room, it would be a bit crowded but they would manage. Willie and Tommy and their families would only be staying for two or three days arriving in time for the New Year they all had cars so didn't need to depend on public transport this was down to a single option, Dr Beeching had closed all the railways down so there was one choice bus only. Sandy hit his first snag as an employee, he couldn't please himself when he took time off and he had been with the Council for so short a period he hadn't accumulated enough holiday hours to entitle him to more than the standard Christmas and New Year entitlement which was two days for each occasion so he had to content himself with what was coming to him. He was experiencing the down side of the Motor Bike Combination now that winter had arrived he encountered a few hairy moments on the icy roads, as soon as he was free of the croft he would almost certainly invest in a car but at the moment he was reluctant to spend until he was sure of how much money he would be left with from the sale of his goods, Meg had already intimated that there were umpteen new items required for the new house they would be moving to, most of what they had was old fashioned items bought by her mother so they were over forty years old.

Meg was having the time of her life sister Mary had a car so they were able to go shopping in various places that were inaccessible without private transport, Mary had been in touch with her twin sister Peg, telling her and Buck she would collect them from Dyce Airport when they arrived which was a couple of days away, the excitement for Meg was getting more and more intense with every day that passed. Mary and Meg had a tricky journey to Dyce that morning there was about four inches of snow on the road and with quite a strong wind it could get worse. It had been over three years since Peg had departed for the States so the re-union with Meg was quite an emotional affair and then of course Buck was something else a big handsome fellow who hugged his future sisters-in-law like he was some sort of grizzly bear, Mary had met up with them when she visited her sister Betty in Canada less than a year ago. The journey back to the Glen was even hairier, the more traffic on top the snow the more slippery it got but Mary was tough and nothing ever seemed to get the better of her the journey lasted about half an hour longer then it should.

Meg soon had lunch on the table and they were just about to sit down when Sandy arrived home form his work, at the moment his job was more about clearing snow than collecting rubbish and of course the conditions on the road led to some hair raising moments, once the introductions were over they spent the next couple of hours at the table eating and then talking, Sandy found Buck to be quite an interesting fellow although he was a skin specialist in the hospital his folks were ranchers in Idaho where they worked a mixed farm of cattle and wheat. Sandy and Buck took to each other like ducks to water and spent hours talking shop or should that be farms the more Sandy heard about the huge farms and ranches in America and Canada the more inclined he felt that one day he would pay a visit, the girls had their own topics to gossip about. Peg was very proud of the huge diamond engagement ring that Buck had given her and then asked her to marry him no date was set as yet but it was sure to be next summer sometime, she told Meg and Sandy that she wanted them there as she would need Sandy to give her away, Sandy felt a ripple of excitement as his dreams of visiting America may soon become a reality. As usual Christmas didn't amount to very much at Hillies Meg cooked a big roast and added all the trimmings the men had a couple of drams and the women had sherry, Betty phoned on Christmas day and Meg ended up greeting as usual otherwise there was little to get excited about they didn't even have a party for the bairns anymore, the few that still lived in the Glen travelled to town everyday and anyhow their town school held a party for them, the village hall was becoming a bit dilapidated but then the hotel now had a function room where weddings were held and any other entertainment that used to be held in the hall, this year for the first time they were having entertainment on New Years Eve. Sandy enjoyed his couple of days off but they soon passed and it was back to rising at the back of four, Buck had told him he would see to the cattle and Meg said she would keep him right, the twenty seventh of December was a pretty dreich morning not particularly good motor bike weather it was a nightmare journey but being Sandy he was at work on time, Derek Wylie was quite amazed to see his tractor driver appear out of a blizzard slipping and slithering all over the street but Sandy was as cheerful as ever commenting that the journey had been "Gie rooch"

Bye the end of the week Willie, Maria and the twins had arrived, Tommy Arlene and young Thomas were due at any time, the roads North were a bit tricky and it was touch and go if they should make the journey, but Meg had a phone call saying they were on their way. Sandy was quite late getting home the Council workers were stretched to the limits clearing pavements and foot paths and they had been asked to work over, but he had no need to worry Mary and Buck had everything in the byre in hand so all Sandy had to do was sit down and have a cup of tea, Meg was getting worried about Tommy it was starting to get dark. Just as they were about to sit down to supper the lights of a car turned in at the crossroads and headed up Hillies road there were sighs of relief all round. Tommy was near smothered when his sisters set upon him hugging and kissing him well it was quite some time since they had been together like this just a pity Betty and Jim couldn't manage, Meg kind of forgot about the supper as she cuddled he little nephew after his mother had been given a Duncan welcome. The supper that night lasted for ages as the family sat and reminisced about things and people that had long since departed the Glen.

Hogmanay night was just like old times as soon as the bells on the wireless rang Sandy got out his old accordion and played some music, just after one am there was a knock on the door and members of the Morrison Family were the first footers, then the Fraser's appeared Albie Grant, Vicky and some of the family were next to help over crowd Hillies, it turned out to be the best New Year that Sandy and Meg had experienced for many along year, it was very late when Sandy finally staggered towards his shackie doon in the sitting room anaesthetised beyond all redemption in other words as fue as a whelk no doubt the after effects would be horrendous but that was another day. The sun was streaming through the split in the curtains, Sandy had to close his eyes quickly as he was sure his head would detach from his neck wow he felt bloody awful, with great courage he opened his eyes slightly and squinted at his watch ten past nine, the bloody cattle will be starving he thought as he dived out of his bed, trying to get his leg into the leg hole in his breeks proved to be rather difficult that morning, and it needed him sitting on the bed before success was achieved, in a rather dishevelled state he staggered towards the kitchen and was quite amazed to see most of the family sitting round the kitchen table, Mary asked if he wanted bacon and egg, he didn't answer but made a beeline for bathroom where he promptly threw up and retched painfully for the next ten minutes, on arrival back in the kitchen he was advised to return to bed and sleep the effects off, he only needed to be advised once and quickly disappeared back towards the sitting room. Meg had a busy morning she had kept one goose with the idea that one day before they left Hillies she would have a full house to feed now it had happened and the goose was browning nicely in the oven of course the rest of the ladies were mucking in and giving a hand, Mary and Buck had done the needful in the byre and Mary was now jogging her way through deep snow as she carried out her fitness schedule she had asked for volunteers to keep her company but got not takers, Sandy Willie and Tommy were still in bed nursing self inflicted pain. Once the dinner was cooking away nicely the ladies sat down at the kitchen table and over a cup of coffee they had a good old chinwag each had some interesting tale about the part of the world they were now staying in.

Come midday and the men were starting to recover, Sandy seemed to be suffering worst but then he never had the practice the others had owing to having led a pretty sheltered life compared to the other two who were much more streetwise than their oldest brother. The dinner was just like old times in the Hillies dining room it was ages since there were eight adults sitting down to a meal, Meg was in her element and wished she could feed this amount everyday she liked a lot of company maybe because she had been used to crowds and then when they all left home it was only herself and Sandy. The dinner lasted for ages and much hilarity took place, it was unusual for the Glen folks to have wine at the dinner table but Willie moved in circles where wine was almost a must at dinnertime so he had brought a few bottles, the hilarity was maybe the result of the wine and the spirits from the night before mixing especially in Sandy's case before long he was feeling quite tipsy again. The dinner over after dinner drinks were offered, Sandy was now heavily sedated and declined, soon he was snoring his head off and slept soundly until the evening, every now and again Meg would give him a kick as she tried to stop the horrendous noise it only worked momentarily. The second day of the year dawned and the weather was in the grip of winter with quite a heavy fall of snow overnight, Willie and Tommy were hoping it would clear up as they both intended travelling back to their home areas next day, Sandy was almost feeling normal again and was up and about around five am he was busy at his animals when sister Mary appeared with the milk pail she shouted that she had given Meg a long lie, as the past few days had been heavy going for her. Back in the kitchen Sandy had another cup of tea along with Mary they discussed the forthcoming move away from Hillies Mary said as soon as the date was set she would get leave and come home and help with the roup and the flitting, Sandy explained his feelings about having to give up his lively hood, he liked his new job and the fact that he got a steady wage but Hillies would always be close to his heart it was all he had known his entire adult life and the wrench of leaving would be very hard to take.

Sandy had to return to work on the second of January, Willie, Maria the twins, would be leaving as soon as it was daylight they had a daunting journey back to London. Tommy and Arlene and the two kids would also have to brave the elements and return home. Mary, Peg and Buck would be staying on until the following week, Peg had them all clued up on her forth coming marriage which she hoped would take place in the fall as she called it, she had decided on having it in Canada in the little church that Betty's family attended her thinking being that Canada was the easiest place for the two families to travel to, it could be exciting times especially for Sandy who had never travelled beyond Aiberdeen, but always at the back of his mind was his need to find a house before the May term arrived so before even considering Pegs wedding he had other priorities.

Time seemed to be whizzing past before they knew it the end of February had arrived and still no luck on the housing front, Sandy was a regular visitor at the housing Department Office he knew the women who worked there. Their usual answer was nothing doing Sandy but don't panic we'll have a house for you in plenty time but for Sandy it was not as easy as that, soon he would have to start making arrangements for holding a roup possibly the second week in May. Tommy Willie and Mary were taking holidays so they could lend a hand.

Sandy was getting ready to go home after his shift when Derek his foreman called him over " Hi Sandy the quines in the hoosin office are wintin tae speak till yea" Sandy felt a flush of excitement run through his body wid they have word of a hoose he wondered he thanked Derek and hurried off towards the Housing Office. As he entered the girls started to take the rise of him saying that they had found accommodation for him " Oh far aboot" asked Sandy, Bell Fraser who was about ages with Sandy and had been brought up in the Glen killing herself with laughter said " Its along the links in a four man commando tent somebody has left it so the bobbies has given permission tae remove it" Sandy had no answer he knew he was the butt of their joke so stood in silence while they had a bit of fun at his expense. Bell continued once the laughter had died down "Sandy what a piety yea couldna see yir ain face it's a picture", "But all joking aside how dea yea fancy a hoose in the country"? " Far aboot in the country" " Yae ken far the agricultural hooses are aboot a mile and a half fae the toon centre" Sandy nodded his head yes he knew that houses they had been built to house farm workers just after the war. "Well continued Bell ane of them will become vacant at the end of the month the only snag is that it's a four bedroom so the rent is a bit dearer than the smaller houses. Sandy was gob smacked for once in his life his luck had seemed to change and he felt even luckier when told it was an end house, which meant it had a huge garden. Sandy was desperate to accept but asked for twenty-four hours so that he could discuss the move with his sister no use him agreeing to something that mightn't suit her but he was sure in himself Meg would be just as delighted as he was to know that they had a home to go to also the fact that they would have two spare bedrooms was just what they wanted, now that the load of being rehoused was off his mind he could get down to the task of getting things ready for the roup (sale) he had been strongly advised that a lick of paint often added a few shilling to an item in a sale so he asked auld Jock Suds if he was interested in earning a few pounds, Jock proper name Sutherland was an odd job man who could turn his hand to many different tasks painting being one of them, he agreed to give Sandy a hand to get organised. Sandy sat down to his dinner and dropped the bombshell on his sister about the offer of a four bedroom house, she was totally flabbergasted to be offered a council house in the country and only a little over a mile from the town centre was more than they could have hoped for, Sandy told her he had to let the office know to-morrow because there were other people just as desperate to get an opportunity like they had been offered. Meg told him to make sure he was at the office as soon as it was open, in her head she was weighing up all the new horizons this move would make one being a much wider scope for her getting a decent job, in fact she told Sandy she had a better idea she would write a letter of acceptance and he could shove it through the letter box on his way to the Council Yard. For the first time in years Sandy felt as though he could see himself getting somewhere much and all as he loved his little croft it had been getting stale over the past few years, he was now content to be looking forward to a whole new era. A week later they received a letter from the Council Housing office stating that they could pick up the keys to their new house on the first of May that gave them twenty eight days to clear up at Hillies and move to number six Bogton Row quite an unglamorous name but what's in a name. The whole Duncan family were coming home for the Grand Finally at Hillside.

Jim and Tina were the first to arrive from New Zealand they had decided to fly over on their own, Meg was disappointed she wouldn't be seeing her niece and nephew but she was over the moon to have Jim and Tina, the two women were able to get things going at Bogton as soon as they got the key it was a long hard slog and with Sandy working Jim and auld Suds had their hands full but bye the middle of the week Tommy and Willie had also arrived so there were plenty hands on deck to get things in order, Mary was due at any time she was capable of helping both men and women she was still as tough as old boots. Finally Betty and Peg flew over together from Canada and America. The saddest thing to greet the family when they arrived at Hillies was the for sale sign pinned to the yard gate, the Estate people had worked a fly move when they got rid of the last couple of crofts they had sold the ground to one of the big farmers and then sold off the Croft house and out buildings along with a couple of acres of ground separately they were asking for three and a half thousand for Hillies and stated that their was the potential for a market garden or a horse riding school, more than likely it would be snapped up by an English Couple who could easily out bid the locals that was the trend in the late sixties, pushing the prices away above the heads of the Glen folks.

The last few days before the roup was busy, Sandy had managed to get a few days off the four Duncan brothers had their work cut out every item had to be numbered and catalogued Jock Suds was a godsend coming up with ideas and short cuts that saved no end of time, Sandy thought he would get a better price for his animals if he sold them at the Mart not that he had many left a few calves, Albie Grant had bought the milk coo much to Sandy's relief knowing she would be well looked after seeing she was as much a pet as a milk coo. For the first time in his life he had to revert to using bottled milk his verdict was when the cream was removed it was like drinking bloo water. With less than a week to go the women moved to the new abode at Bogton Row the brothers roughed it at Hillies not wanting to leave the place unattended over night, some of the household goods were now much sought after antiques so there was a good chance that they would be removed if unattended, after they had finished for the day they sat down and over a dram reminisced about days gone by and of the old friends many of them departed never to be replaced it was a changing world Willie who spent a lot of his time in the Middle East told his brothers that the biggest change to the North of Scotland had yet to happen , it was just round the corner, through his contacts in the Middle East Oil and Gas industry, he told them that the Americans were about to launch a big Oil exploration programme in the North Sea, when they strike oil of which they are near certain, look out it will be a new revolution to the Scottish way of life and money will be no object pointing to his youngest brother Tommy he told him as soon as it happens Tom get in there because it will be a real Klondike just imagine Oil fields with no Arabs in Control it will be a licence to print money.

It was over thirty years since Sandy had taken over the reins at

Hillside but in less than thirty hours he would walk away for the last time, every time he thought about it he felt really emotional to-morrow his whole world would be sold to the highest bidder he had had quite a few offers from people who had called in to view what was on sale, he had to explain that all the goods were catalogued so he didn't want to rock the boat by selling privately.

Chapter Twenty Five

SANDY WAS ON HIS FEET AND getting dressed around five am it was the morning of the roup, he felt quite shattered as it had been a restless night spent tossing and turning he had very little sleep. Meg arrived at the back of six and started to tidy up what remained in the house, make shift beds that her brothers had slept on and other odds and ends. The hotel owner had procured a licence which allowed him to sell food and drinks his large tent was already set up and before seven-o-clock his staff started to arrive getting things in order, the view of sale items was to commence at ten am and the sale at midday. Sandy decided to have one last walk up to the top of the hill he called his dog and he trod a path that he had spent many happy hours on, of course there were also the sad times but he felt happy and relaxed when on his own. The sky larks were twittering away as they hovered many feet above him, there was an abundance of rabbits along with a few hares, his thoughts returned to the days when he and his brothers would set snares, the rabbits caught would be skinned and cooked sometimes it was the best meal of the week, now with myxomatosis the rabbits were left to breed and multiply people would no longer eat them for fear of catching some horrendous disease. One area Sandy always visited and paid homage to was the memorial to the Canadian Airmen killed many years ago as they helped to defend the British Isles. It had taken nearly and hour to walk the perimeter fence Sandy hadn't encountered a living soul it was so peaceful it was unbelievable, as he entered the kitchen he was greeted with a chorus of voices mostly saying " Far the hell hiv yea been so and so's been on the phone or so and so was at the door, " Well I'm here noo if its aw that important they'll call back" replied Sandy, as he proceeded to test the tea pot for contents. Time was starting to drag, there were still fifty minutes to go before the gates would open and allow the browsers to enter at ten am, Sandy was getting restless he decided to have a final wander among his beloved possessions many of them belonged to his father especially the implements used when everything was done by horses the longer he stayed in the field the bigger the lump in his throat became it was hard to bear, back in the farmyard things were even worse, this was where the household goods were on display some of it his mother and fathers wedding presents but it was all old fashioned big and clumsy the modern women wanted the latest designs and materials so the goods that had stood them in good stead for over fifty years were now redundant it would be interesting to see how much would be bought, with a heavy heart Sandy retreated to his bedroom which was now empty except for an old chair, he filled his pipe and enjoyed half-an-hour of peace and quiet he stayed there until three minutes to ten and dead on the hour he opened the gates so that people could enter and rake through his possessions before deciding how much they would bid when the sale started, he wasn't knocked over in the stampede but there were half a dozen or so, Sandy thought to himself when they began raking through his stuff no doubt there are nosey buggers here to see what they can see and no doubt pay as little as possible for any goods they would like to purchase. The Hotel Marquee opened for business at Eleven-o-clock and he was soon doing some brisk business as people dropped in and had what ever refreshment took their fancy, the Duncan Boys wandered about the sale items making themselves available if anybody had any queries, the sale of the implements was first on the agenda.

At eleven thirty the Auctioneer arrive with his entourage, that consisted of an Accountant and four heavies who would be called upon to act as dogs bodies if anything needed to be moved, Sandy was quite annoyed as his brothers and himself were available free of charge to carry out any donkey work that arose instead the Auctioneers fee would be greatly enhanced to cover the expenses of his hired hands but unfortunately Sandy was at his mercy if he kicked up a fuss it could cost him money as the price he received for his goods was entirely in the hands of the Auctioneer he could keep the bidding going or close it at will. As the hands of the clock crept steadily towards midday Sandy began to feel the pressure the last nail in his crofters coffin was about to be driven home, a great feeling of sadness sweep over him, suddenly he was brought back to reality when the voice just behind him spoke. "Hi Sandy it's a very sad day for everybody connected to the Glen I feel rather emotional about the whole scenario" Sandy half turned and he was face to face with Roddy Tracey, " Aye Roddy min fit like"? The two shook hands and then Roddy said, " Sandy many happy hours were spent in your home when we were young and the Glen was a splendid place to live every household made you welcome and they all had youngsters our own age, but alas the wind of change alters all our lives, I fully understand your reason for having to leave, if I didn't have a job with the estate trustees who pay me a wage we would find it hard to continue at the home farm, so sad and all as it is seeing you leaving I am well aware of the current economical climate". Roddy and Willie were the same age and had been great pals up until they both joined the army and of course Roddy had a mega crush on Mary that was until his father Auld Spencer found out that he was cavorting with the serfs and put his foot down and had him marry a woman of his equal standing. Just as their conversation was going well the Auctioneering team burst into life by announcing they were ready to sell the first item, they would sell the crofting items first, have a short break then the household goods would be last.

The first item to go under the hammer was Sandy's old horse drawn plough it brought a real lump to his throat as his mind wandered back to the many miles he had walked behind that old plough over the years but it looked like the packing case had only been removed an hour ago Auld Jock Suds had done a marvellous job restoring all the old rusty implements, the bidding for the plough was slow and the Auctioneer who had started off at one pound had to drop to 7/6 (35p) before he managed to generate interest then suddenly the bidding got very competitive and before they knew it had gone well over £5 not a bad start and even better when it was sold for £8. The last item to be sold from the implement side was Sandy's beloved Davie Brown tractor he had it over fifteen years and had never had to spend a penny on it just kept on going he was delighted to receive £55 for it, that part of the sale had taken just over an hour so the Auctioneer stopped for a fifteen minute break.

Part two of the sale got under way just after one pm, it was strange at these farm roup items that looked like pure rubbish fetched astronomical prices for example China chamber pots (locally known as chanteys) were selling for four or five pounds they were probably bought for a few pennies, the next item you were expecting a good price for was sold for pennies. Sandy needed every penny he could get as he had quite a few pounds to pay out after all this was over.

Just before two thirty the final item of furniture was carried into the arena, a circle formed by eager buyers and spectators the Auctioneer was standing on an upturned barrel ready to spout out his selling repertoire. There was a gasp from the crowd as the Duncan family's pride and joy was carried centre stage it was a Welsh dresser an heirloom handed down from their grand mother, when their mother died it became the property of Sandy and Meg it was a marvellous hand crafted antique but it was unsuitable for a modern house it needed a huge kitchen for its presence to be justified so with a heavy heart the brother and sister decided it would have to go but only if the price was right, Sandy had a reserve price of twenty pounds on it so that was where the Auctioneer started. At least ten hands shot up as the Auctioneer asked for a bid of ten shillings (50p) he was soon going up in pounds and it didn't take long to reach thirty pounds, as usual people began to back off as the bidding kept a steady pace, eventually at forty pounds there were two bidders Roddy Tracey and an unknown person, Roddy seemed determined to have it so he upped the price and they were bidding at two pounds a time at Fifty pounds the unknown buyer back off and Roddy got it for fifty two pounds, Sandy was over the moon his beloved Welsh dresser was staying in the Glen and going to a good home. Sandy had announced he would stay behind until five pm to allow the buyers time to remove their purchases, at three minutes to five he was standing by the gate as usual there were one or two stragglers and of course the ones that wanted to talk to Sandy. He had been warned by his sisters that he was required at Bogton as soon after five as he could get their, by five fifteen with great emotion Sandy closed the gates at Hillies for the last time he would need to return and do a final tidy up but that would more than likely be on Monday after work, without looking back and with tears welling up in his eyes he jumped into Willies car and they drove to the new abode. As they made the short journey Sandy turned to Willie and said " Willie dea yea ken this? For the first time in my life I winna be sleepin at Hillies fae noo on", the rest of the journey was completed in virtual silence.

It was quite a strange feeling for Sandy as he stepped over the threshold of his new abode at Bogton, previously it felt like he was only visiting but now it was for keeps and felt quite creepy, he didn't get long to dwell on his thoughts when sister Mary announced that she had booked a table for ten at the new Chinese Restaurant in town, Sandy screwed up his face and exclaimed gaud! " Yea want tae hear some of the stories gan aboot that place they cook cats and seagulls and the stink roon the back wid mak abody couck" "Well, Well yea'll get a sample

291

of cat or seagull the nicht so yea better awa and get yirsel ready" Mary replied, Sandy was shakin his head as he made for the bath room, before he closed the door his young sister informed him the table was booked in his name so he would be peying. Meg was quite excited it would be the first time she had sampled Chinese food so at least she was looking forward to it, the rest of the family were well versed in eating foreign food especially Chinese. It would be the last family gathering for a few months the next would be in Canada for Pegs wedding when asked why Canada and not America or even here she said she fell in love with the little church near where Betty lived and also it was the most central place for everybody to travel to and they could make a holiday out of it at the same time.

Sandy and Meg were like a couple of sore thumbs when dressed to go out they had never moved with the times and their clothes were possibly ten years out of date Peg shuddered when she thought about her wedding day, there was no way she could allow them to turn up with their present day clothes, she would need to have a word with the others. It was Sandy and Megs first visit to a foreign Restaurant the first comment made by both was how dark it was inside they liked their surroundings to be bright and airy so that they could see what was in front of them and what they were eating. Sandy's first attempt at trying to come to terms with a Menu of the type used by the Chinese was challenging, but he found them very helpful although difficult to understand, he was quite fascinated with the way they disappeared through the bamboo curtain. Mary was an expert at dining out especially when it came to Eastern cuisine, with her help Sandy was able to choose a meal that he would enjoy, the verdict after they had eaten that it was dammed fine. As he had been warned Sandy had to pick up the tab, again he had to call on Mary to explain how it worked, when it came to the bottom line and he was told the cost would be £9.12s he exclaimed " Michty me their nae chape"! But he paid up, he felt he owed his siblings a small reward for all the help they had given over the past few days, soon they would disperse to their various parts of the world once again. This year was not so bad as they would all be attending Peg's wedding in Canada another exciting time for Sandy as he would be flying for the first time, back home after their meal Sandy still felt strange the sitting room at Bogton just didn't measure up to the spacious rooms they had just left at Hillies but he would have to get used to it as there was no turning back. On the Sunday after breakfast the family started to disperse Tommy and Arlene left for Ross-shire by car Willie did like wise heading for his home in London, Mary had stayed back a day so that she could run her sisters Peg and Betty to Prestwick where they would board a flight back to Canada Peg had some wedding arrangements to sort out before flying back to her hospital in Houston Texas. Jim and Tina were staying on another week before making their way back to New Zealand so it was another tearful day for Meg as she hugged her brothers and sisters goodbye, Sandy just took it in his stride and ambled on as usual, he had a bit of work ahead of him as he had accounts to sort out and pay off then he would see how much capital he had left over from the sale of his goods at Hillies.

Monday morning and Sandy returned to work after the usual banter with the early starters he got into his stride once again, he decided to have an easy week as he still had Jim and Tina to entertain when he finished work, Meg had been busy and had got herself an interview with the Social Services she was due to meet them on the Wednesday, she was full of hope that she would be able to start a new job within a week or so, she would need to save some money for their trip to Canada, Meg had no need to worry about waiting a week the Social Services were so desperate for Home Help people that they offered Meg a job starting the next morning but she had to decline as she still had her brother and his wife until the end of the week, so it was agreed she would start the following Monday it turned out that she managed to get two positions one in the town and one at Bogton where she now stayed so it worked out well for her.

Jim and Tina left for New Zealand on the Friday morning, they needed to catch an early bus to Dyce Airport to fly to London their flight home would leave London later in the evening as usual Meg had a flood of tears as she waved the taxi away, she had no need to weep as she would see all the family in October a trip she was really looking forward to, she too felt a sense of freedom since getting rid of the croft, it would be interesting to see what the bank balance amounted to when everybody had received their whack. It was well into July when Sandy received his statement from the bank there had been so many people to square up it had all taken time the bottom line was that when all the accounts had been gathered including the sale of the goods at the roup the top line of the account read One thousand six hundred and fifteen pounds, the total deductions taken away from the top line was six hundred and seventy five pounds this included solicitors fee's Bank overdraft and all the various people involved in winding up the croft. The Duncan's were left with a balance of nine hundred and fifty pounds, Sandy decided to buy a car and then split what was left with his sister, the car cast two hundred and fifty leaving them with three hundred and fifty each not a lot for thirty years hard graft but that was the way the cookie crumbled.

They settled down to their respective jobs, Sandy took a long time to get used to the cramped space around a council house even although he had an end house with a shed and a garage it still felt claustrophobic to him but he would have to get used to it and also the nearness of his neighbours, there never seemed to be a lot of privacy compared to what they had been used to, another factor was the presence of bairns some were pretty wild but Sandy put his foot down right away and let them know that his garden was his private property. His job was going well and he was getting quite friendly with some of the other early birds, his old friend Fred West also started at six-o-clock his summer job was keeping the hanging baskets watered before the streets got busy, one morning he askedSandy if he would be interested in a couple of hours gardening after he finished with the council, Sandy jumped at the chance it would be a few bob extra and would help pass some of his free time, it turned out to be quite handy as it was on the road home, so started a new career for him, as soon as it was found out that he was a hard working honest man he was inundated with offers of more gardening, he didn't want to over burden himself so he picked and chose two or three which he found was just plenty and still left him with plenty spare time.

Time was rushing on and their trip to Canada was looming on the horizon everything was in order, passports, visa's travel tickets etc Mary was meeting up with them in Prestwick and they would travel together, but that was a few weeks away yet. Meg had a ritual or maybe a routine on a Saturday evening, she phoned Canada, New Zealand, America and the family still living in the UK she spent about an hour on the phone, it was now mid August and as she sat down to her usual hour of keeping in touch the phone rang she got a bit of a start as it was unexpected, she picked up the receiver and it was Mary, "Michty me that wis quick Meg yea must have been sittin waitin for a phone call" then she remembered it was time for Meg's weekly correspondence, she apologised but said she just wanted to say she would be home next week-end and would take them to Aiberdeen to get kitted out for Canada then she rang off.

Meg was full of excitement at the thought of having her young sister home for a few days and a shopping trip to Aberdeen was just something else, she told Sandy but he didn't show the same enthusiasm about the need for new clothes he maintained that his fifteen year old Harris tweed sports jacket had nothing wrong with it he had bought it from Humpy Danny the old tailor in the Glen, it was second hand and cost him thirty bob (£1.50p) and his hodden Gray flannels had cost seven and six (35p) and he felt they were as good as the day he had purchased them he had a pretty frugal wardrobe, a suit over ten years old, one white shirt one checked shirt he wore long john drawers cotton in the summer and woollen ones in the winter his semmits(vests) were of the same material two sets worn for a week and changed every Saturday evening so he would be fresh for the Kirk on Sunday he also had a couple of khaki shirts for work again they were changed and washed after being worn for one week, Sandy had never owned a pair of pyjamas his long johns and semmit were worn twenty four seven, worn all day and slept in at night by the end of the week they must have been pretty ripe. Meg was little better she was still about a decade behind times in her dress, she still wore Sties and lisle stockings along with bloomers that had elastic in the legs and came to just above the knee the up to date ladies wore tights, panty girdles and panties that had about as much material in them as a handkerchief, they were in for a rude awakening as their trendy young sister Mary was about to drag them into the twentieth century.

Friday arrived and Meg had an adrenaline rush as she waited excitedly for Mary to arrive she was driving, being stationed in Edinburgh for a few months was just ideal three hours and she was home, expected to arrive around nine-o-clock, the loud blaring of the car horn heralded Mary's arrival as usual she was full of bounce and her idea of a hug as a gesture of affection amounted to the same as a black bear would administer, but she was popular with all who knew her and it was a shining light in the Duncan household when Mary was at home, her first action after the hugging and kissing was to ask Sandy if he had a dram in the house as it was too late to go to the pub, he assured her that the drinks were all taken care of but as he was working in the morning he would only be having a small amount. The programme for the shopping trip was spelled out when Sandy returned from work at around eleven they would have a cup of tea get dressed then head for Aberdeen they would have lunch and then get stuck into the shopping. They left Bogton at quarter to twelve and were parking the car in Aberdeen just on one pm they decided to start off at the British Home Stores where they had a very good restaurant, it was very busy but they soon had a table where they enjoyed their lunch, Mary asked the question where they would like to shop but as neither Meg or Sandy had much experience of city shopping she was greeted with a blank stare, Meg had been a couple of times before but for Sandy it was a first, he always depended on the mobile draper for any clothes he required so he was a bit mesmerised with the choice offered by BHs. They wandered around the aisles for about twenty minutes and then Sandy was told to carry on alone while Meg was kitted out she was a bit horrified when she saw the underwear suggested by young Mary she refused to buy the latest panties on show but agreed to the more sedate ones and insisted they should have elasticated legs, she was eventually kitted out but not without an argument.

Meg still had to buy an outfit for her sister's wedding in Canada, Mary suggested they should buy it over there, it would save them having to pack and unpack and would also avoid it getting creased it was about the only thing the sisters agreed upon all the time they were shopping. Now it was Sandy's turn he looked real ancient in his Harris Tweed Jacket and thick Gray Flannel trousers rather out of place in the BHS. As the three of them met up again Mary asked Sandy if he saw anything he fancied, he shook his head and told her their wis ower muckle tae chaise fae. But he was dragged kicking and screaming along to the underwear department after protesting profusely he was made to purchase three sets of aertex semmits and drawers it would be the first time in his life he would be wearing short underpants, again he protested about having to pay for three sets saying that two sets would be ample, Mary argued that he would have to change every day and he needed a spare pair incase they had difficulty with laundry, Sandy was getting no where fast so he decided the best idea was just do as he was told. The next department they visited was shirts and socks again he reneged but ended up with three of each, on they went to jackets and breeks he ended up buying a tweed jerkin (now a bomber jacket) and a pair of cavalry twill trousers, in the shoe and belt department Sandy voiced his loudest protestations first he said he always wore galluses tae had up his breeks he didn't feel comfortable with only a belt, he was told there would no galluses in his luggage so he better get accustomed to wearing a belt only, finally shoes he only ever had one pair of plain black shoes they had been soled and heeled many times over but it looked like their days were numbered as Mary started to pull down brown slip on's after he had again caused Mary much frustration he settled for a light brown pair. Finally Sandy was dragged to the overcoat department where he was made to purchase a light raincoat, the three of them made towards the cash out Sandy was beginning to fret about what it was all going to cost him and he near collapsed when told the final tally was forty two pounds seventeen and six but to avoid a scene he wrote out a cheque just as his sister Meg was doing the same at the next till. As they drove home Sandy was still moaning about his purchases and what they had cost, when they got home they had a bit of a mannequin parade and both Sandy and Meg agreed that their new outfits fairly took years off their appearances, Mary told them just to keep them on and they drove into town for their supper for which she paid. Monday morning and Sandy was back at work, Mary was going back to Edinburgh in the afternoon she was back on duty on Tuesday morning, she was taking part in the Tattoo in August so would be back and forth to Edinburgh doing rehearsals etc, both Willie and Mary had achieved the highest rank possible in the Military Police to get any higher they would need to take a commission but both decided they were too old to start studying so it looked like retirement for both was just round the corner. Life for Meg and Sandy just ambled on, Meg was bending his ear about getting a Television but he was resisting he was quite happy with his wireless but Meg had the bug she visited friends who now owned a Black and White tele she had been greatly taken with the cookery programmes and some of the quiz programmes, she was sure Mary would be able to pick one up much cheaper than they could so she hatched a ploy with Mary. She would have tele before the dark nights arrived.

One of Sandy's favourite relaxation's was to lie on his bed fully clothed and pick on a subject from his past life in the Glen and reminisce about how things were, how they had enjoyed life in the Glen with all the friends and neighbours, it was a hard, tough, but good life, sadly many of the folks have departed this world and others are scattered around the globe life will never be the same again, Sandy's mind wandered back to his trip to Aberdeen and as he studied the receipt telling him how much each item cost, he had been mesmerised by the sheer size of the stores M&S, BHs, C&A, Burton and Hepworth the list was endless even Woollies was mind boggling he wondered how they all made a living. But then his mind wandered back to the Glen just after the war all their needs were supplied by mobile shops many of them still horse drawn there was the baker twice a week, the butcher, the fishmonger this was mostly elderly women with creels on their backs they walked miles round the country selling their fish, then there was Humpy Danny who owned the mobile drapers shop. Danny was thus named because of a birth defect that left him with quite a large hump, due to his deformity Danny had suffered a lot of cruel tricks during his younger life but he was now the owner of a thriving business his mobile shop was only part time, he was a qualified bespoke Tailor, being the only one in the district he was in big demand, he also made a killing after the war selling surplus Government Surplus forces clothing. Greatcoats were his best seller he could never get enough of them, some of the men would cut the coat in half and make a reefer jacket, so the people of the Glen especially the men looked like a band of freedom fighters when a few gathered together with all their different coloured coats but Danny didn't bother he was getting rich at many of his tormentors expense and if it was in his power to cheat he would, he got great pleasure in getting his own back. But there was a clandestine side to Danny he harboured a great secret few people were aware of Danny was the only means of birth control in the Glen you see he had the agency to sell French letters, to give them their proper title Durex they were kept in a locked cash box under the counter retailing at half-a-crown for a packet of three, Danny being the shrewd businessman that he was kept a list of the ones who were at it, he had two women on that list one was Vicky Grant Albie, s wife, Danny would smile to himself when Vicky left the van clutching her purchase thinking I wonder who has it in for Albie but then he would remember his tormenters, when he was young Albie was one of the worst so hell mend him. Then there was the young Lairds wife she was quite open about it and caused Danny to blush at times he did notice that none of his female customers were locals they would be too embarrassed to do such a thing but Danny hung on to his secret list thinking to himself it might come in handy one day. Sandy's mind cleared and he was back to the present Humpy Danny and the rest of them were all gone but Sandy still had his memories and he felt really relaxed after his hour of reminiscing.

He had been really busy since they moved house, there had been decorating to be done, the garden was now under control, one morning as he turned up for work he bumped into his old mate Freddy Shounders, Fred was into everything and most of his evenings were taken up with one activity or another one of his favourites was Bowling.

Chapter Twenty Six

THE BOWLING CLUB WAS ALWAYS ON the look out for new members so Fred invited Sandy to get involved, he had never been much of an active sportsman, he had been keen on the Tug-Of-War when Lang Dod kept things going and he had played a bit of Football for the Glen team when he was younger, on Sunday he would read the sports pages of the Sunday Post this kept him up-to-date especially what the Football World was up to. He was reluctant to get involved with the bowling club being very shy and self conscious Sandy found it hard to commit himself but Freddie was a very persuasive man so he wore Sandy down until he agreed to go along after work and have a trial go at it. At the bowling green Freddie explained the rules and showed Sandy how to release the bowl, how to make it swerve and all the other moves associated with the game of bowls, Sandy then had a go, on the croft he had been a crack shot with a rifle and shot gun so he already had a keen eye. Twenty minutes into Sandy's practice session Freddie threw down a challenge and invited Sandy to play a few ends, in Freddie's eyes he was natural and could turn out to be a real gem for the club.

A few sessions with Freddie and Sandy became hooked he swept the boards at the Novice competitions and soon stepped up to play in the more experienced competitions, every second Saturday afternoon Sandy would be playing at one of the many Bowling Clubs around the coast, he had found an outlet that he wished he had found years earlier, he was a great favourite with his fellow players not only for his bowling skills but they found out that Sandy was a fairly accomplished Accordion player this was a real boon to a small bowling club when they had readymade dancing music, even better was the fact it was free Sandy refused to accept a fee for supplying music to the club. He had at last found a relaxing inexpensive past time he also encouraged Meg to get involved she had no special interest in playing bowls but she was handy to have around the club kitchen helping the other volunteers making tea and what ever else was required of her. Sandy found himself just waiting for the weekends to arrive so that he could get out on the greens, he was dreading the dark evenings as that would put paid to the bowling until the spring. October was looming big on the horizon their trip to Canada was getting nearer every day. It was decide that Mary would come home pick Sandy and Meg up and drive them to Prestwick where the three of them would fly from, their flight was leaving at two pm so Mary had to leave Bogton at six am it was a good six hours drive, Sandy was quite excited it was the first time he would be farther away from home than Aberdeen, the size of Glasgow had Sandy awe struck and when they did get to Prestwick the sheer size of the Airport buildings had him gob smacked on seeing the aircraft hangers he said to Meg that they made Lang Dods Dutch Barn look like a chicken coop.

Sandy was very nervous as he waited to board the plane but once he was inside he decided it was just like sitting in a bus, they had a very uneventful flight, once they cleared Customs they were just about smothered as Betty, Walter and the two grown up Niece and Nephew hugged and kissed them. Once the formalities were over they headed for the restaurant, Jim and Tina and their two kids were due to land in half an hour so they had refreshment's while they waited, Betty and Walter both had a station wagon that held at least six people in each.

During the course of the conversation Sandy was quite surprised that they had a three and a half to four hour drive before they reached the ranch, but looking around him he could see that Canada was a huge country, he also noted that there seemed to be a lot of traffic and everybody seemed to have huge cars. They had been waiting for just over half-an- hour when the arrival of flight so and so from Auckland New Zealand was announced, the excitement in the Duncan family was about to erupt again as the Kiwi contingent appeared at the arrival gate, the other travellers must have thought they had gone mad as they hugged and danced about, after picking up the luggage they moved towards the car park. Walter senior and young Walter elected to drive young Walter thought his mother would be too distracted as she held a conversation with her sisters, the females being in one vehicle and the males in the other. It was a long but pleasant drive Sandy could hardly believe the size of the fields and the farm steadings it made the croft at Hillies look like somebody's back garden, he shuddered to think what like it would have been having to hoe turnips or lift tatties from one of these huge fields. On arrival at the ranch Sandy was again gob smacked on seeing the size of the place, it had employed twenty two men in the days before mechanisation now there were four, they had a bunk house where the single men used to stay, now it was done up into individual rooms and was used to rent out to tourists this was Betty's end of the business, she had never forgotten her crofting roots as she had a milk cow and a vegetable garden which she looked after herself she still did a bit of part time nursing so she was a very busy lady. With the size of the ranch house and the Bunkhouse there was plenty space to give everybody a bed. Tommy and Willie would be arriving later in the week. The wedding was going to be a real Scottish affair, Peg was due to arrive next day and they needed to have a rehearsal before the big day, which was a week away. They were to be married in the little Church about a mile from the ranch, Walter said they would then have the local Pipe Band to pipe them from the Church to the Ranch but this was a secret as Peg and Buck and their guests weren't aware of this, another surprise for Sandy was that he was giving the bride away, what he didn't know was that they had ordered a kilt for the occasion, he had never worn a kilt so his reaction should be memorable. There was still a lot of organising to be done Meg had elected to bake the cake the flower arrangements had to be carried out in the church so there would be no idle hands especially among the women. Walter owned a mobile home, which they used for holidays and weekends of hunting and fishing he invited Sandy and Jim to get the van ready and they would spend a few days touring around maybe do a spot of fishing, one of Sandy's wishes was to view the Rocky Mountains he had often seen them at the pictures but to see them in reality would be something else. As the men left they were given strict instructions they had four days as they were needed back before Wednesday the day they were due to pick up their wedding clothes Sandy still being unaware he had to wear a kilt he was under the impression it was an ordinary suit. They covered just over a thousand miles the scenery was breath taking Sandy had looked at the Rockies through Binoculars they were still many miles away and time was at a premium, It was late on the Tuesday evening when they arrived back, Willie and Tommy and their families had arrived so it was more hugging and kissing.

Wednesday was the beginning of the count down to the wedding, Sandy and Meg were going into town to pick up their wedding outfits, Sandy was surprised to see a Tartan shop in a mid west town in Canada and even more surprised when they parked the car and started towards the shop. Mary had come along with them, she was sure she would have to calm her brother down when told he was wearing a kilt for the very first time. On entering the shop they were greeted by the owner who was as Heiland as a peat, he was in on the secret of Sandy's kilt, by this time Sandy was starting to get suspicious and when confronted he nearly blew a fuse he ranted and raved and threatened to board the next pane for hame if he was forced to wear a bloody kilt. Mary took the situation in hand and with a bit of cajoling and threats Sandy soon calmed down and was in the fitting room trying on his Duncan Tartan Kilt, Meg was further along the shop getting fitted out in a Tartan Skirt and over her white blouse she was going to wear a Tartan Sash the other brothers and sisters all had their own Highland Outfits and wore them when ever the opportunity arose even Walter had his own Kilt, Manitoba had quite a lot of Scots immigrants Sandy could tell by the amount of Scottish place names he had seen as they drove around the country and of course Banff was a name the Duncan's were very familiar with Banff Scotland being the nearest town to the Glen they were brought up in. Sandy was soon dressed in his Highland Dress and looked good in it, he paraded in front of the mirror and although he didn't say much he felt quite pleased with himself. Friday afternoon was rehearsal time everybody relevant to the wedding party was now resident in the vicinity. Sandy and Peg were to ride to church in a closed in carriage pulled by four grey horses so it was decided to have a dummy run on the Friday the bridesmaids were also in the carriage that was Mary chief bridesmaid and then the three nieces were bridesmaids and the nephews were page boys and ushers, Buck also had nieces and nephews who were given roles in the party. The rehearsal went fine and Sandy had a chat with the minister, it turned out he was a third generation Canadian his great grandfather had emigrated from the Isle Of Lewis at the end of the nineteenth century, they kept up to a date with the happenings in the old country, another coincidence was that the Rev Macleod forefathers had been crofters so he and Sandy had a lot in common. The wedding feast was to be an all Scottish affair the Duncan sisters had prepared everything by themselves Meg had even baked a three tier cake the idea was that they would hire some waitresses from an employment agency to serve the food but they themselves would have everything ready the menu was Scotch Broth made with Hough the second course was to be the Hough served with potatoes and two veg this would be carrot and turnip they would also include a mealy jimmy which was the traditional accompliment to boiled beef the sweet was Clootie dumplin with custard and cream as required, as they were preparing the food Meg remarked " Its jist like getting ready for the threshin mull" only there was slightly more mouths to feed they were catering for a party of fifty. The rehearsal had gone well it was also a chance for Sandy and the rest of the family to renew their acquaintances with Buck and his family they were all invited back to the ranch for tea and biscuits and of course, Buck had invited the men along to his hotel for a bit of a stag party the women were staying at the ranch but no doubt plenty refreshments were available.

The men gathered at the Brown Bear Hotel just after eight pm and before nine thirty you could say they were in good voice, it was quite a crowd as many of the locals joined the party, somebody suggested that it was a pity that Sandy hadn't brought his accordion along but they were told not to worry and soon an instrument was produced and thrust into Sandy's hands he reluctantly agreed to play for twenty minutes but two and half hours later accompanied by two more accordions two fiddles and an array of tin whistles the Celeidh was going great guns until finally just before midnight the instruments were packed away and a very drunken stag party headed for the ranch and bed they had a long day ahead to-morrow.

Saturday the wedding day had arrived Sandy was up around six am his room had tea making facilities so he was sitting having a pull on his pipe and enjoying his first cup of tea when there was a knock on the door, he opened it and there stood Mary with an entourage of athletic youngsters just about to set off on their early morning jog Sandy was invited to join them but very pleasantly told them to b****r off his days of running were over so with much hilarity they set off, it was a nice crisp morning. In the confines of his room Sandy had a wee secret try on of his kilt he was still none too happy about it but was advised by Mary as he was head of the family he was expected to enter the sprit of the day and make his young sisters wedding a day to remember.

The carriage was due to arrive at one fifteen ready to be loaded up and leave the ranch around one thirty the ranch house was a hive of activity the brides nerves were a bit frayed but with the help of her sisters she was ready in plenty time. Peg was thirty nine but she looked as radiant as any bride half her age and of course the young bridesmaids were ecstatic in their long dresses complete with Duncan tartan sashes, Sandy got a round of applause when he arrived in the house wearing his highland dress, when asked how it felt he replied, " Am missin ma lang drawers it's a bit draughty a roon ma erse" Mary butted in and said " Aye hope yir lang drawers are still in your drawer at Bogton yons affa lookin things". Peg and Sandy were the first aboard the coach then Mary once they were seated the younger girls were packed in but trying to avoid crushing their dresses, as they started to move the build up of excitement could be felt, the nearer the Kirk they got Sandy could feel the adrenalin coursing through his veins, Peg of course was a bundle of nerves but Mary as always was in full control as long as she was at the helm everything would be fine. As they neared the Kirk a lone piper was waiting to play them into the service he did a fine job of the tune Mhari Wedding, Peg had to have bit of titillation to her dress to make sure it hung properly but with Warrant Officer Mary Duncan in charge everything was done to Military precision, Peg crooked her arm through Sandy's then they were off no turning back now, the inside of the church looked wonderful with so much tartan on show you would think you were attending a Clan gathering in some remote Scottish Glen, the biggest surprise for Peg was when she looked to-wards the alter and her American groom was dressed in full Highland dress as was the best man, the minister was wearing a kilt in Macleod tartan it was quite an overwhelming experience and Peg needed all her strength to stop her bursting into tears.

The ceremony lasted all of fifty minutes. Peg and Buck looked a splendid couple as they posed on the steps of the Old Kirk to allow twenty minutes of photography and yet another surprise awaited the newly weds a huge American Buick complete with decorations pulled up at the bottom of the steps the chauffeur opened the door and motioned the happy couple to enter, as they drove off round the corner of the church they were given a rapturous round of applause, as the car nosed past the crowd on to the roadway the couple were gob smacked to see a full Pipe band waiting to play them back to the ranch Peg was thrilled what a way to start married life it was just marvellous. The Pipe band were local college kids they had formed the band recently and were desperate to show off their skills, the Drum Major a friend of Walter also an Ex pat Scotsman who attended the Caledonian Society of which Betty and Walter were members had approached them and offered the band services just to enhance the Scottish occasion he assured them the kids would be as thrilled as the wedding guests being allowed to participate in front of real people from Scotland, bye the time they reached the ranch they had proved their repertoire was wide ranging covering many well known pipe tunes. The agency staff hired to serve the food were busy getting everything ready a marquee had been erected and tables laid out for the fifty guests who were invited to the meal. Meg soon found an apron and joined the two chefs who were hired to more or less heat the food which the Duncan's had already prepared the day before, she was just makin sure the Canadians knew how to handle Scottish food. Inside the entrance to the marquee everybody was handed a glass of champagne and lined up either side so that they could toast the newly weds as they entered to the sound of the pipe band playing a selection of tunes that included Mhari's Wedding and various others well known to the likes of Sandy, everybody was then seated at mixed tables the idea of this was to make sure nobody felt left out, various people stood up and made speeches and finally just on an hour later they were ready to be served, Scotch Broth with newly made oatcakes and fresh butter; real figure busting material. The meal would have been more appropriate in a farm house kitchen on the day of the threshing mill it was just good wholesome Scottish fare thoroughly enjoyed by the whole party everybody was mucking in and a lot of hilarity could be heard for the Duncan's this was a family reunion as well as a wedding on the American side there were only fifteen but as Buck explained they were in the middle of a very busy period on the ranches back home in Idaho so quite a few relatives were missing but he announced that all were welcome to come for a holiday when ever they felt like it. The meal lasted nearly two hours and with the speeches they had been seated for over three hours time for Sandy to sneak out and have a session with his pipe the scent of the St Bruno could be felt in the still evening air, he still marvelled at the size of the fields around the ranch he could barely see the fence at the far end he shook his head in wonderment. Soon the noise of chairs scraping across the marquee floor could be heard as they cleared the floor ready for the dancing to start right on cue a van pulled up and three or four men got out and started to unload musical instruments some of the guys were the same ones that Sandy had met and played along with in the Brown Bear the evening before, Sandy crossed over to where they were and was soon told he was expected to take a turn on stage they even brought along a spare box for him.

The musicians had their instruments tuned up ready to start, they called themselves the Lochside Celeidh Band, they had brought along a spare accordion so that Sandy could join them if he so wished, no doubt he would be delighted as he wasn't a dancer, Mary now dressed in jeans and a tartan shirt soon had the dancing under control with the rest of the family joining in they were soon going through a wide range of Scottish Country Dances the Canadian Barn Dance was also a favourite, there was quite a crowd gathering the kids from the pipe band had been invited, the great thing was because the community was made up mainly of exiled Scots most of them were familiar with the dances and the floor was packed every time, by this time Sandy was seated with the band really enjoying himself it brought back memories of Will Watson and himself playing in the Glen Public Hall, one thing that stood out there wasn't one drunk person nor did any of the young ones step out of line it was just a wonderful evening. Peg and Buck had changed into casual clothes halfway through the evening, then about eleven –o-clock a taxi pulled up and the newly weds bade their guests goodbye as they jumped abroad, they were not taking any chances of having their wedding night disrupted so they had booked into an hotel for the night, the pranksters who had their bed in the house doctored were very disappointed that their ploy was knocked on the head, just like at home the last dance was called at eleven forty five. It would be over before the Sabbath day arrived, by twelve fifteen the Marquee was deserted as the throng made their way home. The Duncan family and one or two guests carried on with the party in the house the drink was starting to take affect as one by one they disappeared towards the bedrooms. The matriarch Meg warned them all that they were expected to be ready for church parade next morning she had promised Murdo Macleod that the whole family would be there. Groggily they started to appear in the dining room the next morning, Mary had already been out and done a five mile run she had been accompanied with one or two of the younger ones, she had the coffee pot ready as the hung over brothers made an appearance with that all too familiar remark "never again". Meg and Betty were already in the kitchen preparing a good wholesome Scottish breakfast staring off with a plate of porridge followed by bacon, egg, sausage black and white pudding beans and a tomato, it was not appreciated by all especially by the ones with a khaki stomach. Half past ten and Meg was mustering them all to get ready to leave for the Kirk, she was not the most popular person at that point but everybody knuckled down and nursing their sore heads made their way to Sunday worship, just as they reached the gates of the churchyard a taxi pulled up and Peg and Buck disembarked full of the joys of spring there was much hugging and kissing you would think they had been missing for years. Murdo Macleod had been the parish minister for near thirty years and for the fist time ever he had to find extra seating for his congregation that morning, the church had never been so full, he started his welcoming speech by saying that if this was the effect that the Duncan family would have on his weekly attendance he would make arrangements for them to stay. The Church service over the crowd began to disperse, Buck and Peg were the centre of attention as congratulations were heaped on them, as they made their way back to the Ranch Buck announced that they had ordered a local catering company to hold a barbeque.

Buck explained that the BBQ was his family saying thanks for the wonderful day that the Duncan family had laid on to celebrate his wedding day, the sisters thought it was a wonderful gesture, (secretly thinking great it lets us off the hook from having to feed this mob again) the full wedding party had turned up again so they might as well make the best of it and before long a full blown Celeidh was going strong, the Marquee was still erected so there was plenty seating, Mary was having the time of her life as she organised the young ones into groups where they participated in various games it didn't take long for the adults to join in the hilarity and fooling about went on until the caterers announced grub up causing complete silence for a while as people got tucked into a galaxy of food. After a most enjoyable afternoon it was time for the wedding guests to start departing and go their separate way to their various parts of the world, Peg and Buck would be leaving in the morning heading for Hawaii where they were to spend a week on honeymoon, Bucks family were heading back to Idaho and Texas where they lived and the Duncan's were departing at various stages during the week, Willie and Tommy were also leaving on the Monday back to the Uk but to different ends of the country, Jim and Tina and the family were staying until Wednesday and Meg, Mary and Sandy were staying until Saturday, Sandy was cramming as much sightseeing into the few days left as was possible, Walter was a brilliant guide and he showed them as much of the country as was humanly possible, but like all good things it came to an end they were flying home on Saturday . Friday night it was early to bed as they had to leave the Ranch at four am the drive to the airport lasted approximately four hours depending on traffic and weather conditions, it turned out an uneventful journey Walter was driving and Betty had come along to say goodbye to her family, the big station wagon was soon eating up the miles and they arrived at the airport with plenty time to spare, allowing time for something to eat before the flight to Prestwick was called, as usual it was a tearful goodbye especially with Meg and Betty shedding tears as if it was the final meeting, Mary stood back and shook her head she wasn't the emotional type.

The flight back to Scotland could be described as rather hairy with the plane being buffeted about, a bit nerve racking for the novice fliers like Meg and Sandy they were glad when they felt the bump of the plane hitting the runway, once they cleared customs and picked up the car they would head straight up the road to Banff-shire it looked like it would be around mid-night before they finally reached home. The drive north was fine but the three travellers were glad to see home it had been along stress full day, Mary suggested the best idea of the day when she produced a bottle of whisky from her luggage and poured three stiff drams what a wonder full booster a drop of the cratur is, in next to no time they were fully revived and ready to have something to eat before getting ready for bed. Early next morning Sandy awoke he could hear Mary as she prepared to go for her daily run, he would wait until she was gone then rise and have a cup of tea ready for her coming back, no doubt Meg would be wanting to attend the Kirk it was a big part in her life and of course she would be dying to tell her WRI friends all about Canada, after the Kirk they intended having some lunch then Mary would depart she was heading for Edinburgh for an overnight stay then on to Catterick on Monday morning.

Chapter Twenty Seven

ONDAY MORNING SOON CAME ROUND AND Sandy was back at work it didn't take long for him to realise he was back home in Banff-shire among the Doric speakers the first person he met in the yard was Derek Wylie the foreman, " Aye, Aye Sandy fit like min? Fu did the holiday gang", Sandy explained that it had gone well and the eye opener he had received at the size of the country Canada turned out to be, Derek continued, " Fit aboot the fleein fu did yea get on wi that" " Och it wis aw richt a bit hairy on the wye back a could feel a erse nippin at times but it wis fine". Ach weel yea'll be gled tae get back intae the harness efter aw yir excitement" with that Derek headed for his office leaving Sandy to prepare for work. It was a great feeling as he drove along the main street waving and shouting at his fellow early morning colleagues, especially a very secret friend of the female variety. For quite some time Sandy had become very friendly with a war widow by the name of Vera Simpson, Vera was about ages with Sandy, her husband had lost his life at Normandy and she had brought up her two bairns on her own she had a job as a cleaner in the Bank which she had held for the past twenty years, starting at six am, it had been very handy when the bairns were in school it allowed her to be at home when they were getting ready, now they were left school she found herself on her own quite a bit, up until she had met Sandy she had been quite happy to be on her own, but over the past few months as she walked to work she found herself timing her arrival at the Bank to coincide with the time Sandy would be sweeping the street in front of her patch, it really struck home during the past fortnight when she found herself longing for the day he would return, her heart missed a beat when she turned onto High Street and there was Sandy making his way along to-wards her she felt her face blushing as he got nearer with the huge Sandy grin on his face, he stopped beside her, she felt like rushing over and giving him a big hug but that was not becoming of a widow woman in the middle of the High Street at six-o-clock in the morning, further more

Sandy would maybe have had a fit he was still a very shy reserved sort of fellow especially around females. Vera asked how the holiday had gone, he told her it would take hours to tell her the whole story but it had been fine and he had really enjoyed the experience. Vera saw a chance to spend a while longer with Sandy by inviting him to sit down and tell her all about it, she thought for a few seconds and then said she would meet Sandy after work down by the harbour, there were benches set out along the back wall, Sandy was caught unawares and he stammered his way through his reply but the bottom line was ok he would see her at two pm. As he drove away his head was in turmoil you see at the age of forty five his experience with the female species was nil, when his father had died Meg and him had only one thought on their minds that was to provide a home and food for the other six members of the family plus their mother so it didn't leave much spare time to pursue members of the opposite sex. In fact Sandy's marriage spanner was never used as a means of reproduction and still brand new never out of the box, then when he did attend social functions he was always the one supplying the music so his opportunities were pretty limited, this left him very shy and backward when in the company of women who were not related, his sister Meg went through a similar dilemma so from the age of fifteen until they were around thirty they cared for the rest of the family which left very little time for their own needs.

As Sandy left the council yard he was very apprehensive about his clandestine mission to meet Vera, but then he wondered if she would bother to turn up maybe it was a spur of the moment thing but his fears were brushed away as he rounded the bend heading for the car park he could see her waving to him as if to say I'm over here. Sandy parked the car and feeling rather awkward he strolled over to where Vera was sitting, at her feet was a shopping bag from which she produced a thermos flask asking Sandy if he liked coffee he told her yes then marvelled at how the flask was a real ice breaker. It was their very first meeting where they could sit and discuss various subjects such as Sandy's holiday, one of the items they discussed and it turned out to be a subject they both really enjoyed was the pictures Sandy always tried to go to a movie at least once a week the same as Vera did. They chatted for an hour but were forced to give up as the chill wind off the North Sea started to get the better of them, just as they parted Vera said " There's a smashing picture on in the Playhoose this Friday nicht I wis thinking of going wid yea like tae come wi me"? Sandy was fair taken aback and stuttered and spluttered his answer which was yes he didn't have a lot of options so they parted company after arranging their very first date, by the time they had parted Sandy was feeling very comfortable in Vera's company. They continued their morning ritual of having a quick word as she scurried up the steps of the bank and he passed along the street with the street sweeper, but he was now counting the days to Friday when he would once again be able to be in this fascinating woman's company for at least a couple of hours, of course Sandy would have to keep their meeting low key he was fearful of what sister Meg would think of a man of his age going out on dates, but it would be dark when he met Vera and he would make sure they were near the back of the cinema where he was sure nobody would see him he felt obliged to opt for the more expensive seats it would look bad on his part to seat her in the scratchers (the name given to the front half dozen rows).

On Friday morning the two met as usual at the bank, after their brief chat Vera asked if they were still on for the pictures in the evening, without showing a lot of eagerness Sandy said yes and went on his way, actually he was feeling quite excited about the whole scenario and was happily whistling away as he carried on his days work. At home in the afternoon he was having a quiet nap when Meg arrived home she had bought some fish for their tea and asked Sandy when he would like to eat, he said five-o'clock would be fine as he was going out, " Oh far are yea gan"? Enquired his sister, " Am gan tae the pictures" (he was holding his breath incase she wanted tae go with him) but she never asked any more questions, but she did have a WRI meeting in the Glen Village Hall so that maybe saved him a big predicament. Sandy parked his car on the main street and walked towards the picture house, he felt his heart skip a beat when he spied Vera waiting for him just inside the door, they greeted each other quite formally and then moved towards the kiosk, just as he was about to pay the young lady usherette, in a rather shrill voice said " Aye Vera you're the deep ane yea never mentioned that yea hid a date the nicht," Vera quickly answered " Oh a dive hae some secrets ah keep till masel"The young lady replied " Vera when ah see fowks your age picking up a lumber aye ken there's hope for me yet, dive yae want seats in the back row" she said winking at Sandy.

Sandy had never been so embarrassed in his life he was just thankful there wasn't a big queue behind him, he paid for the tickets and scurried off behind Vera dying to get into the darkness of the picture house before he had to withstand further embarrassment or so he thought. The usherette with the torch turned out to be an acquaintance of Vera, "Aye Vera fit like the nicht, oh! Yiv a man wie yea, aye supposes you'll be needin seats in the back row that's far aw the love bird's gang." Sandy had never faced such an embarrassing ordeal in his life he just thanked his lucky stars it was almost dark he was trying to keep this evening low profile but the usherettes were determined to broadcast it to the world that Vera had a man for company that evening, but Sandy's embarrassment was not over yet most of the back four rows of seats were used by young couples sixteen to twenty five, so Vera and Sandy were sticking out like a sore thumb, plus the antics of the courting couples were very distracting, Sandy found himself fascinated and at times wondered how far the couple were prepared to go he was getting hot under the collar and was glad when the final credits appeared on the screen, of course it was the last house so the lights came on, Sandy was amazed to see how little clothes the lassies were wearing of course it was the sixties and the mini skirt was the uniform of the day but not only were the skirts short the tops were pretty skimpy as well. Sandy kept his head down as they shuffled to-wards the exit. Out in the cool evening air Vera was standing pretty close as she asked Sandy if he wanted to come up to her place for a coffee before he went home, he turned down the invitation but offered to run her home, his excuse was that he was working in the morning and would need to get to bed.

Sandy was playing hard to get, he had a real dilemma on his hands he was really fond of Vera the night at the pictures had been great but he was keeping his distance, his dilemma was sister Meg she had stuck with him through thick and thin during their thirty years at Hillies, never complaining although the work was hard and her days were never less than fifteen hours, on top of this they never received a proper wage it was only in the last year that they were given a pay packet every week and could use the money as they pleased. In that era there were many men and women like Sandy and Meg who never married, living together like a married couple some would even be with their parents until they died, neither Meg or Sandy really had an opportunity to get involved with the opposite sex due to their circumstances being the bread winners of the family. Now Sandy had a guilt complex every time he was in Vera's company, he was running out of excuses as to why they could not go out together. He was given a real boost when Vera announced she was going to Edinburgh for Christmas and New year to stay with her daughter that would let Sandy off the hook but first she wanted him to come to her house so that they could have a meal together before she went off, Sandy agreed he couldn't see any harm in that but he did ask if she could make it on a week night as he was tied up most week-ends. On the Thursday evening Sandy made his way to Vera's house it would be his first visit, dressed in his casual clothes he made his way up the gravel path, he felt naked as he was sure he could sense the curtains being moved back so that the neighbours could get a better view of Vera's new companion, he felt it quite nerve wracking and even more embarrassing when she threw her arms round his neck and gave him a huge hug and a kiss.

Sandy felt more at ease when he heard Vera close the door, but his ordeal was not over yet Vera asked if he wanted to remove his jacket which he did, she hung it up on the coat stand in the lobby then directed him towards the sitting room he commented on the aroma of cooking as he passed the kitchen door, she asked if he would like something to drink while she finished cooking the meal. He decided he would be safe enough to have a bottle of export ,while he waited his eyes wandered around the room, he was very impressed with the way Vera kept everything so tidy and clean he started to study the photographs she had framed all around the room, a couple of teenagers with mortar boards on their heads, he was sure it would be Vera's kids the girl was a teacher in Edinburgh, the boy was a civil engineer working in the Highlands somewhere. Then Sandy focused on a wedding photo on the sideboard it was Vera and her husband he felt a funny sensation running through his body, like the man in the photo was staring at him and asking what bloody right have you got sitting in my house I don't even know who the hell you are. Suddenly Vera was at his side holding a glass of beer in one hand and a small glass of sherry in the other, she noted Sandy was gazing at the wedding picture and went on to explain what happened. "That's Andy and me on our wedding day it was nineteen forty I was eighteen and Andy was twenty one the war was just started, but he was exempt until he was called up in time for the Normandy invasion, a year after we married we had young Andrew life was not easy, we had a room from my mother who was a widow so she was quite happy to have us but we were living under the threat that Andy would be called up. Suddenly the inevitable happened Andy was called up and off he went he was away for ten weeks then he was allowed home for embarkation leave they called it, it was a very emotional two weeks and they flew past, he left not knowing what lay in front of him, he had been gone a month when I discovered that I was pregnant again my girl Maryann was the result, unfortunately poor Andy didn't survive the first twenty four hours of the Invasion". Vera sprung up from her chair shouting "michty me the tatties i'll be ruined" well at least it broke the ice for Sandy and for the minute he didn't have to carry on the conversation about the late Andy. Vera had gone out of her way to cook a lovely meal she had chosen roast beef as she was sure they would be fed up of Turkey and Chicken by the time Christmas and the New Year were over. It was a five star feast with all the trimmings they spent quite some time over it discussing various aspects of how life had treated them, Vera said she remembered the day Sandy's father was taken into hospital she had just started work as an orderly they were all praying for him to survive although none of the girls on her shift knew who he was they were all very sad when word came round the hospital that he had failed in his struggle. As they sat and talked it was inevitable that they would eventually get round to the fact that Vera had been a widow for over thirty years, Sandy asked if it was choice, Vera took her time in answering as if she looking for the proper thing to say, "Sandy I was devastated when we received the telegram that said Andy had been K/A as they put it, here I was eight weeks pregnant and now a widow and had never been out of this toon I jist didna ken which wye tae turn but then I was luckier than most quines in the same boat I was staying wie ma mither, what a blessing that proved to be, I decided that I would with the help of my mither bring up my two brains so that their father would have been proud of them, so between us I think we have done quite a good job both went to university the girl is teacher the boy a civil engineer. Oh! I could have re married I had plenty offers but a lot of them were jist efter whit they could get, they seemed to think when you are a widow you are desperate.

Sandy glanced at his watch it was showing quarter to eleven michty me Meg would be going aff her heid worrying aboot him, he hurriedly thanked Vera for a wonderful evening and grabbed his jacket, he was just about to receive the most embarrassing moment of the evening when Vera handed him a small parcel wrapped in Christmas paper " Just a wee pressie for Christmas" she said as she planted a kiss on his cheek, Sandy was thankful the hall was quite dim and he managed to hide his blushing cheeks he felt absolutely terrible and couldn't escape quick enough. He managed to mutter thanks and to tell Vera to enjoy her break in Edinburgh. He would have to take his time on the way home it was frosty and he had to scrape the windscreen , he was hoping Meg was in bed as he would no doubt get an ear bashing one for being out so late and driving on the frosty roads and for another thing he had left in the evening without a word of where he was going, peering through the sitting room window his worst fears were allayed when he saw the light was still on. Meg had been dozing off so she was not in the best of humour when she was startled awake by Sandy nosily bursting through the door she went right into attack, " Far the hell hiv yea been till this time oh nicht she berated her brother, I've been up tae high doh windering if something hid happened tae yea", Sandy shook his head and gave an explanation that had absolutely no bearing on the real reason for him being late he declined his sisters offer of a cup of tea and went to bed. Sandy tried to avoid his sister for the next couple of days in case she started to pry into his whereabouts the evening he spent with Vera as far as he was aware it was still a secret that he had a female friend. Mary was due home for Christmas and New-Year this would ensure that it would be quite a lively affair this year, she always injected a bit of fun into life when she was around. It was now over a year since Sandy and Meg had given up the croft they were beginning to come to terms with a life that didn't involve working every waking hour of the day. Sandy was getting slightly worried about his liaison with Vera the morning after she left for Edinburgh he couldn't believe how he was missing her cheery smile and found himself staring up the steps towards the door of the Bank in case she had changed her mind and stayed at work he was feeling like a love struck teenager, he had never felt this way about a member of the opposite sex before he would need to get a grip the last thing he wanted was anybody to find out there was a possibility that at the age of forty eight he had fallen deeply in love, he just wouldn't manage to handle the embarrassment and leg pulling he was bound to receive when the news eventually got out, if the partnership continued no doubt it would become headline gossip he could just imagine it " Dea yea ken the latest" " No fits that" "Dea yea mind on Sandy Hillies he wiz in oor class at the school, well he never merried he's cumin up on fifty and I hear he's courtin and will get married jist shortly, the worlds fu oh surprises yea niver ken whit'll happen next" . "By the way fa's the lucky quine?" "Ach yea'll ken her tae she wiz widowed in the war and never merried again, Vera Simpson a richt hard workin quine she wiz, brought up twa bairns single handed and pit them through the university they shid make a good match" Sandy's imagination was running riot as he turned over in his mind what people would be saying and thinking about him and then he would think damn the bloody lot of them it's my life and I'm free to do what I want with it. Mary was due home late in the evening she was driving up from her base in Catterick and the roads were pretty treacherous she had phoned to say if it got any worse she would get a B&B somewhere and stay the night it would be easier driving during the day, as she hadn't called back they were expecting her to arrive at anytime.

Mary arrived home around eleven she was shattered it had taken her ten hours to drive a seven hour journey she said it was the worst journey she had ever had to make on icy roads and not much sign of them being gritted, Meg rushed to put the kettle on and asked what her young sister would like to eat, Mary being Mary told them the first thing she could do with was a large dram to calm her nerves down, she reached into her bag and handed Sandy a bottle of Antiquary stating that it had been ordered since last Christmas that's how scarce it is, Meg settled for a sherry and Sandy had a small dram as he was still working in the morning, he pointed this out to Mary it was also a chance for Meg to get a dig at him about being late the night before, but he let her remarks pass over his head not wanting to open a can of worms. After Sandy had gone to bed Meg and Mary sat chatting into the wee sma oors, they covered a multitude of subjects one brought up by Meg was her brother Sandy's strange behaviour, " it seems to be since we got back from Canada he is hiding something but I canna pit my finger on it". Mary looked at Sister Meg and replied "Maybe he's got himself a woman". Meg felt a strange sensation running through her system the thought had never occurred to her but it made her think, then after a bit of thought she replied, "I've never had any recollection of Sandy ever being involved with a woman we were always that busy working on the croft and when he did have free time he would be playing his accordion so his opportunities were limited." But it was something for Meg to chew over and try and broach". Mary asked if Willie had been on the phone, he was in Sweden at Maria's folks over Christmas and New Year but was due in Aberdeen in the first week of January, Mary was to meet up with him they had some business to attend to Meg didn't ask what it was but it was another item she would spend time trying to fathom out. Sandy had to work his full shift on the thirty first so it was late afternoon before he was finished but then he had three days off, he was looking forward to the break, when he arrived home he decided to have a quick snack then have a lie down because there was no doubt it would be long a night bringing in the New Year. He fell into a deep sleep which; lasted for three hours his young sister Mary was shaking him trying to waken him as his dinner would be ready in twenty minutes, he roused himself up and after a shower and a shave he was ready to face whatever was thrown at him, they were about to spend their first Hogmanay at Bogton and were unsure how many first footers they would have if any. They had become reasonably friendly with most of the people who lived in the row of houses but they all had their own interests and not all of them were country folks so there were conflicting back grounds and though hard to believe it did make a difference how people reacted to each other but anyhow Sandy and Meg had extended an invite to them all and assured them they would be most welcome to call over the festive week-end. Meantime in the Duncan residence they were sitting waiting for midnight to arrive, Sandy had given in to them having a television a while back and so they sat speechless watching the black and white images flickering on the screen eventually Sandy was chastised by his sisters when he started to snore, now being in a rather grumpy mood he stormed off to his bedroom where he would get peace and he could listen to his wireless there was a Scottish Dance music programme on at nine thirty just as well listening to that because when the telly was on and everybody was glued to the screen nobody spoke if Sandy had his way there would be no place in the house for the damned anti social contraption, how he missed having a good old blether with a house full of friendly people. Sandy reappeared at quarter past eleven just in time to watch Andy Stewart and his cast of all the top Scottish celebrities of the day he could enjoy that sort of thing but it still didn't compare with how they used to do things.

One minute to midnight and the show stopped and all their glasses were charged ready to toast in the New Year Sandy didn't't like this idea either in the old days the New Year was heralded in by a resident of the Glen blasting off a shot gun then the rest followed suit until everybody who owned a shot gun had taken their turn to greet a New Year the television made it too clinical in Sandy's mind but this was progress. As the bell tolled on the television and rang out midnight the two sisters and their brother toasted each other then hugged and toasted their absent siblings and their families in their world wide residences, Meg even managed to shed a few tears. It was nearly ten past midnight by the time they had settled down again and proceed to enjoy their drams, just getting comfortable when the phone burst into life the first one of the family to ring which one could it be, it generated a bit of excitement Mary was first to the phone, "Mary Duncan here who is it please who? Ok I'll get him for you" Sandy could feel a rush of adrenalin Mary stuck her head round the door covering the mouth piece with her hand she whispered " It's a lady called Vera for you Sandy" Sandy rose and headed for the hallway his face boiling with embarrassment this was not how he intended to start the New Year. He closed the door between the lobby and the living room trying to keep the conversation as private as possible, Meg was staining her ears trying to find out what was being said but it was a usual Sandy conversation " Aye fine aye a richt jist my sisters Meg and Mary ok then cheerio" and so it ended not giving much away. Sandy decided to delay his re-entry into the living room by heading for the bathroom he had a wash and was delighted when he heard the door bell ringing that would delay the embarrassing situation he would have to endure when the sisters started the interrogation. He arrived at the door almost the same instant as Mary they opened it and the elderly couple from two doors along were standing with their carrier bag bearing their hogmanay drinks after wishing each other a Happy New Year Sandy set about pouring drinks, Mary sidled up to him in the kitchen and asked was Vera ok, that was when he was aware that this was just a taster of what was ahead of him so he just replied she was fine and scurried away with a tray of drinks there didn't seem to be an escape route his secret would be revealed as soon as these two women had him alone. By two am they had quite a houseful of people and as was the norm in the Duncan house whenever there was a bit of a crowd Sandy would be hounded to play some music he was delighted to be asked this year as it was the best he had experienced for quite some considerable time of course his neighbours were middle aged or elderly so they were well experienced on how Hogmanay should be celebrated, the exiled members of the family had all called home and as usual Meg had tears streaming down her face, Betty had been away for well over twenty years but Meg still found it difficult to come to terms that things would never go back to what they were. The first footers stated to drift off home and some time after three am the house was back to normal, Sandy was well oiled and gibbering a bit so Mary thought it may be a good time to tackle him about Vera, he wasn't as drunk as his sister envisaged and even well oiled he was giving nothing away, much to Mary's disgust all she found out was that she was a widow who was a cleaner in the Bank and started work at the same time as Sandy did every morning.

Willie phoned on the second of January to say he would be flying up from London the next day he had decided the roads were too treacherous to drive, so he asked Mary if she could pick him up at midday to morrow and also told Meg he would be requiring a bed, he would be alone as Maria had to get the kids back to school on the fifth. Sandy was already back at work he only had the one day off his main task at work was clearing the pavements of snow in the middle of the town but it was good warm work so he didn't't mind, he was hard at work oblivious to what was going on around him when he received a slap on the back he jerked up right and was facing Vera, " Michty me Vera yea nearly gave me a heart attack, I didna think yea would be back yet, are yea started work?." " No I dinna start work until next Monday but av missed yea so I thought I would jist hiv a walk down the toon tae see yea." This made Sandy blush a bit but then he went on to thank her for her phone call and added that it had caused him a bit of hassle wie his sisters. " Bit yer nae ashamed oh me or anything like that are yea"? she asked. Sandy shook his head, " Its jist that ither fowk canna mind their ain business and tak great delight in poking their noses in far there nae wanted." " Oor Mary takes great delight in annoying folk she's never happier than when she is up tae some devilment or ither, nae doubt she still has some mischief up her sleeve but that's jist the kind she is a devil may care sort of person and nothing is ever too much bother to her so I'll jist hiv tae pit up wie her ragging until she leaves at the end of the week. Willie was sitting in the living room when Sandy returned home from his work he was late, due to the work load, they had asked him to work over, Meg was busy in the kitchen she always made a special effort when Willie her twin brother was home one of his favourite meals was scotch broth made with a skirt of beef stuffed with oatmeal and onions to-nite he would have his speciality set in front of him, over a cup of coffee Willie explained that he needed to have a little meeting he had a couple of surprises to tell the family but he decided that he would wait until the meal was over then over a dram he would reveal the mystery, he also added that he had hoped that Tommy could attend because it may involve him, but he had phoned earlier to say that due to the condition of the roads he was unable to attend. The dinner over Meg and Mary cleared the table while the men listened to the news at about half six they were ready to listen to what Willie had to say although Willie stressed that he never had anything to drink when he was conducting a meeting, seeing it was a family get-together to-nite he would make an exception so while Sandy poured the drams Willie arranged his notes on the table. He stared off by asking if Sandy and Meg remembered him telling them about the Americans drilling in the North Sea for oil , Sandy nodded and said he remembered vaguely, Willie continued " Well they have finally found enough to start a worth while venture in Oil production at the time I said to you and Tommy if you want to end up rich get in there at the start". " That's just what Mary and me have done we are on our final leave from the army and as of the first of February we will be civilians that is also the day our business kicks in we have started a business dealing with Security, Protection and Courier services. We bandied a few names for the new company about and nostalgia persuaded us to call our firm Hillside Securities, Protection & Courier Services." There was silence for a few minutes until Willie asked " Well fit div yea think oh that". Sandy said he wiz flabberghastet and had nae idea that any moves had taken place. Willie went on to outline what would happen how they would have an office in Aberdeen which they were going too sort out the next day also an office in London, Mary would run the Aberdeen one and he would have a manager in the London office as he would continually be on the look-out for work he also stated that both him and Mary would be millionaires before they were sixty, he then offered both Sandy and Meg jobs with the company but both declined Sandy was quite settled working for the Council and Meg wanted to think things over.

Chapter Twenty Eight

WILLIE MENTIONED THAT HE WOULD HAVE liked Tommy to be present as he is also getting the offer of a job but anyhow there was time to get things sorted out. Next morning Mary and Willie left at eight- o- clock bound for Aberdeen they had an appointment with an agent who rented office space at nine thirty, the roads were really bad so they gave themselves plenty time. Mary phoned home to let Meg know that they had been delayed and it would be after six before they would arrive back at Bogton, when they arrived back Willie was furious and ranting and raving about the inefficient Aberdonians, " They'll need to buck up their bloody ideas if they are to make anything oot of the Oil that's on their doorstep, they hiv nae idea" with that he reached for the drinks cabinet and poured himself a stiff dram asking if anybody else cared to join him, while he was away having a wash Mary explained to Meg and Sandy how their day had more or less been a wash out the letting agents were way behind the times and didn't seem to be bothered that they would soon be dealing with high powered Oil Companies who didn't suffer fools gladly and if the locals couldn't supply the goods they would soon import people who would, it looked like Willie and Mary would have to stay put until the week-end they were due back in Aberdeen in the morning. Willie got on the phone to Tommy asking if there was any possibility that he could come down before Sunday he was desperate to have a talk with his young brother he had him penned in to be a driving force in the Courier part of their business, Tommy said he would, but he may have to take the train to Aberdeen as the roads were still a nightmare, Willie said that would be fine Mary or himself could pick him up, it was agreed he would come down on Saturday morning, Meg shouted over the phone would he be bringing Arlene and the bairns but he said no it would be bad enough bringing himself down. Willie had arranged to catch the evening flight to London, he decided that when they picked up Tommy they would go to a hotel and the three of them could sort out what had to be sorted and that was that, Tommy was wanted to take over and run the Courier side of the business at the moment of arriving in Aberdeen he wasn't sure what his mission was. Meg had accompanied them into town she would have a great romp round the shops on her own nobody to hinder her in any way. Just after eleven Tommy stepped off the train and was immediately whisked into a taxi and driven to the Athol Hotel where Willie had arranged for them to have lunch, over a cup of coffee he out lined his plans he wanted Tommy to move either to Aberdeen or London he needed somebody who would push the others to the limit, Mary was quite taken aback at how ruthless Willie sounded but when he put his cards on the table she assumed that he knew what he was talking about. They sat down to Lunch and Willie explained what the Courier side of the business was about, " According to the Americans North Sea Oil is going to be big; at the moment at least six Rig Builders are looking for deep water sites so that they can build rigs and ship them out to the oil fields, let me assure you the Yanks don't throw money into projects unless they are certain there will be big bucks to be made, now the machinery they use will be running twenty four hours per day, no machinery can stand up to what theirs has to withstand so inevitably they end up with break downs, break downs cost money so the race is on to get started again, they will pay all sorts of prices to keep everything running so that's where our Courier Service kicks in it is up to Hillside Courier Services to supply the goods, we will pay top dollar but we need to employ class acts, men and possibly women who are not afraid to put themselves about. If we can survive for ten years we could all retire well off personally I am looking to be a millionaire before I'm sixty which is in thirteen years time. What do you think Tam could you handle the pressure?. Tommy looked at his brother and said it looks good but what do I ken aboot being a courier, Willie butted in yea winna be a courier you'll be makin sure the rest are good couriers and if they dinna shape up to our standards they can ship oot simple as that.

Willie went on to outline how the company would operate i.e. all they employees would be self employed on a daily rate except for any office staff that would be required, by operating this system the employees would be responsible for their own stamp and insurance we will pay top dollar by doing this we can hire only class one people and we won't have the problem of Unions interfering in our operation. He turned once again to Tommy and asked what he thought about the proposal, " Well its like this Willie this would be a whole new ball game for me, would I get any training? and another thing I would have to move house something I would need to discuss with Arlene she might not be too keen with the kids soon to enter the higher education system so it's a big step for me it will need a bit of thought when would you like an answer?" Willie put on his ruthless cap once again and without looking up said " In twenty minutes would be fine" Tommy shook his head and told his brother he would need a week before he could give an answer Willie accepted this and reminded Tommy that he would probably treble his wages and being a director of the company he would qualify for a yearly profit bonus. The meeting broke up just as Meg arrived laden down with carrier bags she had had a field day, Tommy was heading back home he didn't want to leave Arlene alone as the weather conditions in the North were difficult, Willie was flying back to London, Mary picked up her car and did the needful first dropping Tommy off and then Willie the roads were clear so she anticipated the journey back to Bogton should be without any hazards.

She was going to stay till Monday then travel down to Catterick and look in past her office she was still in the army but she was free to do as she pleased while she was arranging a job. Sandy had spent Saturday afternoon at Vera's house while the rest were in Aberdeen but he made sure he was home first, Mary asked what he had been doing with himself all day, his story line didn't include Vera so he got peace and no leg pulling. Tommy's mind was in turmoil as the train sped towards Inverness he was keen to take up Willie's offer but the disruption of moving to the other side of the country frightened him and what if he didn't like the job or worse still if he was useless at it, it was a worry but never mind it would be up to Arlene to help him decide. Mary decided to wind Sandy up a bit by asking him to invite Vera out for her dinner the next day which was Sunday, " Why wid I dee that"? he asked, " Ach jist so that we could hiv a look at her and make sure she is suitable for yea" Sandy hesitated deciding whether he would take the bait or not he knew his sister too well and if she could get him going she would be in her element so he pretended he didn't hear her, she gave up but she would be back he knew that. Tommy arrived home late in the evening the journey from Inverness by road had been a nightmare but he was home and overjoyed to see Arlene and the kids it had been a long harrowing day but a good glass of Morangie and the supper that Arlene had prepared perked him up no end and he was ready once the kids had gone to bed to enlighten Arlene about Willie's offer. The two of them kicked it about for at least a couple of hours before they decided on an answer, Tommy with Arlene's blessing would take the job on for a trial period of three months if it wasn't working out he would just jack it in and go back to driving earth moving equipment the job he had been trained to do in the Army, with that decision taken they retired to bed with Tommy deciding to phone Willie early the next day, he wanted a decision with-in a week so he would get it early. Willie wanted to get the business up and running on the first of February which was still three weeks away so he was delighted when Tommy called, although Tommy sounded apprehensive and still unsure of himself he put his proposal to Willie, Tommy thought there was a sharp edge to Willie's voice when he said, " Michty me Tam Courier sounds a real posh name but at the end of the day its only delivering bloody parcels". Tommy committed himself to start in two weeks time.

Mary was due to end her association with the army at the end of January she would have completed her twenty two years and was free to go although her boss's did everything in their power to get her to sign for a further three years, she had had enough and needed a new direction in her life the thing was, was she taking the right direction only time would tell. Tommy and Mary were going to lodge at Bogton until such times they had the business up and running, Willie was coming to Aberdeen to be with them to get things kicked off, his London office was so busy he had to recruit a manager to run the place as he was being pulled all over the world the need for security and protection was becoming big business especially with every re-newed Terrorist Attack Willie felt as if it was like winning the pools, he had a job supplying enough people to cover the requests he was being inundated with, Northern Ireland alone was big business and what the money companies were prepared to pay was obscene at times. The Oil industry around Aberdeen and the Highlands was beginning to gather momentum, Tommy had settled in like a duck would take to water he had with Willies help bought an old farm house on Deeside and moved the family down from Ross-shire, Arlene could see the house as a potential tourist establishment, she had declined getting involved in Hillside S.P.C. as office work was not her scene. Mary continued to commute back and forth to Bogton a round trip of eighty miles per day eventually she would need to think about moving nearer to where their premises were but in the mean time she was quite happy to commute. Sandy was still discreetly seeing Vera, they spent quite a few nights at the pictures of course Sandy still had to endure Mary's funny but snide remarks.

Over the next three years Hillside S.P.C services expanded and grew at a frightening speed the Aberdeen branch covered the whole of Scotland from Wick to Leith. The London office covered the whole of England and World wide operations where ever Willie had managed to place his Security and Protection guys it was big business. Arlene had managed to establish a lucrative niche in the tourist trade so she could lead an independent life, of course the Oil Industry also helped her in as much as the oil people booked up all the rooms around the city leaving people like Arlene to scoop up the over spill the Duncan's from their humble beginnings at Hillies were flying high, that was all except Sandy he was quite happy turning up at the council yard every morning and his clandestine meetings with Vera, he wasn't interested in the riches the rest of the family were enjoying, when there was a family gathering Tommy, Willie and Mary would park their latest BMW,s while Sandy parked his ten year old Ford Anglia along side but he was quite content with his lot, he preferred the simple uncomplicated life he was used to.

Bye nineteen seventy six the Oil Industry was in full swing there were fabrication facilities all over the country Hillside SPC Services were expanding daily and the money was rolling in. Tommy and Mary were stretched to the limits as they were inundated with demands for their services, in London Willie also controlled a huge Empire it was a high powered stressful business to be in but the stakes were high, the company was now four years old and was drawing admiring attention from their competitors with at least one unsuccessful take over bid, Willie wanted a few more years yet.

Sandy was still seeing Vera and spending a lot of time with her but being of the old well disciplined school he returned home every night it never entered his head to stay over, people of his era just didn't do these things. Vera did have thoughts that he might ask her to marry him but Sandy never mentioned the idea, she had a bit of a dilemma if she married or co-habited with a man she would loose her widow's pension which along with her part time job made her quite well off.

The emergence of the Oil Industry was nearly as disruptive as the Second World War had been with people moving from all over the world Aberdeen was expanding at a fearful rate, some the schools were multi national so the face of the North Of Scotland was changing daily. The Duncan's themselves were caught up in the upheaval Willie was never out of the air flying all over the world attending to his business interests, Mary and Tommy were still dealing with the pressures of the latest technology. Because of her work load she decided to buy a flat just on the outskirts of the city not too far from the Airport. When she moved from Bogton Meg decided to go with her she was offered a job helping out around the office and looking after the flat. Sandy would stay on at Bogton and the sisters would use it as an escape from the turmoil of the city, this arrangement suited Sandy just fine, Vera said she would make his dinner for him so he ended up sleeping and having his breakfast at Bogton, then after work he went to Vera's, great he didn't't have to explain his where abouts to his nosey sisters.

Sandy could hardly believe the difference the riches of the Oil workers would make to the environment but it did, things got so bad that he was asked to join a rota working on a Sunday morning clearing up the debris left by the Saturday night revellers fast food containers, beer cans, plastic bags just dropped where they were emptied it was disgraceful, Sandy was reluctant to work seven days a week he had suffered thirty years on the croft of working round the clock he didn't't really want to go back to that way of working, but with a bit of friendly persuasion he finally agreed to take his turn.

Into the New Year and Sandy was having an evening with Vera in her house she had made a huge meal they were sitting with a coffee and an after eight mint when Vera looked over and said to Sandy, " Sandy I am going to ask you a very awkward personal question will you mind?" " Oh a dinna think so jist ask awa" she was stammering a bit when she blurted out, " Hiv yea ivver thought of asking me tae get married " Sandy near chockit on his after eight and didn't really know what to say he was quite overcome. "Michty me Vera what a bloody shock yea gave me, bit the answer is Aye av thocht aboot it quite a lot bit I hiv always thocht that yea wid niver merry again after being a widda for sae lang". "Well it's a leap year this year so I'm entitled tae ask you" with that she knelt doon on her knees and asked, " Alexander Duncan will you take my hand in marriage before this leap year ends" Sandy was red from embarrassment and told her to get up aff her bloody knees in case anybody was lookin in the windie . " I will stand up when I hear the answer I want to hear." " Aye ok Vera fan wid yea like it tae happen", poor Sandy was all flustered he had never ever seriously thought he would get married he was quite happy glorying on treating Vera like a pal rather than a lover, he had a real predicament on his hands now he would have to get Vera involved with his sisters what an other ordeal for Sandy, he was still living in the early twentieth century where most people were living in the fast lane of the mid seventies. After getting over the initial shock of being proposed to Sandy needed to do some serious talking he was still living at Bogton mostly on his own although Meg spent most week-ends there so he would need to take the bull by the horns and talk to her about what would be happening. When he arrived home that evening he called his sisters in Aberdeen and asked when they would be coming home as he had some urgent business to discuss, Meg said she would be home on the Friday evening but she was unsure about Mary as she was in London for a couple of days, Sandy said that would be fine and he would look forward to Friday evening, he had another dilemma, should he invite Vera to Bogton when he was breaking the news, he would discuss this with her the next day. The two of them discussed the situation and decided that Sandy should break the news on his own on the Friday evening and then bring Vera along to Bogton on the Saturday evening, she had a better idea why not invite the sisters out for a meal a sort of engagement party that may be better than sitting around the house.

Vera said she would book a table in the Royal Oak Hotel and they would have a proper sit down meal, that agreed upon they had a discussion about when they would hold the wedding and the venue, Sandy said he would like to go back to the Glen and have the wedding in the Kirk there and then they could have the reception in the hotel, Vera was quite in agreement with this suggestion she asked about a guest list, Sandy said he would need to involve his sisters about guests but what ever happened he wanted a quiet affair the preparations were left on hold until Sandy had informed Meg and Mary about his forth coming marriage he was keen to see their reaction. In the house at Bogton alone Sandy was getting agitated as he waited for his sisters to arrive, the nearer the time the more the adrenalin pumped he was up to high doh wondering how he would break the news and also how they would react, he was his usual self very unsure what to do when he should just have taken the bull by the horns and told them what was happening but this was just not Sandy's nature he needed reassurance that he was doing the right thing. He heard a car pull in the drive, looking out through the curtains he had a nervous attack when he confirmed it was Mary's Mercedes with the Hillies Logo emblazoned along the side. He was as up tight as the strings on a fiddle when he heard the front door open and Mary shouted is anybody hame, " Aye am am in the living room"

Sandy stammered " Wid yea like tea or coffee the kettle's biling?" " Oh coffee for me fit aboot you Meg?" " Aye coffee will be fine". Sandy made the coffee and handed the cups to his sisters who were settled each side of the fire Mary had already kicked her shoes off. Meg always the nosey one was dying to hear her brothers problem and could contain her self no longer as she asked " Fits so important that yea need us hame tae discuss it" Sandy could feel the blood rush to his head as he carefully thought how he would put his news across stuttering and stammering he finally blurted out, "Vera and me hiv decided tae get merrit bit we've nae made any plans yet ah thought it would be better tae speak tae you twa first". The two sister's looked at each other in amazement, Meg was first to speak, Well,well Sandy Duncan aren't you the deep one when did this plan materialise, " Oh jist last nicht Vera invited me to her hoose for ma denner and during the course of the evening we decided tae get hitched" Mary always the one for winding her brother up and knowing how shy he was asked, "Fa asked fa, we ken it's a leap year so did you ask or did Vera ask." This put Sandy in a real embarrassing position but he pulled himself together and stated it had been a mutual agreement, Mary then owned up that she was just taking the micky and congratulated her brother in his forth coming marriage, she then asked when they would finally meet the future bride, Sandy had done a great job keeping his family away from Vera. "Well we have decided to take the two of you out for a meal to-morrow evening in the Royal Oak the tables booked we just have to let them know the numbers". The two sisters were in agreement this would be a good way to break the ice with their future sister-in-law. Meg was now desperate to get on the phone so that she could spread the news to the rest of the family most of them thought it was a huge joke, Sandy getting hitched and him into his fifties, Meg assured them that as soon as she found out the dates and details she would let them know she was sure some of them would like to be present the day big brother tied the knot. The three of them sat round the sitting room fire into the early hours and discussed Sandy's plans for the future where would Vera and him live etc but Sandy just shook his head and said they had discussed nothing other than the fact they would be getting married later this year. Meg touched a raw nerve when she hinted at Sandy that he was maybe already staying with Vera he took the bait and exploded how could his sister ask such a question, when he queried why she thought that she explained that the house at Bogton was always spik and span which was unusual for a man living and eating on his own, at that point Sandy owned up that he had his dinner most days at Vera's but he came home every night.

Sandy and his sisters had agreed to meet in the Royal Oak at six thirty they would have an introductory meeting over a drink then dinner at seven, Sandy left Bogton ahead of his sisters he was picking Vera up and taking her to the hotel. They walked to the hotel it was just a couple of hundred yards, as he neared the Royal Oak he had another of his adrenalin rushes the nerves were really strung taut, it was like he was about to be executed. They handed their coats to the receptionist then with Vera in the lead they proceeded towards the cocktail bar, Sandy felt a real surge as he spotted his sisters seated by the fire, luckily Vera had no inhibitions about meeting her future sisters-in-law and held out her hand as Sandy introduced first Meg and then Mary, of course Mary soon broke the ice and the three women were soon chattering away like long lost pals. At around ten to seven the waitress called them through to the dining room and Sandy was taken aback to see the table was set for six people, before he could say anything Mary said there were another two guests arriving at any moment, Sandy went into shock who the hell could have been invited he looked at Vera who in turn shrugged her shoulders. Just as Sandy was about to protest he heard a voice behind him on turning round he was confronted by young brother Tommy and Arlene they apologised for being so late as they smothered the family with hugs and kisses, then Tommy shook hands with Vera before giving her a big hug as well. The meal lasted over two hours as they chatted away got to know each other Sandy as usual didn't have a lot to say but his sisters made up for any shortfall, Vera asked if they would like to go to her house for a coffee before they went home, nosey Meg was all for it she was keen to see her future sister-in-laws house the old saying went that you could judge a person by the type of environment they lived in. Before any of the rest could get hold of the bill Mary had grabbed it as she went to pay she told them that she had instructions from Willie, he was sorry he was unable to attend but the next best thing he could do was pay for the meal, Tommy's comment to that was, " If I had kent he was peying I would have had another bottle of wine". Arlene dug him in the ribs and told him not to be so ungrateful.

Vera opened the door to her house, you could smell the waft of polish as she stood back and allowed her in-laws to enter, the living room was faultless everything was sparkling the Duncan ladies were really impressed with brother Sandy's choice of wife, he had waited a long time but Vera seemed the perfect choice, and by the way she looked at Sandy and touched him at every opportunity she looked like a lady in love.

Over a coffee and then a couple of drams they blethered into the wee sma oors, Mary had told Sandy to leave his car at Vera's and have a dram with the rest of them she would drive him home and he could pick up his car to-morrow, before they left to go home Vera was invited over to Bogton for her dinner the next day she could come with Sandy when he picked up his car with that they headed for home, Tommy had to leave the driving to Arlene as his state of inebriation was well above the drink driving threshold. After the Kirk on Sunday Mary dropped Meg off at the house at Bogton then headed for the town with Sandy to pick up his car, on the way Mary started to try and find out the plans for the forth coming marriage but Sandy in his usual laid back style hadn't really thought about it, he said that Vera and him would have to sit down and work things out, Mary pointed out that she was sure Betty would be over from Canada but she was unsure about Peg and Jim at the moment but she did emphasise that they would need a bit of warning to allow them time to book and make arrangements. Meg had the Sunday lunch well under way bye the time Vera, Mary and Sandy arrived back at the house, she had Arlene giving a hand but with a crowd of people to feed she was in her element, Mary and Vera were told they weren't needed as it was a very small kitchen, they settled down with Tommy and Sandy and had a little discussion about the forth coming wedding it was decided they would keep the wedding party at about forty and maybe the evening entertainment at seventy five.

Chapter Twenty Nine

Sᴀɴᴅʏ ᴀɴᴅ Vᴇʀᴀ ᴡᴇʀᴇ ᴍᴀʀʀɪᴇᴅ ᴀᴛ the Easter week-end everything went to plan, Sandy's family except for Jim attended, Jim was at a busy time of year and couldn't afford to take time away from the sheep farm, he did ask for Sandy to bring his new bride over and spend his honeymoon in New Zealand. It was a great day for the Duncan's the ones that were abroad were able to catch up with old friends. Vera looked splendid in her light violet coloured costume she was given away by her son and her grand daughters acted as bridesmaids, Sandy had been persuaded to wear the kilt as did the six nephews who acted as best men and ushers. During the meal in the hotel there were exactly fifty guests, many of them stood up and gave speeches told funny stories etc, finally Willie called for quiet and after speaking of his brothers struggle to provide a good home for them after their father was killed he thought his brother deserved to find a lovely lady like Vera, he had to stop while the guests applauded. Willie continued " To show our families gratitude and as a little thanks to Sandy for the scarifies he made in making sure we were all well looked after we have clubbed together and bought tickets so that Sandy and Vera can fly to New Zealand and spend their honeymoon with Jim and Tina and while there they can also visit relatives of Vera". The whole place erupted and the emotion overcame Sandy he was seen to brush away a tear from his eye, worse still he had to get up and reply not one of Sandy's strong points, he could provide music to audiences of any size but to get up and talk was an ordeal in its self but he felt obliged to struggle through even though his emotions were running high. The whole day had been a roaring success both families mingled with each other, and the reception at night was of the old style even though it was Sandy's wedding day he was requested to get on stage and play a few tunes on his beloved button key accordion. He managed to extract an extra week of holidays from the council, their flight tickets were for three weeks and they were flying on the Wednesday. It would be

Vera's first flight but Sandy was a seasoned traveller having flown to Canada to Pegs wedding although he was not a very confident aviator, but Willie had promised he would be at Heathrow to make sure they got their flights it was along haul of around thirty hours which neither of them had experienced before, they had two stops on the way but it was all a new experience for them. They were absolutely shattered when they reached their final destination, as soon as they cleared customs they found themselves in a sort of rugby scrum as Jim and the family hugged and kissed the both of them it was a wonderful welcome with nearly all of Tina's family there to join in the welcoming party. As soon as they collected their luggage they boarded a station wagon with Tina driving and headed for the sheep station which was a good three hours drive from Auckland, Jim was having problems with his wounded arm which was pretty well useless and preventing him carrying out tasks like driving etc. It was quite overpowering with all the Kiwi's trying to speak at the same time Sandy could well have done with a lie down he was nearly out on his feet, Tina eventually showed them their room and suggested they have a shower and a couple of hours kip she would call them in time for dinner, Sandy thought it was the best suggestion he had heard in a long time, he was no sooner showered and into bed before he was snoring his head off. True to her word Tina gave the honeymooners a shout in time to get dressed for dinner what she didn't't say was that she had laid on a spread and invited quite a few friends and neighbours over making sure her Scottish relatives had a real Kiwi welcome. After a huge feed and quite a few glasses of intoxicating liquor Sandy was ready to sleep again that was until somebody suggested a sing-song then as if by magic a button keyed accordion appeared and Sandy's tiredness was forgotten as he got into the rhythm of the music for the next couple of hours many of the old Scottish dances were performed, not maybe to the Scottish Dance Associations standards never the less the young ones were enjoying the Celeidh.

The New Zealand Duncan's spent as much time as they could afford driving Sandy and Vera all over the place showing them the beautiful countryside that New Zealand is famed for, Sandy was still a farmer at heart so his interests were taken up with the N.Z way of doing things, Jim and Tina had a holiday chalet in the mountains where they spent a lot of their free time, Sandy was greatly taken by their way of doing things, the chalet was near a river which was teeming with fish, this was a favourite past time so quite a lot of the meals were fish based, trout and salmon being the most abundant. Sadly like all good things the holiday was at an end and they were soon boarding the plane for home a journey neither of them were looking forward to. Willie was meeting them in London as they had nine hours to wait for a connection to Aberdeen, where Mary was waiting to pick them up and drive them home, Meg had a meal ready at the flat, after eating Mary told them to stay the night she would take them home in the morning, the four of them sat and talked for hours as Sandy told them all about Jims family and how they had enjoyed their time with them.

Back home the next day, Sandy surveyed his surroundings nothing but houses and cars not his idea of an early morning view, Sandy was a country boy but when he married Vera he broke one of his vows by moving into her house in the town it seemed the most sensible move at the time as Vera owned the house she lived in. Their holiday well and truly over it was back to auld claes and porridge as Sandy prepared to return to work it was almost a month since his last shift. He had still to face his work mates who no doubt would have some uncouth comments to make about his honeymoon. One of the first he met was his old pal Freddie Shounders, "Weel,weel Sandy Hillies fu did the marriage go and did yea enjoy New Zealand, better still are yea enjoying merrit life?. I kwid hardly believe fit aye wiz hearin fin fowk said yea wir getting merrit, I said fa, Sandy Hillies, never Sandy's a confirmed bachelor bit how wrang can yea git anywye the best oh luck tae you and Vera."

Sandy and Vera settled down to married bliss, she got herself another part time job as she had lost her widow's pension when she got married, Sandy was quite happy to plod on working for the Council and was never tempted to join the exodus earning huge amounts in the Oil Industry. It didn't take long to show the wealth being generated from Oil all along the North East coast as far North as Wick where men were employed in the facilities required to keep the industry going. Over the next ten years Sandy and Vera covered quite a bit of the world as they visited relatives all over the place and of course they had done quite a bit in the Spanish resorts.

Willie had achieved his goal of becoming a Millionaire, on his fifty-eighth birthday he had the company valued and got quite a shock when he was informed that it was worth between two and three million the protection side of the business based in London was a gold mine and every terror atrocity made Willie millions, as the demand for experienced men capable of protecting people and property increased.

He decided to call a board meeting with Mary and Tommy, the business was still owned by the three of them Willie being the majority shareholder. The meeting was held in Aberdeen Willie wanted to keep it short, he didn't't beat about the bush and told his siblings what the company was worth and he was sure if he announced it was up for grabs they could probably get over four million for it, the Aberdeen Branch was on its own worth about a million their main earner was the courier service but others were beginning to muscle in and under cutting rates, as this happens it becomes more of a struggle if you're not making money you cant pay top wages so you don't get top class people. "What I want to ask the two of is what is your feelings about selling up and getting out for myself I have had enough hassle, travel and arguments with employee's and clients to last me a life time. What do you think its up to you two lets enjoy it while we can" .

Mary and Tommy didn't need much time to make up their minds everything about the oil industry was stressful long hours, hassle you name the down side and the list was endless. Tommy aged fifty and with a good going tourist establishment was all for getting out, Mary aged fifty four was the same she had done her twenty two years army service often working long hours felt the same lets enjoy the benefits. It was a unanimous decision to sell the company and go their separate ways. With that decision taken they retired for lunch and to discuss the way ahead, Willie was quite certain it would take most of what was left of the year to finalise everything, after lunch it was carry on as normal with Willie catching the afternoon flight back to London.

Willie's prediction was correct he was inundated with offers most of them asking that he stay on as Managing Director but that was not what he wanted his mind was set on a life of leisure doing what he wanted; being the efficient man that he was his future was all mapped out, his plan was to buy a villa in the South of France where he could potter about growing grapes and lapping up the sunshine. Finally he got an offer of three point seven five million the only request the company had was that Willie would act as an advisor for four months and be available if there were any queries that needed answering, he faxed the Aberdeen Office asking if they were agreeable, by return wire the answer was yes. Tommy was offered the job of managing the Aberdeen branch after Mary had made it clear she had no intentions of being involved longer than was humanly necessary, he decided to carry on until he had discussed with Arlene what the future held for them. As of the last day of December Mary would be unemployed she decided to spend the Hogmanay with Meg, Sandy and Vera then she would take off and have three months holiday visiting her family in America, Canada and New Zealand she offered Meg to accompany her but she declined she was looking forward to having some quality time on her own the past few years as Mary's dogsbody had been hectic at times, that was her plans anyhow.

After a life in the fast lane the Duncan's who remained in the North East of Scotland settled down to the more leisurely way of living that they were used to. Mary returned just before Easter full of stories and photo's of her world wide adventure she had also managed a week in Japan visiting people she got acquainted with while stationed there with the Army. She managed a week of the life where you sit around doing nothing but watching telly drinking cups of coffee and reading, not Mary's cup of tea and soon she was itching to get her teeth into something useful, little did she know that she was about to hit the jackpot.

One Sunday morning as they drove up to the Glen Kirk in the distance up the road to Hillies their old home she thought she could make out a for sale sign, possibly for fresh eggs or something like that she never gave it another thought until she spied Roddy Tracy the laird Meg nearly had heart failure as Mary grabbed him and gave him a big hug (you just didn't do that to the laird) but Mary being Mary had her own form of protocol, and anyhow Roddy had been madly in love with Mary when she was still in school. During the conversation Roddy asked her if she had noticed their old family home was up for sale. When the Duncan's left the new owners who were English had bought five acres of ground along with the house and out buildings, they made the ground into paddocks and started a trekking school, but they were getting on a bit and had decided to sell. Mary's eyes lit up when Roddy told her they were looking for offers over forty five thousand for the business, Mary was interested it would suit her fine, something to constructively pass her time. She was chattering on and asking all sorts of questions, Roddy offered to introduce her to the current owners advising her to get in quick and maybe broker a private deal. The couple were a Mr and Mrs Bostock, Mary put their accent down to being from around the Norfolk area, Roddy told them Mary was interested in buying Hillies from them.

Mary said she didn't't want to interrupt their Sunday but would it be ok to visit Hillies next day, the Bostocks told her just tell them a time and they would make sure they were available, she asked if ten am would suit them they both nodded in agreement and parted company, Mary felt real excited about the prospect of returning to Hillies and pestered Meg all the way back to Bogton asking her opinion, Sandy and Vera arrived shortly after they were having Sunday lunch with Meg and Mary, as soon as Sandy entered the house Mary pounced on him asking if he knew Hillies was for sale and what he thought about her buying it. Sandy thought it was a good idea and pointed out that the whole place had been done up and modernised, the people that had it ran a kind of outdoor activities centre based mostly on pony trekking, but he thought it was worth a look.

Next day Mary could hardly contain herself as she waited for the clock hands to move to nine thirty the time she would be leaving to travel to Hillies Meg reluctantly agreed to go with her. They were in familiar serroundings as they entered the yard at Hillies they were overwhelmed with dogs as they tried to get out of the car they were a mixture of Shiz Tzu and Lhaso Apso.s all milling around seeking attention, Mrs Bostock ran over and shooed them away until the sisters managed to get out of the car, Meg told her not to worry they were well used to dogs. They were invited into the house which had under gone a big transformation from the days they lived there all Mary could say was wow! this is nothing like the home we were used to. The Bostocks introduced themselves as Brian and Jean both were semi invalids hence the reason they were being forced to sell Hillies, Mary thought they were the most helpful couple she had ever come across she explained her situation being newly retired and still mid fifties she was looking for a challenge and Hillies looked just right, they went on to tell the Bostocks how they had been brought up at Hillies and would really love to come back as the Glen would always be home to them. Mary asked about the price they were expecting for it and near collapsed when told the price was offers over fifty five thousand, but it was a business and there was room for development, two and a half hours after arrival they were back in the car, Mary shouting that she would be back in touch as soon as she had spoken to her solicitor. Mary drove straight into town and parked in the solicitors car park, the girl at the reception asked if she had an appointment she then looked at Mary and said " Your Mary Duncan frae Hillies aren't yea"? Mary nodded and asked the girl who she was, " my mither and father are Vicky and Albie Grant" Mary recognised her right away she was her mother's double after asking how her parents were she told young Miss Grant she needed to see the property solicitor as soon as was possible. "Bye the way I'm caed efter ma mither" she informed Mary as she excused herself and disappeared into an office. She returned a few minutes later and said Mary could see somebody later that afternoon at four pm she nodded her head and said that would be fine and left. Mary was on tenter hooks as the time seemed to drag, at quarter to four she made her way to the solicitors office, young Vicky Grant didn't stand on ceremony as Mary opened the door she was greeted with " Hi Mary" as though they were life long friends she seemed a very bubbly young lady just like her mother had been. " Jist go in Mr Still is ready for you", Mary knocked and was told to enter, the office was very modern and didn't't befit the outside which still had a medieval look about it. The young man behind the desk stood up and shook Mary by the hand " I believe our firm have already done business with the Duncan family Miss Duncan, bye the way I'm David Still the third generation so it would have been either my father or grandfather who would have been running things then, it will be a pleasure for me to continue where they left off." He then asked what he could do for her now, she explained that the old croft was up for sale it was now a small business and she was keen to purchase it.

He asked who the selling agent was but he told her not to worry, he phoned through to Victoria and ask her to get details on the property at Hillside. With in fifteen minutes there was a faxed sheet of paper on his desk, he read through it and took a sharp intake of breath when he saw the asking price, offers over fifty thousand. Looking at Mary he asked if she had seen the asking price, she nodded her head and said yes she was aware of the price and that she wanted to put in an offer, one they couldn't refuse. Young Davie Still hesitated as he asked Mary how she would finance the buying of the property and how big a mortgage she would require, she had been waiting for this and had a well rehearsed answer, " Oh ! I never thought about a mortgage as I intend to pay cash, I have just sold my business and am now a millionaire in fact three of our family are". Mary was enjoying this she could see young David squirming in his seat and felt like asking how many millionaires he normally dealt with in a week. Stammering a bit over his words and looking rather unnerved he continued by asking how much she was prepared to pay over the asking price, she played the ball back into his court by asking his opinion, he pointed out how fast property was rising in price due to the influx of oil workers and the fact that there was outline planning permission to build chalets at Hillside she would be securing a good return on her cash much more than what the banks would pay so in his opinion two and a half thousand over the odds should be enough to secure a purchase. Davie Still asked if there was any other help she required, she shook her head but said she could do with a quick reply as she was anxious to get her future sorted out, he said he would put the pressure on them and demand a quick response, he stood up and shook hands saying they would be in touch as soon as any developments took place, Mary had the feeling that now he knew her financial status he would have jumped through hoops for her, as she left the office young Vicky called bye bye then Mary we'll be in touch. Mary had time on her hands she was very restless, sitting around the house was not her style but as she took time out one afternoon she began to plan in her mind what she would do if she was successful in purchasing Hillies she would probably keep on the pony trekking, then there were people who liked to go walking and there were plenty places to walk and hike so she started to write down ideas, a youth hostel type place for walkers, chalets, there was outline planning available, yes there was potential for quite an interesting venture. She was tapping her writing pad with the end of her pencil as she wracked her brains thinking up other ideas, she suddenly thought of her niece, Arlene, Tommy's daughter she had recently received a degree in Equestrian Management but was having difficulty getting a job it was not a very common event in the North East of Scotland so it looked like she would have to move south to full fill her ambitions, Mary had an idea she would talk to Arlene to get a feel for the need for Equestrian facilities around the area. Later that day Mary called her niece and asked if she fancied coming over for the week end she never mentioned her reasons, Arlene said yes she was getting a bit frustrated with all the knock backs her job applications were getting, she was doing office work for her father and helping out her mother but that was not what she had trained for, she said she would see Auntie Mary on Friday evening and would stay the week-end. Late on the Friday afternoon Mary received a phone call from the solicitors office it was Davie Still himself, " Hallo Miss Duncan I have some pleasant news, your offer for Hillside has been provisionally accepted and there is a written acceptance in the post so it looks like your dreams have been full filled, if I make an appointment for you on Monday can you come in and see me".? Mary could hardly contain herself " Yes just let me know the time and I'll be there", he told her Vicky would phone and let her know the time. ,Mary laid down the phone and let out a whoop we've done it Meg we've done it, owners of Hillies once again.

Chapter Thirty

ARLENE ARRIVED ON FRIDAY EVENING SHE parked her little car in the driveway and headed for the house, she knocked and entered and was immediately attacked from all sides by her spinster aunts and a couple of dogs the formalities over she was told to remove her jacket and come through to the sitting room, Meg was still fussing about asking if she had eaten then offering tea or coffee. Mary decided the time was right to crack open a bottle of champagne she had been keeping it for a special occasion, what could be better than to-days occasion, over a glass of bubbly she outlined the set up at Hillies, although Arlene was virtually inexperience practically she had all the theoretical qualifications to set up and manage Stud, Equestrian and any other establishments where horses were kept. This meant that she would be quite entitled to give an opinion on what could be achieved at Hillies, after finding out her Aunt Mary's ambitions. First question she asked was if Mary was interested in setting up an Equestrian Centre it would cost for a middle of the road set up about sixty thousand but if it were to be set up to cater for disabled people the Government would probably pay for two thirds of it in grants, but you would need to allow disabled people a certain amount of time to use the facility, Arlene pointed out that the pony trekking was ok but if the weather was bad especially in winter they would need to shut down but with her proposal they could be open seven days a week if need be. Mary thought the Equestrian Centre was a good idea and there was no competition for miles around, it would be six weeks before Mary got the keys to Hillies, but Arlene told her to start the ball rolling with planning permission and of course she would need an Architect to draw up the plans. With the champagne bottle empty and the three ladies talking twice as fast as was normal they decided to call it a day. Mary and Arlene decided to have a run along to the Glen in the morning and run an eye over what they hoped to eventually achieve, Meg had made sure the rest of the family were aware that the Duncan family name would be appearing on the title deeds at Hillies again.

After a late breakfast the two sisters and their niece piled into Mary's car and had a leisurely drive along the coast until they arrived at the cross roads that led them to Hillies, they drove slowly up the hill past the entrance and carried on to where they encountered the Mansion house of course the gates were closed, they by passed the estate entrance and kept driving until they hit the main road again, just after the junction to the main road was the entrance to Burnside, Mary asked her sister if she had any idea how Betsy Wilson was getting on, Meg told her she didn't't often see Betsy but that she was now a granny and no doubt the grand children kept her busy, she quickly added that Betsy still did a good bit about the farm driving tractors etc. The ladies carried on and had their lunch in a small country pub near Fraserburgh, they were meeting Sandy and Vera for dinner in the evening , after lunch they carried on past Peterhead then headed back home through Ellon arriving back at Bogton late afternoon, they had a lovely evening with Sandy and Vera.

Arlene left for home after lunch on the Sunday as she departed she asked Mary to keep her informed as to how things were progressing, she needed to carry on working in order to earn, Mary's new venture was a turn up for the books and she was looking forward to setting up a whole new project this was a chance of a lifetime. She was wondering if she should advise Mary to seek professional advice on how to set up the building etc, on the other hand consultants were expensive bearing in mind they were spending other peoples cash, it maybe wasn't such a good idea. Mary had a busy time ahead of her as she arranged to move to Hillside, the fact that she had her sister Meg with her was a major boon it allowed her to concentrate on getting organised. The Bostocks had offered to give her tuition on how the Pony trekking business was run they had booking's to full fill, so all in all it was a busy time.

Arlene also wanted to have some time with the Bostocks so she managed to get a weeks leave from the jobs she was working in, that week proved to be really help full and some very good ideas were passed between the two families. Mary had managed to get an architect to start on her plans, she would like to have them ready for the next planning authority meeting, it would be difficult but the architect said he would pull out all the stops, she wanted to incorporate Bunkhouse style accommodation where people could come and stay for their vacation, this was an idea Mary had seen in Canada at her sister Betty's place, it would push the price up considerably but she was sure that after they got established things should work out just fine.

Mary received the keys for Hillies on the twenty eighth of November although she was thrilled to be back the house just didn't resemble what they had been brought up in, it had been completely gutted and fitted with all the latest gadgets but still this was progress, she would have to wait until mid December to find out if her plans had been accepted, because she was upgrading the facility and creating a leisure complex everybody was more or less certain it would go through no bother. They had handed in the keys at Bogton and Meg had thrown her lot in with Mary, Sandy was also a regular visitor as he helped his sisters to get things going, there were still a few bookings for the pony trekking but mostly at week-ends. It had been thirty two years since Mary left the Glen to join the Army and over ten years since Meg and Sandy had moved from Hillies so even though they still attended the Glen Kirk most Sundays they had lost contact with what took place in the Glen. It was quite a shock when they found out that nothing took place, the village hall was more or less derelict the school was now a craft centre, there was nothing for the few youngsters who remained in the district and the few women who still kept the WRI going held there meetings at Betsy Wilson's house so the social side of things were pretty grim. The same two families from the original fifteen that was the Grants and the Morrison's were still there but when Mary asked Vicky what had happened to the community spirit she replied " Mary have you heard of the Highland Clearances well that's what its like here now, all the property is being snapped up by the Bloody English who don't want to mix the only time you hear them is if they want to protest and that's usually when the government want to bring modernisation to the district like the new electric line the Hydro want to install because the wooden poles are obsolete and need replacing so they were going to install pylons but our English colleagues are protesting about it spoiling the landscape just you wait till they have no power then we'll hear all about it, Mary that's what your up against now, I'm surprised they haven't protested about your plans." Mary didn't't really have an answer to what Victoria had told her but she was going to try and re- kindle the spirit of the Glen, at the moment she didn't know how but once she had Hillies established that would be her next project.

Finally on the twenty first of December Mary received the go ahead to start building her Equestrian Centre, the first thing she did was to contact Arlene and tell her the good news, she was delighted as it had been agreed that she would get involved as soon as the building work started this would be the first week of the new year, weather permitting the contractor had promised they would be finished by the end of April so that Mary would be in business for the summer, she also received permission for the Bunkhouse which was an added bonus, she still had the outline planning for six wooden Chalets but they were on hold at the moment. Things were going better than she expected. Willie had purchased a Villa in France and would be moving in the New Year he was still involved with Hillside Securities so that was holding him back in the mean time. Tommy was doing well running the Courier business in Aberdeen he had invested some money in the business so he was Managing Director of the Scottish end of things.

Meg had invited the UK residents of the Duncan clan to celebrate the New Year with them at Hillies she was predominately the house keeper so she busied herself getting the house and the food prepared it was expected that there would be twelve people for New Years dinner, Meg would be in her glory she loved catering for large crowds especially if it was her own family. Mary had spread the word around the Glen that Hillies would be hosting a New Years day party in the afternoon, every body was welcome. The family had all gathered on the thirty first, the last to arrive was Tommy and his family he had some last minute hitches, Willie was quick to point out that it was one of the joys of being M.D of the company. Meg had plenty helpers one of the first to offer a hand was Vera she asked for an apron and was soon stuck in helping Meg get a supper ready, of course Arlene was always ready to give a hand while Mary preferred to sit and have the crack with the boys, and indulge in a bit of horse play with her three nephews who were now teenagers but found that Auntie Mary had a few tricks up her sleeve where she could get the better of them.

As was now the norm the television dominated the evening until well after midnight, how Sandy wished he could turn the clock back and make their own entertainment but sadly that was all water under the bridge. The bell struck heralding in the New Year, Sandy was at the back door waiting to see if any body was firing a shot gun as used to be the norm, years ago there would be fifteen to twenty guns blasting away for the first five minutes of the year, he was just about to give up hope when bang somebody still remembered, coming from the direction of the Home Farm probably Roddy Tracey. By two am it was obvious that there would be no visitors to Hillies the family Duncan were in good spirit as they prepared to retire for the night it would be interesting to see how many would accept the hospitality offered on New Years Day.

Mary woke with a start she tried to sit up but her head was throbbing over indulgence in the red wine oooooooohhhhhhh!, it was still pitch black outside she peered at her watch it was just after eight am, she could hear movement through the house most likely sister Meg would be getting the lunch organised. Arlene who was in bed next to Mary stirred and sat up in bed switching the lights on, Mary did a bit of moaning about her eyes and her head which Arlene found quite funny and burst out laughing, she asked Mary if she would like a cup of tea as she bounded out of bed as fresh as a daisy, a cup of sweet tea tasted like nectar as it wet Mary's parched lips thankfully it was very rare for her to indulge as much as she did last night, but she would need to pull herself together as she had six trekking ponies to feed and exercise before she did anything else. She had a quick shower, felt much better then a cup of black coffee and she set forth to the stable, there was quite a covering of snow and she could see fresh foot print somebody had beaten her to it, she opened the stable door and just like the olden days brother Sandy was busy mucking out she grabbed him and gave him a big hug at the same time asking how his head was. Sandy said he was fine although feeling a bit ropey but nothing that wouldn't go away as the day progressed. The ponies were restless they hadn't worked for nearly a week although Mary could have had bookings she decided to close down until the end of the first week of the year. Suddenly she had an idea she would offer the nephews a chance to come out with her they could saddle up and walk the ponies up as far as the Canadian Memorial she was sure they would be thrilled and it would give the beasts much needed exercise. Meg had the breakfast table set and some of the family members were already seated, when Mary announced that she was going to walk the ponies she was overwhelmed with offers, soon all six places were filled, Willies boys Billy and Heinz young Tommy, Arlene, Mary and Maria were the six volunteers, so after breakfast they saddled up and had a wonderful trek to the top of the hill round by the memorial and back home the cold frosty air had blown the cobwebs away and Mary felt very near back to normal.

Chapter Thirty One

THE NEW YEARS DAY DINNER AT Hillies was just like the olden days, fun and laughter, Meg was in her element she just loved having the family around her and having to cook for such a large family brought back many happy memories, Willie had brought a case of champagne back from France which was used to wash down the goose and of course no doubt contributed to the hilarity. Dinner over and the family settled down, the men for a nap the youngsters to watch a film on the tele, the women had to clear up the dishes, then they sat and had a good chin wag bringing up various subjects.

Suddenly they heard a vehicle pull into the yard seconds later there was a loud knock, Mary answered, it was Betsy Wilson from Burnside the two women hugged and wished each other Happy New Year, Betsy then pointed to her jeep and said she had brought visitors, Mary looked at the jeep and recognised Hans and his wife Mary she rushed over and hugged the two of them then headed for the house ushering the three some in front of her she wouldn't't allow Hans in first as he was a little badly fellow and not the required stature for a first foot i.e. tall dark and handsome. There was much hugging and kissing especially for Sandy he was a great favourite with Betsy who although over sixty was still a stunning woman, Hans and Sandy were also great friends although they didn't see each other as often as they should have done. Shortly after that there was another knock at the door when Mary opened it she went weak at the knees for there stood her heart throb Roddy Tracey he got a special hug and a kiss, unfortunately for Mary he was a happily married man but he fitted the bill as the ideal first foot. The house was getting a bit crowded so the young ones made themselves scarce by going to a bedroom to finish watching their film. The next family to arrive was Albie and Vicky Grant, Albie who weighed almost twenty stone needed a good bit of room for himself, Jock Morrison and his good lady also appeared and a rip roaring party was taking place, Sandy was soon persuaded to get his accordion going and a real old fashioned New Years party was in full swing, a few more Glen residents appeared, namely the hotel keeper and the shopkeeper they both brought replenishment for the drinks cabinet. By eight-o-clock people were beginning to drift off home one or two were quite inebriated but everybody had to agree it had been the best New Year in a long time, Mary had also bent a few ears with the idea of holding a meeting to try and revive the old spirit that used to exist in the Glen, so it was on the agenda for early in the New Year. By midnight Hillies was in darkness everybody had retired early as the past twenty four hours had been rather hectic and quite a lot of the sleeping draught had been consumed. Into a new week and Hillies was back to normal the digger was creating the trenches required for the new building, up to now it had been a mild winter so no reason for the contractors to be held up, Mary was looking to start up her business for Easter week-end, Arlene was now on the books so she needed to be paid wages, the Pony Trekking didn't't generate a lot of income especially after the feed and other odds and ends were taken into consideration. What Mary really wanted up and running was the bunkhouse it could cater for twenty four people and was self catering she would soon be advertising it in the Bird Watchers, Hikers/ Walkers and any other magazine associated with out door activities. Arlene was experienced in the use of computers although they were fairly new lots of business's were installing them so they were toying with the idea of using this as another means of drumming up business.

The contractor was true to his word and had all the construction work finished by mid April the Bunkhouse would be ready for use at Easter week-end, Mary could hardly believe that she had almost filled it with some of the people staying for a week or more the majority were bird watchers, the cliffs along the coast seemingly was an ideal place to see all sorts of birds especially different species of Hawks, Mary's business also had spin offs for the hotel people who were doing a roaring trade in meals, things were looking up.

By the time the summer arrived Mary was real busy she had the whole family employed, Sandy spent all his spare time helping out after he finished his council work, Vera would travel out on the first bus her domain along with Meg was running the bunkhouse, the two old ones got on well and had plenty time to gossip as it was not always busy but a fairly steady turn over. Mary and Arlene were kept fairly busy with the Horsey side of the business they had employed a young girl who Arlene was training. Mary decided the time was right to do something about restoring the Glen to its former glory, she invited the residents to meet at Hillies, they would try and form a committee with the idea of reviving some of the old customs that had made their lives so enjoyable when they were young. The evening of the meeting arrived and Mary was in for a shock when only six women turned up and they were all residents from Mary's childhood days. Betsy Wilson, Mary Morrison (Hans) wife, Vicky Grant, Fiona Tracy, Dr Isobel Findlay, Isobel from the hotel and one English resident who owned the Filling station. It was obvious at this stage that the English White settlers were not interested in the welfare of the Glen to them it was a life of peace and quiet and they did not want any intrusions. The first item on the agenda was to elect a Chairperson, as it was Mary's idea she was voted in to run the show, they were all given ten minutes to have their say as to what should be done, the majority had the same idea's, the last one to speak was Isobel Findlay, Dr Issy as she was affectionately known. Issy felt at home in the sitting room at Hillies she had spent many hours of her childhood in that very same room she was ages with Jim and being an only child she enjoyed the company and warmth of the Duncan girls especially Mary and Peg who were only a year younger than she was. Issy cleared her throat and started to give her input as to what had gone wrong with the Glen she started to speak " Ladies like the majority of you here I am a Glen girl born and bred my childhood could not have been better as the Glen folks were a special breed and we looked after each other. Sadly due to circumstances beyond our control those days are gone and I don't think they will ever return and hear are the hard facts." "When the estate was sold off all the croft houses were snapped up by middle aged English people, when I was young there were fifteen crofters each with an average of six children that was ninety children the English invaders were past child bearing age so now we have very few youngsters growing up to take over from us. The English invaders came here from the bustling areas of London and the South East where they had spent a life time of commuting over crowding and queuing so to come to this little quiet corner of Britain was heaven to them that is why they are opposed to any new development in the district, another thing it is so easy to get to their English home area even by car it is achievable in less than twelve hours, the next problem even if we had youngsters coming through is the television, due to it we no longer have a picture house along the whole Moray Coast and further more I am led to believe that the next gadget for nearly every home in Britain will be the computer they were now a common part of the furnishings in most American homes." Issy had spoken for twenty five minutes but all her findings were correct, so resurrecting the Glen was a task that was neigh on impossible they badly needed new blood, breeding families but for the present generation this was maybe a step too late. Mary had decided to hold an open day to try and test the water and just to see the response she would get one of the other ladies suggested they could hold an amateur flower show all it needed was a few tables and somebody to donate a cup or a rose bowl pointing out that if there was a prize to be won it always encouraged people to enter, Vera said she would get Sandy to put up a poster at his work , the final item on the agenda was the state of the village hall it was totally wrecked the only solution seemed to be to raise it to the ground and build a new modern facility but that would cost money, it was left in abeyance until the next meeting which would be convened in a month.

Mary would have her work cut out to organise her open day before the harvest was finished, especially if they were going to have a small Flower and vegetable show but the ladies who had turned up for the meeting threw their weight behind Mary and each was allocated some part of the proceedings. Fiona Tracy had volunteered to look after the Gardening part, Meg and Vera the home baking section, Sandy and Arlene had arranged to have pony rides for the kids along with swings and slides, Mary was inundated with requests from people willing to take part. The people who ran the craft centre in the old school asked if they could have a stall they were willing to make a donation so things were looking good all they needed was good weather and it should be quite a success. It was agreed that there would be an entrance fee of five shillings 25p, for adults and two shillings 10p for the bairns if there were more than three bairns the whole family could get in for ten shillings 50p.

After a lot of hard work the great day arrived the gates were to open at eleven am, Mary was taken aback by the amount of families inside the fields before one-o-clock there seemed to be bairns everywhere getting involved with as much as they could. One of the old traditions that was revived was the Hill Race it was the highlight of the afternoon due to kick off at four fifteen that would allow them to wind up at five. Mary a real tough nut had entered herself for the race, even at the ripe old age of fifty six she was still as fit as ever, there was quite a good turn out with fifteen adults and about twenty youngsters.

347

Roddy Tracy was in charge of the starting pistol, the bairns were given a five minute start then the four ladies three minutes later, then the eleven men. This was the most supported event of the afternoon with mothers going hysterical as they urged their youngsters towards the finish line, it was pretty gruelling stuff as the out ward journey was quite a steep incline, Mary and Arlene were the leading Ladies and finished in a dead heat, its amazing how quickly an event closes down and everybody disperses one minute the place is seething next they're gone. The Marquee which housed the Flower Show was being left in place until Monday, Mary had one of her brain waves why don't they invite the committee members back in the evening and they could have a dance just like they did in the old days, she cajoled brother Sandy into supplying the music and Albie Grant who was a keen fiddler offered his skills as well. Eight-o-clock in the evening and a good old Celeidh was in full swing it was amazing how many people turned up quite a few of Sandy's work mates and their wives had made the journey out from town they were mostly middle aged folks so they were all skilled at the Scottish Country Dances the evening was going great guns when suddenly the flashing Blue Lights of a Police car was lighting up the night sky as it headed its way up the road to Hillies. The police car drew up near to where the Marquee was erected and out stepped two bobbies they asked who was in charge, Mary stepped forward and took responsibility, the older of the two stood back and let the young one talk his first question was how much it cost to get in, Mary said it was a private party and wasn't normal practice to charge friends, this kind of took the wind out of the bobbies sails as he must of felt he had a good capture. The older fellow stepped forward and spoke for the first time "Aye Mary I micht of kent you wid hiv ah the answers yea werna an Army bobby all that years for nothing". Mary peered at him under his peaked cap and it suddenly dawned on her who he was, " Ach its yirsel Tam fu are yea dein and fits this visit aw aboot". Tam Reid had been in school with Mary but she hadn't seen him since their school days, " We've hid a complaint fae some of your neighbours aboot the noise so we had tae hiv a look, try and keep it doon a wee bitty and don't be too late in closing doon enjoy the rest of yer evening" with that they left. Mary was seething and wondered who the sneaky pig was that would have reported them anyhow they now knew where they stood with their neighbours and would no doubt find out who.

Mary decided to start a fund with the idea that one day they would be able to build a new village hall , from her open day she had made one hundred and thirty pounds profit which was a good start. She could just see a chink of light at the end of the tunnel in her quest to resurrect the Glen. The open day had been a huge success considering the short space of time she had had to organise the event, to attract five hundred people was encouraging , her goal for next year was to pull at least one thousand.

Now the Oil industry was in full swing the young people had money in their pockets, riches they had never dreamed of, and with these riches they no longer wanted to rent Council houses, they wanted to buy their own, there was a boom in private housing, to get a mortgage was simple, just tell the Authorities you were an Oilman and they would crawl over broken glass to get your business. It was only human nature that people were cashing in and charging extortionate prices for their properties none more so than the English people who owned the croft houses in the Glen. The first to go on the market was Frankie Smiths old place the owners had bought it for six hundred and twenty pounds, it was on the market for fifteen thousand pounds. Mary had never really had a chance to get to know the couple who owned Frankie's place they were very anonymous and kept to themselves, maybe Mary's party after the open day had frightened them away.

Rumour had it that there were over two hundred offers for the croft house , and it was finally sold for over twenty thousand pounds. The couple who bought it were young, mid twenties and the parents of four young bairns, could this be the start of re-populating the Glen. It was exciting times and Mary made sure she afforded the new owners a very warm welcome to her beloved Glen and to Hillies.

Amid Mary's euphoria Arlene dropped a bombshell when she announced she had become engaged to her long term boyfriend, they had met at college when he was training to be a vet, Mary was gob smacked as she dreaded loosing Arlene whom she depended heavily on, but she had no need to get alarmed as the boyfriend was trying to get a post locally, and was thinking along the lines of setting up his own surgery.

When word got round at the price Frankie Smiths old croft had sold for there was a bit of a rush on as other owners decided to cash in and sell their places, with-in a year at least six other young families had moved into the Glen, they were all of an age where they were still breeding. The population of the Glen had now been boosted by over twenty youngsters ranging from babies to ones newly into their teens,

Mary was overjoyed, she encouraged the older children to come to Hillies and allowed them to go trekking giving her ponies much needed exercise. Arlene was also very good with the youngsters teaching the older ones how to handle the equestrian ponies and to groom and keep the stalls clean one or two were recruited and given Saturday jobs, Mary felt as though the Glen had been given a new lease of life. The Glen continued to flourish, Mary's business went from strength to strength, and her fundraising for the new village hall was achieved in under five years . Eventually Scottish National Heritage chipped in some funds in return for some space, they were lucky in as much as they had people like the Duncan's, Albie and Vicky Grant, The Tracy's and Betsy Wilson still alive and were able to relate to historical events that had happened in the Glen. Arlene was now married and expecting her second child, she and husband Robin were very much involved in the running of Hillside Equestrian Centre. Sandy was retired he also spent a lot of time at Hillies doing odd jobs, himself and Vera would also spend a good bit of time with Willie in France, Meg was her usual busy self making sure every body at Hillies was well fed and looked after. But for all Mary's hard work and organising the Glen would never return to its former glory, life had moved on even the bairns had a different outlook on life, probably the fact that she never bore any children of her own made it difficult to comprehend the difference of her impoverished life compared to the luxurious lifestyle enjoyed by the modern generation but that was how it was life was changing daily not always for the better.

Chapter Thirty Two

MARY HAD MADE PROGRESS IN TRYING to restore some of the old ways of life, but lots of things had her baffled. She managed to form a youth club, at first she was over whelmed as most of the youngsters now resident in the Glen were eager to sign up, what Mary couldn't understand was that if there was a decent programme on the television the kids just wouldn't turn up, they showed very little interest in the old skills such as knitting and sewing but they all had their little Nintendo boxes and would sit and stare at the tiny screen for hours on end, she tried every trick in the book but to no avail although she did keep the club going for the sake of the few that did show willing.

Life is very strange and unpredictable at times and quite often people who do their utmost to help others are for no known reason stuck down, often they die or are crippled for life, fun loving people who did more good than bad. If you remember back to the beginning of the Duncan family shortly after their move to Hillies Mrs Duncan the mother was struck down with a mysterious illness that rendered her helpless for the remainder of her life. Then their father seriously injured under mysterious circumstance which were to prove fatal. Well in this part of the world people are very suspicious and believe in fate i.e. two deaths in the one family will most definitely be followed by a third. Quaint ideas like that so when a serious accident did happen to another member of the Duncan family you could hear the few locals that still remained in the Glen whispering it was bound to happen, Hillies is bad luck for the Duncan's I cant understand why they ever came back after what happened to their father and mother, but happen it did.

Mary was her usual cheery self as she entered the stables, it was well before seven am but brother Sandy was started to muck out, Mary gave him a big hug and asked if he had a problem sleeping, Sandy explained that he was in the habit of getting up at the back of five and it was such a bonnie morning it felt great to be out and about. The girls who assisted Arlene were next to arrive and got stuck in helping Sandy and Mary, there was the usual banter between them and Sandy being the lone male had to endure quite a bit of leg pulling but all in good fun. Suddenly Mary asked if any of the girls fancied a gallop up to the Canadian Memorial before breakfast, there was never any problems getting volunteers and all four put their hands up, from then on it was a kind of game, a race to see who would be saddled up first, they had to be properly clad with safety helmets etc before they were allowed to start racing, it was normally a close run affair, but although the girls were at least thirty years younger than Mary she was hard to beat once she got going, as usual she was first to leave the stable the other girls were almost a dead heat as they jostled with each other to get started . Mary was just through the yard gate ahead of the others, there was along steep incline as they approached the Memorial as it was a sharp turn they had to slow down until it straightened out again. Mary was slightly ahead going round the bend, then tragedy struck her horse stumbled and fell rolling over on top of her. The girls pulled up and hastily dismounted, Karen the most senior told one of the others to get to the phone and get medical help urgently. Mary was in a critical condition, Karen told the other girls not to move her as she could have spinal injuries so they removed the horse blankets and covered her. Karen feared the worst as Mary was still unconscious and looked a terrible gray colour no doubt she would be in shock. The girls were getting anxious it now felt like hours since the accident and no help had arrived, Karen looked at her watch and was relieved to notice it was less than twenty minutes. Suddenly a Land Rover was racing up the track, it screeched to a halt, Dr Issy jumped out and raced over to her friend Mary, she was shocked to see how badly hurt Mary was and still unconscious she had already called for expert help fearing Mary had spinal damage, which she was helpless to handle alone.

Dr Issy was at a loss, her friend was lying helpless on the ground her colour was alarming, Issy was worried, she didn't't want to move Mary until expert advice arrived , she was well aware that if the spine was damaged or broken the least movement could be fatal. Suddenly in the distance she could hear the sound of an ambulance, it was going real fast and had a police escort in front with blue lights flashing and sirens wailing. Issy was relieved as the ambulance pulled up she recognised Bill Brown a surgeon from the local hospital he did a quick check of the patient then sprinted over to the ambulance, over their radio he made an emergency plea for urgent help. Mary was still unconscious, her head had taken a severe bash hard enough to damage her safety helmet, she was showing signs of shock so Issy sent the girls back to the house for additional blankets and if any hot water bottles were available they would help. Mr Brown the surgeon was the son of the surgeon who had treated Mary's father over forty years ago, he pulled Issy away to one side and more or less confirmed that Mary had broken her back he was also afraid of possible brain damage as her head was swollen he said he was waiting for an air ambulance to appear. Suddenly the air was filled with the noise of a chopper fast approaching from the east with-in seconds they were on the ground as well as paramedics they had picked up a surgeon who specialised in spinal injuries, they were soon pulling out all the stops getting Mary strapped into a special stretcher ready for the journey to a hospital in Glasgow. Meg and Sandy were quite distraught as their young sister was whisked away, memories of their father being removed in similar circumstances over forty years ago came flooding back. Issy put her arm round Meg and led her to the Land Rover by the time they had reached the house Meg had regained her composure she made a pot of tea, as she handed Issy a cup she thanked her and stated a good stiff dram would have worked wonders but she had a surgery later in the day so alcohol was out of the question.

Mary was flown straight to Glasgow Southern General where she was stabilised, she was still in some sort of coma, the decision was taken to fly her south to Birmingham where they had the best spinal injury team of surgeons in the world, they were standing by ready to begin treatment as soon as she arrived her fight for life would then begin. She regained consciousness three days later, one stroke of good luck was that although her brain had been injured she had escaped lasting brain damage. Her spine was a different kettle of fish, she was paralysed from the waist down, the surgeons were working hard to get some feeling in her lower body, and Mary being the strong willed character that she was would fight to the bitter end. Willie had flown over from France and was at his sisters bedside when she emerged from the coma, she was very vague about what had happened and what was going on around her, it took a few minutes to recognise Willie, but by being patient she gradually began to realise she was in hospital. Willie was only allowed ten minutes with her before the medical staff asked him to leave, she was about to have further treatment especially to her blood system as she was in danger of blood clots forming especially in the brain. As soon as he found a call box he phoned Hillies to let them know the latest they were over the moon when told Mary hade regained consciousness. Meg was over come when she heard the news, Willie said he would return to the hospital later on and give them a call in the evening with the latest bulletin. With-in a week it was established that Mary would never be able to walk unaided she was paralysed from the waist down. Seven months after her accident she was back home charging all over the place in her wheelchair, the girls christened her Ironside after the actor Raymond Burr who played a bossy wheelchair bound detective in a TV series. She was to receive physiotherapy many months after returning home and with the Mary Duncan guts and determination eventually managed to walk short distances with the aid of two walking sticks with elbow supports. At the age of sixty two she handed over the reins of Hillies to Arlene and Robin.

Mary still had a controlling interest but left the running of the place to the young ones. She had a specially adapted bungalow built in a New Retirement Housing development where Meg and her moved to enjoy their retirement it was close to the Glen and could have been named after the Glen because most of the residents were retired Glen folks. Near neighbours were Issy Findlay, Cliff Paterson, Betsy Wilson and others were waiting for the builders to complete more houses.

As in all walks of life age starts to take its toll and there is no escape, the first member of the Duncan family to pass away was Jim in New Zealand he had suffered a stroke a while back but when hit with a second one he failed to respond and passed away at the age of seventy his sisters were distraught even more so that they would be unable to attend the funeral. Willie and Betty along with husband Walter were able to attend.

A few years later Sandy was the next victim he also suffered a stroke which left him in a very poor state of health virtually helpless, Vera did her best to make life as easy as was humanly possible but with-in three months Sandy succumbed to his poor health and died aged seventy nine.

Meg the matriarch of the family lived well into her nineties she ended up in a Residential Home where one of her fellow residents was her sister-in-law Vera who passed away in her mid eighties, of the rest of them they passed away over the years until Tommy and Meg were the only survivors.

The Duncan family had enjoyed a colourful life, Sandy was as poor as a church mouse the day he died, Meg was the same but they had shown their true Christian unselfishness by caring for the younger members of the family instead of chasing wealth as Mary and Willie did, both were multi Millionaires who in all fairness made sure that Sandy and Meg never wanted for anything and here ends the story of the Duncan's of Hillside. The family name Duncan died with Sandy as neither him Meg nor Mary ever bore children. Tommy ,Willie, Jim and Betty all produced sons but they were street wise as to what lay outside the boundaries of the Glen so the chances of any of their off springs taking up residence in the vicinity were pretty remote.

THE END

About the Author

I WAS BORN 14/12/1937 OLD ENOUGH to remember the Second World War. Eight years of my life was spent living on a small holding (croft), living from hand to mouth through the six years the war lasted. I left school at fifteen with no qualifications, worked for forty seven years mainly in Construction and Heavy Engineering. In 2000 I suffered a heart attack that left me unable to hold down full time work. To pass the time I bought a computor and decided to write poetry and short stories. My first book is my own autobiography Tigers Under The Turf, it sold five hundred copies hopefully this one will do better. A Way Of Life Disrupted is meant to be a humourous but often sad look at life just after WW2 until the present.

Lightning Source UK Ltd.
Milton Keynes UK
UKOW051843290911

179516UK00002B/17/P